i

Halo Valley

The Legend of the Stolen Children

Louise Furley

Halo Valley

ISBN- 978-1-7349807-2-1 (Paperback)

Cover design by Pixel Mischief Design

ALSO BY LOUISE FURLEY

Solitar

Halo Valley

Isle of Orainn

Anastasia

The Kissing Number

Wrath of Wolf

Devil's Prince

Devil's Seed

Jungle Treasure

Adara

The Poser

Her Gangster's Winnings

Dedication

As always, to my Heart, Bob.

Chapter One

In the early morning twilight, remnants of a campfire burned behind Sergeant Michael Kelly like an orange halo. Outlined in the wavering glow his silhouette created the illusion of an ancient Celtic warrior standing strong on the shore.

Blustering in from the north, a coarse wind snapped whitecaps on the water and rifled his hair. He was oblivious to the whirling sheets of sand that stung his face, the wind was already losing its bite.

In the predawn dimness, he appeared to wield an axe in his iron fist as if awaiting Viking invaders to come slashing from the mist-cloaked waters.

Watching the rasping sea lap at Kelly's boots, Garda Lucas Bregg waited a few meters behind his boss like a blocking fullback. Inland, there were no medieval campfires smoldering in the dawn, just vacant modern houses.

A tangle of abandoned homes with their windows and doors boarded up, looking like a string of blind people waiting for a leading hand. A veritable ghost town.

Bregg coughed and rubbed his arms. "I should have dressed like you, Michael." He blew warm air into his cupped hands.

Instead of chain-mail armor and a helmet of olde, Sergeant Kelly wore black jeans, a brown bomber jacket and steel-toed boots.

Only rare occasions did he wear the standard blue and yellow uniform like Bregg was of a 21st century policeman in Ireland, An Garda Síochána. In his hand, Kelly clutched not an axe but a long black flashlight.

Michael shot Lucas a slight smile eyeing his uniform that was not as neatly pressed as it had been a few days ago. "You can't help it, Lucas, even though you're an ex-football player you still have more of a sense of pomp and circumstance than me. I told you not to leave your jacket in the truck, that the rising sun made it look warmer than it was."

He glanced around. "Anyway, officers and CSI scoured the area all the way to Halo Valley. There's no signs of the rest of the body that belongs to that skull."

Lucas shoved his hands in his trouser pockets, hunched his thick shoulders and stamped his feet. "The rumor was that it was ancient, you know, part of the legend."

The pair surveyed the nearby area. The homes bunched in clustered knots around the village, some crowned with the old thatched roofs, normally housed mostly fishermen and others that made their livings from the sea.

Oyster shells, fish remains and nets left unrepaired strew forgotten in back yards.

Michael shot his officer a crooked smile. "Yeah, well, the ME put that lunacy to rest. The skull has only been around since around the time of the evacuation. If Pierre Doin hadn't come back for his tool box the skull undoubtedly would have gone by the way of the rest of the body.

"Wild animals, or even local dogs likely unearthed it from a shallow grave and dragged the skeleton off. The remains are probably scattered for miles. Marta says she is unable to determine cause of death, but since the teeth were all knocked out I'm going with the homicide theory."

"I agree. It's pretty unlikely the animals pulled the teeth out. I read her report, Marta said it looked like some of the teeth were just smashed out like possibly with a hammer. Someone didn't want the victim, she says it was male, to be identified."

Nodding, Michael said, "Anyway, for now we have nothing to go on. At least our cursory inspection to make sure everyone did evacuate looks okay. Everything seems secure, at least for now." He glanced around. "Let's pack up and head out."

2

Normally, sheep would be grazing, fuzzy white dots against the green muslin of the mountains, but today the unadorned mountains rose stark against the dark dawn.

Because potatoes were so prevalent, the two policemen had searched for evidence of poitín distillations, but if there was any illegal moonshine the stills were hidden or dismantled for the mass evacuation.

When done loading the cruiser they trod back down to the shore and checked around to see if they left anything.

The emptiness of the town was numbing, even the sea seemed subdued now, like it was lonely.

Craning his ear, Michael imagined the music of the wind flowing over the water sounded like a mermaid playing an ancient crumhorn, the reedy horn blowing mournful and forlorn. Smiling, he shook his head, he was being whimsical, the local leprechauns must be spreading their enchantment.

"You're not crazy, Michael, I hear it too," Lucas grinned at his boss' expression.

Pulling off his black leather gloves, Michael stuffed them in his jacket pockets. "At least the rest of the citizens of Cleasaí should be safe now. The plans have been in the works for quite some time. They have been worked and reworked to ensure a smooth transition. As soon as we return to Halo Valley I'll review the fusion to see that everything has gone according to plan."

He unzipped his jacket and peeled if off, the sun was lasering holes through the haze, starting to heat the morning as Lucas had predicted, but low clouds still smudged full light.

Lucas sighed. He stared glumly at his phone. "Yeah, tensions have always simmered between the two towns, it's to be expected there could be all sorts of problems and fighting, hopefully nothing life threatening or irreparable, but we'll know soon enough. At least we have enough officers on guard just in case."

He glanced around, squinted up at the mountains. "I don't know how Cleasaí gets by with such lousy cell reception."

Nodding, Michael considered the gloomy day. It brought to his mind the grim fable on everyone's lips. Pushing aside the feeling of doom, he set his hands on his hips, raised his face to the sky and breathed in the tingling salty air. The surf calmed even more, the waves mellowed as the tide receded.

He turned on his heel, Bregg alongside, their boots pocking prints in the hard sand behind like two Hansels leaving a trail, winding back up to where they'd left the truck.

It had taken them several days to tour Cleasaí, the coast side of the Maru Mountains. They had slept in sleeping bags on the pebbly sand beside a homemade campfire not for the first time in their careers. Another degree colder and they would have bunked in the cruiser.

Verifying the town was veritably uninhabited, they climbed in the truck. Bregg unlatched the lid to a cooler on the seat beside him and took out two sodas. "Here," he said to Michael passing him one.

Michael cracked the tab, quickly sipped the liquid that fizzled up, took a couple of healthy swigs then set the can in the cup holder and drove out of the area.

Nearing the foothills, they passed orchards of hazelnut trees bereft of their fruit, deadened fields of barley, and stark berry patches. It took several hours to get around the craggy, bare mountains that were emerald and soft in the summer, and back into their valley.

Finally nosing the truck into the park where the party was in full swing Michael smiled at the white lamb sitting just outside the entryway, one rogue, weak ray of sunlight stroking its face.

Lucas laughed. "Oh yeah, your Irish is showing. I can tell you're seeing that lamb with the slight sunbeam on its face as a superstitious good luck sign."

A corner of Michael's lip pulled in, he let the comment go.

After parking the truck, a heavy aroma of tangy barbequing ribs wafted straight from the first food booth in a row of many. "Wow," Lucas sputtered, "my mouth is watering!"

Pulling his jacket back on, Michael took in the various food kiosks. "What I really could use is a hot cup of coffee. No offense, Luke, but your weak campfire caffeine water could use some work."

His nose in the air like a dog sniffing, Lucas muttered, "Yeah, yours is worse, always burnt. See ya later," and headed off to the smoking grills, bits of his blond hair gleaming in splinters of burgeoning sunlight.

Waving off his friend and his own stomach rumbling, Michael passed booths of sugary cotton candy and greasy fries, ducking flapping streamers in search of coffee.

Blaring foot tapping music assailed the airwaves mingling cheerfully with the uninhibited laughter of children. Smiling at the gaiety, the sergeant sidestepped a group of giggling and shrieking children chasing each other in a zigzag race through the park.

Still, the archaic nightmare hovered, a chill pall over the festivities like the misty halo cleaving to the Maru Mountains.

Shaking off the foreboding feelings, Michael pushed the jacket sleeves up exposing rock hard arms. On the eve of winter, the crisp morning was giving way to an unnaturally warm day.

Rippling muscles and a fresh vitality, Michael Kelly could be a poster boy for the police. A hair before thirty, he was still young but with some wars etched on his face.

Having been gone for a while, he and Garda Bregg had decided to stop by the party in the park and see how the town was handling the advent of the newcomers.

Skin still holding bronze color from the summer, blessed with a strapping height, glinting black hair and midnight Irish eyes, heads turned when Michael Kelly strode through the park.

He nodded greetings here and there. As soon as he spotted a booth selling coffee he made a beeline for it. Before he could get there a woman he didn't know stopped him.

She seemed a little distressed. A slight tightness in her voice, she said, "Hello, Officer, I'm new here." Somewhere in her thirties she was neatly attractive, a tad overdressed for an outside festival in a black sweater, skirt and heels. She straightened a hairband tidily holding back collar length auburn hair. Her smile wavered, as if she wanted to trust but not sure.

Michael dipped his head towards her. "Ma'am. Sergeant Michael Kelly. What can I do for you?"

5

"Sir," she said, setting fingernails on his arm so red and sharp they looked like burn marks on his tanned skin, "I've heard terrifying stories. I'm worried for my family, my children, and now I've locked my-"

Disturbing sounds across the park caught Kelly's ear distracting him. He cocked his head to listen while looking around.

Smoothing her annoyance at his averted attention, she said louder, "I've heard since there had been fighting between the towns for years, the people of Halo Valley thought it a great idea to have a welcoming affair for their temporary residents from the coast side. Personally, since I'm from Cleasaí, our tiny coastal village on other side of the Maru Mountains, I think it's lovely for you all to hold this party for us."

When he didn't look at her she poked a couple of fingers at his arm again, the sharp nails leaving real marks.

A little louder with a stronger hint of irritation she said, "A party sounded like fun, you know, the last outdoor event before the dark frigid days of winter keeps everyone inside toasty and cozy by their fireplaces."

Her voice softened, "It's blossoming into a lovely day, don't you think?" She gestured to the sky.

The sun's bleak rays pushed through the low clouds like a yellow comb through thick grey hair. In the past months the earth cooled in the village of Halo Valley, rustic autumn was setting on the horizon of a frosty winter white.

The snow had yet to make an appearance, it hung just offstage, tantalizing with unseasonably warm days sprinkled in between with evenings growing chillier and chillier.

Michael didn't respond to the woman's rambling. He watched a hundred plus people scattered throughout the square wandering about eating hot dogs and salty pretzels, playing games and visiting, getting to know each other.

It appeared folks were trying to make an effort to pull together the frequently feuding two towns divided by the mountains, and prepare for the impending catastrophic storm and the heart breaking devastation it was predicted to leave behind.

Again the sound- his ears pricked, he swiveled trying to pinpoint it. Easing through the heavy air, an unsettling odd noise spurted between scales of laughter sounded to Kelly more like frantic screams than yelps of joy.

He scanned the nearby surroundings for the cause of the disturbance but only saw people mingling, eating and laughing. Blocking his view, tied bubbles of balloons like square dancers dressed in their colorful outfits bounced everywhere, straining in the wind to escape and journey across the land.

Turning a circle, Michael searched the heavily populated park for the cause of the troublesome noise.

All around the park people peeled overcoats and hats like monkeys in a basket of bananas. Still scanning, everything appeared innocuous to the sergeant.

"Sergeant," the woman complained, digging her nails deeper into his arm a hair's breadth from drawing blood.

Still he ignored her, she went back to her initial issue. "Listen to me, I've locked my keys in my car and I can't find my husband. I need you to help me!"

Kelly looked down at the woman, he couldn't ignore her pleading. "Sure, Mrs... Miss, uh..."

Smiling, she drew back but kept a few fingers lightly on his arm. "I'm Herodias Troicasi. I know," she laughed at his surprised expression. "My mother was immersed in the Bible while pregnant with me. I don't even want to tell you what my sisters' names are!"

The sergeant laughed. The laugh froze when he heard the odd noise again in the distance. He couldn't make it out, but it didn't sound like joyful partying. He craned his neck to hear better. "I'm sorry, Mrs. uh, Miss-"

"Please call me Dee, my husband-"

"I'm sorry, really, I don't mean to be rude." Kelly hated to step away from a damsel in distress, but- "I've got to go see if there's trouble. Please excuse me, I'll come back and help you when I make sure all is well."

Dee frowned as Sergeant Kelly turned from her. "Hey," she said, "I hear your transfer here to Halo Valley wasn't a promotion,

Sergeant. That a man is dead because of you," she gripped his arm again.

Aghast, Kelly looked at her, his mouth pulled in tight. Stiffly he pulled his arm from her hold and very politely said, "I'll return and assist you as soon as I can." Without waiting for her to respond he jogged away, towards where he could discern the disquieting noises generated.

Following the sounds, he clipped through yards of park and crowd. It sounded like the trouble was inside the park and not the business section surrounding it or the woods beyond.

Kelly hoped there wasn't anyone in distress in the woods. Dark dense forests, thick with secret hiding places and mystery would be laborious to search for someone in trouble.

Chapter Two

Tired of just standing around, three-year-old Stormie Dodge tugged her chubby hand free from her mother's grasp and toddled off along the walk, winding her way through dozens of centipedes of legs.

Her mother, Carnie Dodge, hardly noticed, she was involved in a spicy conversation with newcomer, Champ Clyde.

Champ had moved over to Halo Valley from the coast with his fellow residents in anticipation of a predicted storm that could be so ruinous, according to the legend-tellers, that his hometown might be completely destroyed.

Champ's body was a perfectly muscled V. Dressed in black like a velvety villain, pointy-toed boots, tight jeans and silk shirt unbuttoned almost to his navel showcased Champ's hot bod.

Carnie Dodge couldn't tear her eyes off his fine face, long silky black hair and eyes so blue the sky was jealous. Preening, she about swooned in her obvious desire.

He swaggeringly unbuttoned another button. Her eyes dropped to his hairless chest and then down further. His jeans were so tight little was left to the imagination.

Carnie, plain as a stout brown bush, had no plans on letting this gorgeous hunk of man get away. Graham, her hardworking geeky husband, stayed stuffed in the back of her mind.

She never noticed the blonde hair and blue dress bouncing and skipping away, off towards the creepy dark woods.

Her tiny arms out to the sides like a little ballerina, Stormie's patent leather shoes tapped along the cobblestones as she danced further and further from her mother and the crowd partying at the park square.

Layers of businesses and shops circled the center of the Lilliputian-esque town. The center of the town was a square, inside the square the large park dotted with antique statues, splashing fountains and benches for people watching stayed open year round.

Plumy maples and oaks canopy the park in the summer. The little girl kicked at shed leaves spread all over the ground like curled red and yellow hands.

Singing a merry song she learned in Sunday school, Stormie skirted the cobblestoned square skipping along the path leading out of the main park area.

Older folks resting on the benches feeding the birds smiled at Stormie as she danced by.

At the edge of the woods, workmen pulled a heavy metal cover off an old well. Dragging it to the side, they left it to go in search of lunch before coming back to put on the new cover. The old cover was rusted and had holes and the people in the town had complained for a long time that it needed replacing.

It was a danger and an eyesore. With the winter season on its way, the mayor had ordered the town to replace the cover ASAP. The well should have been filled in, but the taxpayers demurred when they heard the cost. The new cover would make do.

Stormie danced and twirled and skipped, a pretty blonde fairy twinkling across the parking lot towards the woods. Her mother had read her a book last night about the magical leprechauns that frolicked in the woods with other elves and sprites that rode frogs during the day and snoozed under toadstools at night. Trees that had in the past few weeks dropped basketfuls of leaves beckoned from the gloom with gnarly grey fingers to the little girl promising enchanting adventures.

One of the construction workers snapped his fingers and stopped walking. "Damn."

Another worker slowed. "What's the matter, Ian?"

"I forgot my wallet, man. I left it back in my pack by the worksite. Hang just minute I'll run and get it." He turned and started back, then hesitated. His eyes widened, his mouth popped open like he'd sucked in a bee. He started running, yelling-

"No! Stop! Get away! Stop!"

The other workers turned to see what the commotion was. They watched their co-worker running and screaming across the parking lot. Then they saw why- little Stormie Dodge was skipping right towards the open hole, she was only inches away.

Ian Smelter screamed and waved while running as fast as he could, the hole was an old natural well, no one knew how deep it was.

They had goofed around tossing in rocks to see how long before they heard a splash or a clunk when they hit hard earth, but no matter how many rocks they dropped they never heard any of them hit bottom.

The other workmen ran after Ian, yelling and screaming- but they were all too late-

Stormie's toe caught a tool lying beside the hole, she flew a few feet into the air over the hole, like a baby bluebird taking flight for the first time- then – she dropped, disappearing into the black hole. Her screams hurled into the air after her.

Carnie Dodge's head jerked up. A familiar sound hit her ear. "Stormie?" She tore her eyes from the peacock Champ Clyde and glanced around looking for her tow-headed three-year-old, to no avail. "Stormie?" she called out louder frantically looking around, but no child.

Pushing people aside, following the screams she ran to the open cobblestoned path leading to the woods.

"Stormie! Stormie! Oh my God someone help me, my baby my baby! Help! Somebody help me!" Her heart racing, Carnie booked down the path towards where the screams were coming from. Puzzled people close by dropped what they were doing and followed her.

Carnie saw the group of workmen standing in a circle around the old well. Some had their hands together like they were praying, others were bent over looking in shock and fear inside the hole. Carnie ran over and shoved through the men to see. Clutching the arm of the man next to her, she covered her mouth with a hand and peered over the side. Eyes widened into terrified saucers, screams burst through the fingers clenched over her mouth.

Inside the black dirty well, Stormie's dress had caught on something protruding from the side. A blessing, an old shard of metal stuck out from the wall.

The shard left from a ladder someone years ago had tried to install but gave up when there was no discernible bottom. The rest of the ladder had rusted and fallen into the well.

Thankfully, the metal piece had grabbed Stormie's dress just as she was plunging down the hole. The bad news was that the child was too far down to be reached and the dress was beginning to tear. Peels of screams emanated from the hole.

Mother and daughter shrieked in unison. Stormie was hanging face down in the well with her arms and legs dangling. Her screaming and writhing and kicking caused the dress to tear faster. Her little face was as red as if stung by a wasp.

Champ Clyde ran up to the group. He shoved the workmen aside to get to Carnie. Carnie was mad with fear, shrieking hysterically, her muddy brown eyes blind with horror.

Champ noticed people with cameras and cell phones snapping pictures. He saw an opportunity to be a hero and decided in an instant to exploit it. The town would surely reward him for the daring rescue of a beloved local toddler!

"Step aside! I have long arms, get out of my way!" Champ shoved violently at anyone sorry enough to be within arm's length.

"Oh my God, save her! Save her! I'll do anything if you save her!" Her hands clasped in front of her begging, Carnie screeched at him.

Champ winked at Carnie. "I'll hold you to that, babe. Now get outta my way." His eyes rolled, after he's tomorrow's headline he won't need anything from frumpy Carnie Dodge, all the girls in both towns will jump at him.

He needed a new sugar mama anyway. Moneybags Gladys Crimpshaw was tiring of his laziness and spendthrift ways. Plus, she was beginning to catch on about his other female 'friends.' It was in the cards that she would soon be giving him the boot.

He dropped down on his hands and knees and looked over the edge. Little Stormie hung from the wire, bouncing from her frantic moves, wailing and screaming. She was further down than he had thought. He got down on his belly and snaked to the edge of the hole.

"Someone get a rope!" a voice in the crowd yelled.

"There's no time, she's falling!" another cried.

"She's too little to be able to hold on to a rope and get pulled out!"

"Okay everyone, you all need to shut up. You too, Mother," Champ shouted out to the crowd and to Carnie, her hollering was deafening his ears.

"You need to be quiet so I can concentrate. Shut up down there little girl. Can you hold still and just shut up for a second?" he yelled down to Stormie. The toddler screamed louder.

"Mama, Mama, Mama, Daddy!" Stormie shrieked, her arms and legs flailing like wild puppy tails wagging. The dress tore another few inches, her screams went up a notch.

Champ let out a heavy agonized sigh, and leaned over the hole. "Here goes. I should put cotton in my ears. Okay, kid, I'm coming." Under his breath he muttered, "You're gonna be my meal ticket, baby."

He wriggled further over until the top part of his body was hanging over the hole. A couple of workmen dropped down and grabbed his ankles to hold him steady.

But Champ didn't want help. He wanted the headlines to shout 'Hero Champ Clyde rescues baby from certain death!' He had no plans to share the keys to the city he was certain to receive and maybe even a parade in his honor!

He did not want to share his notoriety with a couple of yahoos with hammers and saws. He kicked at them. "Leggo, back off, buggers." Grumbling, they let go. Half a dozen people got on their hands and knees around the hole to watch the rescue.

Champ leaned over further and further on his stomach, he squirmed to his hips, his long arms reaching down for the tot. She was inches away. He swung a hand at her, swiping at her back...if only he could grab a handful of hair...he slid over further...

Half of the crowd hushed, holding their breath, the other half yammered asking each other what was going on. No one except the workmen circling the hole could see what was happening. The clouds thickened and lowered, growing together closing out the sun. The park darkened, condensing haze pressed down on the people dampening hair and clothes making it hard to breathe.

"Dammit, I've almost got her," Champ cursed, sweat slid down his forehead into his eyes. Making one last lunging grab at Stormie, it was enough to off balance him, he was now top heavy, he started sliding into the hole, over the edge went his stomach, his hips, then his thighs-

"Help me! Help me you bastards!" he yelled, desperately trying to dig his toes into the solid earth, his frenzied fingers scraped frantically at the rocky wall.

The men jumped forward on their hands and knees and grabbed at Champ's ankles, but he was sliding too fast, the toes of his pointy boots sliced trails in the dirt, then kicked in the air as he went over the edge-

"*Ahhhhhhhhhhhhh...*" Champ's screams reverberated down the well, down and down and down. Breaths sucked in and held as those nearby listened for a thump or bang or a splash. But there was no sound, only the absence of sound when his screams could no longer be heard.

No sound except from little Stormie who stopped moving when Champ hit her on his way down, now she kicked and wailed up a storm.

Carnie stood still, white as a ghost, shaking.

The crowd hushed, all eyes riveted on the hole that Champ Clyde had just disappeared into.

Chapter Three

"Outta the way! Let me through, I'll get the baby!" A man muscled his way through the stunned crowd.

He dropped to the ground on all fours. The plight of the baby in the well had quickly spread through the park.

"Hold off, sir!" Sergeant Michael Kelly rushed up after him. People shouted to him what had happened as he made his way through the park to the hole.

"I'll do it. We don't need to lose another citizen." He tore off his jacket throwing it on the ground about to drop to his knees.

"No," the man objected with a shake to his head. He leaned over the hole. "You're a tall fellow, but I've got these crazy double-jointed legs, I can lean over the hole in a better position to reach the child." He crawled to the edge of the hole then lay down on his stomach.

Not wanting to waste any more time, Sergeant Kelly sat down on the cold hard ground, rolled over on his stomach and took a hold of the man's legs. He looked up at the man nearest to him. "Grab a hold of my legs, Stan. You, Glenn, hold onto Stan. Go on, we need to make a chain."

"Hurry! Hurry!" Carnie screeched. "She's falling, my baby's falling! Hurry!"

Indeed, Stormie's blue dress was almost torn in half. Another second or two and she would be following Champ Clyde down the big black hole.

Lying on his stomach, the man inched his way over the well, just like Champ had. He reached out a long arm to the flailing child. His fingertips brushed the back of her dress.

He shrugged forward an inch. Half his body hung off the hole, his legs frogged behind him, oddly anchoring him and allowing him to reach down further.

"Steady man, steady," Sergeant Kelly called to the man whose legs he strained to hold. Another man held Kelly's legs and others rushed up making links in a human chain. Some men dropped down and sat on men in the chain to help anchor them, keep them from be pulled forward.

Off to the side, other workers were furiously trying to untangle an old length of frayed rope. Frightened people in the crowd yelled out encouraging words to the men, "Hold on! You'll get her!"

Hands wringing, feet pricking with pins and needles, hearts raced up clenched throats, one woman bit her lip so hard it bled.

The blocked sun bore oppressive shadows forcing a chilly pressure on the crowd.

Half the park had fled to the scene. Some cried, some prayed, some called out encouraging words, others expecting the worst murmured pessimistically about the child's probable demise while others froze into scared silence.

Parents held tightly to their own children in desperate fear that they could magically be pulled into the well with Stormie.

Like there was a magnet in the bottom of the well and he was a chunk of metal, the man was pulled further into the hole.

With a last huge effort and a huge grunt, "Oomph!" he threw his arm out and down.

Stormie's dress tore, only one thread held the squirming girl, her arms swinging madly in the air, he grabbed at a tiny wrist- the dress tore through- she fell- he held on-

"Pull me out! Pull me out!" the man yelled. Holding the slippery wrist with one hand, he dug into the earth with his other to stop his forward slide. Stormie jerked and twisted squealing like a greased pig, she was slipping out of his grasp and pulling him in-

"Pull us back, hurry boys, pull!" Sergeant Kelly shouted.

16

The momentum of the man clutching the falling child was pulling them all forward into the yawning mouth of the bottomless well. The sergeant's cramping fingers were losing their hold as they slipped from the man's legs to his ankles as the man struggled to hold onto the writhing toddler.

The chain of men jumped up and pulled as one like a human crane. Ferociously they pulled Michael hard- like the winners of a tug-of-war, the man came back with him lickety-split shooting out of the hole onto his belly.

"Help me!" he cried, his arms still in the well. People charged over, reached into the hole, able to reach her now, they latched onto the child he was still gripping and yanked her up and out. The men collapsed to the ground in relief.

Snapping out of her shock, Carnie snatched a grubby crying Stormie from the people that held her. Hugging her until the child couldn't breathe, Carnie sobbed into her daughter's dirty hair. In motherly relief, she sniffed the dank soil smell of her child's hair like it was the most expensive French perfume.

The man who rescued Stormie Dodge lay panting on his back, one knee raised. Michael sat catching his breath waiting for his thumping heart to settle.

Fragile strands of sun filtered back out, pushing through the swollen clouds, shining feathered streaks across the crowd. A coolness brushed through, people shivered, then, the streaks grew bolder, wider, stroking the crowd with gentle warmth.

With a quick toss of his head, Michael flicked back his hair like shiny molten oil, stood up, brushed off his shirt and pants and held a hand down to the man. The man took it.

The grateful sergeant helped him to his feet. Michael vigorously shook the man's hand and clapped him on the shoulder.

"What a brave act, sir, a very heroic act. They told me as I was running here that another man had just fallen into the hole trying to rescue the child. You, sir, are a helluva hero!" Michael grinned, nodding emphatically.

The man brushed dirt and old soggy leaves off his jacket then wiped his hands on his pants. Both tall men, they stood out in the center of the crowd.

"What's your name, sir?" the sergeant asked.

The man appeared embarrassed. "Oh, I didn't really do anything but pull a kid out of a hole." He ducked his head then grinned up at Michael holding out a long narrow hand. "My name is Troicasi, Dusja Troicasi. My friends call me Dusty."

They shook hands, Kelly's brow rose. "That's an unusual name. If I may say so, you don't look Irish, Where're you from?"

Troicasi smiled. "Oh no, I'm from here, good old Eire but my parents originated from Egypt. My wife, Dee, was born in Dublin."

"You must be from Cleasaí on the coast, you don't look familiar," Kelly said. He smoothed his jeans back down from when they pushed up while he had squirmed on the ground.

He brushed dirt and crinkled leaves from his tousled hair then tried to smooth it back with his palms. He bent and scooped his jacket off the ground.

The crowd swelled around the group at the well, people chattered excitedly in amazement about the stranger's daring rescue. They had quickly forgotten Champ Clyde's tragic attempt.

Rotating back and forth, Troicasi shook hands with people eager to congratulate him.

He nodded shyly at their ecstatic praise of his courage and heroism. Several young women exclaimed wonderment over his long arms and funky double-jointed legs, unabashedly flirting with the new hero. Taking a quick breather, he responded to Michael's question, "Yes. I've come here temporarily like the others to wait out the storm."

It grew louder as more people gathered congratulating Troicasi and jabbered about the shocking incident. "Well, you are a champion, Dusty, a true hero. But they should call you 'Crazy Legs!' Thank you for your courageous deed." Something behind Troicasi caught Kelly's eye.

"I see a reporter making her way through the crowd," Michael told him. "You can recognize that red hair for miles. I'll leave you to her. I'm going to see that Mrs. Dodge and Stormie get to the hospital and get checked out and then get them home. Hey," Kelly hesitated, "I think I met your wife a few minutes ago. Something about her keys locked in her car? Is your wife a darkish redhead?"

Dusty grinned showing lots of choppers. Brown eyes in a long sand colored face darted in the direction of the rapidly approaching reporter. A flock of cameramen and other reporters hurried behind the flaming redhead.

He replied, "Isn't practically everybody here a variation of red? Yeah," he nodded, "that sounds like my wife. She is absentminded, every morning she's searching for her keys, purse, shoes, whatever. Knowing that, I always keep my keys in my pocket." He patted his pants pocket and held up a key ring.

"I'll go take care of her. It'll give me a chance to give the press the slip!" He slid a four-leaf clover out of his pocket and showed it to Michael. "I know it's bad luck to show it, but I always keep one with me. See, it was my lucky charm."

Kelly returned his grin. "Good thing we're not superstitious," he laughed. "Well, *fáilte*, welcome, and again, thank you for your selflessness, you could have easily been killed."

He shook Troicasi's hand again, then Troicasi quickly moved into the crowd to go find his wife before the reporter could get to the scene.

Kelly turned to his gardaí, policemen. Several had been stationed at the party as security, and they had raced to the well during the commotion. Lucas Bregg came right behind them.

"Lucas," Kelly said, with his hands on his hips he nodded at the hole while talking to the husky blond officer. "We need to make a report on Champ Clyde and contact any kin. We also need to find a way to get to the bottom of that well and see if we can retrieve his body. And make sure when it gets up here that the body is covered and taken straight to the morgue.

"You know that people in this area still think that parts like the hand of the deceased can cure diseases and stuff like that, we sure don't need any missing body parts issues. Can you get that started? I'm going to see to the Dodges."

As soon as the officer nodded his acquiescence, Michael went over to Carnie and her daughter who were being hugged and kissed by the crowd.

Middle-aged Babby Bianchi separated from the crowd to meet the sergeant. Saffron hair rolled in a high bun on the top of her head like yellow wool on a spinning wheel's spindle, and a full flowered skirt swinging like a hoop around her sturdy legs, Babby's brow wrinkled in unease as she approached Michael.

"Sergeant," Babby said in a low voice. "The panic mill's whispering is already cooking, saying this is an evil omen." Full blown figure, feet in white frilly ankle socks stuffed in maryjanes, sweepingly long false eyelashes and a beauty mark dotting one cheek, Babby loved to look like she stepped out of a Grimm's Fairytale book.

Michael slowed, his ear tilted to the older woman, he frowned then his chin went up. Crossing his arms, muscles bulging through the flannel shirt, he shook his head, a thin shag of dirt sprayed from his ordeal to the ground.

"It's just foolish ghost stories to stir people up, there's nothing to it. We need to ignore them, they'll stop. Right?"

Chapter Four

Months later in the police station, the double windows burst open crashing against the wall so hard the glass crackled. Curtains blew in an uproar like blue flags whipping in the crazed wind. Squawks of dissent erupted around the room as snow and icy air rushed in.

"Oh hell, it's begun-" The first to react, Garda Lucas Bregg jumped to his feet. He hurried over to secure the windows while the freezing wind and curtains beat at his face.

In the middle of the room, Sergeant Kelly leaned a hip against a desk, one hand in his trouser pocket and the other cradling a mug of hot coffee. The steam rolled up soft and warm moistening his face, he took a sip. In a blue flannel shirt with the sleeves rolled up, black slacks and boots, he watched the uniformed officer tussle with the banging windows.

He said mildly, "Don't be an alarmist, Lucas, it's just a little wind. Winter is upon us you know."

Holding a football sized hand against a window pane, huffing and grunting from his exertions, Garda Bregg raked his other hand through his thick, wavy blond hair trying to neaten the wanton locks. Snow dusted the shoulders of his uniform like a light case of dandruff before quickly melting, leaving his collar damp.

Securing the window, Bregg tramped over to stand beside the sergeant who was now gazing out the front glass window. "You know it's time, Michael," a hint of panic edged his voice. "They say it's in the books, when the snow starts, they're doomed, the children are-"

Not unkindly Kelly rebuked him, "Get a grip, Lucas, it's a fairy tale." Moving closer to the window he watched the activity outside. Sipping slowly, he savored the strong brew, hot and black, the steam flowing softly to the sides as the air from the heater pushed it around like a lazy ghost.

Outside, snowflakes popped then disappeared. Bundled in winter wear, people scurried along the brick sidewalks lining the quaint village, heads bent against the bitter wind. Except for the vehicles and some modern buildings, the hamlet didn't look much different than it had a thousand plus years ago.

When restructuring, the town kept the old buildings just updating them to retain their ancient charm. In the distance, the mist-shrouded Maru Mountains appeared invulnerable, like an immense black castle formidable against the horizon, a mirage of solid strength and security.

Inside, a dozen or so beat up desks were scattered around the room armed with computers, phones, files, and all the accessories that pack a police department. The antiquated heater thumped, rattled and banged against the wall.

On the desks phones rang sporadically, the calls going straight to voice mail. Only two of the desks were occupied, one officer was working on a computer, the other was reading a book.

Michael and Lucas shared a chuckle at the voices streaming from the hall leading to the kitchen in the back, it was lunchtime and part of the crew was eating. It sounded like they were having a bit of a wild time playing cards hooting and hollering.

Bregg straightened a picture on the wall tilted from the sudden gust of wind. Awards, framed pictures of past sergeants and inspectors, and posters advocating the war on drugs and other community service programs decorated the pale blue walls.

Those that had desks near walls had haphazardly taped forms and papers and sticky notes to remind them of a million and one things they felt they needed to remember.

"I see you're avoiding the paperwork as usual, Michael." Bregg nodded towards a hallway. Back across from the kitchen and down a ways, the door to Sergeant Kelly's aggrieved office stood half open. Once a week he labored to clear his cluttered desk, trying to mingle the crime files into one organized pile. Further down the hall, way in the back was the 4-celled jail, empty, which was mostly the norm.

"I know you prefer to be outside on the street like me," Bregg continued when Kelly remained silent. "So, did you get any update from Doc Marta on the skull?"

The sergeant shook his head. "No. Nothing new. It's still an unidentified male, cause of death undetermined. There's no DNA for her to process yet. She did say it's a Caucasian male probably between 25 and 40."

"Huh. That's fits half of both towns."

Michael nodded. Standing near the window he could feel the chill come through, but the sun warmed him at the same time. "I know. Not much to go on. We've interviewed everyone. No one saw anything, no one knows if anyone is missing. Due to the evacuation, half of Cleasaí came here and the other half scattered to towns north. Everyone just gives crazy stories that it's the legend that murdered the victim, and worse is yet to come. What a bunch of-"

"Listen, Michael, aren't you just the tiniest bit concerned? I mean, the prediction of the storm, and the horrific legend and, well first Stormie Dodge and then this week little Sissy Cardsdale went missing, the whole town is up in arms about them being harbingers of-"

The sergeant cut him off, "Stormie was an accident and she was saved, and Sissy was found, Lucas, a few hours after her parents called it in. She was down at a neighbor's house and she was fine. She's not a harbinger, she's simply a child that should have told her parents where she was going."

"Now," Kelly went on, turning to squarely face his garda. "Stop buying into this superstitious BS. It's for hysterical little old ladies that have nothing better to do while playing bridge than rehash ancient events and whip everyone into a freaked out frenzy with their silly story telling."

Not looking the least bit reassured, lodged somewhere between his late twenties and the brink of his thirties, even in the small town

23

of Halo Valley, policeman Lucas Bregg had enough law enforcement experience to feel guilty about being anxious over make-believe stories. Hunching his shoulders, his hands deep in his pockets, maple eyes flit to the window that had earlier banged open.

The wind beat fists against the thin glass trying to get back in. Just as Bregg turned, something dark, like the shadow of a large twisted bird slid across the sky… Bregg blinked, and blinked again. There was nothing there. He decided it was just a black cloud rolling past, heralding the storm.

Michael asked Bregg, "So, are they all finally here and settled in?"

Bregg nodded. His husky build belied his speed, a great hidden tool when he had played football in high school. He went to college up in Glenfall on a football scholarship but missed his family back in the Valley.

Large square head on thick shoulders, a twitch of blonde hair above his chin, he stroked it with a finger when thoughtful, like now. Maple eyes and fluffy blonde hair brought on the nickname of Waffles when he was tearing up the football field. He did his college in Maine in the States on a football scholarship.

Leaning over his desk he picked up a clipboard. He only glanced at it because he had reviewed it again and again until the pages were smeared and wrinkled.

Rubbing a stocky thumb against the side of his nose, he tapped his knuckles against the paperwork. "Yeah, it's a good thing we started the relocation process almost a year ago. As soon as the weather people forecasted that the impending weather patterns jibed with the almanac advising it would be looking good for a cataclysmic storm to hit this year, the Upper Region sent down a young lady to get the ball rolling and do the heavy organizing and transitioning.

"They're also prophesying that we're going to get a lot more snow than our normal mild dusting." He pointed to a newspaper sticking out of a trashbin. "So, did you see the paper before you left, about that guy, what's his name, our town hero rescuing little Stormie Dodge?"

"Yes, um, Dusty, uh, Troi…Troi…casi." Michael smiled. "He should be honored for that act of bravery. Maybe when all this other business settles down we can give him a proper reward."

Lucas agreed, "Sure. I don't think the picture of him did him justice. You can only just make out his features in the grainy photo. But at least he got some recognition. His family must be so proud. He has two teenagers, must be why he jumped in with both feet so to speak."

"Anyway," Michael asked, "since you were involved in helping move the people before we went out and surveyed the coast, had there been any problems convincing the people in Cleasaí to evacuate here? I was gone before it started and sent back right after we returned from our survey. We haven't talked about it yet."

Still leaning against a desk in front of the window, he crossed one foot over an ankle. His fingers wrapped around the coffee mug, the heat felt good on this cold day. The hot coffee warmed his insides all the way down his throat to his stomach.

Sun streamed through the filmy glass glinting off the black waves on his head, outside it sparkled over the blowing snow.

"No," Bregg shook his head. "Not really a lot. You would think people would be reluctant to leave their homesteads and schools and businesses as small and remote as they are, to live here until the threat passes, but most did it with little protest. Of course there were a handful that wanted to hold out, but we told them there would be no one to come and save them, and there was a strong possibility of a killer tsunami predicted following the storm.

"They could be cut off from the mainland with no food or water, medical care, and no shelter if the wicked squall destroys their homes. That pretty much moved the hard core reluctant folks."

"Were there any reports of trouble while I was gone, after the blending of the towns? Everyone get along?" Michael asked.

"Ah," Lucas answered ruefully. "Nothing much changed there. Fortunately just mostly minor spats."

He thought for a second recalling what other officers said of some tense incidents that flared between some people. "Maybe it's escalated a little. It seems every day there's more and more fights breaking out. Swift Sam's convenience market and Jerry down at the Things and Stuff mini plaza complained that shoplifting and arguing between customers and clerks is rising. There have also been reports of people fleeing after getting gas and not paying for it then denying it later when tracked down. I mean, this small of a town it's loony for anyone to think they can get away with it."

Michael acknowledged, "There's bound to be conflicts. Most of Halo Valley residents own businesses or are teachers, more white collar type jobs, where most of the work in Cleasaí is seafaring and fishing or something to do with it, fish markets, net and sail repairs, or farmers."

Forking his fingers through his thick mane of yellow hair, a corner of his lip curled, Lucas nodded. "Yeah, conflict's a nice neutral word to use. Anyway, the fishing of course dies down some in the winter. We started the transferring paperwork to our schools here in the summer so it would be an easy assimilation for the new school term.

"And because so many people had moved away from here when that new factory opened up in Glenfall in the upper western region, we had plenty of vacant houses for families to move into. And that meant there was space for people to fit into jobs where employees leaving caused a shortage." Bregg continued raking his fingers through his hair vainly trying to flatten it.

"It's a good thing both villages are small so there are less schools and things to have to shuffle and deal with," Michael said thankfully.

Noise buzzing in the room went unnoticed by the two men used to it. Dispatch radios crackled in the background, two operators mustered over in one corner periodically answered calls, mostly about cats in trees, frozen pipes and normally, before the move, once in a blue moon shoplifting from a mom and pop shop on the strip.

The crime activity in Halo Valley consisted mostly of nuisance calls, domestic disturbances, or searching for someone lost in the woods, which more often than not was tourist campers, buzzies and hikers failing to follow maps and guideposts.

Then there's the occasional drunk and disorderly call for teenagers feeling their oats and acting like *balubas*.

Sergeant Kelly contemplated his coffee, swirling it before taking a last gulp. He peered at Bregg over his cup. "We can work on helping the towns get along during this transition. Maybe have some meetings or workshops or something, we'll brainstorm with the crew. I should have thought of this before I went on that last mission. Maybe we could put a notice in the paper for suggestions."

Michael shot a look at Lucas' rumpled hair that resisted the officer's attempts to tame. "Stop primping, Lucas, for Pete's sake, you'll never get that great glob of yellow mop to behave." A half smile touched his lips before he turned his attention back out the window.

Bregg ran fingers like large clothes pegs one more time through his thicket of curly locks then dropped his hand to his side. He looked at his boss and friend.

"Yeah, easy for you to say, Michael, not everyone is blessed with your wavy hair. It's bad enough all the girls go agog over your dark eyes and lean mean machine that the rest of us slobs always have to take your leftovers. It's time you get yourself nabbed up by a local and settle down and give us regular Joes a chance!"

"Oh give me a break, Lucas. I saw you and Kenzi coming out of the movies the other night hanging all over each other, looked pretty serious to me. Besides, you know I hardly ever date." Sergeant Kelly frowned down at his inch shorter equally muscled but huskier friend.

Bregg nodded. "Yeah, you don't date. You just take a lady- and I use the term lady- loosely- out for a short evening. It's like you put a wall up, bro, no emotions, no feelings, don't get involved, heaven forbid you start a real relationship. When are you going to realize you're better than that?

"You need to let the secret out, tell the truth, so you can get on with your life and kill the rumors and speculation, no pun intended. People will understand what led to what happened. You deserve a decent girl, a decent life with kids and-"

Tuning out Lucas' words, Michael finished his coffee and set the mug on the counter. "Never mind, Lucas, let's get back to the transitions. Update me on how many families there are and where most of them have relocated. I've been gone so long on the government special task force I have no idea what's been going on. I need to get out and meet our visitors. It helps that I do know some of them from frequenting Cleasaí."

Bregg dropped his head to his clipboard and tossed some papers back and forth. Without looking up he said, "You haven't even met the Regional girl yet," he grinned. "Huh, yeah, you're in for a treat."

Snorting his mirth, he glanced up at his boss and best friend, then quickly straightened his mouth. "Seriously, Michael, you don't need to worry about it, it's all under control."

The front door opened and another garda bustled in with more wind and snow. He grinned at Kelly. "Michael, welcome back."

Kelly returned the smile. "Thanks, Justin. How're Emmy and Simone?"

Snowflakes salted hair as red as the tip of a burning cigarette. The officer's grin widened like a proud rooster, freckles stretched across his pale white face. "The wife is doing well, Michael, she's got our daughter entered into the beauty pageant, she's pretty excited about it, says she promises she won't be a stage mom.

"And Simone is growing like a weed, she's 8 going on 19, you know? She can't hardly wait for the first show of the season with make-up and high heels and all that girlie stuff."

"You did all right in that department, Justin," Bregg told him. "Every time I see Simone she's prettier and prettier. That blonde hair is like silk and those baby blues, she'll be a handful someday, I don't envy you when she hits her teens."

Mournfully, Justin Zeall looked at his feet. "She's already a spoiled handful. Man, the way the sass zings from that girl it's like she's already a teenager. She's getting smartass with a big time diva attitude. I have to take away her cell every other day as a sanction for being disrespectful to people.

"I mean, seriously, a cell phone, twenty pairs of shoes for an eight-year-old? Geesh. If she's anything like her drama queen, shopaholic mother I'm in for a lorry full of trouble!"

All three men laughed together. Wiry as a pipe cleaner, snapping his fingers the garda remembered why he came in.

"Oh Mike, there's a reporter and cameraman out on the front steps of the Town Hall. It's that O'Leary woman, she says she wants to interview you and, well, you know, there's a crowd gathering. Everyone's on tenterhooks waiting, the anxiety level is rising like the smell off a fat man in a sauna."

"The media is already congregating? She here to talk about the storm, the evacuation or the legend?" the sergeant asked.

Zeall shrugged. "Dunno. Probably all of it. I'd use the term 'media' loosely if I were you. In this rural town it consists of a few gangly reporters and a handful of interning college kids from the university up in Strowell with cameras. They have more spunk than know-how."

Deputy Bregg piped in, "You said the reporter is Mallory O'Leary? Dude, she's hot, but a snotty bimbo, you know, like has a real mean streak sometimes. She's got a long bodacious body but her face kinda looks like a fox, or a wolf, almost pretty but not quite. But her face does exude sensuality, like on an almost porn level, ya know?"

"Oh yeah," Zeall agreed, "she's always made me think of like a hunk of rich red velvet cake, that white skin and red hair, all sweet vanilla on the outside and inside juicy red, oh yeah, she knows she's hot and lords it over people. Gives the rest of us redheads a bad name."

The slightly smaller thinner Zeall ducked as the bulkier Bregg swiped a brawny hand at his head.

Laughing, Bregg said, "Oh yeah? You can be snotty on occasion too. You're just pissed because when you were in high school before you got married to Emmy you asked Mallory out and she laughed you out of town. Now she flirts and teases you because she knows there's a ball and chain on your ankle."

Justin Zeall scowled. "That's not true-"

"Okay, okay, pull 'em in boys, let's get on over to Town Hall and wrestle with the press. I want to put a lid on this foolish legend before folks get carried away and let their fear drive them amok. It'll cause nothing but a pack of trouble. Let's roll."

Sergeant Kelly strode over to the hat rack and pulled off his jacket and Stetson. The only time he wore full uniform was for formal events like funerals or commencements.

He turned briefly and called over to one of the females on the dispatch, "Dacia, I'll be over at Town Hall if anyone's looking for me."

Her head down with a phone to one ear, Dacia Smoot nodded. Dark twists of hair jumbled around her round, milk-dud colored face. Tapping a pencil on the notebook in front of her, she was listening to whoever was speaking on the emergency phone line.

By her expression, it didn't look like it was a life threatening call. Lips twisting wryly, her eyes rolled heavenward and she muttered, "Uh huh," about 10 times.

Kelly shrugged into his jacket, set the hat on his dark hair then headed out the door with his two gardaí at his heels.

The three LEO's walked briskly down the street, boots clomping on the cobblestoned sidewalk heading towards the Town Hall only a few blocks away. A rare airplane droned overhead halting conversation. Nearing the end of the block they could see a small crowd had gathered around the steps of the two-story red brick building.

White shutters framed the front windows and the weathered double door entrance. Walls of rhododendrons, flowers wrapped tightly in green gloves closed up for the winter, and red-berried hollies hugged the building. Alders, English elm and wild cherry trees punctuated with Norway maples and chestnuts studded the lawn through to the back.

A good lot of the branches were bare, yet some had one or two tenacious scarlet leaves still stubbornly clinging, flapping in the brisk wind. Although winter had been moving on for a few months it had been very mild mostly, like Indian summer, until now.

Attention was on the young woman standing with the mayor on a platform outside the doors of the Town Hall. A semi-circle of five steps made of stone led up to the threshold from the sidewalk. Although ensconced in a belted, long heavy coat, it was clear the woman had a good figure. She was tall and well built, with long red hair snapping around her head in the wind.

But it wasn't the wind that blew red spots on the mayor's chubby cheeks. The woman held a microphone up to the mayor, Ashton Whitworth.

As the three officers reached the crowd, they could see that the mayor was arguing with the reporter. Keenly aware of his constituents' attention, dressed like a baby blue and white 1950's Plymouth buttoned up to his neck in a woolen overcoat, the mayor was desperately trying to control his temper.

Clutching a pair of reading glasses in his hand, he tried to use his arm to smooth down the sparse graying hair flying in all directions. Vain at 50, Mayor Whitworth only wore his glasses when necessity deemed it, otherwise he used them as a gesturing tool.

Michael Kelly gently elbowed his way through the crowd, then with laid back authority he long-legged up the five steps to the platform to greet the reporter and the mayor.

Mallory O'Leary turned immediately to the sergeant. "Hi handsome," she favored him with a full wattage smile, gleaming over-bleached white teeth for miles, her hair redder than the scarlet leaves clinging to the trees.

In the small town most of the residents knew each other from childhood, but Michael Kelly had been transferred in and appointed sergeant of the sub-district five years ago. Mallory leaned in close to him and stuck the mike in his face.

"Hey, Sergeant, long time no see. The people would like to know what precautions you're going to take regarding the legend," she grinned full again, knowing she was putting him on the spot.

A cloud of overpowering, sweet rose perfume coiled around Michael, stifling him. He unconsciously leaned away.

Her face was just a tad too long for her to be called beautiful, more like a pretty fawn or wolf like Lucas had said. Brazen eyes stroked him from head to toe and back, a blatant invitation; *take me now*, screamed from those hazel eyes.

Chapter Five

Michael could feel the pull from her like a bear to honey. Promised fire burned in those hazel eyes. Obtaining his sexual relief with loose women from out of town was one thing, but Mallory was a cunning agitator he wanted no part of.

He shuddered, realizing if she ever got her talons into him she'd dig straight to the bone and never let go. More shady than lady, he found her cloying and annoying not sexy or sweet.

The corner of his mouth pulled in slightly. The description Justin Zeall gave of her and the red velvet cake came to mind. He shook his head, he had sworn just last week to lay off sweets, they're no damned good for you.

Feeling soiled from her flagrant desire for him, he stuffed his hands in his black leather jacket pockets, he'd forgotten his gloves. The action also kept him from wrapping his fingers around her long, lily white neck and throttling the life out of her for getting the town all stirred up and anxious. That red hair of hers was like a big warning red flag, waving stop-danger-danger-

"Well?" Mallory prompted, red shiny lips pursed in a smirk. The long shamrock green coat darkened her eyes to more green than hazel.

The crowd pressed closer together and inched nearer to the Hall steps. More people joined the throng, murmuring, the murmuring grew louder like tree frogs in the night.

A few bold citizens yelled out to the sergeant, "Yeah! We wanna know what you're gonna do to protect our kids from the threat!

What's your plan? Danger's gonna start soon, it's already snowed for two days!"

As Sergeant Kelly opened his mouth to speak, Mallory shifted the microphone back to her own wide lips heavily coated with glossy red lipstick, and turned theatrically to the throng. "Let me bring those folks up to speed that may not know about the legend."

Kelly cut in, "Mallory, wait-"

But the girl shook her head, a sea of brilliant faux red showering her shoulders. "No, Sergeant, the people have a right to know. Right?" she cawed to the crowd, stirring them up more.

The people cried, "Yeah, yeah, we got a right to know! You need to tell us!" More people spoke out, a few shook their fists. Snowflakes fluttered down swirling around the group. Late midday and the shadows were growing long, the wind had picked up even more. The frigid air bit at exposed fingers and noses.

Off to the sides and back behind the crowd, small clumps of teenagers huddled, laughing and jiggling, sneaking smokes, trying not to let their parents see them, showing zero interest in the adults' antsy perturbation.

Up on the exposed platform, the mayor and Mallory had their backs to the wind but it struck Michael full on. In the grey sky, the sinking sun sliced weak stripes through the frosty clouds lighting the jumble of store fronts along the street on both sides of the Town Hall, and reflecting off the bare limbs of the trees that stood as skinny soldiers lining the streets.

Yellow streaks slewing through shadows over the citizens made them look like prisoners behind bars.

Wishing he'd worn sunglasses to stop the glare reflecting off the white shutters, Sergeant Kelly started again, "I wasn't-" but again the girl cut him off. She kept the mike close to her lips, grinning over it like the Cheshire and turned her back to him.

"So," Mallory said, swinging her hair behind her shoulders she smiled broadly at the crowd. The wind pushed the bottom flaps of her long wool coat back. She swept an arm out to the audience. "Most of us grew up hearing the Legend of the Stolen Children, right?"

Kelly rolled his eyes heavenward. Snow fluttering on his face made him blink, then he stared transfixed up at the deep violet afternoon sky. Around the winter sun, a hazy gloriole spread in a diaphanous ring, weakening as it diffused across the lowering clouds.

Snowflakes drifted down in a misty web, twinkling as they passed through faint threads of diminishing sunlight, twirling down and around the crowd like frigid Thumbelinas, piling around the audience's feet as if they were standing in white grass.

A gust of wind whooshed by blowing the falling snow like a sleet blanket. Michael closed his eyes wishing he was anywhere else but there.

Cocooned in the silently falling snow, the crowd shushed, nodding their heads at Mallory's words. Faces paled, fear shone in every eye. Hats were pulled down tighter, mittens tugged out of pockets and slipped on, jackets zipped tight to the neck, they waited.

"The story goes," Mallory regaled the crowd, "every 150 years, towards the last days of winter, it doesn't snow until almost the end of the season, but then the snow comes. When the third day of snow passes, for no rhyme or reason a child is stolen from a family. From what we've gleaned from the reports, altogether, the number of kids taken averages twelve.

"Family members, neighbors and the gardaí, do a diligent search for each child, but to no avail. They're all ages, races, both genders, good kids, bad kids, smart, not so smart, talented or not, rich, poor, there's no commonality in them other than they are under the age of 13 and old enough to walk."

Mallory's voice grew quieter as she spoke affectedly. She played to the audience like she was on Broadway. The crowd gazed back in reverence, hanging on her every word even though most had heard the story told to them by their parents as they grew up.

The legend was scary fodder for campfires, not a sweet fairytale bedtime story, because this legend was different than a fairytale. It was not a made up story about some banshee or monster or mysterious prince or princess in peril in a faraway make-believe land, this was true and it was about them.

People shivered, remembering their terror when hearing the story for the first time as children.

The reporter's head drifted back and forth slowly across the mesmerized crowd. Leaning forward, her eyes narrowed penetratingly at each and every enthralled person.

Her voice strengthened, "After the onslaught of a dramatic and devastating storm, an avalanche of boulders breaks loose, hurtling down the Maru Mountains causing horrendous mudslides, and then the tempest of flash floods and killer tsunamis wipe out any vestige of lingering life.

"Soon, Cleasaí, the coastal side of the mountains is utterly demolished, flooded, uninhabitable. Those smart or lucky enough to get away early have to wait for the waters to recede and the last days of winter to wane, before they can come back and begin the endless, dreary cleanup process to make their destroyed homes livable again.

"Then, the sun appears and with it comes the *te mhor*, a super-hot wind that forces an unnaturally swift, premature spring. It's in the spring when-" Mallory hesitated for effect, it worked, the group collectively held its breath.

She waited a few beats. In the silence, the noise from sporadic cars passing by and birds chirping as they flew in to roost made an edgy day seem a bit more normal.

But pinpricks bristling on arms already forced from the hostile wind ran up their necks when Mallory continued in a hushed voice, "It's in the spring when the people return to their destroyed village to reclaim it."

Mallory shook her head ever so sadly, her lids lowered. Red hair covering her sly face lay on the lapels of her coat like spilled Chianti. "That's when the children are found." Slowly raising her head, shaking back her hair she solemnly looked out over the crowd. Some were weeping.

With great sorrow, she gazed back down at her feet. Shaking her head again, a tormented catch in her voice, "The tiny, lifeless bodies found crushed against the rocks at the foot of the mountains being washed out by the licking sea."

Tears fell from many an eye as everyone hung on her words. Sergeant Kelly watched the crowd, he glanced at his two deputies. Their anguished faces were glued to the reporter like she was Rachel from the Bible crying over her babies dashed against the rocks.

As if she could read his mind, Mallory continued, "But, to quote Jeremiah, as the days follow the days in the Bible we read that 'God will turn their mourning to joy, the abundant crops of grain, new wine and olive oil, healthy flocks and herds, our lives will once again be like a watered garden and our sorrows will be gone, we'll dance for joy and we will enjoy abundance and feast on the good gifts.' "

Kelly grabbed Mallory's wrist to get her attention. "Oh come on now Ms. O'Leary. Just because the almanac is predicting a devastating storm to strike this winter so the upper region decided Cleasaí should evacuate like they did the last time it happened 150 years ago, there's nothing in the almanac about the legend and the children going missing.

"We're just taking precautions against the possible destruction of Cleasaí. It's insane that you're saying that the children in this town are doomed before the storm hits, but then afterwards our anguish will turn to joyful rewards? What kind of garbage is that?"

Mallory swung her fawny face to smile at the sergeant, five teeny freckles drizzled across her nose wrinkled in fun. Her shamrock coat tightly belted and buttoned up with the belt ends jerking in the wind, the big collar pulled up around her neck, the tip of her nose and cheeks bit pink by the thrashing wind.

Whistling around the steps the wild wind ruffled hair and clothes and flapped those scant leaves that still clung on trees.

"But Sergeant, the documentation is there. It's in the record books. Some call it The Sacrifice, some call it The Legend of the Stolen Children. Whatever, it happens every 150 years after the first snow. It has to happen. I think it's kind of a cleansing, you know, washing us of our sins like the Noah's Ark event, then we begin anew, better, cleaner, happier, wealthier."

She hadn't pulled her arm out of Michael's grasp. She looked down at his fingers wrapped around her wrist. Strong fingers, big hands. Rough hands unafraid of hard work, held her like a vice but not hurting.

Kelly let go of her wrist. His black brows daggered down in fury, he growled, "Ms. O'Leary, that's a bunch of bull crap to say that good folks are going to lose their children as a kind of a greedy sacrifice so all our sins are forgiven and we all can live better, richer lives.

"That's the stupidest thing I've ever heard. You're needlessly frightening the town with this kind of foolish talk. It's a bedtime story, a legend, a fable, there's no proof any of it ever happened."

A man from the crowd set his foot on the first step of the Hall. The planes of his olive-skinned face sharpened in anger, dark eyes stormed with fear.

Black hair slicked back, a hint of Spanish laced his taut words. "You know nothing, Sergeant. You're not a native, you're a newcomer. Childless, you have no dog in this show. There is proof. For the census records everything is written down, all the family members, goes back to the last 700 plus years. It's all true!" His breath pooled out white vapor in the cold air.

Michael turned to the man. "Zeb Trueno, you're going to stand there and tell me you believe this BS story about children snatched off the street, being held captive somewhere and then after a great storm they're tossed off the cliffs to die, and then somehow we all become richer?"

Zeb shook his head, one hand raised. "It doesn't matter how much of it is true, or who or what is responsible, I got a right to have my kids protected. I don't care about the riches after the- the- event, I care about my boys, Juan and Santiago. They're both under thirteen, the right age group to go missing. You need to do something before it's too late!"

Up on the platform, Mayor Whitworth sucked in his cheeks and tried to pull himself up closer to the height of the reporter. He tipped his head back so it appeared like he was looking down at her when she really had a good couple of inches on him.

The wind had lessened slightly, he unbuttoned his coat. When he pulled his head back, his open coat and his suit coat slid back causing his round stomach to protrude further, the buttons on his starched white shirt strained, his belly bounced slightly against Mallory.

The reporter glanced down, a mocking smile of contempt at the belly brushing against the front of her belted jacket. The contempt turned into a jeer. Red struck the mayor's chubby cheeks first then blossomed across his face and down his neck. He coughed, loudly cleared his throat.

He cajoled, "Ms. O'Leary," the balding mayor sucked in a deep breath, his neck wobbling he gestured at her with his eyeglasses. "Now, I must insist you break up this melee and move on. Can't you see you're frightening the town half to death with your talk? Sergeant Kelly is right, there's no proof of- the- of the uh, legend as it were, there's only scribbles written down for a few generations.

"Who knows who wrote the notes, it could have been a feudal lord that wanted to obtain prime property so he was trying to scare off prospective buyers, or to keep strangers out of Cleasaí, you know there'd been smuggling, or-"

Mallory slanted her head back and looked down at the mayor, mimicking him. The crowd snickered. "Mayor, the events are clearly documented in the town ledgers and almanacs. 150 years pass, it snows for 3 days, then the children go missing, one by one. Then a big storm hits, devastation follows. Afterwards, bodies are found, and the town is reborn.

"I've done my research, Mayor, you might want to run your little round self down to the public library and check out all the books that I did. Old biddy Miss Marscrumb will certainly have kept a record of everything I did so she can spew her share of gossip at her weekly Bingo.

"Already this year she's intimated that I've had an affair with practically every married man in town, including you," she jabbed a gloved finger into the mayor's plump chest.

Whitworth's mouth dropped, the red in his round cheeks burned from radish to purple beet. "Me! But that's not- you don't know what you're- my wife will-" he sputtered leaning away from the imperious redhead.

Mallory's lips bent up in a cherry bow. "That's not all I researched in this town, boys. I've got dirt on everyone, the locals, the coastal transplants, as well as…" snide eyes slid to Kelly, the cherry bow grew wider.

Sergeant Kelly moved his broad shoulders slightly between the reporter and the mayor so they each had to back up a step. "Okay, that's enough."

The bow turned down. "You can't make me disband, you can't stop me from reporting the news, the people have the right to know." Mallory gazed at the crowd willing them to join with her, they did.

People called out from where they stood on the brown grass now dressed with snow. "Get off it, Sergeant, let her alone, she's just doin' her job, we got a right to know, to ask what you're gonna do about our kids!"

Mallory smirked at Kelly. She held the mike under her slick lips. "Yeah, what are you going to do, Michael, find the villain and kill him like you cold bloodedly killed your cheating sweetheart's paramour?"

The color drained so fast from Michael's face he looked like he'd been hit by a snowball. The crowd gasped, the mayor's brows rose to the top of his receding hairline.

Mallory stood with one hand on her hip and the other holding the microphone in front of Michael's mouth, cunning green eyes waiting for his response.

Chapter Six

A young woman emerged from the crowd. She stepped awkwardly up onto the first step of the Hall then gingerly moved up another step. Thick ribbon of dark hair waving to her waist, gentle brown eyes, her clasped hands shook.

"Miss O'Leary," the petite woman's shy voice started out hushed, hesitant. The long beige coat almost covering her boots brushed the step, plaid scarf wavered in the harsh breeze.

Fingering the silver cross hanging around her neck, she grew a little bolder yet spoke softly. "There's no need to attack the sergeant. There's a force here bigger and stronger than any human being that has ever existed and tortured long before Sergeant Kelly or any of us ever came on the scene. To throw out innuendo like that can only harm, not help."

Mallory raised a disdainful pencil-drawn red brow. Before she could respond, a man jumped onto the step next to Zeb Trueno and shot a finger into the smaller woman's face. Zeb jerked his collar up around his neck and stepped down moving back into the crowd.

The man said to the petite woman, "You mind yourself, Mary Montebello, there's no cause to be disrespectful to Miss O'Leary." In his late thirties, Paul Philo, earmuffs over dark curly hair and rubber boots squeaking with his every move, crossed his arms the best he could in front of his huge oxen chest.

The husky man scowled at Mary but he smiled up at Mallory, his round, dirt brown eyeballs trained on her chest.

Mallory rewarded him with a beaming beguiling smile.

Louise Furley

He took that as encouragement to continue. He scowled again at Mary Montebello. "You need to just stay home and take care of those nuisance- er- that-foster brood of mixed kids you got living there. They should keep you freakin' busy enough to help you mind your own p's and q's." He swiped a handkerchief at his round nose dripping from the cold.

Mary's mouth dropped, no words came out. A hand fluttered at her lips. She tightened the flowing plaid scarf tighter around her neck and fumbled with the buttons on her long coat. Eyes like chocolate drops blinked anxiously at him.

Paul Philo shooed at her. "Go on now, leave the brain work to those of them that's got 'em." The magoo man smiled smugly at the reporter, she returned a conspirator's smile. Mallory was happy to stay back and get the action on tape. Live unscripted action was always better than anything she could stir up.

Mary's face darkened, her hands balled into fists, she planted them on her hips and glared at the thick man, they were almost eyeball to eyeball as she was on a step above. "Paul Philo, my children are not troublesome, why, they are the best behaved-"

Paul leaned his doughy face into Mary's, his lips pulled back in a troll's grimace, moisture dripped from his runny nose over his thick upper lip. Snow clinging to his fuzzy brows shook off as he stood on his toes to tower over her, she cringed at his vehemence.

"That boy, Jessy U," he snarled, shaking a stout finger in her face, "he alone is trouble enough for ten kids! My boy, Pilly, keeps getting into trouble in school and he tells me it's all your boy Jessy's fault, so you take yourself on home and give that boy a good wallop, he'll straighten out believe you me. In fact, I'll come over and give him a good bangin' every day if need be! It's worked on Pil it'll work on your boy."

Mary shrank back, her shaking fingers steepled as if in prayer. Then, she pulled herself up as tall as she could, her face the image of a sternly proud Madonna.

Snowflakes laced her long lashes like gossamer; she brushed angrily at them. "My gentle Jessy U is a good boy, Paul Philo, you know darned well that your Pil is a bully, all of the younger kids say-"

"You shut up right now, you hear?" Paul's voice pitched high like a girl's, his face thundered, he shot out a hand and shoved little Mary's shoulder. "My boy ain't done nothin' of the kind! Now you get yourself on out of here or else I'll-"

Sergeant Kelly jumped down from the landing to catch Mary's arm before she toppled off the cement steps. "Here- Mrs. Montebello." He pulled her back onto the step and steadied her. Shaken, her legs turning to water, Mary clutched at Michael's sleeve.

He held her firmly and stared down Paul Philo. "Or else you'll what, Paul?" Michael's voice was low and even but the dangerous edge was unmistakable. Black hair sweeping over one eye, his granite expression and slashing black brows, arm muscle bulging as he held onto Mary, to Philo he looked like a fearsome renegade pirate.

Suddenly unsure of himself with the angry lawman threatening over him, Philo dusted at his jacket and pulled the sleeves taught. He fumbled with the buttons on his jacket looking everywhere but at the broad shouldered sergeant still holding Mary. He could feel Mallory O'Leary's derisive stare burn the back of his head. The crowd twittered.

Philo shot a glance at the sergeant then down at his shoes. "Whatever. The whole town knows she's got a bunch of derelict no good kids she's fostering over at her place. Who cares, they're all nothin' but trouble. You'll see, that punk boy Jessy will be in juvy before he's 12, mark my words. He ain't got no real parents, he's just a foster brat, so who cares anyways."

Philo brushed the top of his head. In the time they were standing there the snow had picked up and his head and shoulders were heavily powdered.

Kelly turned his back to Philo. Letting go of Mary, he leaned over so he could be face to face with her, his forehead wrinkled. "You all right? I'll run him right in for battery, you don't need to be afraid."

Mary shook her head, large dark eyes like a child's welled with tears. "No, I'm fine, please, let him go. He's just overreacting because he's scared. We all are."

Michael patted her on the shoulder then holding her steady by her elbow he helped her down off the steps.

In a flash she melted into the crowd, which now looked like a field of snowmen and women. Kelly made a cutting motion with his hand across his neck to Mallory to end it.

She pulled the collar of her jacket tighter around her head, buttoning it under her chin, her shoulders hunched from the cold. Statuesque nose red, saucy hazel eyes watering, she smiled at Kelly like nothing had happened.

Turning from the rabble rousing redhead, Kelly faced to address the crowd. "Okay, that's enough now. Everyone go on home now or about your business. We should be watching our children and getting ready for a chilling night with this rare snow. I'll meet with my staff tonight and we'll work on having extra patrols around as much as possible.

"But we can't be everywhere all the time. You parents need to keep your kids close at home. Instruct them not to talk to strangers. Later around eight tonight we'll have a peaceful town meeting back here at the hall for parents and officers." He motioned to Whitworth. "And the mayor will discuss creating an outline to protect the children."

The mayor had moved back in nervous dismay at the citizens threatening each other. Now he pulled himself together and nodded loftily at the sergeant.

Bregg came to stand beside his boss. "You know, Mike, that's going to be no small task now with the coastal people here. They're all pretty much strangers even if most have been here a few months already." He stamped his feet and slapped his gloved hands together to warm them, his breath puffs of vapor.

Kelly's gaze roamed the crowd. Most of the faces were familiar. Even though he'd only resided in Halo Valley for five or so years, and part of that he was gone the last few months with the task force, it was such a small rural community he pretty much knew most residents by face or name if not both.

He noticed a good amount of strange faces mingled with the locals. Those would be the coastal people. Although he already had met a bunch of them, he still planned to get on the horse and get to meet all of them. It was imperative that he speak with everyone, try to relieve some of their anxiety over the foolish legend.

He also needed to check on something closer to home, something no one in the town knew about. Or at least until today he thought so.

His sight settled on Mallory. He shook his head slightly. That girl was trouble. Was it always this way with reporters? They get to ask private, personal, raw- sometimes painful questions, tossing rudderless half-truths into the public air, letting words tumble down into fables that suddenly become real.

Like that game of gossip kids played. Everyone sits in a circle and one person starts whispering a brief statement into the ear of the person next to them, then that person whispered the same statement to the next person and so on until the last person hears the statement and repeats it out loud and it bears little if any resemblance to the statement the first person had uttered and everyone would laugh.

Sure, it was funny then, as pretend. In real life, false stories blended with half-truths and half-lies can cut a person's soul like a knife, and tear people apart.

As if feeling his angry gaze on her, Mallory cranked her head in his direction. The heat from her eyes burned down the steps at him, daring him to- to what? Kelly tossed her a vague frown and clapped a hand on Garda Bregg's sturdy shoulder, and the shoulder of his other officer, Justin, who had joined them.

"Come on, Lucas, Justin, let's unwrap this party and mosey these good people on home."

He called out, not loud, but enough most in the crowd could hear him. "Let's head on home now, folks."

Grinning at those he knew the best, he said, "Joe, Gary, Roslyn, Pang, hey D'Wayne, I bet Quineisha's got a big pot of hearty stew heatin' on the stove. Sounds belly warming to me. I can practically smell those hot buttered biscuits baking in the oven ready to sop up that rich gravy. What do you say, let's all go home and take care of the business of tackling a hot supper to hold us through our meeting later this evening."

Kelly carefully pushed his officers forward hoping the momentum would carry and they would push off through the crowd peacefully rustling people on down the street towards their homes.

Mayor Whitworth hurried down the steps and across the grass to catch up with the long-legged sergeant who separated from the pack and was already striding down the street heading back to the police station.

"Michael," he called, body jiggling, Whitworth panted trying to match his chubbier legs to Michael's stride.

The sergeant slowed his pace. "Mayor."

"What, uh, do you think we have anything to really worry about? I mean about the children, not the storm, we're prepared for that. But the children, what if it's true?"

Digging his hands deeper in his pockets, Michael strode faster, the tips of his ears red under the brim of his hat, white puffs came out with his words. "We'll do our best, Mayor, we'll do our best to keep the children safe."

"But Michael, what if-" the mayor called out to Michael as he melded into the crowd that had caught up and moved down the street.

Chapter Seven

He knew it was a mistake the second he went in.

Goosebumps ripped up his spine and down his arms. The door opened right after he'd gotten halfway across the gym.

Jessy dashed over to the rack of weights and threw himself behind them. Rolling into a tight ball he held his breath. It wasn't that bright in the room, only half the lights were turned on. Maybe he had a chance. He clenched his eyes and teeth, and waited.

Boys' jabbering voices filled the air, a couple of female voices joined in, all young, boisterous, teasing. More lights switched on. Sneakers squeaked and balls bounced.

Jessy could hear basketballs smacking the floor and the walls and hands that threw and caught them. Yells, whistles, shrieks and balls bouncing echoed the tiled walls.

He willed himself to disappear, vanish. Suddenly it was silent. He peeled one eye open slowly. An inch from his foot was a sneaker, bigger than his own.

"What have we here, boys?" An adolescent cocky voice said from above him. Jessy didn't dare look up. The crowing voice continued, "Hey fellas, I think I found a mouse! No, it's bigger than a mouse, must be a rat! I found a big rat!"

Sneakers slapped the floor as another boy ran over. Jessy could hear the sneakers squeak to a halt next to him.

"Nah, Drew, that's a weasel!" Laughter reverberated around the hard floor and bare walls. "Pull it out, Drew, so we can squash it with a bat!" More laughter.

A hand grabbed hold of a hunk of Jessy's hair. "Come on outta there, boy," Drew ordered, yanking Jessy's hair.

Wincing, Jessy bit back a yowl and threw his hands up to grab at the hands that pulled his hair but they pulled harder, his neck twisted back until he was forced to stand up.

"Grab him, Rocky bro, help me haul this rat out of his rat hole!" Another pair of hands grabbed at Jessy, latching onto his arm. Then a third set of hands grasped his other arm.

Together the three boys pulled Jessy out from behind the weights, dragging him out until they stopped in front of another boy.

The boys held Jessy so tightly he couldn't move his arms. Juan Trueno snatched up Jessy's hair again wrapping the locks around his fist, he jerked his head back.

Jessy couldn't help but look up at the boy who stood in front of him. He was probably two years older than Jessy, making him around twelve.

"Ahh, *el raton es grande*!" Juan claimed.

"What?" Rocky Artzi scowled. "What'd you say, Falcon?"

His ball cap on backwards, Juan's angled features sharpened when he scowled at Rocky. "Quit calling me Falcon, Rocky, I ain't no stupid bird, I said he's a big rat!"

Rocky made a face. "Falcons are cool man, they kill snakes and frogs and other birds and rats, just like little Jessy here. It ain't my fault you look like a Latino meat-eatin' bird of prey, dude. 'Cides, you know you're cool looking, all the girls in my grade say so!"

Juan scowled, all the boys laughed, they were too young to care about girls yet.

"Screw you, Rock, c'mon guys," Juan said. "Let's flush the foster kid!"

The group dragged Jessy across the varnished yellow gym floor to the bleachers.

Panicking, Jessy yanked his arms out of the boys' grasp and made a sudden run for it- surprised, after a few seconds the boys ran after him.

He got half way across the room when husky Pil Philo leaped at him. Catching Jessy around the waist he tackled him, slamming Jessy to the floor.

Landing hard he banged his elbows and hip, the rest of the boys piled on top of him, kicking and punching and yelling. At first Jessy fought back, but he was drastically outnumbered. Covering his head with his arms he curled back into a ball. When he stopped fighting, the boys let up. They stood in a circle laughing down at him. Then they jerked him to his feet and held him from fleeing.

Short for ten-years-old, but resembling his nick name with brown hair, Rocky said, "We flushed the mixed breed orphan last week, Falcon, I mean Juan, sorry dude, you know it's your little brother Santy that made that up." He grinned meanly at Jessy. "Let's do something more fun! Who's got an idea?"

Two girls had followed the boys into the gym. They linked arms, giggling. Lin-Lin Ming at the ripe age of seven said, "I think we should tie him to the flag pole, and like put a dress on him."

The other girl, eight-year-old Teddy Keegan, joined in, "Yeah, yeah, then we can like put makeup on him, we can make him look really pretty." Braided pigtails, pencil thin with light brown skin, she looked like a cinnamon stick dressed in blue jeans and a blue sweater.

Teddy took a timorous step forward as if she was afraid Jessy might break away and spring at her. Realizing he was held fast, she reached out and twined one of Jessy's dark curls around a finger.

"Them big black eyes," Teddy giggled, "we can put like you know, liner and shadow over those chocolate-drop eyeballs, and some lipstick on 'im and make 'im look like a model. He's so pretty, with his light skin and dark hair, maybe like a Goth princess, ya know?"

Lin-Lin Ming's older brother, Jamie who was eight like Teddy, with her same porcelain complexion, arrow straight jet black hair and crescent eyes, giggled nervously. "Yeah, yeah, let's put makeup on him!"

Juan and Drew held Jessy taut. Jessy's lip was swollen and a big gash slashed in a red jagged line under one eye that was already turning purple. Dressed in a shirt of horizontal black and white wide stripes, and creased black slacks, Drew, resembling an Italian artist ducked and stuck his face under Jessy's to get a good look at him.

"He ain't so pretty now, is he? But I like the girls' idea, what do you guys think? We can tie him to the pole, pants him, gussy him up and leave him in his underwear for when the bus comes, then everyone can have a thrill!" A half smoked cigarette tucked over one ear, twelve-year-old Drew Artzi guffawed, his brother Rocky joined him, laughing like a pair of hyenas.

Pil Philo, a smaller version of his oxen-chested father, Paul Philo, snickered like a stocky monkey. Solidly husky for his age, Pil's round brown eyes half covered by a messy mop of curly dark hair, licked his thick fingers and smoothed Jessy's hair off his face.

The ten-year-old dough faced boy teased, "Oh yeah, let's get a-- whaddya call it, a- a barrette for his pretty hair, he's got girlie hair with those black ringlets! You just know his foster ma cuts it herself, they're too poor for a barbershop!" Jessy struggled again, but his arms were held tight behind his back.

"Yeah, let's hope he's wearing underwear when we string him up!" Plump Tom-tom guffawed so hard his glasses fell off.

The boys dragged Jessy across the floor, he fought them but they pulled him along. The kids all gathered around him in a taunting group, chanting not for the first time, "Mixed breed, mixed breed, gonna make you bleed, keep your face hid, foster kid, 'cause we gonna make you bleed."

Tom-tom Two-Feathers' wide set eyes and mouth opened into an O, one front tooth prominent, the other missing, a perpetual look of dim astonishment on his round face snatched his round glasses off the floor and pushed them up his long nose, the lenses making his eyes look huge.

Short, pudgy reddish-olive skinned Tom-tom ran to the side door that opened to the outside. It said *open only in an emergency*, but all the kids knew no alarm would go off. Tom-tom pulled the door open and peeked outside. He looked around, seeing no one in sight, he waved to the others. "Coast is clear, let's go!"

The group dragged Jessy out the door, laughing and taunting him and teasing each other.

Linking arms again, Teddy and Lin-Lin skipped behind the boys, sing-songing the same chant, "Mixed breed, mixed breed, gonna make you bleed, keep your face hid, foster kid, 'cause we gonna make you bleed!"

Dragged by his arms, he couldn't get traction with his sneakers on the polished floor to slow them down or get to his feet to run, Jessy's stomach coiled, *What are they going to do to me*?

Icy air blasted their faces as soon as they left the warmth of the gym. Being kids, they hadn't thought about how cold it was outside.

Shrill wind knifed right through sweaters and jeans. Teddy and Lin-Lin squealed when the freezing air hit them, like lightning they rushed right back inside.

Juan's ball cap flew off his head exposing his short buzz cut to the wind's wrath. He let go of Jessy to make a grab for it, it sailed off along with the wind, Juan ran off after it.

The rude wind slapped Rocky in the face, swatting his curly hair in his eyes, blinding him. Releasing his grip on Jessy he tripped over a stone and he fell forward landing hard on his hands and knees.

Suddenly set free, Jessy scrambled out of the way of the grasping kids and ran like a deer with bullets whistling past its head away from the jumbled fray.

He tore across the schoolyard, around the building, past the one school bus idling out front with its tail of exhaust streaming behind it, and into the woods.

Running so fast his legs peddled in a blur like spokes on a bicycle, his shoes crunching in the snow, he kept his head low to avoid branches. Never slowing to look behind him, he ran and ran and ran, fear galvanized him, squeezed his throat, energy struck him like a flame from a flicked match.

Fight or flight, he chose flight. If only he had wings, wild wings to carry him above the trees, over the school, skimming house tops, through streaming smoke from chimneys, sailing along with the soaring birds carrying him swiftly and safely home, to his mom, Mary. His foster mom.

His toe caught a root, he tumbled head over heels down a small ravine, bumping and banging and scraping until a boulder stopped him.

When he crashed, his head banged against the boulder. Stunned, he sat unmoving. In a minute, he blinked, trying to clear his blurred vision and catch his breath.

Sitting absolutely still, his head pounding in pain, he listened. He didn't hear any running footsteps, no one peered over the bank at him, no one came sliding down the hill screaming and taunting, ready to string him up a pole or flush him down a toilet. The only sound was the wind whistling through the bare trees and crows cawing in the distance, and his breathing loud in his ears with the clattering of his petrified chattering teeth.

Gritting his teeth to still them, a big heavy sigh of relief drained his tightened body. He put a shaky hand to his head, it hurt. Blood from another gash transferred to his hand.

He stared glumly at the reddish goo. Rubbing the blood on his pants he tried not to picture his mom when she saw the stain on his new jeans.

Now relaxed, he felt the cold. Shivering, he wrapped his arms around his body and pulled his knees to his chin. He had left his jacket at school. Never mind. At least he was safe.

Jessy set his hands in the fluff of snow he was sitting in and tried to stand up. Legs like rubber slipped out from under him, he plopped back down with an 'oof.' He decided he'd wait a minute, catch his breath, wait for his head to stop spinning. Just a minute. In a minute he'd be okay.

Soon he'd be back home, safe with his mom and dad in their cozy kitchen and his foster siblings laughing and playing. His mom would hug him and make him a sandwich, and maybe a bowl of hot soup and some cookies. She'd watch him eat. Occasionally she'd reach over and lovingly sweep a lock of hair out of his eyes.

His head drooped, shoulders slumped, *Just for a minute I'll rest and then I'll be fine...* his eyes closed. He didn't see the shadow move over him.

Chapter Eight

Emmy Zeall parked in front of the auditorium, taking up her parking space and half of the one next to hers.

Pressing the release button to open the back of the huge SUV, she jumped out quickly stepping around to the back of the truck. The hatch had automatically opened by time she got there.

She immediately started pulling things out. Tossing a huge, stuffed tote bag over one shoulder, she grabbed a bunch of pageantry outfits laying them one by one across an arm.

She abruptly stopped pulling out items. Frowning, she peered around the hatch to see the passenger side of the vehicle. Her footsteps crunched impatiently across the gravel as she briskly made her way over to the passenger side of the truck.

Yanking the door open, she frowned at her daughter still sitting in the seat holding a cell phone to her ear.

"What the heck are you doing just sitting there? We've got to go! Get out now! Put down that damned cell phone before I take it from you!" Emmy threatened her eight-year-old daughter in a loud whisper. Other people exiting their vehicles turned heads in their direction.

Simone Zeall ignored her mother and kept chatting on the phone.

Emmy looked about to explode. Suddenly hot inside her down ski jacket, she reached in and snatched the phone out of her daughter's hand.

"You spoiled brat, no eight-year-old child really should have a phone! If you don't get your butt out of that seat right now and help me, I swear to God we are going straight back home and you will not enter the Miss Irish Bright Pageant now or ever, do you hear me?"

"Hey! Gimmie back my phone! Give it to me right-" Simone shut her mouth, crossed her arms and dropped her head letting her long hair hide her petulant expression.

Taking a deep breath, with tiny hands she smoothed her silken blonde locks back in ladylike fashion then turned her head up and smiled brilliantly at her harried mother.

"I am so sorry, Mama, I didn't mean to misbehave. Please, let me help you!" Grabbing her pink winter jacket she slid out of the car onto the graveled drive. Slipping into the jacket and pulling on matching pink mittens, she stood primly with her hands clasped behind her back, smiling up at her mother.

Cold air patted roses onto her pretty cheeks, her big blues flapped innocently, snow lingered on her lashes and flaxen hair turning her into a little snow angel.

As usual, Emmy's heart warmed at her beautiful young daughter. As usual, she gave in. She handed Simone her phone encased in its pink sequined cover. "I'm sorry I lost my temper, baby. Here's your phone. You know these pageants always get my nerves jangled and I guess I become a little irritable."

Simone took her phone and tucked it into her tiny, sequined pink purse. She headed for the back of the car, crafty smile unseen.

They emptied the car and with their arms laden, they pulled the wheelie-carts, filled with Simone's pageant costumes, shoes, makeup bag and accessories bags. They made their way inside the auditorium.

Once inside, Emmy's heels rat-a-tap-tapping on the tile, they called out greetings here and there as they followed the other hopeful little girls and their mothers, everyone's arms piled high with pageant gowns and necessities and pulling the rest on wheels down the big hall to the dressing room.

Her boots off, Simone's slippered feet moved faster like a hamster's on a wheel, she said to her mother, "Let's try to speed up,

Mama, and get past that dumpy Janet John and her tubbo mother. Let's go!"

The pair picked up speed scurrying down the hall passing many of the other women, trying to get ahead of everyone that was already entering the auditorium.

Locals and girls from the coast side as well mingled in the crowded dressing room. The volume was loud with females scuttling about and talking over each other.

The room teemed with mothers giving instructions, girls whining, singing, and practicing their talent, the aids handing out name tags and directing people where to go pointing and shouting. Emmy and Simone joined the exuberant throng.

"Hey, Mrs. Zeall."

Emmy was bending over a bag, rummaging through looking for Simone's makeup kit. She glanced up through a wad of cashew highlighted hair. Pushing aside some of the wad she frowned slightly at the young girl standing there beaming at her with wide, almost exotic almond shaped eyes against an oval of sand colored skin.

The girl shook her head, shoulder length razor straight brown hair swung across her shoulders. She giggled apologetically. "I'm sorry, Mrs. Zeall, you don't remember me. I'm Belle Troicasi. We're new here, me and my family. We came over from Cleasaí because of the storm that's coming. I'm assigned to Simone. I'm supposed to help her get ready for the pageant. What can I do to help?"

Emmy sighed, annoyed. "Thanks honey, but even behind all that eye liner and lipstick I can see you're-"

Simone cut in, "I love your makeup, Belle, can you do mine like yours?"

Belle put a hand up to Simone's face and held her lightly by the chin. She turned Simone's head side to side. "Well, you're kinda young, I mean I'm thirteen and you're like, what, nine? Ten?"

Happy someone thought she looked older than she was, Simone stood up tall. "I am eight and a half. Please do me like you."

Belle hesitated. "Well, if it's okay with your mom…" She looked in Emmy's direction.

Emmy grunted. "It's girl eat girl here, Belle, do whatever needs to be done for Simone to win the crown. We need this win to go on to the next Miss Emerald Princess then on to, well, I'm sure you know the drill, hon."

"Here, Simone, I have a place saved over by that big light and counter, come on." Belle grabbed Simone's arm pulling her to a counter a few feet away. It was set up with a chair and big mirror. She tucked a white towel around Simone's neck and got to work.

"Don't hold back, Belle," Simone said admiring her reflection, "I love a lot of glitz and glam! They call me the Darling Diva around here!"

Less than an hour later the show began.

Each girl came out as called wearing her own pageant creation of bright colors and exquisite sequins, voluminous petticoats, satin ruffles and flashy bows, dripping with glitter, tripping about in sparkly high heels, even the littlest ones at three years old. They strutted and giggled and answered questions with silly thoughts.

Then the talent part began. The dancing and singing and baton twirling. Some just stood there frozen, eyes wide with fright being on stage. Mothers cooed and threatened and madly gestured, calling out instructions.

Some of the mothers standing offstage or in the audience were trying so hard to direct their child they looked like miming clowns.

Lucina Gribble elbowed Katy King aside so she could motion to her daughter, Sally, to smile bigger. Affronted, Katy King gave Lucina a little shove back. Lucina stumbled backwards, just catching her balance by grabbing the curtain. Clutching the curtains,

Lucina pulled herself upright, her high heels turned pigeon toed and legs knock-kneed, glaring daggers at Katy.

Katy turned her nose up, sniffed at Lucina then turned her attention to her own daughter, Megan who was also on stage. She put her index fingers to each corner of her mouth, pushing them up to indicate to Megan to smile more.

Megan glanced nervously at her mother while trying to keep up with her music. Wearing a black sequined tuxedo bodysuit with a satin bow tie and top hat, she tapped a cane. Hopping around, missing every other beat, she looked like a tuxedoed heron stumbling through the swampy weeds jabbing at fish.

Katy whispered loudly, "Faster, Megan, you dope, you're losing the beat, smile, smile, smile, *ooah-*"

From behind Lucina suddenly shoved Katy hard causing her to tip sideways with one foot waving in the air, she tried to catch her balance, hopping on one foot. Her arms flailing, Katy accidentally slapped Emmy in the face.

Emmy snarled at Katy and gave her a good shove from the opposite direction causing Katy to lurch backwards- right into Lucina, knocking her into Roslyn. Roslyn struck out at Lucina, missed, and hit Emmy on the other side of her face.

In seconds all of the stage mothers were brawling. Mrs. Peabody, the director of the pageant stood off to the side, appalled. She couldn't believe the riot she was witnessing.

Megan ran off center stage to help her mother. She took her cane and walloped Lucina in the leg. The other girls took this as a sign and they all rushed over to join the fracas.

Mrs. Peabody ran out on the middle of the stage waving her arms frantically, it was pure pandemonium!

"Bob! Cut the music, stop the music! Ladies! Girls! Please, stop! This is not a saloon- stop fighting this instant!" She started out with a steady voice, but it quickly grew loud and shrill. The members of the audience jumped to their feet, yelling at the mob scene adding chaos to mayhem.

No one noticed Simone, her skit done, slipped out to the dressing room and changed her clothes.

She was going to meet Teddy Keegan in the cellar where Teddy promised she had a cigarette and they were going to try smoking!

Chapter Nine

Joseph Solomon came in through the kitchen door. Slamming the door behind him, he stomped his feet on the mat to shake off the melting snow then kicked his boots off leaving them in front of the door. He dumped a six-pack and his lunch box on the counter.

Pulling off a beer, he shrugged out of his jacket and dropped it and his hat on the kitchen table. He padded through the kitchen in his stocking feet into the living room.

His son, Barty was slouched on the couch playing a handheld video game. Beeps and rings bounced around the room.

"Earphones," Joseph barked. Crossing the room, he slapped Barty on the side of the head as he passed him on his way to his reclining chair.

Plopping down, he pulled a lever along the side of the chair making the back recline and the foot rest pop up. He yanked the tab off the beer and chugged half of it.

Relaxing back into the cushions, he yawned, belched, took another swig and scratched his belly.

Barty immediately plugged earphones into the game effectively silencing it.

Yawning again, Joseph studied his son. He shook his head. He never was big with the video games, didn't see any sense in them. At least billiards or cards took skill.

He finally gave up on pushing the boy to get into sports. All bones and no meat, Barty broke a leg playing football, got hit in the head with a ball playing baseball, basketball- well, the kid couldn't throw, toss, jump, catch, run, he was a totally useless son. Joseph's stomach turned at the thought of the boy being representative of him. *Burp. Damned whore of a wife, the kid's probably the mailman's.*

His mother had warned him not to marry a dancer but he'd gotten trashed and wasn't about to fight off the bleached blonde with the enhanced bosom who dropped in his lap at the pub. She got pregnant the first time they did it, and they got married.

"Barty," he called to his nine-year-old son. The boy kept playing. This annoyed Joseph because he knew even with the earphones in the boy could still hear him. Very quietly he said, "I guess I need to git up and git that belt-"

The boy turned off the machine and pulled the plugs from his ears. "Oh, hi Dad, I thought you were in the bathroom." The skinny kid, floppy sandy hair and ears, and big teardrop shaped brown eyes smiled limply at his father.

Barty had Joseph's coloring but that's where it ended. He looked more like a refugee raised in a destitute country whereas his bloated father could have been an ancient King of England complete with gut, gout and bleary eyes.

Joseph snorted. "Yeah, right, ha ha the bathroom. That smell ain't me boy, it's your baby sister needs changing." Burp. "Listen, you hear the talk about the legend?"

Barty nodded. "Yeah." Hearing his sister whimpering from down the hall in her crib he slid to the edge of the couch to go fetch her.

Joseph pushed the lever on the side of his chair so the back returned upright and the legs slammed down. He got up, trudged over and flopped down next to his son blocking him against the arm of the couch.

Ignoring the boy's cringe, Joseph said, "So, ya worried or anything, about the, you know, kids getting snatched off the street and stuff?"

Barty stared down at the shut off game in his hands. He pulled his knobby legs up, wrapping pin thin arms around them. He shrugged. "I dunno. Kids are talking at school and stuff. Some say it's true and some say it's bogus like Santa Claus, that adults made it up to scare us into behaving. I don't know. Do you think I'll get swiped, Dad?"

He turned vaguely concerned teardrop eyes half covered with long thin bangs up to his father. The baby still whimpered, but Barty had long since learned not to run from his father.

Joseph swigged his beer and slapped the boy hard on his bony leg. "Don't you worry, boy, I'll keep an eye on you. I need your ass here to work that farm out back yonder. If we're lucky, the poor devil will take one of your sisters, that'll teach him a lesson, huh!" He sniggered.

Barty moved a hair away from his father. "Yeah, can you imagine, Da, if he grabbed Rachel? She'd talk him to death. He'd toss her out to shut her up! But she's too old, she's a teenager. And Persia's too little to get grabbed. I heard that the legend guy only takes kids from 12 to like 5 or something, they gotta be able to walk and Persy's just a baby."

Joseph wound a beefy arm around his son and squeezed Barty's skinny shoulders hard until they cracked then he leaned back, his body sinking deep in the old couch causing the cushions to push Barty up like he was sitting on a hill.

Belching between sips of beer Joseph said, "Yeah, what guy in his right mind would snatch a baby he has to feed and change and burp."

"And drool, Da, Persy drools somethin' awful. And she pukes a lot too. So I think she's safe."

"Well kid, you just come straight home from school, and always walk with your buddies. Don't be talkin' to them strangers from Cleasaí. They're all assholes you know. You'll be safe here at home until after the storm. Besides, we need you to get them sheep sheared and who's gonna pull all them potatoes and hoe that back field before the ground gets too hard?

"Which reminds me, don't think I didn't catch that you slept in some past 5 this morning. I need that fence repaired, so you get yourself up tomorrow again before school and get to work on it. So, don't you worry, yer mom and me will be keeping you safe. Speaking of your mother, where the hell is she?"

Without waiting for an answer, he finished his beer, playfully punched the boy's arm and headed off towards the kitchen for another beer.

Barty rubbed his arm, pulled his sleeve up and looked. Tomorrow there'll be another bruise to match the many others that peppered his body. He slid off the couch and hurried down the hall to change his sister before his father returned.

Another few beers and his temper usually raged before he passed out.

Chapter Ten

Before leaving the mayor in his dust, Sergeant Kelly had helped his gardaí disperse the crowd.

He avoided Mallory O'Leary and her cameraman as they loaded up their news van and drove off. Mallory had tried to engage him in conversation but he cut her dead with 'no comment' at every question.

Michael knew she was going to try to pump him for information that he had no intention of providing. Anything he told her would be creatively taken out of context and splashed all over the headlines tomorrow.

His meeting with his staff lasted over an hour. Then after patrols he went to the public meeting at the Hall. A last quick patrol and it was long after midnight when he took off for home for a short night's sleep.

At dawn the next day, he showered, gobbled down a bowl of Cheerios, grabbed his hat and jacket and a thermos of hot coffee and was out the door.

Long strides took him quickly to his snow covered police vehicle, an SUV cruiser. Fortunately the windows hadn't iced so he hopped right in.

After arriving at the precinct, he checked in with dispatch then rushed through some backed up paperwork.

An hour of signing and correcting, he plunked the pen in the holder, shoved the tedious paperwork and files aside and pulled out his cell.

"Hello, Gram, it's me. Where's Matty? She's home? Keep her there, I'm on my way over. I'll explain when I get there. Don't get shook up, Gram, there's nothing wrong. I'll be there in 45 minutes give or take. Put the coffee on."

The sergeant pulled up the snow covered driveway of his Grandma Zinny's beige, A-framed house and parked in front of the garage. As soon as he shut off the wipers the windshield was fully covered with snow.

In the window box, dried primroses, their shriveled, pale yellow blossoms hung over the sides. Many Irish people did this to ward off malevolent fairies. Gram says she doesn't believe in fairies, but why take the chance?

Inside the gingerbread white trim and shutters, the ruffled kitchen curtain moved, Kelly could see her kind face peering out. She smiled and waved.

By the time he got inside the garage she was there with the kitchen door open. Inviting warmth, and the aroma of fresh coffee brewing wafted out, lingering long enough to make Michael's stomach rumble.

Removing his boots, he tucked them behind the door and hung his hat and jacket on the doorknob. He followed Zinny's fairy godmother figure into the house, straight into her comfortable kitchen.

The room with many windows was as sunny as a winter morning can be and cheerful with bright yellows and reds. Two coffee cups, cream and sugar, two plates, cutlery, potato chips, pickles and a platter of sandwiches waited invitingly on the table.

Kelly went straight to the table and pulled out a chair. Grandma Zinny picked up another platter, this one held chocolate cookies. Michael made a grab for one as she came to set them on the table.

She slapped at his hand. "No sir. You need to eat your lunch first," she rebuked him and set the platter down out of his reach.

"Now Gram, isn't it great that now we're adults we can eat anything anytime we want? Besides, have you ever known me not to clean my plate? And I am starving. I could eat the coffee cups!"

"Oh!" Grandma Zinny jumped up. "The coffee-" she ran and grabbed the pot and poured them both a cup, returned the pot and sat back down.

Kelly had already demolished half a ham and cheese with lettuce and tomato and was picking up the second half. He licked a glob of mayonnaise blobbing out the side before biting into it. "I appreciate this, Gram. How did you know I was hungry?" He picked up the pickle spear, it was devoured in three swift chomps.

Zinny smiled and reached for a sandwich. "It's called 'grandma radar.' Besides, it's past noon and it's quite frequent that you show up during the lunch or dinner hour. You need to get yourself a steady girl, Michael. You need to put the ugly past behind you, you are a good man no matter what happened."

She patted his hand when his brows drew down and he started to speak. Her kind smile widened, she assured him, "Of course darling, my door is always open to you." Her smile dimmed. "Plus, you sounded serious, and serious business should never be discussed on an empty stomach. So, what's up?"

Michael's cheek bulged like a squirrel hoarding nuts while he chewed his sandwich, the crisp lettuce crunching. He washed it down with a swallow of coffee. Two more huge bites and the sandwich was gone. He licked a couple of fingers, snagged some chips and tossed them in his mouth.

Sitting back with a handful of chips, he said, "Well, I feel kind of silly coming here now. But," he shifted in his chair. "Well, I just don't want to take any chances with Matty." He tossed a few more chips in his mouth and reached for some more.

Munching the crisp chips he leaned back, stretched his long legs out in front of him and crossed his ankles. Zinny filled his already empty cup.

Surprised and concerned at his words, Grandma Zinny, a retired teacher born with an affectionate smile and sweet disposition, turned at the sound of the phone ringing. Zinny let the machine pick it up.

It was Nelda from the church calling about something. Nelda called at least 6 times a day, every day. Zinny was quite popular and active at her church where she spent a great deal of her time.

63

The elderly grandmother sat forward, age spotted hands gripped the chair arms. Brows slivered with white drew down between compassionate suddenly worried blue eyes. "What are you talking about? What about Matty- is she in some kind of danger?" The long puffy gingham dress pouffed around her legs and out the lower back opening of her chair.

Kelly heard the catch in her voice and hurried to reassure her. Shaking his head he leaned forward resting his forearms on the table, bridged his fingers. "No, no, Matty is fine. I told you I feel kind of stupid now for- well, you know about that ridiculous legend about the stolen children? You may not know because we didn't grow up here. But, ah…"

Zinny nodded. Her coffee sat untouched. "Sure, sure I know about the legend. The entire town, residents and the Cleasaí people alike are talking about nothing but. I dismissed it as just a local fable, do you- do you think there's anything to it? Do we need to take Matty somewhere?"

She leaned towards Michael, curly hair fluffed around her head like silver cotton. Her fingers twisted at the latticed apron she wore over her blue gingham dress. She was the perfect picture of a pie-making grandmother.

Michael scratched the back of his head and plucked two cookies, one disappeared whole into his mouth, he'd hardly swallowed before tossing in the second. The kitchen still smelled homey from the baked cookies. One shoulder raised in a half-shrug.

His fingers too big to fit into the looped handle on the coffee cup he held the cup with his thumb and two fingers and drained it. "I don't know. I don't know what to do. It's probably just a fanciful mythical tale. Except they claim there's logged documentation in the local chronicled history records and almanac. But, I'm sure there's nothing to it…still…"

Zinny picked up an empty plate and stacked it on another one. She gathered crumbs that littered the table, brushing them off the tablecloth and into her hand then dusted the crumbs onto a discarded plate. She picked the plates up, set them down, picked them up then set them down.

Hovering like a nervous helicopter, dawning panic chased away her naturally friendly expression. "First there's that dead guy's skull found in Cleasaí, then little Stormie's mishap...What should we do, Michael? If anything ever happened to Matty, why, I'd never forgive myself! It's bad enough what happened with your sister Kayleen, what with the murder of poor Ceire and your arrest, prison, I-"

Michael held up a hand, glancing around to ensure they were alone. "Shh, Gram, you know I don't want Matty to know what her mother did. I was, well you know, and Kayleen is-"

"I know, I know," Zinny whispered nodding vigorously, sympathy pulled her face down. "I'm sorry, it was all so- so horrible and tragic, what it did to you, it'll never be in the past, Matty is an eternal reminder."

"Yeah, I know. And I don't want her to feel tainted or – or whatever, she needs to feel loved and cherished and safe. I think I'll call Cousin Korey over in Glenfall and have him come down here and stay with you two until this legend-horror business is over. That's okay with you?"

"Of course, Michael, of course. The hair is rising on the back of my neck as we speak. What if-"

He shook his head gently. "Let's not go there, Gram. Let's stay in the present. I wish I could be here but we're doubling up on patrols and this place is too far out of town for me to get back and forth swiftly, which at the time of course we did on purpose. I didn't want anyone except Lucas, Justin and Hollis knowing about Matty and, the, uh past business. It was better that way."

Wringing her veined hands, Zinny nodded. "Of course, we agreed it was the best way."

"Yes, but now I admit I'm growing concerned." His words tumbled slowly, thoughtfully, "It's like there's something in the air, a heaviness, a- a dark panic simmering under the atmosphere. People, even the animals seem agitated, there's fear in the wind," he shook his head again.

"I'm probably just getting spooked by all the talk and the residents and their worry and fighting. Whatever." He wiped his hands on a napkin, tossed it on the table, pushed his chair back and stood up. He gathered up the stacked plates and coffee cups and took them to the sink.

"I'd move you and Matty in with me," he said, "but I think it's still better no one knows who she is. I don't want our past thrown in her face. What do you think? Maybe I should. You guys can start packing and I'll come back later to-" rolling his sleeves up he looked around the sink for detergent and a sponge.

Zinny got up as well and came over to stand behind him. "Don't bother with them Michael, just leave them on the counter." She fluttered nervously around him like a fly around a horse. "Matty won't be any safer there with you gone all the time. We will be just fine here. Korey will come and watch over Matty.

"Besides, the heater's bad in that empty cavern of an old house you live in and the whole place is too- too in disrepair it's downright dangerous and it's, well, it's dreadfully stark. You have only creature comforts and nothing else. You need a girl to come and put in some flowers and lacey curtains and some pictures on the walls.

The corner of Michael's mouth tugged in as Zinny took a breath and went on, "And you need to fix the plumbing and stairs and heat and, well, the other myriad of things that need repairing. It's too dangerous for a child to run about in.

"The stables and barn are sturdy but not the other outbuildings, and you know how curious and adventurous our Matty is. Anyway," she returned to the table and pushed her chair in, "you couldn't dig me out of here with a shovel. I love my home and refuse to be scared out of it or in it. We'll take every precaution with Matty.

"I wouldn't want to ever have to use the shotguns in the basement, but my daddy taught me to shoot straight when I was just a tiny girl. Living out in the rural countryside the danger from coyotes and rattlers was too real, the farm animals needed to be protected. So, don't you worry about us."

Michael grinned, setting the dish soap down. "I know, you might look soft and squishy but you have a spine of steel."

He turned back to his Gram who buzzed around him again. "By the way," he said, "I've gotten several of the rooms in my house nicely done up, especially the kitchen and den and a couple of the bedrooms. I've been waiting to surprise you with a visit."

He smiled but then turned serious, "Anyway, I can't see that there's anything to this legend. But, I can't disclaim anything that may affect the citizens of this town, including my own family. I can't take Matty and sequester her somewhere safe and sound away from Halo Valley without telling the entire town to do the same. Maybe I should evacuate all the children of that certain age group."

Zinny set a hand used to working in the garden on the counter nudging him away from the sink with her rounded hip. "I've already seen the news today. The mayor refuses to execute a mass evacuation and there's nowhere for folks to go. Especially with this storm coming and we're pretty far from a bigger town like Strowell or Glenfall."

A wrinkled hand went to her throat, "But Michael, still…" worried blue eyes gazed up at the sergeant through wire rimmed glasses, the elderly voice quivered.

Michael set both hands on Zinny's round shoulders, the worn gingham soft under his calloused fingers. "Everything will be okay. I'll stop by every night to check on Matty. Korey can walk her to and from the bus stop every day. I think there'll be a lot of parents doing the same thing, of course the schools will be on lock down with extra security.

"We'll start a parental neighborhood crime watch today. Once she's in the house, she's not to leave, not to go to her friends' houses or to the store, not even with you or Korey. Understood?"

Zinny nodded silently, wringing her fingers, crinkles around her eyes deepened. Her fingers twitched nervously, she repeatedly smoothed the apron with her hands, a worrying habit Michael had only seen her do infrequently over the years.

Last time was waiting at the hospital after Matty broke her arm flying off the swing when she was six. Matty had told everyone she was practicing to be an acrobat.

They moved from the kitchen to stand under the arch to the living room.

"And, she's not to answer the door." His face hardened. Rubbing the sides of his jaw with his knuckles, he hadn't shaved this morning in his rush out the door, his stubble made a sandpaper sound.

His voice low, urgently he pointed at Zinny, "You tell her until the spring comes, she isn't to speak to anyone, even if she knows them unless you or Korey or I am present. She has me on speedial. Any of you need me, you know to tap 111 on the phone and I'll know it's an emergency. All right? We clear?"

She nodded again, they stepped into the living room stopping near the stairs. "Sure, Michael, we'll be dog wide extra vigilant, we'll never take our eyes off of her. She-"

"Uncle Mike!" The person of interest came bounding down the stairs, leaped off the third last step and hurled herself into her uncle's arms.

"Hey poppet!" Kelly caught her then tickled her- she squealed with laughter, kicking and squirming until he set her on her feet.

A slingshot sprouting from one back pocket, nine-year-old Matty stood with one hand on her waist, the other pointed at Michael. "You were going to eat and run, Uncle Mike, and not see me?" she scolded him. Twin stumpy red ponytails jumped as she gestured.

Michael Kelly chuckled, a deep sound bubbling in his throat. He threw his hands up like an outlaw giving up. "I'm sorry, poppet, I stopped in for a quick bite and I've really got to go."

Holding her pigtails out to the side he joked, "If these were braids you'd be my very own Pipi Longstocking. Now they're just long red puppy ears."

Matty giggled. "Are not, you're silly Uncle Mike!" She grinned, two prominent chicklet teeth gleamed at him.

Michael knelt down in front of his niece. Setting his large hands gently on her small shoulders, he pulled her in and hugged her tight. She smelled of bubble bath, bubble gum and possibly of frog.

He was careful not to touch her pockets. Zinny stood smiling contentedly at the pair.

Matty threw her arms around his neck and hugged him. "I wish you could stay longer, Uncle Mike. You and me and Banny and my dolls can have tea and cookies."

Paving his expression to still the smile at the cheerful red poppy she invoked, he said, "I'll come by Sunday and do that. But right now, I want you to really listen to me, poppet."

His expression serious he went on, "I know you're always a good girl. Your Great-Grammy Zinny is going to have a very serious talk with you after I leave. She is following instructions from me and I need for you to promise me you'll obey everything she says without any argument. Do you promise me?"

Seeing how serious her uncle was, Matty nodded emphatically, strawberry ponytails hopping. Red ribbons tied in bows became merry exclamation points every time she moved. They coordinated with her red sweater and blue jeans and a red spot of something sticky on a knee. "I promise, Uncle Mike." She said, crossing her heart.

"Okay poppet, I trust you. Now I've got to go. You listen to your grammy, I'll stop back by and read you a story before you go to bed, okay? What do you say about that?" He tweaked a tail.

"Yippee!" The child clapped her hands and leaped in the air. A big toothy smile broke across her face, a smattering of freckles trickled over her snub nose.

"Okay, now walk me to the door, poppet." Michael kissed Zinny's soft, aged cheek and told her, "I'll see you later, Gram." He took up Matty's small hand while she skipped along beside him to the door.

After he left his Gram's, Michael spent the next couple of hours driving around the countryside of Halo Valley and the surrounding foothills of the Maru Mountains, and back across the brown heath.

He didn't know what he was looking for, just something amiss, or something that didn't belong, or maybe something that was missing.

It felt like eerie fingers tickled the hair on the back of his neck, but everything appeared status quo.

Chapter Eleven

Jostling across the rocky shrubby land in his cruiser, Michael avoided known areas where peat bogs lay in wait to suck in some poor unsuspecting hiker.

Finding nothing out of order to cause a second look except a spare swallow, and surprisingly a red fox dashing across the road, a red slash on the white snow that should have been nestled sleeping in a den somewhere.

Michael headed back to town. Hours had passed since his sandwich at Gram's. He left the heath and drove into the forest.

Little snow had drifted or fallen through the canopy of dense tree-tops he was able to follow a wide, brown grass trail that ran only a few feet in from the edge of the woods.

Enjoying one of the few bits of forests left in the land, he covered a few miles of timberland moving slowly through the sea of winter stripped trees.

Emerging from the forest, he drove over bumpy meadows and back to the main road. Now he cruised along narrow country lanes half covered with flowing winter grass and scattered pebbles until he finally reached the business circle in the center of town.

A quarter mile down the street he parked in front of Dandy Tandy's Diner.

Every booth was taken so he ambled over to the sandwich counter. Shrugging out of his bomber jacket, he dropped it over the metal back of a stool and sat down on the red vinyl cushion. A waitress in a pale pink polyester dress and white apron came right over.

Louise Furley

"Hey Sergeant, what can I get you on this blustery day? Something to warm yer cockles?" Wendy Ooi set a napkin with cutlery rolled up in it and a menu in front of him.

She leaned one arm on the counter and leered at the Sergeant. "I can think of many ways I can warm yer cockles there, Sargi boy."

Twining a loose black tassel of hair around one finger she gazed directly into Michael's eyes. Tilting her head back, minty black eyes stroked his rugged face. Her tongue rolled around wide lips making no mistaking her offer.

"Ahem," Michael cleared his throat. He opened the menu and stuck his face in it, mumbled, "I'll have coffee if it's fresh, Wendy, thanks."

Wendy waited in her pose for a second. When he continued to ignore her she unfolded lazily and went for the pot.

"I wouldn't recommend the coffee, unless your stomach is made out of cast iron," A derisive voice next to the sergeant murmured.

Black brows rising, Michael looked over at the young woman sitting next to him. His dilating pupils were the only thing to give him away.

He couldn't stop his eyes from rolling down the slender figure encased in a white angel hair sweater, white jeans and white hi-heeled boots. A white fur trimmed jacket with tiny braiding of black hung over the back of her stool.

Conversationally, Michael said, "My mother would never let me wear white as a child, unless it was to church or a wedding, and then I still managed to spill soda or lean on something black and inky." He eyed her outfit. She smiled. Against his will, Michael's heart beat faster.

A beauty with plush red lips, eyes the color of the sea in the dawn's light and lush hair, to call it brown would be like calling Shakespeare a jingle writer. Rich chocolate with natural steaks of sun and champagne swirled through the wavy tussles. The sea eyes merrily teased him.

"Mine neither," she concurred with a smile. "That's why I do. Wear white I mean. Don't worry, by the time I get home tonight everything will have to go straight to the laundry basket and soaked."

The waitress returned, her face pursed as a lemon peel when she saw the interest the sergeant had in the lady next to him, she hurried right over to interrupt. "Well, Sarg, what can *I* interest you in?" She positioned her body so her back was to the young woman, leaning her arm on the counter she tried to further block Michael's view of her.

Michael's lip turned up at the chuckle he heard behind the waitress. He said, "Uh, well, Wendy, never mind the coffee, I've lost my taste for it. Um, bring me a cup of hot chocolate. I'd like some fresh whipped cream on top, okay? And I'll take a bowl of that chili, is it hot, you know, spicy?"

Wendy discreetly pulled the button at the throat of her uniform open and leaned over further. "I got something spicy for ya, Sarg-"

"Wendy! Get yer blimey arse to work! Get off that bunk now ya hear me, girl, get to those customers!"

Wendy Ooi moaned, scowled. She threw the finger and made a face at the cook behind the counter who yelled at her. An immense man with a pillow of a belly bulging against the white apron that stretched tight across his stained white t-shirt and pants. A grimy chef hat covered half his huge head.

Glaring at Wendy, the chef growled, sweat dripped off his round nose and cheeks catching in the stubble on his face. He wiped the sweat off his forehead with the back of his hairy arm, in his hand a spatula dripped with grease.

He scooped up then flipped a burger onto a bun, dressed it with lettuce, tomato and onion, plopped it on a plate with fries, and slapped a ticket next to it. "Order up!" he bellowed.

"Ah, screw you, Ham Porter," Wendy snapped over her shoulder at the fat man. She turned and smiled down at Michael. "Okay doll, I'll get you some chili and chocolate. Want anything else?" She tugged at the lacy lapel on her pink uniform, trying to expose a bit of cleavage.

Louise Furley

"No, the chili and hot chocolate and some oyster crackers will do." His eyes on her face, with a vague smile, Michael handed her his menu.

Wendy took the menu, sniffed and sashayed off, long black hair in a braid swatted her rear every other step. The cook crabbed at her from behind the line. She snapped back, they continued to bicker while going about their business.

"I've heard about you, you're Sergeant Kelly, right?" The woman beside Michael nibbled on a tuna fish sandwich and periodically sipped at a cup of tea. She picked up her pickle spear and bit off the end.

Michael eyed the pickle the woman was enjoying. He liked it that she picked up the whole dripping spear in her fingers. Most women he knew would have neatly cut it into bite-sized pieces. "You have me at a disadvantage," he said, his smile tilted friendlier.

Wendy plodded over and set a cup of hot chocolate in front of him so hard the liquid sloshed then she stalked off. It was dark and silky with a big swirl of luscious whip cream on top and sprinkled with cinnamon.

He looked down at it, reaching for a spoon. "Gee, this looks more like dessert than a beverage." He dug in. "Mmmm, this is decadent. So, you are," he slurped another spoonful, his eyes rolled sideways at the woman. "You're American."

She set her pickle down and sat back, observing the man beside her. Her lips curled up in a soft red leaf as she watched him lustfully attack his hot chocolate.

"Good investigating, Sergeant. You're pretty observant for a policeman," she teased. "Yes, I am an American, but I have dual citizenship, I was actually born in Ireland but raised in America. My family lives in America."

Her smile rueful, she said, "Far enough away they can't nose into my business, but," she tilted her head with a crooked grin, "too far away that I miss the heck out of them."

She nodded gracefully to him and introduced herself, "My name is Cataleigh Sylvester. I've been sent down from the West Region to help the Cleasaí residents move, get settled and assimilate

73

comfortably here. My family call me Cataleigh, my lazy friends call me Cat."

Michael almost choked. He turned grinning at her. "Cat Sylvester? Notwithstanding the belief is that cat means bad luck in Ireland, that's a heck of a moniker. You must have gotten a lot of ribbing growing up, huh?"

She frowned. "Excuse me. My daddy named me. We can't all have common names like Michael and Kelly."

Michael's lower lip stuck out. "Hey. Those are good old Irish names. Nothing to be made fun of, Miss *Cat*aleigh *Sylvester*." It seemed the Sylvester the Cat thing was lost on her, maybe a sheltered childhood. He shrugged, letting it go.

Wendy set his chili down, hesitated, when he only said 'thank you' without looking up, she swooshed off in a huff. Instead of oyster crackers Wendy had brought him Saltines.

He opened the pack of crackers, crumpled one and dropped it in the soup. Stuffing the other whole cracker in his mouth he stirred the chili. Blowing on a spoonful, he gingerly took a sip. It was good, spicy, hot and meaty.

"So, how is the transition going so far?" he asked without looking at Cataleigh.

She sat silent. Breaking off a corner of her sandwich she popped it in her mouth then picked up her tea cup but didn't drink any. Chewing thoughtfully, she swallowed and set the cup down.

Noting her silence, Michael glanced at her. The side of her mouth pulled in, blue eyes roamed around the counter in front of her. She held half her sandwich in one hand but didn't eat any more. The lighthearted bantering was replaced by an uneasy air.

"That good?" Michael forced a shallow chuckle. He set his soup spoon on the saucer. Brushing aside a lock of black hair that had slipped down his forehead, he turned his full attention to the beauty perched on the red cushioned stool beside him. Her attention was now concentrated on the rest of the diner.

Booths with red vinyl benches and white tabletops lined two walls, and a smattering of tables filled the middle of the diner. Beige

Louise Furley

linoleum that had seen better days covered the floor, the sandwich counter stained cream was dotted with gold flecks.

The kitchen in the back had an open window so the staff could pick up their food from under the heating lamps and stick new orders on a metal wheel that the two cooks could easily reach.

"What's up, Miss Sylvester?" Michael asked when the young woman hadn't responded. He spoke a little loudly over the clanging from pots and scraping the grill and yelling orders back and forth, and the general hum of conversation in the diner.

She hesitated like she wasn't sure if she should share what she was thinking. She watched the front door where a harried hostess took names as people waited for a table. Even at three in the afternoon people still came in. In line, there was a college student with his laptop tucked under his arm, two construction workers in tool belts with construction helmets yawned, behind them a businessman in a suit typed on his phone.

Cat pulled off a chunk of sandwich and stuffed it between bare lips shaped like two halves of a ripe red peach. Chewing pensively, she swallowed hard. Turning towards him, she laid her arm on the counter.

Even speaking softly she could be heard over the hubbub of the diner. "It's kind of crazy." She hesitated carefully choosing her words.

"Well, I was sent here to, you know, the Region sent me to organize the transfer of people from Cleasaí to Halo Valley. I thought the actual finding places to live and work and getting the kids into school would be the hard part, but…" she trailed off, the bustling in the small diner a vague white noise in the background.

Michael made fast work of his chili and was now enjoying the rest of the hot chocolate. "But?" he encouraged.

Cat stirred her tea but didn't drink any. Setting her elbow on the counter she rested her head on her hand and looked at him sideways. Then she sat upright, a small jerk of her head sent her long hair swaying to her back. A slight smile, she shook her head. "But, all that stuff went smoothly. It's the fighting that's a problem."

"The fighting?"

75

"Yeah. You'd be surprised at grown adults. There's like a- a kind of prejudice between the towns, or a feud, kind of like the Hatfields and the McCoys."

"Who?" Michael's brow wrinkled.

"They were American- never mind," she shook her head. "But, then again, both townsfolk also fight amongst themselves. It's funny, some people act like I'm invisible, a servant to do their bidding, or like I'm a plant. They talk and do things in front of me they probably wouldn't do and say in front of most people.

"And some people think I'm their shrink and they tell me things they really shouldn't." She sighed, picked up her sandwich and took a big, yet ladylike bite.

Michael slurped the last of his chocolate and set the mug down. He pushed the mug and soup bowl away. Resting his hands on the counter he twined his fingers and seriously perused the young woman.

"They are *claonta*, prejudiced. Apparently there has always been feuding between the towns. I've struggled to set up programs for both towns to get involved together, you know, trying to foster camaraderie. But residents on both sides fight me on it. It's a work in progress.

"My deceased Ma used to quote the Bible relentlessly," his sigh laborious, he told her, "one of her favorites was Mark 3:24, 'A kingdom divided against itself, that kingdom cannot stand.' We're so far away from other bigger cities that we really need each other. Anyway, what have the people told you that they shouldn't?"

Cat raised and lowered one shoulder, mulling over her words.

Holding her hands around the sides of her plate she told him, "Oh, like this one's having an affair with that one, this guy's *borrowing* money from his job, that one beats her kids, this one's cheating the government, another one is hiding out from the law from another country.

"There's talk of drugs, smuggling, gambling, another robbed and assaulted up in Dublin and came here to start over. Then there's just small mean things like deliberately tripping people and stuff like that, it goes on and on. There's something else a little strange I learned. You are aware that I had to know people's bank accounts and marriage licenses and birth certificates?"

"And?"

"Well, everyone goes on and on about being a local, a native, a *duchasach*." She ignored Michael's smirk at her distorted accent.

"Yet, after pouring over records of both town residents, I learned that there's actually a great many people that have come here from all over the world. It seems they came here to these- these- two miniature villages divided by the mountains to- to, I don't know, I think they came here it seems to hide."

His brows flew up, his grin crooked, he ribbed, "Your accent needs some work." Then he repeated her words with confusion, "But, you said, to hide? Hide from what?"

She shrugged again. "They're hiding from a myriad of things like I said, debt, affairs, theft, abuse, the law. It's like they think they can come here, meld in like they've lived here all their lives. That's why there's such a mix of Irish, Scots, Italians, Latinos, Asians, Jews, Americans, etc. there's even a small group of Native Americans that live further up on the outskirts of Halo Valley."

Michael nodded. "I've met them, they're always the first to volunteer for neighborhood crime watches. But why do you think all these foreigners come here in particular?"

Her brow furrowed in thought, she chewed her lips reddening them more. "I think it has a lot to do with the legend. From what I can glean, they think that records are not kept that strictly here, they tend to be vague, even specifics lack about the legend.

"And maybe they're waiting for the cataclysmic storm and flooding predicted, hoping records will be destroyed and they can become brand new people in name as well as in, well, in mind, in spirit. To be cleansed and their sins forgiven. Beat the law, and, in a strange way, to reinvent themselves.

"Even with modern computers and the cloud and such, these are small towns that haven't manifested a lot of their information into the digital world."

Michael unbuttoned the cuffs of his flannel sleeves, folded them up to his elbows and smoothed his hair back off his temples. He crossed an ankle over one black jean clad knee, his boots still damp from the slushy snow made a small puddle under his stool. Crossing his arms over his big chest, he leaned back so he could see more of her.

He said, "It doesn't make much sense, some of them have been here for years and years. It's kinda farfetched to believe they deliberately blended in to appear as natives, yet the storm hasn't happened for almost I understand 150 years give or take."

"Exactly." She nodded. "They came here to wait for the storm. The prediction that the weather is right for circumstances to cause a catastrophic storm this winter has been on the worldwide news for the past year. The almanac forecasted it long ago. There've been articles on the net for years about it."

"I know, but-"

She interrupted him, a seriousness set in her pretty lips, "I think you guardians need to be highly cognizant, and be prepared that there could possibly be, oh I don't know, thefts, assaults, maybe even murders during or after the storm, if it comes that. It does seem as if the storm truly is coming.

"This whole...scene kind of makes me think of that song, you know, One Tin Soldier. Where the mountain people had a treasure the valley folks thought they wanted, so they killed the mountain people to get it. And the treasure was just a piece of paper that said 'Peace on earth.' I hope this isn't our case here where the coastal people go after the valley people or vice versa, for whatever crazy reasons." Using her pinky she femininely curled a strand of hair out of her eyes.

Michael nodded with ambiguous agreement. "There is a change here, I can feel it, simmering anger, tension, fights springing up everywhere, the trash piling up. Let's hope things don't become lethal. We have enough to worry about with the deadly storm predicted."

"Yes, let's hope so. We need to do some heavy praying."

He leaned in and said, "I need you to compile a list of some of those people that, uh, I want to check out the backgrounds on the people you think might be wanted or, you know, could be dangerous or fugitives, or frauds or grifters, whatever."

She could see her reflection in his clear eyes, like black mirrors so dark they matched his midnight hair. Cat dabbed her mouth and fingers with a napkin and dropped it on her empty plate.

Pulling her jacket off the back of the stool she shrugged it on. Looping the chain strap around her wrist she opened her purse, took out her wallet then waved at the waitress.

"Oh Miss, may I have my ticket, please?" She tried to get Wendy's attention but the waitress was down at the end of the counter flirting with another male customer.

"I've got it," Michael tapped her arm gently. "Yikes-" he pulled his fingers back quickly from the tiny shock when he touched her.

She laughed, joking, perfect teeth shone in a wide smile, "It's kismet!"

"More like static electricity," he replied, then grinned. "But I like your idea better."

"Just call me Sparky. Thanks but I pay my own check, Sergeant."

"It's Michael, and really, I'd like to take care of it. Take it as a thank you for all of your hard work. It's appreciated. I've heard nothing but good things about you. The females call you *aingeal*, an angel, and the men are all smitten. My garda, Lucas, is quite enamored with you, and he's a tough sale. So, please let me, Miss Sylvester."

She smiled. Buttoning her jacket she stood up. "Well, if you insist, thank you then. Please call me Cat. And stop laughing at my name." She playfully batted his arm.

"Sure." Standing up politely, he watched her walk out the door, all dressed in white like an *aingeal*, her hair a *cailin caille*, a brunette veil flowing behind her.

"Stick those eyeballs back in yer head, me boyo," a low voice next to him mocked.

Chapter Twelve

Michael turned to the familiar voice. He grinned when he saw who was in the booth he was standing next to.

"Hey, how're you doing Hollis? You're looking tanned and fit for a man claiming to be pushing 70."

Hollis Hunter set down his coffee. A half smoked cigar set on an ashtray on the table. With a grin he said, *"Céad míle fáilte,* a hundred thousand welcomes, Michael. I've had a full day so far, a couple of hours at the gym, then a hike up the mountain, a massage and a haircut, then here I am at an early supper. Not bad for an old retired Chief Superintendent, eh?

"I highly recommend the squeak and bubbles." A burly tanned hand gestured to his empty plate. He stuffed the unlit cigar in his mouth, threw some bills on the tab, shuffled to the end of the booth and stood up with a grunt.

The men bumped fists then Michael crossed his arms in front of his chest and leaned back against the booth's table. "Old? You're way too healthy and active for a retired Chief. And a haircut? How many was it exactly?" He eyed the man's tanned and shiny bald pate. "You should have considered a moustache trim instead."

"Oh come on then, Michael. I'm trying to grow them into a full handlebar moustache," he stroked one end of his thick white moustache. "Let's go outside."

Catching up his jacket and hat off the seat next to him he walked around and pushed the door open. He let Michael pass through first and then he followed him.

Both men quickly zipped and buttoned their jackets and dropped hats on their heads. Michael's a Stetson, Hollis' a fedora.

The chill wind cranked through the dimming late afternoon, striking their bare skin like a belly flop on an icy lake. On Main Street buildings partially blocked the wind.

Moist clouds drizzled florescent dew that turned into snow on its way down to becoming frozen splinters, settling like a lace comforter, bleaching the winter grass and parked cars.

Turning a corner, Hollis pulled his collar up and fedora down tighter against the brisk wind and turned slightly to look at the sergeant. "So, who's the skirt with the moonbeam smile and rollercoaster body?"

Michael choked. "When did you become a damned poet?" Hollis smirked beneath his hat. Vexed because he could feel his face warming, Michael said nonchalantly, "You, uh, you mean Miss Cataleigh Sylvester? She's the agent they sent down to organize the transferring of the Cleasaí residents to Halo Valley, you know, because of the impending storm."

Hollis snorted. "Impending *legend* you mean. So Miss *Cat*-aleigh Sylvester dressed all in white and black? *Ni me*, I wonder, do you think that was a deliberate cutesy thing?"

Michael shook his head. "No. More of a rebellious thing I think."

"Was it to match the Sylvester the Cat key chain in her hand?" Hollis asked.

Michael almost tripped. Hollis' sly grin teased him. Michael chucked wryly, "I guess she got it after all. I thought she was obtuse, but she was pulling my leg. She must think I'm a real dolt." He shook his head.

"Aha." Hollis pulled at his moustache. "She, like a lovely, slender white Persian cat, and you like a lithe black panther, you will make a great pair, peas in a bud as it were."

Laughing, Michael corrected him, "You're nuts man, and that's peas in a pod, not bud, Bud. And there's not going to be a pair of anything. She's here to do a job and then off she goes, back to wherever she came from. Poof- gone." He snapped his fingers.

"Even better, Michael, a couple of hot torrid nights and then she leaves, you don't even have to remember her name. That's the way to go."

"Listen to Mr. Married 4 times talking," Michael gibed his friend.

"That's five. Like a bad cliché I married Lorielle twice. We keep forgetting we make better friends than lovers. I take that back, we make great lovers too. She's sort of half staying at my place again. I can't help it," he whined manfully, pained at Michael's shaking head. "Gawd man, the sex is sizzling with Lori, it's hot like red ants."

Michael threw his head back and boomed a laugh. He dropped his head, bouncing it then shaking it. "You mean red hots, the candy, Hollis, not the bugs!" He wiped an eye and pushed his cowboy hat tighter on his head.

"Ah, boyo, I might have meant the ants. There's a close relationship between pain and pleasure, you know. Anyway, you can stick to your pattern of never letting anyone get too close. I'm honored that I'm one of the few you trust and confide in." Hollis pulled out the unlit cigar he was chomping on, studied it then stuffed it back in his mouth. Michael said nothing. They walked on.

A horn honked, they both turned. A friend of Hollis' waved. Hollis saluted a wick of two fingers to his temple. A loud pop like an air gun sounded, making them both look back at the car, the tires had run over a beer bottle.

Paper cups, newspapers, plastic grocery bags swept against their legs shuffled along by the wind. Hollis snatched another beer bottle off the sidewalk tossing it on top of an already overflowing trashcan.

"Listen, Michael, seriously, have you taken a look at our town lately? There's a nasty growing abundance of rubbish everywhere. This town used to be neat as a pin, now, every day there's more and more trash on the street. I mean look around, boyo."

Michael didn't have to look around. He'd noticed it too. He had picked up bottles and newspapers strewn in front of the diner before he'd gone in. In the short time he'd been in the diner the entrance was already littered with garbage.

"Again, Hollis, I think it comes back to the damned storm. It's like people have given up, or don't care, they think every bad thing will just go away, disappear with the storm and everything will be washed new and clean and shiny again."

Hollis grunted. "I hear from the Dash Thru Shoppes fellas that people are spending money like it's water. It's as if they think they won't have to pay for things when the bills come due."

Michael shook his head. "I know, it's bizarre. They think their accounts with their credit companies will just vanish? And what about the children that are threatened by the so called legend? Don't they realize it can happen to their child, not necessarily someone else's child?"

Hollis' white brows rose. "The children? Have you changed your mind about the legend? Last week you thought it was a bunch of flooey, and now?"

Rubbing the side of his face, Michael's lips pursed then released. "First, it's hooey, not flooey. Second, I can't take chances on it being malarkey or real. If it's true, these are our innocent vulnerable children. I'm hoping it's not real but what if it is? No," he shook his head, "I can't take any chances. We're battening down the hatches at the station.

"We've had a few meetings and we're upping the crime watch and working extra hours patrolling the neighborhoods. We've sent gardai to schools, churches, businesses, everywhere to talk with kids and parents on being careful. Always staying in pairs, don't talk to strangers, you know, all the stuff."

His hands in his coat pockets, wool collar pulled up around his neck, Hollis nodded his agreement. They continued down the street, heads bent against the biting wind shrilling past.

Kicking trash off the sidewalk, his head down Michael said, "If we all keep vigilant, keep our eyes peeled, what could happen? There's no such things as monsters."

Chapter Thirteen

As they passed a pharmacy the door opened. A man clutching a plastic bag hustled out, the door whooshed behind him clicking closed. He stopped and greeted the two men. "Hello Sergeant, Chief. Gettin' cold, ey?"

Michael nodded, tossed him a short smile. "Hey John, how's the family?"

John Artzi switched the bag from one hand to the other. "Family's good, good. What are you go-"

"Sergeant Kelly!" A woman screamed.

The three men turned. Mary Montebello was running across the street towards them, narrowly missed getting hit by a car. Long dark hair flying loose behind her, her face red and wet with tears, she threw herself at the sergeant.

Kelly gripped her arms and held her back, tears streaked down her pale Madonna face screwed up in anguish. She sobbed and hiccupped trying to catch her breath to speak.

"Mrs. Montebello, what is it? What's happened?" Michael asked, still holding her as if he let her go her legs wouldn't be able to hold her up.

Hollis reached out and very gently touched the side of Mary's face. He held his hand against her skin, warm even in the cold air, who knows how long she'd been running? Taking a long, deep breath, he spoke low and slow.

"She's hyperventilating," Hollis murmured, without taking his eyes off the young woman. Then he said, "Mary, take a deep breath with me, deep, listen and do it with me, honey." He held her face and breathed deeply, loudly so she could hear. She followed him until the hiccupping waned and she calm somewhat. She swiped at her eyes with her hands.

Michael let go of one of her arms and Hollis patted her shoulder gently.

Hollis spoke quietly, "There, there, Mary, take another deep breath and tell us what's going on."

Mary shuddered, tears still poured down her face. Petrified eyes like dark shoals washing up on a beach flashed from Hollis to Michael. "Sergeant, please, it's my boy, it's Jessy, help us-" sobbing again, her hands balled into fists, she pressed them hard against her mouth like she could keep the panic in.

"Tell me, Mrs. Montebello, tell me about Jessy U, what's happened?" Michael gently prompted her. "The sooner you tell me the sooner I can help."

Mary nodded vigorously. Her coat had come undone in her dash across the street, the belt held only by the loops, her long woolen scarf brushed the ground on one side, the other end laid across her shoulder, the fringed end like crooked plaid pins against her heaving chest.

"Yes- yes- help us, help Jessy." She blinked rapidly, wiping the overflowing tears, hiccupped, "He's missing. He's gone. I'm sure he's been taken!"

Ignored, the short Italian's anger ripened. Crossly slapping the paper bag against his leg, eyes spitting thunderclouds, John Artzi grated, "Oh geez, up the yard with you, for crying out loud. All this for that gammy foster kid?" His scathing voice fouled the air like choking exhaust.

"You know damned well that he's playing in the woods, or over at a friend's house for the love of the saints." Black hair greased with heavy gobs of gel combed straight back dried clamped around his head like a granite helmet. The mischievous wind pushed at pieces, loosening them then blowing them into curls.

"No!" Mary turned furiously to Artzi, her arms fell rigid to her side, hands still clenched in fists, she stamped her foot, snow flew up like a sneeze. Long hair shaking, coat flapping, she stomped again. "Jessy always, *always* comes straight home from school. It's a house rule. I've called his friends, no one has seen him since school. That was hours ago. There was some kind of- of altercation at the school, they say Jessy ran off into the woods-"

"You see, just like I said. The homeless urchin is hanging out in the woods, probably hiding up in a tree house reading nudie mags like we used to," Artzi snorted.

"No," Mary shook her head. Catching the short end of her scarf she twitched at it, yanking it until the other end came up evening them. Unconsciously she fingered the fringe, twirling individual woolen strings between her trembling thumb and fingers.

"No John," her pale white face set with brows like inverted parentheses, fine lines knit across her forehead. Shaking her head again, her expression cleared, the lines disappearing like the end of a pencil erased them.

"Jessy knows the rules, and he's not homeless, he has us! We legally adopted him." She turned pleading eyes back to Michael. "Sergeant, he has no jacket, no hat, gloves. It's freezing out and almost dark. His brother Jackson rushed home and said that Jessy was bullied again today, and there was an incident and Jessy ran off into the woods.

"Apparently Jackson came across the aftermath on his way to catch the bus. A couple of little girls, that Teddy girl and the youngest Ming, I forget her name, anyway, they told Jackson that the kids, *your* boys," she shot an accusing look at Artzi. "They said Drew and Rocky were in the thick of it." She pulled her coat closed and tied the sash belt. Pointing at Artzi, "Yes, John, your boys-"

"I-"

"Whatever," she cut him off, a shuddering breath cascaded. "What happened at the school doesn't matter now. We will forgive your boys, pray for all of the kids to grow up good and straight like strong oak trees. But now," tears fell again.

"It's freezing out, Sergeant, he'll die, *please*, maybe it's the monster, they say that it's time, it's time, Jessy's the first to be taken-" Mary begged, her hands clasped in prayer.

"You're bollocks girl, you've gotta be kidding, Mary. The *razzers,* ah, the police have better things to do with their time than chase after juvenile delinquent runaways. The kid's no good, just a little *git,* he's just a bloody foster kid for Pete's sake, who cares anyway." Scornfully, John Artzi dismissed the hysterical mother.

He rudely turned his back to the petite woman to face Michael. "Sergeant, don't be wasting your time, our taxpayer's time, with her folly-"

Hollis crossed his arms in front of his chest, his legs akimbo; he narrowed a look at Artzi, his face impassive but his brown eyes blazed. "What's the problem, John, you created kids just like you, brutish little rocks that bully when in the safety of a crowd but *babby* cowards when one on one?" The unlit half-smoked cigar stuffed in a corner of his mouth barely moved.

"*Amadan-* idiot- *pog mo thoin,* Hunter," Artzi scowled at the older man, slashing his hand in the air dismissing Hollis. Slapping his arms against his sides he turned back to Michael. "Sergeant-"

"Kiss your ass? You're brave in front of the active police." Hollis nodded his head at Michael, taking a step towards the shorter man. His brogue thickened, he cursed, "Artzi you scurvy block of wood, close your eyes Mary and Mikey boyo, me and John here need a moment alone."

Hollis' face hardened, vigorously chewing the end of his cigar, a vein pumped over one ear. Snow covered the top and brim of his fedora.

Shorter and less fit than the older man, Artzi's eyes widened, he took a step back from Hollis and closer to the sergeant.

"You stay away from me, Hunter. You touch me I'll have you arrested for battery, I don't care if you are an ex-chief." He inched closer to Michael. "Really, Sergeant, it's nothing but a big *fribble,* why waste the gardai's time with this kid. Who cares, I-"

"*I* care, John." Michael glanced briefly down at Artzi then smiled kindly at Mary. His smile turned serious.

"Mrs. Montebello, I need you to go home and wait for one of my men to come by. I need Jackson to tell the officer the exact last place that anyone saw Jessy. I'm going straight to the woods now. I want you to double check with anyone he might possibly be with at their home."

Michael gently touched her arm when she started to object. "I believe you that he wouldn't do that, but it's procedure. We have to be able to log that all parties were questioned and all possible locations noted. Okay? Go straight home now and make a nice thick meatball doorstep and mug of hot cha for that hungry boy. We're going to bring him home."

Hollis raised one grey brow at Michael's pledge, a promise he couldn't realistically guarantee.

Artzi broke in, olive skin darkening as if left out in the sun too long, "Listen, Sergeant you can't take this ridiculous wo-"

Ignoring him, Michael pulled out his cell.

Mary swept the plaid scarf over her head tucking a blowing wisp of dark hair inside. She tightened the scarf around her head and neck then smiled weakly at Michael. Her dark eyes wobbled with tears. "Thank you, thank you."

She stood on tip toes, pulled his head down and kissed his cheek then did the same to Hollis then she turned and ran back across the street.

Reaching his dispatch, Michael instructed Dacia to send a garda to the Montebello home to question Jackson, and Jessy's friends and other foster-siblings. He told her he was going to saddle a horse and head to the woods to search for the boy.

He couldn't ask for volunteer searchers until daylight, the forest could be a dangerous place in the pitch of night and he needed his officers out watching the streets and protecting the other possible at risk kids.

Hollis set a rock hard hand firmly on Michael's shoulder and announced, "I'm going with you."

Still holding his cell open, Michael looked at Hollis, he opened his mouth but Hollis cut him off.

"I'll saddle up Timber and meet you behind the school. I expect you'll be riding your Rossie. I'll grab some spotlights and flashlights and call Lorielle and tell her to fill a couple of flasks for us, hot tea in a thermos for the boy, and slap together some sandwiches."

Michael's brow shot up. "Lorielle is at your place?"

Hollis looked sheepish, the moustache ends turned up. He pulled a knit hat out of his coat pocket and slid it on his head under his fedora to cover his bald pate. Michael surmised it was more to cover the spreading red embarrassment than to warm his head.

The older man remarked, "I like a warm bed and a hot dinner and she's one of the-" Hollis shook his head ruefully and grinned. "Never mind. I'll meet you at the school."

Smiling, Michael shook his head as well. "Damn, Holl, I'll have to think of a wedding gift, what do you get a guy that marries the same woman four- five times," he ducked as Hollis slapped at his head. Laughing, Michael said, "Okay, let's roll. I'll grab a blanket too, when we find the boy he'll be cold."

He hesitated, grinning. "I need a new pitchfork, mine seems to be missing, so I think I'll get you one too as an engagement gift, to give Lorielle a little poke…"

"Yeah," Hollis grunted. "You're a funny, funny guy. You shoulda been a comedian. Let's go before I have to endure anymore of your…humor." Shaking his head again this time with affection, Hollis started off down the walk.

The two men set off in opposite directions.

John Artzi stood stupefied holding his bag. Everyone had totally ignored him, left him standing alone. He muttered, "Harrumph. Waste of good policemen for an ignorant orphan git. Wait'll I tell Francine and the boys all the trouble that miserable delinquent is causing!"

He glanced around feeling foolish for talking to himself. Pulling the collar up around his neck, he tugged his hat down over his brow bracing against the blowing wind and stalked off towards home.

Chapter Fourteen

Rossie hoofed under a crystal clear black sky, trailing along the fieldstone fence that began at the dirt road on the upper ridge of Michael's property heading to the stables.

Both man and horse's heads bent, their silhouette a dismal picture of a long fruitless journey.

Like a mini fortress wall, the fence was forged with rocks culled from the hard earth by hardworking pioneering families hoping the sturdy tapestry of rocks would last possibly for eternity, the same as they hoped for their home, farm, and descendants.

When he got near the stables, Michael slid off his horse leaving the reins draped over the worn saddle.

Tramping wearily towards the barn he didn't look back, knowing his horse would follow him, and the clip clops and snorting did sound close behind him.

Lining the right side of the long dirt drive were rows of winter bare trees. On the left rolled open pasture, the rivets and rocks and hills creating scattered misshapen shadows in the silver moonlight.

Rossie's snorts and clip clopping steps on the dirt and gravel were the only sounds breaking the silence, the dense huddled trees of the forest too far away to echo back the beats.

The quiet was actually comforting, opening the night wide and clear, an infinite crisp vastness where anything, real or imagined was possible. Man and horse trudged to the stables.

Distressed wood, paint peeling in grey strips, gangly strands of tan grass stroked the weathered barn attached to the front of the biggest stable. The barn and other outbuildings, shaggy concoctions of old, haphazardly nailed uneven beams of sun-bleached wood, cropped like cracked toadstools behind it.

By the time they reached the end of the long dirt road descending clouds blew in, quickly banding together in dark opaque walls as if hiding secrets and hopes pinned in the night sky.

In the dark, trees, shrubs, sheds, loitered like irregular chess pieces paused, waiting to be moved. A faint drizzle started, mists of fine pellets fell lightly making ticking sounds on the dirt and pods of snow.

The wind puckered an aroma of hay and old wood. Ancient and misfit, the rugged barn welcomed the tired horse and disheartened man.

Before he had gone to search for Jessy, Michael had stoked hot coals in the old wood burning stove and lit oil lamps. The old barn glowed warm and cozy drawing man and horse to its rustic breast.

Michael rubbed down and brushed the horse, cleaned up Rossie's hooves and was filling the feed-bag when he heard a car crunch on the gravel drive. Recognizing the sound of bad shocks he didn't go outside to see who had arrived.

Leaving his horse to feed, Michael put up his tools and the saddle and looked around for his pitchfork. Remembering it was missing, he grabbed a rake to move some extra hay into the manger when someone entered the barn blocking the light from one of the lanterns hanging inside.

Without turning around, Michael said wearily, "Hey Lucas."

A slight pause, then the policeman wearing off duty jeans and a leather jacket, his boots clumping on dirt and straw stepped inside the barn. "Hey Mike."

Rubbing his hands together to warm them, Lucas moved further inside. He waited until Michael had completed his chores and came to a standstill in front of him.

"No luck, eh?" Lucas asked. "It's warm in here, you know, the walls stop the wind and I guess the lanterns and the animals give off a lot of heat." Occasional stomps, snorts and whinnies and a few bleats purred in sporadic symphony from the rest of the darkened stable. Lucas unzipped his jacket.

Michael reached for his own jacket hanging on a hook but didn't put it on. His lips pulled in, he wordlessly shook his head once. "I hated to stop, the longer the kid is missing, the less chance of, well, you know." He ran his arm across his forehead to hide the trepidation in his eyes before setting his hand on a lean hip. He knew Lucas felt the same concern for the missing boy.

Michael kept his expression stoic, he believed the gardai and the town looked to him for strength, guidance, leadership, not mewing his fear like a kitten.

Setting his blocky hands on his hips, the blond officer wore a concerned expression. "I heard over the dispatch you called in to have search parties and volunteers gathered before dawn, as well as for the extra duty for gardai to monitor the streets."

He squinted at Michael. "Geez, Mike, you look like shit. Your eyes look as tired as sand sucking down in a bog. You been out all night?"

Michael nodded and shrugged into his jacket. "Yep. Hollis and I scoured the woods behind the school. We figured about how far the kid could have travelled if he was running. We trod in a small circle then widened the circle, fanning out like an unfurling hose."

He rubbed his brow, a clump of black hair whisked over his eye, he brushed it back.

"Not a sign of the boy?" Lucas grazed his blond goatee with the side of his finger.

Michael covered a yawn with the back of his hand and shook his head again.

"It was so black out there from the heavy cloud coverage we could have missed Old Saint Nick himself if he was there. After a couple of hours the sky cleared and the moon lightened up the woods a bit. When the clouds closed in again it was pure pitch, too foolhardy to be stumbling around in the dark with the danger of falling down a ravine or worse."

"Thankfully it hadn't rained until now and snowfall has fluctuated enough that it melts some in between," Lucas said.

"Yeah, it was bad enough without the weather being against us. We did find Jessy's footprints in the mud on one of the trails leading into the forest and followed them about a half a mile in. That poor kid must have been frightened out of his wits to run that far. The prints ended at a boulder.

"We could see where he'd sat against the rock. But," he sighed. "It has snowed some since he was there. The land leading to the boulder was wetter so the prints were still there.

"But the ground hardens as you move up so with that and the snow we lost any trail that would have been there. We circled out from the boulder. And, there was some blood on the boulder. Not a lot, and we didn't see any on the ground, but…there's nothing good to tell Mrs. Montebello."

He went over and led his horse into its own stall and closed the gate. Then he extinguished all but one lantern and made his way to the entrance of the barn. Lucas followed him.

Breathing in deeply, Lucas said with a half-smile in reminiscence, "Boy, I sure love the raw smell of hay. It's earthy and welcoming, brings me back to when I was a Boy Scout. My best times were at horse camp, after riding all day we'd sit around a fire cooking dogs on sticks and singing, it was-" his lips pursed.

"Sorry, how selfish of me to recollect happy times when young Jessy is likely in dire danger. Was there only the boy's tracks?"

Once they emerged into the frigid night Michael closed the door to the barn to keep the heat inside. They stopped next to Lucas' car.

"Yeah, just the boy's footprints. Mary told us what sneakers he was wearing so we're pretty positive they were his. Jessy must be out of his mind with fear, and freezing, the poor little guy.

"Maybe the search party can come up with something tomorrow, I hope. They'll bring the dogs. I'm gonna go catch a couple of hours of shut eye then I need to meet with the mayor and decide what to do before another kid goes missing."

Lucas opened his car door. "Yeah, his poor mum must be beside herself. After our shift today Justin, me, Babby Bianchi, Dacia and the luscious Miss Sylvester met to organize the searches in case you and Hollis didn't find Jessy. I'm gonna catch some Z's too and then

I'll be there to lead one of the search teams myself. So I'll see you at the school at daybreak."

Clasping his hands behind his back he pulled his arms back to stretch them. Yawning, he stretched his neck, cracking it, twisting it side to side.

Michael bit back a yawn. "I gave Mrs. Montebello a call, you know, keep her up with what we're doing. Her sobs, man, broke my heart. I could hear his brothers and sisters crying in the background, just about killed me, those little kids…" Sighing, "I didn't tell her about the blood of course. Anyway, yeah I'll see you tomorrow before dawn."

Lucas got in his car and drove away, the shocks squeaking off into the dark distance as Michael headed for his house.

Dragging himself up the steps he didn't bother with the lights when he got inside, just showered, pulled on shorts and a t-shirt and fell on his bed face first on his pillow, too tired to get under the covers.

Chapter Fifteen

It seemed like only minutes later the alarm blared. Michael palmed his eyes, massaging them open. He sat up, pushed a swatch of hair back off his forehead and swung his legs over the side of the bed.

He checked the time on the clock on the stand beside the bed. Two hours had passed like a minute. Surprisingly, he'd slept like the dead and didn't feel a bit groggy.

Twenty minutes later, a feather stroke of sunlight trickled through the pre-dawn clouds guiding him out his door and into his car.

He didn't stop to eat or grab a coffee. He went straight to the station, picked up paperwork and 15 minutes later the sergeant was in the midst of a crowd made up of police officers and the public.

Michael looked around. Half of Halo Valley was present, ready to volunteer to search. Seeing a good measure of unfamiliar faces, he figured half of Cleasaí was there too.

"Hey, Sergeant," a soft voice sounded from behind him.

Michael turned as someone mustered up beside him. He looked down into the smiling face of Cat Sylvester. "Miss Sylvester," he greeted her. She was smiling but her creased brow revealed concern for the situation that brought them all there.

He said, "Are you here to-"

"I'm here to assist in organizing the search parties. I have a log already of everyone present," she indicated her clipboard. "Each person has been assigned to a color and the color to a grid," she grinned, "you know, basic search party set up. If I can, I hope to search as well. I've worn my sturdiest boots." She turned a heel, they both looked down at her feet.

Michael's eyes travelled from her boots up over the body hugging jeans to the brown fur-collared jacket. The soft collar framed her face like a renaissance painting. She'd tied her hair back but loosened strands teased out and around in the breeze.

Someone had set out coffee and tea urns and boxes of doughnuts. Michael poured a cup of coffee and checked out the doughnuts. After considerable consideration he chose a chocolate filled doughnut dusted in powdered sugar. It looked like it had dropped on the ground and rolled in the snow.

Talking through a hunk of doughnut he said, "I see no white this time, Miss Sylvester."

She chuckled, pretty teeth gleaming. "No, I don't do white all the time, I'd be spending all of my time in my laundry room. However, I see plenty of white from here." She brushed powdered sugar off the side of Michael's mouth. "Please, call me Cat, Miss Sylvester is too many syllables this early in the morning."

"I-" Michael started to respond when several of his gardai approached.

"Sir, we're gathering the volunteers in lines to get started. Per Miss Cat here," the policeman nodded to the young woman, "each group of volunteers will be headed by a garda. We don't want anyone getting lost or hurt, plus we must protect anyone, uh, you know, like a female getting harassed by a lout or, uh, you know." The man blushed.

"Yes," Cat stepped in. "Since we don't know everyone, we must make sure the volunteers themselves are safe. Everyone either brought their own or was given a whistle. Jay at the Slipin and Pickin came in from way up the interstate and donated them.

"Also, we have not allowed any child under 18 to be involved, and all adults have signed a paper swearing that while they are searching if they have any children under the age of 18 at home that they are supervised by an adult.

"I've set up a care center inside the school with some of the volunteers that will be babysitting for anyone that wants to search but doesn't have someone to help watch their kids."

"Great, Miss... Cataleigh, I see you have everything under control. That frees me up to join a search team myself." He motioned to her clipboard. "Which team am I assigned to?"

One side of Cat's lip pulled in. Her eyes moved from his to a group of excited jabbering volunteers walking by.

The air was static with nervous energy, scores of people wandered around the schoolyard, a few acting like it was a big social function.

"Well, I know every person is needed for a search this vast, but, I think you're really better off here, answering questions, organizing, manning the radios. Your strong presence will relieve a lot of anxiety."

She prepared herself for his angry barrage. It was obvious he was a man of action and might resent being hemmed in.

Michael thought about it. Reluctantly, he acceded with a beleaguered sigh, "All right. I see your point. Okay then, let's get this thing rolling."

Not expecting him to give in so easily, Cat's rigid shoulders released. She dropped the clipboard she hadn't realized she held tightly against her chest and smiled. She walked briskly to the center of the yard where the command station was set up, Michael striding alongside her.

When they reached the station, she held up her hands, the clipboard clutched in one hand. "Please," she called out loudly. "Can I have your attention please, let's get started."

The crowd immediately quieted each other in waves and gave Cat their attention.

"Okay," she said pleasantly, her tone slightly authoritative. "Everyone has been assigned a color, and you know your team leader. Leaders, please hold up your flags."

Each officer assigned as a leader was given a flag tied to a stick denoting their team's color. Raising their arms, they held the flags up for view giving them a few exuberant waves.

"Very good. So, everyone, please remember the orientation from this morning. Follow the rules, they are for yours and the missing child's safety. You stay with your team. Everyone has an assigned buddy, no one is to get out of sight of your buddy. Stay together. If you see anything of note, you blow your whistle. Your leader will review your finding and contact us by walkie-talkie."

Cat glanced around at the crowd. "Any questions, ask now, or ask your team leader." Pausing for a second then she said, "Are there any questions?"

People that didn't have cell phones were also given walkie-talkies so no one would be out of touch. Anything could happen in the woods. They'd already gobbled up one person.

There was a wee bit of murmuring but no one spoke out.

"All right then, everyone go to your team leaders. Team leaders, review your rosters then go ahead and start out. Remember the scheduled break times, please, and the check-in times. Everyone grab at least one bottle of water and a power bar before heading out. Good luck and God Bless." She indicated for people to start leaving.

The chaplain had led a prayer just as Michael arrived for the search to be successful and for everyone to return safely, especially Jessy U. Montebello.

The murmuring of the crowd grew as everyone located their team leaders and their names were checked against the roster. Their direction and area to search were previously determined. The teams immediately marched to the woods and pastures. Within a few short minutes, the people melted into the forest.

It was eerily quiet as the volunteers had been told to keep talking to a minimum so they could hear if Jessy called out, or to hear someone shouting or whistling if they found something. At least it would be easier to see in the forest thanks to the denuded winter trees.

Cat and Michael made their way over to a fire pit in the command area. A robust fire billowed in the chilly wind. Heads turned as a car came speeding up the driveway. The car screeched to a halt. Both front doors popped open, two people jumped out and hurried over to the pit.

"Mr. and Mrs. uh, Troicasi?" Michael left the fire and approached the couple.

"Yes, Sergeant, please forgive us for being so late. Our son Red ate something and was dreadfully ill, he-" Mrs. Troicasi apologized.

Mr. Troicasi touched her arm to quiet her/ "Hush, Dee, they don't want to hear all the gory details." He turned to Michael and told him, "We rushed over after making sure Red was all right. He seems to have recovered and is with his sister, Belle. We really want to help. Tell us what we can do."

He scanned the area. His Egyptian, horse-like face fell. "It looks like we're too late to join the search parties?" He looked hopefully at the Sergeant. "Can we still participate?"

"Please?" Dee Troicasi joined Dusty's plea. "We'll do anything we can to help." Even with a two inch heel on her boot, Dee's auburn head barely reached her slim husband's shoulder.

Cat regarded her clipboard then smiled at the couple. "Sure. I have a team that has less people on it than the others because it was made up of latecomers, like-" her smile broadened.

"Like you two. They're the violet team; they're searching closest to the edge of where the woods join the school yard. I'll call them."

She opened her cell and spoke briefly into it then said to the couple, "See over there," she pointed towards the forest. A person stood right at the clearing, waving a purple flag.

"I see him." Dusty Troicasi shook Cat's hand vigorously. "Thank you, Miss, thank you. We so wanted to do our part." His long pointed chin stretched with his grateful smile.

Returning his smile, Cat said, "Go ahead and join the violet team. Boone Hicks will give you a quick review of the orientation we held this morning before dawn." She pointed to a cooler. "Don't forget to get bottles of water over there, and grab a couple of power bars. Oh, and help yourselves to doughnuts."

"Thank you!" Dee chirped. They grabbed up water and bars and some doughnuts, then the pair ran off to join the violet team.

"What're their names, Sergeant?" Cat asked, pen poised over her graph.

"That's Dusty and Dee Troicasi. They're from Cleasaí, I can't remember their real first names, they were kind of complicated. Wait, Dee is Herodias, I think she said, and," his lips pulled in, he shook his head, "nope, can't pull out his name. Just make it Dusty and Dee Troicasi." Michael reminded her, "You know him, he's the guy that risked his life to rescue little Stormie Dodge. His picture was in the paper."

Cat nodded her head vigorously. "Oh yes, now that you mention him I recognize him. He was a true hero! From what I heard you were involved as well." Her lips lifted mischievously at his discomfort.

He looked away, the tips of his ears reddened. "I was just doing my job, actually I was just an anchor. That guy Dusty was amazing. He didn't think twice, just dropped to the ground with his crazy frog legs and practically fell in trying to get Stormie. I was only an ankle holder."

Cat smirked at him. "Uh huh." She scribbled their names, then frowned. "I should have gotten their address and phone number, oh well, I guess we can always track a hero..." She finished and they moved back near the fire.

A few of the people from both villages that were disabled or too elderly or not fit enough to be active in the search were scattered around the fire.

They wanted to volunteer and help in some kind of way. They made sandwiches and poured hot drinks for when the search parties took breaks, and handed out flyers, kept track of who was where, manned phones, anything to assist.

Standing in the center of the group, Cat felt like she was at a quilting club. People chatted amiably, gossiping and sharing stories. After pacing for a few minutes, Michael strode off.

"What's with our sergeant, Miss Cat? Does he dislike feeble folks?" An elderly lady questioned as the group watched Michael stalk away.

Cat sighed, she wished she could move around too like the free sergeant. She loved to run but there had been no time this morning. She ached with the desire to hit a trail, go running through the

100

woods. But it was her job to control the search parties and be available to answer questions and to handle anything that may occur.

She watched Michael moving quickly towards the woods. A corner of her mouth tugged in. Obviously he was the kind of guy that had a hard time sitting on his hands when something needed to be done, like finding a missing child. He wanted to be actively out looking, not standing around chit-chatting and answering phones.

It was warm near the fire. Cat opened her jacket, her mind wandered. *Michael Kelly was probably the type that ran from commitment too. At his age he should be thinking about getting married and having- oh-* she bit her lip- *what do I care what the man is like!*

"Miss Cat?" The elderly lady tugged at Cat's sleeve.

Cat blinked, then realized she hadn't answered the woman's question. "No, Mrs. O'Rielly, I think he's just jam-packed with energy and can't stand to sit around twiddling his thumbs. He's a man of action I've been told."

The group around the fire watched Michael faint into the forest.

Several hours later, after teams had come back in for lunch and gone back out, some people grew tired and went home. Another couple of hours passed and the teams wandered in to refill their thermoses with hot tea, coffee or hot chocolate.

By four o'clock the lawn was freckled with tired volunteers sitting in lawn chairs sharing their views of the search.

Thankfully it wasn't snowing, and surprisingly low clouds caused a humidity that actually warmed the area a little.

Vehicles continued coming and going. A car roared up, swerved around the other cars and stopped so abruptly the car bounced. John Artzi scrambled out of the vehicle, a stricken white-faced woman exited right behind him.

"Where the hell is the sergeant?" Artzi yelled at the crowd milling about, slapping his hand on the command card table.

Cat separated herself from the group and trod calmly towards Artzi. "What is it, sir?"

Slicked back black hair, winged black brows, eyes like dart boards the brown irises with ragged lines of red veins streaking from them, sweat streamed down his face. He shook his head back and forth like he was violently denying something.

Arms bowed, hands clenched, he practically hopped from one foot to the other. "Where the hell is Sergeant Kelly?" He demanded, "I want to see him now!" and slammed his fist on the table, everyone jumped.

His wife, a female version of the short Italian, stood beside her husband wringing her hands. Hair escaping from her black bun swarmed around her head in the wind.

Keeping her voice low and hushed, Cat calmly set the clipboard down on the table. "Sir, please tell me what you need, I will contact Sergeant Kelly immediately-"

"Now!" Artzi screamed. "I want him now!" Slamming his fist on the table again, everything on it jumped. "He's out wasting his time looking for that git foster kid and my own boys are gone!"

Grabbing Cat's arm, his fingers dug through her jacket cutting off the blood to her hand, he bellowed, "You get him here now!"

Cat froze, staring Artzi in the eye.

Furiously, Artzi shook her arm, but she refused to respond. "What's the matter with you, girl? Are you a deaf mute for crying out loud? What the-"

She stared at his hand squeezing the life out of her arm.

He growled and roughly shoved her arm away.

Cat could feel the emotion vibrating from the man, obviously greatly disturbed. When he let go of her, she pulled out her cell and pushed Michael's number. She spoke low but tight and brief, "You should come here right away."

She closed the phone and slid it into the case clipped to her belt. Her face soft yet bereft of any hint of a smile, she said quietly, "He'll be here immediately."

Francine reached her husband's side. They clutched each other. The pair resembled two brittle lollipops. Eyes bulging, Francine's face was white as a sheet and John Artzi's was red.

In minutes they could see Michael emerging from the woods. He approached them with quick but controlled steps. John shook off his wife and stormed up to Michael.

His face a blank, the sergeant glanced briefly at Cat then to Artzi.

"John?" Michael addressed the obviously flustered man.

"My boys! It's my boys!" he yelled hysterically, his face bursting. The anger switched sharply to fear. "Please, Sergeant, please, they're gone, they're gone…" his voice squeezed into a wail. Francine stood next to her husband, her hands twined together so hard her knuckles were white.

Michael gently touched the shorter man on the shoulder. "Okay, John, tell me, you have to tell me exactly what's going on so I can help you."

John's huffing breathing wavered, he wiped the back of his sleeve across his brow. "I, we, uh…Franny and I went to see her sick, elderly Aunt Minna, and, mind you," his brows drew down, he scowled at Michael.

"I strongly admonished the children to stay inside and don't answer the door to nobody, not even you buzzers." He looked sheepish. "No offense, Sergeant."

Michael made no comment.

Artzi went on, "Anyways," he took a shuddering breath, "me and Franny got home, we was only gone an hour, and, and, our girl Salome, and our youngest boy, Alex, said Rocky and Drew were gone. Gone? We asked. Whaddya mean gone? Didn't we tell you kids to not leave the house for any reason?"

Gritting his teeth and shaking his head, Artzi groused, "Them kids I tell ya, I'll thrash the daylights outta them when I see 'em. Little bastards, giving their mum and me such a fright, they forget the last whipping for the last time they-"

"John!" Francine squawked.

Artzi took a breath. "I just don't understand, Sergeant," he turned a grievous face to Michael, to Cat and back to Michael.

"All right, John, simmer down. Have you looked-"

"Looked! Goddammit Kelly, of course we looked. We called their friends, we searched the neighborhood, the house, the cellar, the yard. Frankly, there's no reason for them to be out. With the curfew on and everyone making their kids stay home, there's nowhere for them to-"

Michael interrupted him, "Kids always do things that don't make any sense, that's what makes them kids and unpredictable. Tell me what your other children said, like did they leave the house, let someone in, climb out a window? How did they go missing?"

Artzi shoved his hands in his jacket pockets and opened his mouth but his wife spoke over him.

Francine glared at her husband. "You wasted so much time, John, threatening and slapping Alex and Salome, thinking they were playing us, or protecting Rocky and Drew, we could have-" breaking off in a sob she pulled her hood up over her hair and tightened it against the chill wind that had picked up.

John turned on his wife, his fist in her face. "You shut up, Fran, it's not my fault it's the-"

"All right folks, please focus. Tell me the specifics, you're wasting more time bickering," Michael rebuked the couple, stepping close to them to prevent any assault.

"We," John started, heaved a deep breath, let it out. "Okay, we came home. Salome and Alex were in the den watching the telly. We changed our clothes, got a snack and joined them in the den. We don't have a large house. We noticed right away, because of the quiet, that the two boys weren't around. So I asked the others where were they?"

Francine stepped in her voice shaking, "You could tell something was up. They acted scared. They were quiet and staring blankly at the TV. We have four kids, the house is always noisy, but, but not this morning…it was different…" Tears streaked down her face, she tucked her arm through her husband's and looked up for him to continue.

Artzi turned his palms up. The steam drained out of his anger. His voice trembled, "There's nothing, really, to- to say. I asked them where the boys were, they said they didn't know. After ten minutes of questioning them, you know kids, ya gotta drag everything outta them inch by inch. It boiled down to Salome got them all breakfast, she's the oldest at 15.

"They ate then she cleaned up the kitchen. Alex says he went to his room to listen to music, and the boys, they told us, went into their room for- for whatever kids do in their rooms. Salome said after cleaning the kitchen she went to her room and went on her Fakepage or Faceoff or whatever that chat thing online is.

"Somewhere around an hour later she came out to get a drink, noticed the boys' door was open, the room empty, she figured they were in the den or the kitchen. She joined Alex who had come back downstairs to the den to watch the telly. I guess after 20 or 30 minutes one of them said vaguely to the other, 'where are the boys?'

"Then, after another 20 or so, they got a little suspicious that they were up to something, and decided to look around the house. And," Artzi glanced down at his tearful wife.

"They discovered the same as us, the boys were nowhere to be seen. Salome said they neither saw nor heard a thing. One minute they were there and the next minute- they just weren't there." He sighed heavily, his eyes aggrieved. Even in the chilly air, beads of sweat rolled down from his temples.

"You have to help us Sergeant, please!" Francine cried. Long grey skirt tricked around her calves, her long coat buttoned unevenly over it. Part of the collar of a blue sweater stuck messily out of the top.

She had thrown the coat on her plump body as they dashed out the door in a panic and buttoned it as they hurtled to the school with her husband driving like a maniac.

The car had swerved all over the road, tires screeching he ran red lights and stop signs, he was speeding so fast Francine prayed the police would pull them over, force him to slow down.

"Yes, you gotta find my boys, Sergeant. It's not some snotty nosed, git foster kid missing, now it's *my* boys!" John jammed his fists to his sides, his face darkened again.

Cat remained silent. John Artzi seemed to get agitated easily and she didn't want to antagonize the situation. She realized the people still scattered around the premises were watching them. Some were starting to drift over, they could see something was obviously amiss.

Michael called out to a garda, "Jarislov, please come here."

The garda hurried right over. "Sir?"

"Jarislov, go over to the Artzis' house with them and check out the scene. Two of his boys are missing. Take, uh" Michael scanned the area. Everyone was busy doing something. "Lucas!" he called over to the beefy blond. Lucas had just exited the woods with his search team, he immediately came to them, boots sloughing over the wet grass.

When the garda approached, Michael told him, "The Artzis' oldest boys are missing. Go with Jarislov and do a diligent search of their house, yard, neighborhood, call all their known acquaintances, family in the area and interview the neighbors. And do it fast. Keep me abreast of everything as it's happening. Got it?"

"Yes sir." The two gardai and the Artzis promptly left for their respective vehicles and exited the school area.

Michael chewed the tip of his thumb for a second, the area had quieted so much a dropped pin could be heard.

He pulled out his cell and dialed. As soon as his dispatch picked up, he said, "Get me MI 5."

Chapter Sixteen

The bartender punched the keys on the cash register, the drawer sprang open banging to a stop an inch from his stomach. He slipped the money under the clips and shoved the drawer closed.

A few steps to the right and he snatched two beer mugs out of the crushed ice. His Irish ancestors traced back for generations.

Karl's red moustache flowed under bright red round cheeks, and hair like a curly orange collar circled the lower part of his head leaving the top bare and shiny like a bowling ball.

Holding the mugs in one hand, Karl filled them with draft beer. Foam rolled up and over the lip of the mugs, streaming down his hand.

Dripping a trail across the floor, he set one in front of a heavy man hunched over the bar, and one in front of a thinner man perched next to him.

The thin Native American man yawned and reached for his beer. Ignoring the inch of froth, he slurped, the foam layering his upper lip like a white moustache. The heavier African American man gulped his beer, belched, gulped some more until he drained a third then set the glass down.

"Yer don't know beans about football, D'Wayne Fady," the Native American slurred to the other man.

"This ain't real football over here, Jim Two-Fedders, ya dumb fu-"

"Come on, boyos, keep it clean. I don't go to your country and foul it up, now do I?" the bartender interjected. He wiped his hands on a towel, threw it over his shoulder and picked up some glasses. He held the glasses over a glass washer, pushed a pump with his foot and plunged the glasses up and down to clean them.

"*Is Cuma duit*, that's none of your business, Karl,"

The bartender set his wet glasses on a towel then leaned over the bar, spear-eyed at Jim Two-Feathers. "My bar, my business, you gee-eyed bag of crap, yer fiery just like your real first name, Hakan, everybody knows Jim is a nick-"

The skinny man cut in, "You bet I'm fiery. Gimmie some more of this fire-water and I'll do a rain dance on the bar!" He joked laughing loudly swigging his beer.

Karl the bartender snorted. Pulling the towel from his shoulder he picked up a glass to dry it. "Fire-water! Ha- you dumb plonker stereotyper, it's just a grimmy bit o' brew."

With only a short counter lined with a handful of rusty colorful stools like tarnished plastic jewels, and half a dozen wooden tables, the dimly lit tavern had one picture window.

Grainy sun struggled to push through the grimy window to light up the clichéd dusty painting of a voluptuous naked woman on the wall behind the bar.

D'Wayne Fady said, "We both have lived here for so many years we're practically Irish. Anyway, it don't matter, Karl. He's a sissy-pants redskin, anything with 5% alcohol, hell he could get blustered on Nyquil."

Draining his mug he slammed it on the bar. "Another!" he roared. Then asked quite peacefully, "You got any barmbrack for us to nibble on?"

Skinny Jim's head drooped and bobbed a bit. He tried to train his intoxicated cross-eyes on the man next to him, "You quit calling me a redbin you-"

"Ha!" D'Wayne blurted. "You can't even speak English, it's redskin you moron." Karl brought him another beer.

"Come on fellas, we'll have no name callin' and ancestry bashing, no racist crap, you guys are best friends when yer sober. This whole dang town is just jarrin' with fights. What's goin' on?" Karl stood back, knuckles curled back on his hips, shaking his head.

D'Wayne pulled some crumpled bills out of his pocket. He stared at the wiggling money bleary-eyed, separated a few and set them on the counter.

"You're the moron, moron." Jim Two-Feathers raised his mug in a mocking salute to his friend then drained most of it.

"Oh yeah?" D'Wayne responded, "Well you're as stoopid as that boy of yours, Tom-tom. My girl Teddy who is eight is in class with your nine-year-old and she says he's not skinny like his da, can't even throw a ball, he's a chubby yella boy with a mouth like an O and one tooth hangin,' even with glasses he's blind as a bat."

Jim hesitated. Blinking hard, has face turned severe, red blotches popped out all over his ruddy face. He stumbled off the stool and to his feet, black hair sticking out all over in messy spikes. He jabbed D'Wayne awkwardly in the arm with a fist.

"Don't you talk about my boy like that, you- you plonker you!" He almost fell backwards but grabbed at the bar to steady himself.

D'Wayne swiveled on the stool then pushed himself off. His legs wobbled, his belly and neck jiggled while he gained his balance on feet as big as tires. He stuck a fat finger in Jim's face and waggled it. "Don't you call me a drunk you drunk. Yer kid Tom-tom is stoopid cause of all the times you done swatted him in the head."

His long nose in the air, Jim pulled his skeletal frame up to his highest height and looked up at his large friend. "Do you think if you let those bushy eyebrows keep growing up that they'll cover your receding hairline? Huh?

"And talking about being mean to your kids, Tom-tom told me one day you were teaching Teddy to ride her new bike for the first time and she fell and scratched your car, so you took the bike and dumped it right into the trash can. Now that's parenting!"

D'Wayne's jowls jiggled, brown eyes squinted, hands like pork shoulders rolled into fists. "Why you-"

"Hey now boys," Karl coaxed, setting his palms on the bar he leaned over to break up the two friends. "Come on, let's have another Guinness and watch the game."

"I'm a good da." D'Wayne jabbed a beefy knuckle in Jim's bony chest.

Jim stumbled back against the bar. He shook his head to clear it. "Hey, what the-" Blinking hard, Jim pushed against the bar throwing himself at the heavier man.

Taken by surprise, D'Wayne grabbed at Jim, wrapped his fat arms around the thinner man and squeezed. Angry, but too drunk to feel any pain, Jim kicked D'Wayne in the shin, D'Wayne yowled and let go.

Jim threw himself at the fat man again, this time using momentum he knocked him backwards.

D'Wayne grabbed at Jim, catching his shirt, he pulled him down with him. The two brawling men fell to the floor kicking over bar stools rolling and crashing against the bar, tables and chairs skidded over the worn wooden floor.

Karl rolled his eyes heavenward. "This town, it's outta control, like a demon is taking over everybody's good sense." He sighed, baffled, "This is the third fight this week."

Tossing the towel on the bar he went over, lifted up the counter top and came out to break up the fight.

By the time he reached the two men rolling and punching and cursing in the middle of his barroom floor, the front door flew open.

Two women, one Native American, the other African American, pushed their way inside, screeching at the top of their lungs.

"D'Wayne!"

"Jim!"

The brawling men stopped and raised their bruised and bloodied heads.

"Adoette?"

"Quineisha?"

Quineisha Fady marched over to her husband with her hands on her hips. She glared down at him. "D'Wayne Archibald Fady, what do you think you are doing down there?"

D'Wayne blushed, his eyes darted to his friend Jim. "Uh, we're uh, Jim's drunk and he slipped and fell, he pulled me down with him, I-"

"What?" Jim turned to him. "I did not! You-"

"D'Wayne!"

110

"Jim!"

"Ladies." Karl approached the women with his hands out, palms up. "Ladies, come in, can I get you something to drink?"

Adoette screamed, "Shut up all of you!"

Her trembling hand over her mouth, Quineisha put her arm around Adoette. The pair looked frantic.

Quineisha cried, "We're here because, the kids, our Teddy-"

"And our Tom-tom-" Adoette chimed in.

"Are missing!"

Chapter Seventeen

On her hands and knees, her head upside down, Matty inveigled the dog to come out from under the bed. "Come on, Banny, come on out here, I got somethin' for you."

The small fair dog with one brown ear hunched on the floor under the middle of the bed warily eying the girl.

"Seriously, Banny, I won't put the bonnet on you again, just the cute little jacket. Come on, baby." She flattened onto her belly to crawl close to the dog. Stretching out her arms she caught his legs. The little redheaded girl pulled the dog out from under the bed and scooped him into her arms.

Cuddling him in her lap she sang an old poetic prayer to him. "Leprechauns, fairies, fun and laughter, lullabies, dreams and happy ever after, for Banny boy…" Humming she brushed his back with her hairbrush. He allowed her to snuggle him without squirming.

"There, there, Banny my baby, I love you. Look at this pretty jacket I got for you. You can wear this for the holidays. In the spring you can wear it for Easter and we can take a lovely walk out by Ells Glen and look for fairies.

"Gram told me they run along the tops of the fieldstone fences that line the green pasture. Lookit-" holding the dog with one hand she picked up a tiny green jacket.

Realizing he'd been had, the little dog yelped, leaped out of her lap and scurried back under the bed. He backed in far away from the frilly bed linens that draped to the flour.

"Banny! Bad doggie!" Matty stood with the jacket in her hand. She bent over, lifted up the white linens and peered back under the bed. "Come on, Ban-" hearing a sound at the window, she stopped and stood up. The little lass skipped over to the window, pigtails bouncing, she pushed back the frilly curtains and looked out.

"Oh my gosh! That's so cool!" She unlocked the window.

****

"Sergeant!"

Standing out on the acre of lawn that surrounded the Hall, Michael and Cat were surrounded by gardai, residents and reporters.

Hearing someone calling him, Michael turned his attention from the hub-bub and towards one of his officers rapidly approaching, his face showed it wasn't good news he came running to share.

The sergeant tried to circumvent him from blabbing whatever horror was written all over his face to the crowd, but he wasn't quick enough.

"Sir! There's more gone missing! There's more kids taken! D'Wayne Fady's girl Teddy, and Jim Two-Feathers' boy, Tom-tom are gone, Sergeant, they're gone! Like- like they vanished, poof, like mist in the air like-"

Michael touched the garda's shoulder, said quietly, "Okay, Kullen, okay, take a breath, calm down, you're frightening the people."

He leaned in close to the guard's ear and whispered, "Officer, get a grip, behave like a policeman, take a breath and close your mouth." He patted the officer on the shoulder.

Kullen realized he was out of control and freaking out the townspeople. The crowd grew silent and was staring at him with terrified eyes like hundreds of fireflies abuzz in the bushes. He coughed an apology, "Uh, yeah, sorry sir, sorry, I-"

Reporter Mallory O'Leary chose that moment to stride through the crowd like Moses parting the red sea. Long hair a flame flowing behind her, she cut in between the two policemen and thrust her microphone in Michael's face. "So, Sergeant, more missing kids, how many does that make? What's your strate-"

None too gently, Michael pushed the mike away from his face. He glowered at the irritating redhead. "Miss O'Leary, I am ordering you not to put that thing in front of my face again."

The reporter smirked. "Or you'll do what, Michael, hit me? You're certainly not the kind that hits a woman. But apparently you have no compunctions when it comes to men," she smiled a mean little smile, her hazel eyes narrowed. "Apparently you did lose it one day, I know what you did, I know what happened, I know-"

Cat stepped up to face Mallory, her arms straight at her side. Her cool gaze belied the anger she squashed in the pit of her stomach.

"This is not about you, Miss Peacock, I mean *O'Leary*. This is bigger and much more important than," her eyes swept the reporter's long, busty figure wrapped up in an ankle length coat, "you and your little story."

Her gaze angled coolly back to Michael. "What are we to do now?" she asked, letting him take calm control of the arena.

Michael didn't thank Cat, he barely glanced at her. He didn't want any rubbish about him and Cat and a relationship or anything like that going around.

Knowing Mallory, if she sniffed an inkling of a thought that he and Cat were an item, which they weren't, and are not going to be, she would splash a horrible gossipy headline taking attention from the important issue at hand, which was of course the children.

Meanwhile, a fedora on his tanned bald head and unlit cigar clamped between his teeth, Hollis Hunter edged his way to the group, surreptitiously nudging himself between the reporter and Cat and Michael. Rotating his muscled shoulders slightly back and forth, he casually pushed the reporter out of the small tight group.

Dropping the microphone to rest on her hip Mallory scowled. "Hey Hollis, you can't just barge in here looking like an old time western barkeep with your mustache and gold chained pocket watch, who the hell do you think you-"

Hunter ignored the reporter's griping. With crossed arms, he stood as a stalwart sentry, blocking Mallory from any further interviewing. She would have to literally shove Hollis out of the way and make a scene to get to Michael. And she would need an army of men to do that.

"All right." Sergeant Kelly's head dropped, he raked his fingers through his lengthening black mane, sucked in a couple of deep breaths. He looked around at his gardai, and Cat and Hollis. In a low voice he said, "I called in MI 5."

Gasps, then nodding heads from those close enough to hear. The word spread through the crowd like locust in a vegetable garden, the air literally buzzed.

"All right, listen up everyone. You too, Miss O'Leary." Michael motioned to the reporter.

She was standing outside his circle next to her cameraman, sulking and trying to figure out which garda would be the weakest link that she could interview and get inside information from.

When Michael signaled her out, she tried to keep her face from lighting up, but any attention from the hunky, handsome, and from what she'd heard, dangerous sergeant, good or bad- was good.

She moved closer. Hollis still blocked her from getting too close to Michael more to annoy her than to protect his friend. She threw back her tangle of red hair and scowled at him. Not even trying to hide his sneer, Hollis didn't budge.

Michael held up his hands for quiet.

When he had everyone's attention, he pulled at his lips then set his hands on his slim hips. "I am right now making, what's called Martial Law. Forget about a curfew. Everyone goes home now and stays there. No one is to be out on the streets without permission from the police."

"You can't do that, Sergeant," Mallory said. "You've got a hospital, jobs, pharmacies, grocery stores, you can't close them down and you can't keep people from getting necessities, we are expecting a killer storm you know."

Murmuring and head nodding travelled around the yard as everyone at rapt attention considered the consequences of a locked-down town.

Icicles hung from the Hall's windows that were hazy with frost, the trees stiffened in the frigid air, footprints froze as soon as someone moved, the crunching of feet in the snow like a million people chewing at the same time never quieted as people milled about.

Michael's shoulders pulled up rigid, then lowered. He shared a look with Hollis and Cat. "Okay, you're right. But then I will inflict a curfew. Anyone out after 7 p.m. will be subject to providing identification and proof of why they need to be where they are. There will be no room for error on this.

"We'll need every garda on the streets, over-time be dammed. MI 5 will bring in more help. Children should not be out of their houses at all for any reason and they should be in their parents' sights at all times. School will be suspended indefinitely. Garda," he said to Kullen.

"Sir?" Built like a bull, the short haired, dark skinned officer snapped sharply to attention.

"Set up a few people to go around with speakers instructing about the curfew. Get notice to the hospitals, schools, Mallory-" he swiveled to find the reporter.

She stepped around Hollis. Wide glossy grin ear to ear she got as close to Michael as she could without actually touching him. "Yes?" It wasn't lost on her that he'd used her first name at last. Things were looking up for her!

She was a tall girl, yet Michael still looked down at her long fox face. "I need you to contact the head of the station, and the papers and radio stations to put it out that there is a curfew. Have them reiterate to keep their kids inside and close. And," he absently raked at his hair, wishing he had remembered his hat.

"You might as well tell them we've contacted MI 5. Maybe that will alleviate some anxiety."

Mallory's grin widened to reveal her bushel of blindingly bleached teeth. To Michael it looked like she had a lot of extra teeth crammed in there, like a crocodile. "I'll get right on it," she crowed. The grin grew bigger, more glistening teeth, *better to eat you with my dear* "You coming by the news station later to see how things are going? I'll buy you a drink if-"

Michael brushed her off and addressed the rest of the group. "Okay folks," he raised his voice, "there is hereby now a curfew. We're ending the search now. Everyone pack up and go home and stay there unless you absolutely have to be somewhere else. And in that case you must have proof of why you are not home. Is that clear? All right, head on out now, drive with care and go with God."

Unsure of the situation, people wandered around in a kind of daze, some just stood frozen. Cat and Babby Bianchi calmly but quickly went around gathering people trying to herd them to their cars.

As soon as he completed his speech, Michael leaned in close to Hollis Hunter. "Hollis, I'm going to go get Matty. Can you help?"

Hollis shrugged. "I'll do anything to help, Mike, you know that. Are you giving up on searching for Jessy U?"

Michael paled, nodded. "If the boy is still out there, he's, well…" he sighed, eyes like sad bruised coals. "Well, I just don't know. But it'll be dark again soon," he grimaced at the gnarly fingered shadows the bare trees drew on the ground like they were gouged in the white snow with a black finepoint.

The shadows crept creepily around the lawn when the wind blew.

"We can't have volunteers out searching at night. I'll have Davey get the dogs and flashlights and see if he can continue for a bit longer. I'll call Lucas to help initiate the curfew, he's good with people, he'll make them see it's for their own good."

"That's a good idea. I'll pick up Davey and go back out with him, you go ahead and get Matty," Hollis offered. "By the way, any new info on the skull that was found in Cleasaí?

Michael looked grim. "Nothing. It's a damned mystery."

Twisting the ends of his long moustache, Hollis pulled the unlit stubby cigar out and stuffed it in his pocket and took out his car keys. "It is that. All right, we'll get in touch in a couple of hours."

Michael bleakly smiled his thanks. Hollis tramped briskly to the parking lot. Michael peeled off his gloves and pulled out his phone. He hit Gram's number on speedial. She answered after two rings.

"Gram?"

"Hya honey, what's up?" Her granny voice came through, kind and welcoming like a hot cup of tea on a winter's morning. Michael allowed himself to relax a hair.

"I'm coming to get you and Matty, and Korey too if he's still there. You're coming to my place, no excuses. Be ready when I get there." He heard Grandma Zinny's swift intake, but the tone in his voice held her tongue.

"O-ok, we'll be ready when you get here honey," worry serrated her words.

Michael closed his phone and put it away. He searched for Cat's burnished head. She had managed to herd most of the people to the parking lot.

He zipped his jacket as he strode towards her then his phone rang. He took it back out.

"Sergeant Kelly," he answered without looking at the Caller ID.

"Michael, oh my God, Michael-"

Kelly's heart skipped a beat. "Gram? Gram is that you? What's wrong?" He heard heavy breathing and a sob.

"She's gone, Michael, she's gone!"

"Matty's gone?"

Sob, "Yes! Our baby is gone!"

"I'm on my way." Shoving his phone and gloves in his pocket, Michael ran to his cruiser, yanked the door open and threw himself in. Jabbing the key in the ignition he flipped the swirling blue lights on at the same time.

The passenger door opened. Michael shot Cat an anguished look as she climbed in the seat and slammed the door.

"Darn but you run fast, Sergeant." She hooked her seat belt and dropped her purse on the seat next to her.

Chapter Eighteen

"Geez, Cataleigh, I don't have time for any crap, you need to get out, I've got to go-"

Cat stared straight ahead, interrupting him, "Then go. I'm going with you. I saw the look on your face when you answered the phone. Hollis is going to keep looking for Jessy and all the gardai are busy, you need a friend and you'll just have to make do with me. Now, go." She nodded forward.

"You can't- I don't have time for- shit-" he threw the vehicle in drive and hurtled out of the school drive and down the road, heading towards the highway.

Speeding along the highway, Michael dragged a hand through his hair. He shot a quick glance at Cat. She sat calmly, silently, staring straight ahead.

She hadn't asked him any questions, he couldn't believe a female could sit there so quietly and not nosy in. "I- I can't tell you anything, at least not now, maybe never, so, don't ask me," Michael stuttered. His hands gripped the wheel so hard Cat thought he might break it right off the stem.

"I'm not asking you anything, Sergeant Kelly, I'm just coming with you. Keep your eyes on the road please." She pulled her hair forward over one shoulder and ran her fingers through it, trying to undo some of the snarled damage from the wind.

If he wasn't so frantic, Michael's lips would have twitched at her bossing him about his driving. But he *was* frantic, Gram had said Matty was gone.

His throat tightened, his chest compressed, he wiped a sleeve across his forehead, his brain rattled a mile a minute. *Not Matty, how could he have let this happen? He should have listened to the people espousing that damned legend. But, it just couldn't be true, how could it?*

He shook his head. *It doesn't matter if the legend is true or not, or if there's a- a human or animal or- or monster at work. All that matters is that Matty is okay, and all the other children are okay. He's got to make sure no other kids are taken!*

His heart squeezed, he couldn't imagine his little niece in danger, scared, calling his name to come get her, he angrily brushed at a damp eye. Damn, crying like a baby, that won't help Matty.

Silently Cat patted his knee.

It took fifty minutes to get to Gram's house. Michael burned rubber up the driveway then slammed the breaks coming to a sudden, screeching halt inches from the garage.

Gram had been watching from the kitchen window, she flew out the door. Wringing her hands, she hurled her fairy godmother body into Michael's arms as soon as he left the cruiser.

"Michael!" She sobbed into his chest, "She's gone, our baby's gone! "

Michael cradled her briefly then holding her upper arms he pulled her from him. "Okay Gram, come on, I, we, Matty need you to hold it together. You need to tell me what happened."

Gram briskly nodded her head and dabbed at her pooling eyes with the bottom of her apron. "You're- you're right, Michael. My falling apart won't help, won't help our Matty…" Her words were brave but her heart was jumping out of her chest.

"Let's go inside, you need to show me where you last saw her…uh," Michael brushed his mouth with his hand, he regretted using the word '*last saw.*'

Cat stepped close to Michael's Gram. She held out a steady hand. "Hi, you must be Miss Zinny. I'm Cat Sylvester."

Tears blurring her eyes, Zinny offered a tremulous smile and warmly shook Cat's hand.

Cat covered Zinny's cold, elderly soft hand with her other hand. She patted the hand lightly, reassuringly. "I'm a friend of Michael's and I've come to do whatever I can to help. Shall we go inside?"

Taking off her glasses, Zinny brushed at her tears with the back of her hand. "You have a lovely voice, Miss, uh, Miss Sylvester is it?" Cat nodded. Zinny wiped her eyes as a new torrent of tears fell. "Please forgive me. Thank you for coming, your tone is soothing, it's nice. Please, let's go in."

Rummaging in the pocket of her apron she pulled out a tissue. Holding it up to her nose, she dabbed at it and her leaking eyes, and put her glasses back on, and marched into the garage with Michael and Cat right behind her.

The threesome entered the house, it was cozy inside, like a large country cottage one might find on softly green Irish hillside.

"Okay," Michael said once they reached the kitchen and closed the door against the cold wind. He stamped his feet on the mat to knock off the snow. "Tell me when and where was Matty when you saw or heard her last?"

"Ohhh…" Zinny's voice wavered, the tissue wadded up in her hand she plucked at the front of her apron. "Uh, she was playing in her room with Banny. The poor dear, Banny that is. Matty was trying to dress him up again. I think he gets embarrassed at the little outfits she puts on him. I think she thinks of him as a little brother or sister that-"

"Gram," Michael said.

Zinny straightened her round glasses. "Yes of course, I'm sorry, honey. I made Matty her peanut butter sandwich and called her to come and get it. After maybe ten minutes when she didn't come I called her again. Then, maybe another ten minutes went by and I was busy, I didn't pay attention to the passing of time, I'm so sorry Michael I," her voice trembled, she pushed her glasses up and wiped her flowing eyes.

"If only I'd gone right after her, but she's such a good girl you know, she hardly ever misbehaves. I mean she can be quite mischievous and a little too daring sometimes, reckless occasionally, you remember when she-"

"Gram," Michael said.

Cat moved across the kitchen to the stove. She picked up the tea kettle then went to the sink to fill it. She set it on the burner and turned the burner on.

Then she opened a few cupboards until she found the one containing the tea cups. Taking out three cups and saucers she continued poking around the kitchen until she found the flowered ceramic box containing the tea bags.

Gram cried, "I'm sorry, Michael, I'm just so darned scared, my mind just can't settle…"

"It's okay, Gram, it's okay. I'm scared too. Let's go to her room." Michael led his grandmother out of the kitchen and down the hall to Matty's room.

Cat busied herself with the tea. She wanted to be present, a shoulder to lean on or any kind of help she could be. She didn't want to thrust herself into someone else's business. Giving herself the task of making the tea had a twofold motive.

One, it gave her something to occupy herself with, and the other was to just be in the background, there if needed, not being an annoyance if not. Plus, everyone was always better bolstered after a hot cuppa.

Michael thoroughly searched Matty's room. He looked in the closet and under the bed, where he found poor Banny. The dog huddled in a ball as far back as he could get.

"Come here, then, Banny. Come on out," Michael coaxed the dog. Hesitating only a second, the dog crawled out to Michael. The rangy sergeant picked up the frightened dog.

Carrying Banny, Michael searched the rest of the house then returned to the bedroom. He made his way to the window on the other side of the pale yellow ruffled bed.

Scratching the dog's ears, Michael pushed aside the frilly curtains and studied the window. Grandma Zinny remained still in the doorway watching him. But her legs were shaking so she moved to Matty's little desk and gripped the back of the desk chair.

Matty's favorite pink sock doll, Dolly, was on her bed nestled against the pillows. A tear slipped out, Zinny quickly looked away, back to where Michael was at the window.

Holding the dog with one arm, Michael pushed the window, it slid up. Cold air brushed inside, the curtains billowed. Sticking his head out he looked around, and down. He frowned. Closing the window and securing the latch, he pulled the curtains together then walked over to Zinny.

Wringing her hands, twisting them in her apron, the elderly woman could tell something was off. She watched him, blue eyes blurry and soft as a Monet painting through the lenses.

Michael unzipped his jacket, set a hand on the windowsill. "The window was unlocked."

Chapter Nineteen

Boris O'Neil drove slowly down the street, eyes twitching up in the fingerprint smudged rear view mirror making sure he wasn't tailed. The car's musty oily smell rose around him like a well-worn slicker.

Dangling from the mirror the tree air freshener could not mask the putrid whiffs of stale food trashed under the seat, or the filthy ashtray jam packed with cigarette butts. Hairy squat hands gripping the top of the wheel, meaty round shoulders hunched over it to peer out.

The black Cadillac would have been invisible in the black night except for the low beams pointing straight ahead angled down, and the street lights, the glow passing a reflection over the hood then up over the top sliding off the trunk until the next light copied it and the next. Safety lights on a few buildings flickered against the side of the vehicle as it slunk past.

Frost weighed down stiffening the trees. Branches like rigid tarantulas loomed in the black night against the cranny moon. It had stopped snowing, but the damp air made it colder than it was, chilling to the bone. Even with the heat blowing full blast Boris' feet were numb. His breath fogged the glass making it even harder to see out.

He made a fist and wiped circles in the fog on the windshield, leaning to get as close as he could to see out, the wheel pressed against his blimpy stomach. Sniffing, the frigid air made his bulbous snout red and runny, his breath steamed up the window as fast as he could clear it. He wiped the end of his nose with the sleeve of his jacket.

The car slowed, he twisted his head sideways with pug eyes red and watery to squint up at the sign on the building. Shutting off the ignition, he buttoned up his navy blue peacoat and pulled a knit hat over fluffs of wiry grey hair and exited the car.

Crystals formed immediately on his fuzzy grey eyebrows and ice particles clogged his nose and lungs. He hunkered down in his wool coat, pulled the collar up and trudged down the street ducking sharp branches, their claws scraping the air trying to hook unaware passersby.

Moving quickly for a beefy man with a massive chest and short wide legs he passed a few closed storefronts until he got to a gloaming alley. Stopping at the alleyway, he glanced all around, up and down the street.

When he was satisfied no one had followed him, he stepped into the dark alley. A few clammy feet in, he squinted in the dimness at the doors. Finding the one he wanted he knocked, three rapid knocks then two slow.

Hands buried deep in his coat pockets, he stamped his feet to keep the circulation going. It took a few minutes, seemed like an eternity to the freezing Boris before the door opened, he slipped his bulky body inside, the door closed quickly behind him.

Inside, a heavy mushroom haze of smoke hovered over a poker game in the middle of the room that was going fast and furious, the table was covered with drinks and ashtrays.

Patrons sat at other tables scattered around the room shrouded in tarnished grey, dim lights shaded people tucked in corners that didn't want to be seen.

Next to a piano, an Asian girl of undeterminable age, sinuous in a skintight, red satin dress sang low and bluesy. Her accent so thick the words trickled out unintelligible and exotic, infusing mystique to the dark place.

Boris scanned the musky room without moving his head, eyes flit like puggy hands on a clock. He recognized his neighbors, a Leave it to Beaver mom and dad in a half hidden niche, their heads leaning over a table, straws in their noses and white powder on a mirror.

Sidling up to a lone man sitting on a stool nursing a drink at the U shaped bar, Boris slopped on the backless stool next to him. Under his girth the stool disappeared, his short square legs dangled until his cloddy shoes found a rung on the stool.

He leaned a heavy elbow on the counter stained with cigarette burns and spilled drinks to balance himself. Smoke of all kinds, cigarette, cigar, pipe, weed clouded the room, garroting the air.

Boris signaled the bartender who immediately brought him a bottle of whiskey and a glass. He poured two fingers then set the bottle down and left. Boris emptied the glass and poured himself another. "Hey Greg," Boris muttered to Greg Van Ostrand beside him finishing the drink and pouring another.

The man beside him shifted slightly. Sucking a swallow of his own drink, he glanced over at Boris without raising his head. "Wassup," the Dutchman tended to his own drink resting forearms sparsely covered with long blond hair like corn silk tufting along a cob, on the bar, he humpbacked over his drink like he thought someone would snatch it. The hair on his head like on his arms only longer hung limply in his lowered face.

Pouring a fourth glass, Boris drained it before responding. Spits of sweat beaded like boils across his forehead, he blinked at a drop that flitted in his eye. Using the damp cocktail napkin from under his drink he wiped his face with it then tossed it on the bar.

Snagging the knit hat off his head he crammed it in a pocket, grey hair sprung in all directions. Still balancing himself with an elbow the size of a melon on the bar, never letting go of his drink, he turned on the stool to face the other man, careful not to fall off.

"Listen, Greg," his voice hoarse and labored from his weight. "I know you ran from the action in Wales when the coppers started heatin' up and they brought in ones you couldn't pay off so you fled here like I did. I know you're still in the action and I want in."

"Huh," Greg grunted. "Dunno what yer talkin' about."

He raised half-closed bleary eyes to Boris, his back humped over like a curved lamppost. Tall and shaped like a windmill with a big round head and elongated tube shaped body, the Dutchman beside Boris yawned, huge and long and loud, displaying a cave full of oddly spaced yellow teeth so crooked it was amazing they stayed in his mouth. The non-existent lips sure weren't holding them in.

"You heard me. I want action on the smuggling." Boris spotted Becky Solomon half on Antonio Arcangelo's lap noodling in a booth in a dark corner. Another woman he didn't know was cuddled against Antonio's other side.

Greg shrugged, the big head drooped. The palest of blue eyes rolled sideways at the tank of a man beside him. "We cooled dat down, dude. Dat's why we left Wales to come here until the heat blows over. All I'm doin' right now is some books and horses."

He leaned close to Boris in a conspiratorial whisper, "After the storm, some of us plan on takin' over the dead kids' identities so we can go back and do business as usual with a clean record, keep the buzzies off our backs."

Boris slouched back on his stool staring glumly down at the drink in his hand. His hand so big it dwarfed the glass like it was a peanut in a bowl of pasty ice cream.

He picked up the wet shredded napkin and ran it across his sweaty forehead again then tossed it back on the bar. Anxiously he checked out the occupants in the bar. Most were cohorts of Greg's. "What am I supposed to do? I ain't got no action. The well is drying up."

Greg tipped his round head at Boris, looked at him with patriotic eyes so bloodshot they looked red and blue with little white. "I hear they need volunteers to look for dem missing kids," he snickered into his drink. Boris just growled.

Speaking through the side of his mouth, Greg said, "Check with Antonio," he gestured with his big round head to the man in the corner with Becky Solomon. "He's lying low too, trying the same scam we are, but he still has some rackets goin' on and might need some muscle." That said, his head dropped on the bar with hardly a plunk.

Leaning sensuously against the back of the booth, one shapely bare leg dangling over Antonio's knee, Becky Solomon held the glass of burgundy up to the light admiring it, then held it under her nose and sniffed delicately. Swirling the deep red wine she gazed lovingly at it, she just *loved* red wine, the burgundy hue matched her lips, nails and toes, it tasted of oak cask and perfume. Empting the glass in one big swallow, she wiped the back of her hand across her Juvedermed duck lips, set the glass down and laid her hand on Antonio Arcangelo's thigh to get his attention.

Antonio was smooching with a nail thin Asian girl on the other side of him, his hands in her long straight black hair. Pushing the girl away, licking his wet lips, Antonio wormed blowsy Becky onto his legs so her back was against his chest and she was straddling one thigh, his hands lazily surveyed her sybaritic body.

The girl on the other side of him nudged him, she wanted to get out of the booth. Antonio and Becky both had to get up.

They slid out, up, then slid back in, Becky winced when her bare legs in the short tight skirt stuck to the vinyl booth. She went to climb up on his lap again but a server brought over his lamb dinner.

The greasy smell from the meat and parsley boiled potatoes did not appeal to her. She requested another glass of wine. Actually, she asked for two. She settled her back against the booth and watched Antonio eat. He liked conversation when he was eating so she obliged.

Keeping the fact that she knew about Antonio's embezzling schemes and smuggling, that he was a kingpin in at the docks in Wales tucked away for a day she could use the information as blackmail, she said nonchalantly, "So Antonio, what did you do today before I got here?" She asked more because she wanted to know who else he was diddling than because she cared about his itinerary.

He cut a piece of almost undercooked lamb, grease poured out pooling around the pink meat. Skewering the chunk, he bit it off the fork chewing with relish. Shaking his head, he grunted and waved his fork at her. "You talk," he ordered while chewing and cutting his lamb, and sipping his rum coffee.

"Okay, sure." Blonde hair in a bob swished almost to her shoulders, eyes tinted blue with contacts flashed at Antonio. Sexy in a rubinesque way, plump breasts and hips, Becky would turn to real fat by time she hits 40 but she still looked good now for having pushed out three kids. She rubbed a stiletto heel against his calf.

He didn't seem to object so she snuggled closer to him and put her hand back on his thigh. She thought he was so hot. He even retained his original Italian accent. Black hair slicked back neatly, Clark Gable moustache, he always wore a suit and tie. His tailor loved his body, trim, medium height but good shoulders.

Becky thought about what to talk about and decided on her day. "So, Antonio, you hear all that bickering at Swift Sam's market this morning between the coast folks and the locals? I heard there was a helluva food fight, someone cut in line and then someone took someone else's cart, a whole brew-ha-ha hit full on, they even broke one of the windows in Sam's beer cooler.

"There were smashed tomatoes and broken beer bottles and eggs from one end ta' the other. There's trouble all over town they was saying at the Beauty Spot the other day when I was getting my nails done."

He nodded vigorously stabbing a chunk of lamb. "Yeah, some young punks tried to pinch my wallet yesterday, the bastards. Damned cops need to quit worrying about those stupid missing kids and ridiculous storm and get out on the streets and get order back. Ya know?" Stuffing the chunk in his mouth he chewed making squishy sounds until audibly gulping it down.

Twisting a lock of stiff hair around her fingers, Becky nodded. "Whewee, trouble's brewing! You can feel the angry nervous energy in the air, so thick you can practically touch it, it's everywhere. I even heard there was a crazy brawl at the girls' beauty pageant of all places!"

She chit-chatted until he'd scarfed down all his food and finished his rum coffee. The girl singing took a break, the talking in the bar grew quieter now they didn't have to talk over her.

Antonio rubbed his belly. "Ahh, that was good. Now then," he winked at her. "What do you say we nip in the back room for a tussle?"

Becky grinned and slid to the end of the booth. They got up, with their hands all over each other, shuffled out of the bar area and down the hall to a back room. Antonio didn't bother with the lights, he fell on the bed pulling her with him.

Unbuttoning his shirt she said irritably, "We need to make this fast. My husband will be wondering where I am and he won't feed that damned baby. Poor Persy is probably crying and wallowing in her own piss waiting to be changed and fed."

Sliding her blouse off, Antonio asked, not really interested, "Don't you have another older kid, like a teenager to help?"

Unzipping the back of her skirt she squirmed out of it and pushed it off the side of the bed. She was now the way he liked her, naked with just her stilettos still on.

"Yeah, Rachel. She's a princess bitch. She'll be off with her boyfriend smokin' dope somewhere, she better not get herself knocked up like I did at her age.

"At least my boy Barty helps, but he doesn't think on his own, he has to be told. He can hardly add two and two from all the slams to his head from Joe. I'm surprised the kid never runs off, but," she sighed, "he's such a skinny little coward. Okay babe, how's this feel?"

Chapter Twenty

Gram's brows flew up. "But we always lock the windows-"

"I know, the windows are always locked even out here in the country," Michael agreed grimly.

"Especially now, Michael. I probably check them twenty times a day. I've been so worried I've almost compulsively checked them. I don't leave a room without-" her eyes widened. "You think someone- someone came in through the window? But, Matty wouldn't have let-"

Michael shrugged ruefully. "Who knows, Gram? As bright as she is, she's still a child. Children can be gullible. All someone needed was a lure. Maybe they had a puppy or kitten, something that would draw her over and seem cute and harmless. It looks like there're bicycle tire tracks under the window. Maybe it was another kid. I'm going out to have a closer look."

They went back to the kitchen. Cat was leaning against a counter sipping tea. She set her cup down when they came in. The teapot, a saucer of cream and crock of sugar, a plate of cut lemons, and two teacups and spoons were set on the table.

Michael strode up to Cat and thrust Banny in her arms. "Here Cat, hold the dog. He's scared," and he immediately walked out of the kitchen and towards the living room.

Cat turned questioning eyes to Gram.

Gram smiled slightly, cheeks damp with tears. She went to the table to pour a cup of hot tea. "Michael's going to check the rest of the house again, the windows. But, but we know she's gone. It appears someone lured her to her bedroom window and somehow got her to open it." Her voice quivered, she gulped and took a shaky breath, her wrinkled palm on her chest.

She pulled out a chair and sat down. Her fingers worked at her skirt, pushing and smoothing it over her knees, crossing her ankles she tucked her short heeled pumps under her chair. "I'm just so scared. If only I had-"

Setting her teacup on the table, Cat vehemently shook her head, glossy hair swept back and forth across her shoulders. Still holding Banny she sat down.

"Please Miss Zinny," she said, "I apologize for being so familiar with you but I don't know your full name. Michael just kept referring to you as Grammy Zinny. Anyway, there's nothing you could have done. If someone wanted to get to Matty, they would have found a way."

Banny sat quietly in her lap while she scratched his head and played with his ears, one tan the other dark brown.

Gram's head lowered, tears slipped down her cheeks, plopping onto the tablecloth, the tea sat untouched. She lifted her head, sitting in pained silence, sachet of silver hair softly framing her remorseful face. She pulled her glasses off set them on the table and wiped her eyes.

"No, Michael had warned me. I should never have let that child out of my sight. But, but I thought, she's inside her own home, the doors and windows are locked, or so we thought, she'll be safe with me and Korey."

Her lips pursed, white brows drew down. "Korey's been at the store for quite a while. He went to get some milk and bread." Her gaze turned towards the door as if she expected Korey to come walking through. The door opened.

Michael came into the kitchen from the garage.

Cat was confused. "Didn't I see you go into the living room?"

Michael replied, "Yes you did. I searched the rest of the house and basement then went out the front door to search outside the house." His face stiff with worry, he turned to Gram. "There's definitely tire tracks from a bicycle under her window. I'm going to run out and ask your neighbors if they heard or saw anything."

Cat stood up, set Banny on the floor and pulled on her jacket.

"Where are you going?" Michael asked her.

"We can do this twice as fast if I help."

"No, it could be dangerous. For all your sophistication you still only look like you're barely 18, especially with that ridiculous fluffy white knit hat with the fuzzy ball on top. I think you need to stay-"

Cat walked to the door putting on the fluffy hat. "Don't be ridiculous. It's the children that are in danger. You know time is of the essence. Let's go," she opened the door.

Zinny stood up sliding her glasses back on. "In that case then I need to come too."

Michael glowered at Cat, then shook his head at Zinny. Zipping up his jacket, he pulled out his gloves. "No, you need to be here, Gram. Pack yours and Matty's things, and we'll wait for Korey. You are all coming with me. I'm sure Matty isn't going to trot through that door," he glanced at the door Cat was standing in.

"But just in case, leave a note. Pack as much food as you can too," he looked a bit embarrassed. "You know I don't have much at my house, just frozen dinners and beer." He motioned to Cat with his head, "Let's go."

As Sergeant Kelly had expected, their canvassing the neighborhood was fruitless. On an old street enveloped with big yards, saturated with a tableau of trees and bushes even in the nude openness of winter, the houses enjoyed their privacy. No one had seen a thing.

He drove Grammy Zinny, Cat and Banny, and his cousin Korey who finally returned from the store and was guiltily stunned when told about Matty, exclaiming, *"If only I'd been here-"* to his home and got them settled in the best he could.

Michael was a little embarrassed for people to see his living quarters. An old Victorian style house, there were many rooms, three floors of antique rooms to be exact. The rooms were large but they were sparse containing very little furniture, most had no furniture at all.

The walls needed painting and the electric needed new wiring and the plumbing, and well, the pipes groaned and squeaked and twittered so freaky you'd a thought there were ghosts. Which is one of the reasons he hadn't wanted Matty and Gram to stay there.

He figured an old lady and a kid would be up all night with the willies, scared to death of the undead making noise all night long. And it was worse in the winter with the heater on, which chose the moment they walked in the door to whistle and scream.

"What the hell is that?" Korey jumped at the sound. Late twenties, John Lennon glasses, long and lanky and hippy looking with a pony tail, he jerked his head around the room looking for ghosts.

Cat carried the dog which was trying his hardest to bury his head under her arm. Her jacket was knitted with flecks of dog hair that dropped off like tan snow. She took inventory of the room they entered.

They stood in a cavernous elegant foyer, the shape resembling a cathedral, round with an arched ceiling. High dusty windows declared their ornamental status on the once ornate walls like a serpentine of crystal square drops ringing the room.

"Wow." Cat walked in amazement around the foyer. "I didn't know there were such lavish old homes here. This place is, well it's breathtaking."

Korey came to stand beside her. He craned his neck admiring the high oval ceiling and marble floor that when polished to its original luster they would be able to see their reflections. His gaze dropped to Cat's glowing face.

"Yeah, actually this area has quite a fascinating history." He said in his teacher voice.

"Oh? Please tell me!" She turned to him, her smiling face uplifted obviously eager to hear the story, abate some of the gloominess of why they were there. She set Banny on the floor.

He immediately shivered and shook. He stretched his four legs out, invertedly arched his back and yawned. Then, tail wagging he trotted off to sniff his new surroundings. Michael went to the thermostat on the wall and pushed the tiny lever up for more warmth.

Korey shrugged out of a worn suede jacket with patches on the elbows. Laying the jacket over one arm he set tapered hands, the fingers of a piano player on his narrow hips. "Well, in ancient days this corner of Ireland was dotted with castles. The lords that ran the surrounding hamlets were severe, wealthy rulers. This was lush land and vegetables grew by the tons, orchards with a variety of fruit flourished, and the forests were chock full with tasty animals." He said it funny but twisted his lip, quivered and made a face.

"I take it you're a vegetarian?" Cat laughed.

Grinning, Korey said, "Yes, vegetarian and veterinarian, kinda goes hand in hand."

"So you were saying, Halo Valley used to be different?"

Korey nodded, smiling at Cat. "Oh yes, very different. Hundreds of years ago Halo Valley was a rich, thriving populous village. But as was typical in barbaric times, marauding feudal tribes relentlessly, like surging tides one after the other, descended upon the flourishing hamlet, attacking like savage sharks after fat fish.

"They galloped in, killing, committing atrocities we could never imagine and burning the village almost to the ground. The new conquering warrior would rebuild until the next warlord came in wanting to be king and it started over; war, kill, burn, rebuild, rename the town after themselves."

Cat shook her head sadly side to side and clicked her tongue. "What is it with people that we always want what someone else has?"

Zinny joined in, "That's being human I guess."

"Anyway," warming to his story, Korey continued. Mousy brown hair tied back in a ponytail, hair loosened by the wind and travel fluttered around his face, pushed by the warm air coursing through the huge ark-like room.

Mildly, he pushed the loose hair out of his face tucking what he could behind his ears. Everything about Korey was long, lean, beige except for the blue jeans that were so worn they were almost beige too.

Even his voice had like a beige tone. "A Viking invader appeared, a brutal warlord roaring in with his horsemen, stampeding through the town just like the thousands had before him, killing, burning, raping and pillaging. Viktor Henrick, a young and vigorous warrior had been searching for years to find the perfect place to settle and build his own kingdom, so like the others before him he stormed the town raping and pillaging,"

The corner of his mouth nicked in, Michael said, "You seem to like those words, Kor."

Korey canted him a crooked grin. "Well, it kinda fits the story. Anyway, as they were raping and pillaging, a feisty redheaded girl had been captured and was fighting a couple of Henrick's men tooth and nail for all she was worth.

"They toyed with her, pushing her back and forth between them, laughing as they caught then shoved her back again. Valiantly, she scratched and hit them but couldn't get away. They laughed betting who would take her first."

Sucking in a breath, Korey continued, "Viktor Henrick, his comrades called him Viktor the Bear, towered over the tallest and was stronger than the strongest. Engagingly handsome as the Bible's David but built like the giant Goliath. Apparently the second he set eyes on the red-haired girl he was struck by cupid's arrow."

"That's so sweet," Zinny crooned like she'd never heard the fable before.

Korey's eyes rolled. "Yeah, after all the raping and pillaging the enormous man described as a black stallion, bulging with muscles, square jaw and flowing black mane fell hard for the beautiful Chersina.

"A slender supple willow with full breasts and a curtain of red hair that burned with every color of a flame billowed in luscious curls to her tiny waist. Huge child-like eyes in a heart shaped face, skin with the sheen of fresh pearls and lush lips, he was a gonner." Korey slew a look at Michael, they both favored Cat with conspiratorial smiles.

"Uh huh." Looking at Cat, Zinny murmured, "Your description Korey, except for the color of her hair sounds familiar. Are you sure that-"

Korey cut her off. "Yeah, yeah, I got the story straight from Kenzi, my girlfriend, she's a history major you know. So, then this giant bear with a barn of a chest and arms like canons steps in and grabs one of the taunting men, one huge hand around the soldier's neck and the other on his belt, he picks him up and hurls him a good twenty feet," Korey smiled unabashedly at Cat's raised brows.

"Listen," he grinned, "I'm just telling the tale, I wasn't there to verify the facts. So, he then grabbed the other soldier and hurled him in the opposite direction. To the Viktor goes the spoils," he ignored the groans from his audience and went on.

"So he swoops the girl up in his huge arms and takes her to wife. So blindly smitten with his bride he built her the most magnificent castle in the land. They say one look from her lovely crystal blue eyes and The Bear turned to mushy porridge. Soon of course, Chersina was with child. Under Henrick's new tenderized rule, the village grew fat and content and wealthy."

"Oh," Cat said cheerfully, "a happy ending." She frowned at Korey's expression. "No happy ending?"

He shook his head. "No. Viktor was away in a battle for his own chieftain when another vicious warlord came to Halo Valley, killing, pillaging, burning.

When Viktor returned, the town was dust. The beautiful vegetable gardens scourged and the orchard trees chopped to the ground, only stumps remained. Bodies piled in heaps scattered over the ruined land. The woods still smoldered.

"Frantically, Viktor searched for his beloved pregnant wife, but she was not in the destroyed town or in the forest beyond. The only answer could be the warriors that razed the town had taken her. They hadn't stayed to rebuild the village but moved on to even greater spoils.

"Viktor gathered up his men that had been away with him and abandoned the remnants of the glorious castle and no longer verdant land to search for her. He never stopped looking, year after year, town after town. The word was that in his desire to find Chersina, Viktor became reckless and risked their lives too many times so his warriors eventually drifted off choosing to stay at other villages they passed through.

"The tale goes that Viktor never stopped looking, never gave up. He travelled the world forever, spending all the rest of his life looking for her and for his child. The locals claim the loons that sing in the night, that wailing mournful sound is Viktor calling for his bride."

Cat bit her lip. "So sad. What happened to Halo Valley?"

Shaking his head, Korey's thin ponytail flopped back and forth. "The land had been destroyed so the next conqueror moved on. Eventually the forest reclaimed the town. It was hundreds of years before a ship came aground on what would one day become Cleasaí. Exploring the area, some adventurers eventually found their way around the mountain to Halo Valley.

"At some point there was a big skirmish over who owned what property, lines were moved, fights ensued, people died. Half the pioneers settled in Halo Valley farming the generous land and the others stayed in Cleasaí where the ocean teemed with fish and they made their livings from the sea."

While listening to Korey's tale, Cat looked around the once posh room. In the old glory days the antique intricately designed chandelier with draped arms like a golden cypress would have been polished to a brilliant sheen.

After a good cleaning, the dangling layers of glass diamonds would be sparkling rainbows everywhere from the sunlight that shone through the windows.

A heavy scrub and polish and the gold flecks in the white marbled floor would be glittering, adding fresh flowers flowing from vases scattered around the round vestibule would welcome waiting visitors.

But it's been a long time since someone had lovingly cared for the old house. Michael sure didn't have the time. Soon after he'd moved in with plans to refurbish the place he'd been sent out of town on a government mission.

Following Cat's wandering gaze, Korey took in the magnificent foyer actually seeing it for the first time himself. "Flights almighty,

Mikey me boy, what the bloody 'ell kind of crib 'ave you got yerself 'ere?" He dropped his jacket on the piece of luggage he'd set by his feet, put his hands on his hips and checked out the huge empty foyer. He suddenly sounded like carney English.

"Looks like this room came right out of the Henrick Castle. And Miss Cat," he smiled at her, "could be Chersina's great-great-great-great granddaughter. I've seen pictures in books. Blimey girl, except for the hair color you could be her twin." He smirked at Michael, "And Viktor could have been written about you." He laughed at Michael's rolling eyes.

"You sound heavily English, Korey, when you're not storytelling, not Irish," Cat stated matter-of-factly.

He nodded, proud that she noticed. "Ai, I grew up in England." The strong accent softened again. "I moved to Ireland in my late teens to stay with relatives and attend University. I'm actually still in my residency as a veterinarian. I had been shadowing old Doc Perper the last few months around the most rural part of the village as the Doc tends mostly to farm animals. I'm working on my accent."

Ponytail, round glasses, worn blue jeans and a brown flannel shirt, Korey looked like he stepped right out of the sixties. He craned his neck to peer down a hall. "This room needs some furniture but it looks like the rest of the house needs a lot more than just furniture," he grinned at his cousin.

Michael smiled dolefully at Korey's comment about the appearance of his house. He set down the bags he was holding. "Okay, okay, it needs some work. I just haven't had time to-anyway," he gestured with his arm.

"Make yourselves at home. You'll see some of the rooms are done and habitable. We," he looked at Cat, "we're going to the station. I've had my men call in MI 5 and I should get there before they do."

They had emptied Gram's fridge and freezer and half her pantry and brought everything with them in several large coolers.

Turning to his cousin, Michael said, "Korey, help me carry in the ice chests, then Miss Sylvester and I'll get going. The extra keys are over there on the hook by the door. There're towels and sheets and incidentals in the linen cabinet on the second floor. Just poke around to find whatever you need. Make a list of things I don't have- don't say it Gram," he shot her a warning. "Call me and I'll pick up necessities on the way back." He went up to Zinny.

Capturing her veined warm hands in his strong ones, even with the joviality, her forehead wrinkled in deep concern. Michael squeezed her hands reassuringly. "We'll pray, Gram. I'll call you every two hours unless I have any news sooner. Don't leave the house, and of course, don't open the door to anyone, I don't care who it is. If it's one of my men that I've sent for some reason, they'll have a code word, of..." He trailed off trying to think of a word no one would guess. He couldn't use the dog's name or their street name, someone could always take a shot in the dark and guess those.

"Yellow flower," Cat said.

Michael swung his head at her. "Yellow flower? What does that mean?"

She laughed. "Absolutely nothing, which is the point. I made it up now, sort of."

With a slight frown he said, "Ah, all right, yellow flower it is." He turned to Korey who was still gazing around at his surroundings in awe and scorn. "Korey, I need you to not let Gram out of your sight. And I seriously mean that. She's cooking, reading, sleeping, you're there. Got it?"

Korey's hands shoved deep in his pockets. Hair escaped from the rubber band brushed his collar. If Michael was Korey's father he'd see that he got a good haircut. But as they were around the same age therefore he wasn't, so Michael kept his peace about his long slightly unkempt hair.

"Don't worry, Michael," Korey assured him, "we're already missing one too many of our womenfolk. We'll be attached at the hip I promise you." He smiled, then his mild hippie face turned serious. His eyes looked bigger and like they were set closer together behind the glasses.

He said, "I swear Michael, I'm frightened too death about our little Matty, I won't let anything happen to Gram. If you want to leave Miss Cat here too," Korey gave Cat a cocky grin and wiggled his eyebrows.

"I'll be more than happy to not let her out of my sight as well." His hands nestled comfortably in the loose pockets of his well-worn jeans. He pulled a hand out and rubbed his chest over the cotton shirt.

Michael set a hand on Korey's shoulder and squeezed lightly. "Yeah, you're funny Kor, I need Miss Sylvester to keep the public organized. She has some kind of magical calming influence on them and somehow she has the uncanny ability to remember peoples' names, a skill she easily beats me in." He didn't look at Cat. "Righto, Kor, I won't worry as long as I know you're here with Gram. All right then," he turned to Cat, "let's roll." They made for the door when Korey called out,

"Hey Michael-"

The sergeant turned halfway around. "Yeah?"

"Yellow flower." Korey grinned and winked.

Michael grinned back shaking his head. "Yeah, right, yellow flower." He closed the door on Korey's chuckle.

Before they got to the car Michael's cell rang. He answered it. "Oh my God," he paled.

Cat put her fingers tensely to her mouth. "What?"

"I'm on my way," Michael growled into the phone then snapped it closed and slid it back into his pocket.

He opened the passenger door for her and said, "That was dispatch. Justin's daughter Simone has gone missing now. He was too distraught to call me himself. Get in."

Chapter Twenty-One

Michael parked in front of the station. He got out then jogged around to Cat's side and opened her door. He kicked a bunch of trash to the side before she got out.

Cars, marked and unmarked were parked all over the front and back of the station and up and down both sides of the street. Paper cups, newspapers and other flotsam crackled under Cat's feet.

Her face sad, she stepped over the trash in her ankle boots with the four inch heels and walked to the sidewalk with Michael.

"What's happened to this town, Sergeant?" Cat considered picking up the garbage but scanning the area, the sidewalks and swales were so strewn with trash that it looked like a garbage truck had gone down the street with litter just flying off and leaving a hefty trail behind it.

Michael bent to pick up some newspapers but then he realized the trash cans were all overflowing. He stood up, chagrined.

Wiping his hands on his black jeans he said, "It's as if the town has given up. I think people believe the storm will come through and wipe it clean, at the small sacrifice of our children. Well," his face darkened, he angrily kicked at a paper bag. "Not on my watch man, not on my watch. I'm not giving up until we find those kids, someone, something has them somewhere, we have to-"

"Michael!" Lucas Bregg must have been watching from the window, waiting for him to get there. He charged out like a linebacker. Not wearing a jacket he came to a halt in front of Cat and Michael. The wind wailed down the empty street. Buildings were closed and locked up tight, only the streetlights cast their gloomy glow in the violet-hued chilly winter day.

"Miss Cat." Lucas nodded respectfully to her. She returned a polite, friendly smile. He turned an anxious face to Kelly. "Mike, I heard about your Matty, and now Justin's girl, I-"

His suddenly stricken eyes flew to Cat then darted to Michael. "I-I didn't mean to say anything about Matty, I didn't mean to give your secret up, Michael." His worried face swiveled from Michael to Cat, back and forth.

Cat's face showed her obvious interest in the secret. Of course she knew about Matty, sort of. But she was also aware closed mouth Michael and his family were harboring a big dark secret regarding the little girl.

Upset, Lucas said with a resigned sigh, "Someone spilled the beans. I think someone heard you on the phone or something and blabbed and Mallory was around, she seemed to already know something, you know how she digs, and, well, there's a lot of questions..." he trailed off.

Before Kelly could respond, troubled, Lucas twisted his large football catching hands together in agitation. "We're gonna find her Mike, we'll find her, I swear."

Kelly gripped Lucas' arm to steady him and to make him take a breath. "Yes, Luke, we're going to find Matty and all the kids. Don't worry about what gets out, people will gossip, it'll die down. I should never have tried to keep her a secret. Now, I called the Chief Inspector, and he was contacting MI 5 to-"

Lucas frowned. "No, the Chief Constable called the station and said they were sending the RMP."

Michael's brows arched in surprise. "The Royal Military Police?"

"Yes."

Taking a moment, Michael rubbed the sides of his face with his palms then pressed his fingers over his eyelids. Scratching his chin, he unconsciously slicked his hair back, it was beginning to annoy him, black waves catching in his lashes tickled his eyes. He said,

"Fine, whoever is coming, we need to have someone go pick them up, they should be arriving soon-"

"No worries, Mike. Babby Bianchi went to meet them at the airstrip. They should be hitting the Town Hall area in just a few."

"Since they're coming in by private jet, I don't think there'll be an issue what agency they're from. Did you tell Babby to pick up anyone with official ID?"

"Yes, I told her. It's not like a thousand people are coming and going from our tiny little airport as it were. The folks at Cappy's Airstrip must be all a-twitter, nothing this exciting has happened in-" Lucas clamped his mouth shut. It was a tragic frightening time, not a movie event.

"Uh, anyway," Lucas said, "we're putting them up at the Creafog Arms Hotel. It'll be convenient being right between the station and the Town Hall. There's more space for them to work, or whatever they do, at the Hall than here at the station."

Cat's cell rang. She answered it then stepped away a few feet from the men to talk.

Michael nodded, "What else?" He spoke to Lucas but stared at Cat as she stood with her back to the men. Hollis' words describing her as a Persian cat in his mind, his dark eyes travelled the curvy length of her from head to toe. One leg straight, the other bent pointing slightly to the side, she stood in those crazy ankle boots with ridiculously high heels.

Michael followed the line of her long slender legs wrapped in well fitted jeans, the brown jacket cinching her waist. Talking on the phone, one hand rested on her hip, the sugar and spice lush hair blowing a samba in the wind, she spoke softly, the men couldn't hear what she was saying.

Lucas shuffled his feet. He watched Michael watching Cat.

"Yeah, and we're putting the extra gardai from Glenfall and Strowell up at the Creafog. Even with folks from Cleasaí that didn't want to rent staying there, the hotel was practically empty off season like it is. Plus some of our gardai and also some of the public had offered to put up the extra police in their homes. But I don't understand why they sent the RMP?"

Michael's phone vibrated. He took it out, read the text then shoved it back in his pocket. "Apparently MI 5 must just think we're a tiny village filled with loony birds and not worth sending their top agents. I tried to talk as little as possible about the legend and center on the missing kids, but they already knew about the legend.

"I hear Miss O'Leary is sensationalizing this whole legend thing. She calls the newspapers to keep it stirred up. I think she contacted Strowell, Glenfall, Edggreen and as many cities as she could fill ears with the madness. I guess MI 5 thought the RMP better equipped to handle village nuts. Regardless of whether or not there's truth to the legend, the focus needs to be on the children."

Rubbing his hands like two huge pigskins together, Lucas agreed. Even as bulky as he was he had to brace against the wind. "It's just insane that kids are getting snatched off the street and right out of their homes and no one sees a thing. It has to be someone from Halo Valley since someone strange creeping around the neighborhood would have been noticed."

"Yes, but it also could be someone from Cleasaí," Michael inserted gruffly, scanning a sweep of the area. People scurried about, heads down against the chill, not seeming to mind the bogs of trash they scooted around.

"Sure. Of course, due to school stuff, church, community events, and public meetings, the strawberry festival, 4th of July fireworks and things like that we've all pretty much become familiar with each other from both sides of the mountain."

Michael's clenched jaw flexed, the vein at his temple beat. He turned slightly so the wind would blow his hair off his face. "Too bad familiarity is breeding contempt and agitation rather than kindness and friendship. I'm getting constant reports of fights breaking out all over town.

"Trouble with the women at the pageant, fights on the streets, in the pubs, sexual deviancy abounds, family members fighting each other and abusing their kids, father against son, daughter against mother, friend against friend, as the weather darkens so does the mood of the people."

Michael's phone vibrated again. He pulled it out of his pocket, read the message quickly and slid it back inside. He asked Lucas, "Have you heard from Hollis or Davey?"

His eyes bleak, Lucas sucked in a corner of his lip and scratched the thumb of blond hair above his chin. He just shook his head. The brisk wind swooped through his thick yellow mop.

He started to smooth it but Michael always made fun of him when he tried to mash down his thick glob of hair so he resisted, stuffed his hands in his pockets and half-turned like Michael did to let the wind blow his spongy hair back.

It wasn't snowing but the wind whipped around the dusting that was already there. Every few minutes a car passed, every other one beeped a hello to the two LEO's.

"Okay, well," Michael sighed, "let's head over to the Hall. You need to get a jacket and a hat Luke, even though that muff of hair should be enough to keep your head warm. And Cataleigh," he said before Lucas could comment, "you can-"

"Come with you. Let's go," she said, smiling brightly. Completing her call she'd rejoined the men. Pulling her fur hood up over her head, the fur framed her face like a fuzzy halo. Shiny filaments of hair that escaped the hood wisped around her face from the wind. Her round cheeks and the tip of her small nose had reddened from the cold.

"Okay," he gave in, "maybe you can help the RMP's get acquainted with our town." His tone was stiff because weirdly, Michael felt comfortable with her there by his side, like a- a little sister or soft kitten.

His eyes shifted to her comely face then down to her full bust, lower to that hand- spanning waist down to those shapely legs outlined nicely in tight jeans. *Yeah, kitten- more like a cheetah, long dancer's legs, golden brown hair* - Michael shook his head. *Back to the cat synonyms again -what the heck is the matter with me, I'm thinking like an adolescent.*

He was not getting involved, his life was too complicated and she would be leaving. Besides, he had too much baggage, too many secrets. No decent woman would want to get dragged into the darkness that was his life.

Lucas dashed into the station and returned in seconds with his jacket and hat. He shrugged into them immediately, pocketing the sun glasses he had grabbed on the way out the door. Sometimes the glare off the snow could be blinding. He didn't need the glasses though as the clouds blocked the sun, the day loomed grey and frosty.

Vehicles drove by stacked with firewood and plywood. People were methodically stacking firewood inside their homes. Once the cusp of the storm hit it would be impossible to go outside even to the side door to gather wood for fireplaces.

To prepare for the monstrous storm, those that had storm shutters were dragging them out from sheds and cellars, tacking, drilling, hammering, screwing them up over fragile windows. The grinding of metal on metal grated on the ears like a dentist's drill.

Big sheets of metal shutters littered lawns. Each had numbers hand drawn in black marker and laid out in the order they would be put up, which shutter went to which window.

Those that didn't have shutters which were a lot of them, were buying up all the plywood and nails in town to put over their windows to protect them from outside items hurtling and crashing through the glass.

Hammers pounding nails rang in continuous pounding funnels of circles around the village. On the edge of panic, folks were buying up generators up by the dozens, along with gasoline, flashlights, batteries, canned food, battery operated radios.

The earsplitting sound of howling generators roared like low flying airplanes obscenely breaking the sound barrier as people tested them. Everything not cemented down like potted plants, bikes, trashcans, patio furniture, awnings, were removed as they could become deadly missiles.

The three walked briskly down the street, their breaths white puffs.

"Where's Justin?" Kelly asked Lucas. Cat walked between the two men. Both well above average height, it took Cat several extra steps to equal their stride. The men were cognizant of her effort and tried to keep a pace she could manage, but time was urgent.

The blond garda winced. "He's pretty freaked out. At first he drove frantically up and down the streets just looking for any sign of Simone. I heard Hollis left Davey in the woods with the dogs to keep searching for Jessy and tracked Justin down.

"He managed to calm him and advised him he would be a better help by interviewing parents of other missing kids to find a link between them. Hollis thought Justin might catch a similarity that one of us not missing a kid might miss. No offense, Mike." Lucas shot his boss and friend a quick glance.

The three reached the Town Hall in moments. Cars and people, police and civilians, were clustered in the paved square and courtyard adjacent to the Town Hall. The crowd parted as Michael, Lucas and Cat joined them. Several gardai immediately came over to them. Everyone jostled for Michael's attention.

"Have the RMP's arrived yet?" Michael asked the first officer that reached him.

The garda shook his head. "No sir."

Chapter Twenty-Two

At that moment, everyone's head turned as a black limousine with dark tinted windows approached. The car swooped into the front of the paved area and came to a stop.

There were six doors in the vehicle, the four rear passenger doors opened at once.

A man sheathed in a dramatic ankle length, black leather coat got out and stood just outside of the front passenger door. Behind the dark wrap-around glasses it appeared he was scanning the area for whoever was in charge.

"Geez," Lucas whispered. "He looks like an FBI wanna-be, he's sure to blend inconspicuously into the crowd dressed like that."

"Shh, I don't think he wants to blend in," Michael whispered back through the side of his mouth though his lip turned up. He broke from the crowd to greet them. Lucas hurried to catch up, Cat followed more slowly.

By the time Michael reached the long leather man, the other passengers had emerged from the big car. Two more men and a woman, all wearing only the red RMP hat not the full uniform.

Babby Bianchi emerged from the front passenger side, flowered hooped dress whooshing around her sturdy legs, she hid her distress carefully behind her modestly plain face. This was all very frightening for a middle-aged lady with four kids in high school.

Howie Hummel, the owner of the only limo company in town stayed inside behind the wheel.

Michael with Lucas glued to his side approached the leather man with his hand extended. "How do you do? I'm Sergeant Michael Kelly, I-"

Long Leatherman adjusted his wrap-around sunglasses, stood stoic with his legs akimbo and his hands on his hips holding back the opened leather coat, like a cowboy about to draw.

He didn't take a step towards Michael or offer his hand for a shake. A power play to see who was going to be running this show. Dismissing Michael, he barked, "Who's in charge here?"

Beside Michael, Lucas held up a hand whispered behind it, "Reminds me of the movie The Matrix with the FBI dressed in all in black and wearing long coats always trying to get the upper hand."

Michael bit back a grin. "I am," he politely advised the man in leather.

Leatherman tipped his dark glasses to peer at Michael over the rim. His expression made it clear he didn't think much of the young, rugged Irish man standing so politely in front of him. Leatherman had at least ten years on Michael and nowhere near as handsome with kind of a squashed face with prominent round cheeks.

"You run this berg?" Leatherman asked.

Michael flashed a quick smile. "No sir, no. The Upper Region basically owns this town, I just police it. I answer to the Chief Inspector. So, why don't you introduce your people and we'll get you settled so you can get started. We can use all the help we can get. I'm sure you've been briefed, we are-"

"Yes, yes, we know all about the ludicrous legend, the storm, the children, all the bullshit. There's obviously some psychopathic maniac running around trying to get attention by using the stupid fable as a catapult to infamy.

"Or, it's just a big skunky hoax perpetrated by your town for whatever nefarious reason or trying to draw in tourists or whatever. Irregardless young man, we are expertly trained in the serious business of skillful profiling. We will find your kidnapper or whatever doppelganger *drugai* is that's perpetrating this insidious-"

"Micky! I say, the boys and I are absolutely *freezing* in this clammy little borough. Please ask the boy where our digs are to be!"

Louise Furley

The female stalked to where Michael and Leatherman were faced off, eyeballing each other up and down.

"*Ir*regardless?" Lucas muttered under his breath low enough that only Michael could hear him.

One of Michael's brows arched at the woman referring to him as 'boy' but made no comment. Lucas nudged Michael with his elbow but Michael remained stone faced and still. Lucas nudged him again and pointed with his chin at Leatherman's right hand.

The RMP was holding a lunch box. The woman stalking towards them also carried a lunch box as were the two other men that were heading their way.

"This clammy little town does have hotels, restaurants, and grocery stores." Michael looked pointedly at the lunch boxes.

"Yes, yes." Leatherman nodded impatiently, his head jerking up and down with short shots. "We are aware that even the tiniest ruralist towns have diners or burger shacks or what have you, we have stomached some of the most vilest greasy mom and pops all over Ireland. I tell you by now I have a cast iron stomach you know, I can eat almost-"

Thankfully another of Leatherman's people joined them interrupting his diatribe. The skinny pasty-white guy with a fright of red hair piped in sounding quite gleeful, "I always take me pepto with me everywhere I go, I don't know how I'd live without it, because I eat the-"

"Oh shut up Lyell you *redser*, no one wants to hear about your hypochondriacally, never ending ills and damned lousy-" the third man, a black man, interjected.

"No, you dry up you piece of-" Redhead countered.

"Oh shut up both of you! I am so tired of your constant bickering," the female chided.

Leatherman put in his two cents. "You two guys fight like black oil and white water, and you," he said to the female, "sometimes I feel like we're still in training when you-"

Lyell squawked, "Are you calling me a racist, Mick? I don't give two shits that Lamar is as black as the ace of-"

"Hey!" Lamar popped. "That's a racist term, you're just jealous because that pasty white skin of yours burns when you're in a second of sunlight while I have perfect caramel colored skin that the ladies all-"

Appalled at their juvenile behavior, Michael held both hands up. "Okay, okay, we have children's lives at stake here, we need to move along. Now," he turned to Leatherman. "Please introduce yourself and your colleagues. Where are your luggage and materials?"

The four RMP had exited the car but held nothing except the lunch boxes. Michael pretended he didn't hear Lucas mutter, *"Most vilest- ruralist? Irregardless? Where'd they learn their English?"* under his breath.

Leatherman held his hands behind his back, regarding Michael as if he had just informed them his diaper was full. "Simmer down, boy, there is still such a thing as manners. Now, allow me to introduce myself. I am Sergeant Micky Lam, and this is Corporal Lamar Morlock, Corporal Lyell Gilroy, and the lady is Corporal Raveena LaLinn."

The female, face severely sharp angled like a diamond, and dark hair cut so short it was like skull cap scowled at leatherman. "Mick, I have asked you to stop calling attention to my gender. You make me sound as if I have an illness or weakness or have to be taken care of."

"Oh blimey, Rav, get over yourself, I was just being polite," Sergeant Lam's voice fell into a rasp at the end.

"Yeah, after all, Ravy, you are a woman, you need to let it go," the black man with his hair in rows of tight braids offered.

Turning a furious face to the man, diamond planes sharpening, tiny, shiny BB brown eyes sparking, she exclaimed, "Shut up Lamar, I've told you a million times not to call me Ravy, I am not a child or a babe or a dog or-"

"People, *please!*" Michael held his hands up again.

Leatherman held out a knobby fingered hand. "I have everything under control, boy, these are my people after all. Anyway, our luggage and equipment are in the boot. We are holding our lunch bags as it were because as our superior, Major Malkaroy always tells us; eat when you can, sleep when you can because you never know when the next time is you'll be able to. So, we take food and pillows with us everywhere we go. Please have your people get our gear out of the boot. We're exhausted, we need a quick snooze. Where're our rooms?"

Michael's head jerked. "A nap? We have children missing, who knows what's happened to them, they could be-" he stopped, he couldn't bring himself to say what everyone was thinking.

Resisting the urge to suck in a loud deep breath he said, "Listen, time is our enemy, the longer they're missing the less chance of-" he broke off when he heard a woman sob nearby.

"Sergeant," Raveena LaLinn responded. "We can get started right away. We can sleep after the children are found. I think Mick just wanted a moment to get our materials together and conduct a more detailed briefing. We read the paperwork about the legend and the missing kids on the plane, but of course we need more information."

Michael smiled gratefully. "Thank you Miss, um, Corporal. Time is running out for these kids, we must move fast, we can't afford to waste a minute." To his garda he said, "Lucas, please have a couple of officers retrieve these good folks' things. Take the equipment to the Hall and have their luggage brought to the Creafog."

"Yes sir." Lucas jogged over to a pair of gardai standing by waiting for orders.

Cat stepped into the circle with a welcoming smile. "*Céad míle fáilte*, a hundred thousand welcomes. I am Cataleigh Sylvester, please call me Cat." She shook each of the RMP's hands.

"If you'll follow me, I'll get you checked into the hotel. We have a hot lunch prepared for you. The Slippery Egg & Eel Café has prepared skirts and kidneys, colcannon, fresh baked soda bread and goody for dessert for you. It's ready now, they have been waiting for you to arrive. Shall we go?"

She looked at each of the RMP's then to Michael for his permission.

153

Micky Lam moved in close to Cat. His head lowered, clearly behind the dark lenses he was studying her figure. His head didn't rise above her chest. With a smarmy smile, a sexy husk to his voice, he said, "Well there, not only do you look and sound like an *aingeal*, you have the heart of one too."

Lyell and Lamar moved in closer too. Carrot-topped Lyell clapped a hand over his chest and declared, "Miss, I would follow you to the ends of the earth-"

Lamar elbowed him out of the way. "She doesn't want your claggy pasty ass, Lyell, she wants a man like-"

It was irritating to try to speak to Lam with his eyes concealed behind the dark glasses. Michael sighed heavily. "You better go, Cataleigh, the sooner we can get started…"

She grinned widely at him then turned to the four RMP's and swept her arm inviting them to leave with her. "Alrighty then folks, please come with me." Effortlessly she gathered the team and shepherded them to the Creafog Hotel.

As soon as they were out of earshot, Lucas splayed a hand across his stomach, doubling over. "Oh my God, Michael," choking back laughter, he crowed, "are they kidding? Did they send us a comedy team or what? All those L's, heavens above, they're the freakin' L's."

The sergeant ran his palms wearily over his hair, clasped them cradling the back of his head, he stretched his neck back. "My contact at MI 5 said they were sending over what they called 'nonessential personnel.' I guess they weren't at the top of their class. Micky Lam made it to sergeant because, uh, gee I guess that's gossip," he hesitated, dropping his hands to his hips.

He waved at Babby Bianchi as she climbed back into the limo. She was going to see that the RMP's gear was taken to their hotel where officers would help deposit their things.

"Oh, come on, now you've gotta tell me," Lucas pleaded, laughing. "I mean, I thought that Lam guy and the severe looking babe were a tall Popeye and short Olive Oil getting outta that car! That chick scares me, I'd rather tangle with the weird dudes than her!"

Michael ducked his head trying not to laugh out loud, "What did you mean by 'those freakin' L's?" He didn't expound on what he'd heard about Lam.

Tucking his hands in his pockets, Lucas chortled, "You know, they all have L's in their names, Lam, Lyell, Lamar, and the girl, her last name, you know, LaLink or something." The two men laughed together.

"Seriously, Mike," Lucas said, crossing his arms over his big chest. "That face, he freakin' looks just like a tall Popeye, all he's missing is the pipe. And that girl, Ravage or whatever, I'm saying totally Olive Oil but smaller with a really sharp face and no hair.

"With that short red leather jacket she's wearing and the red cap, and those long thin but muscular limbs, I thought I'd die trying to keep from bursting out laughing from the whole leather wrapped pack.

"I don't know why they're not in full uniform, would probably have looked even sillier, they're called red monkeys, the RMP's you know, by geezus, and those two sidekick guys look like half an Oreo cookie with their matching black leather jackets, at least their leather jackets aren't long and flowing like that Mick wank's. And what about that coppertop, Lyell was it, what the- he's an odd flicker of red don't you think?"

Trying to keep from smiling, Michael replied, "*Is Cuma*, doesn't matter, Luke. They're experienced in profiling, that's what we need."

Luke's huge shoulders jerked. "Yeah, profiling what- their asses from a hole in the ground?"

Michael brushed his knuckles off Lucas' arm. "C'mon Luke, let's go hurry their luncheon along and get them set up and rolling ASAP."

"*Luncheon*," Lucas sniggered, "yeah, they'll probably be sneaking left-overs in their lunch boxes to save for emergencies. Ha!"

Chapter Twenty-Three

"Where the hell have you been, Becky?" Joseph Solomon bellowed at his wife when she came through the kitchen door.

Becky dumped her purse and tote bag on the kitchen table. "Who're you, my keeper? I been out, shopping, not that it's any of yer bleedin' business."

Joseph's coarse lips pursed, he sneered, "Shopping at 7 in the morning? What'd you buy, air?" He snatched up her tote bag and started to rifle through the contents.

"Hey!" Becky grabbed at the bag. "That's mine, you got no business-"

Joseph held it out of her reach then dumped the contents onto the table. A book, shirt and a pair of jeans tumbled out. Joseph pushed the items around.

Becky stood with her hands on her hips. "Ya happy? I told-"

Joseph angrily shoved the bag and the clothes off the table. He turned fierce eyes to his wife. "If you were shopping, where's the goods? Huh? I don't see nothin' here but rags. Where's the new crap?" Spittle flew out with his words.

"You are too rummy jealous, Joe, get off my back, yer not my boss-"

Blam! Joseph pounded his fist like a gavel on the table. Becky jumped but didn't back off. "I *am* your boss, Becky, I am yer husband, it's my job to control you and this family-"

"Screw you, Joe!"

"Bitch!"

They both took a breath as a baby's wailing blew into the room from the hallway.

"Barty!" Joseph yelled. "Get yer arse to the baby's room. Take her out for a walk, the cool air should shut her up!"

Barty appeared in the doorway. His thin arms wrapped behind his back. "But Da, I'm not supposed to leave the-"

Joseph turned fast at the boy, his teardrop eyes bulging with wrath. "You arguing with me boy? You telling me what to do? Well? Are you?"

The underweight boy backed away, "N-no sir, no, I- I'll go take Persy for a walk." He turned tail fast and disappeared down the hall, his parent's bickering trailing behind.

"Now, you listen here, you slut-" Joseph cursed a blue streak.

"You leave me alone you son of a bitch! I swear I'll-"

"You'll what? C'mere, dammit, wait'll I get my hands on you-"

Becky's screams diminished as Barty ran out the door with his baby sister, a blanket, his jacket and her bottle in his hand. The stroller was in the garage.

Out in the street, Persia's cries sounded muffled in the cloaked winter day. Powdered snow covered tree limbs and ground and houses, but the sidewalk was clear. The snow cushioned any echo, cocooning Barty as he made his way down the street with the baby in the stroller.

The icy air hurt his lungs at first, but the faster he fled from the hell that was his home the warmer he got. How he wished he wasn't such a coward and could stand up to his parents and tell them what mean jerks they were, but, he shivered just at the thought of confronting them.

Hammering from people boarding up their houses broke through the early morning quiet. Trucks rumbled by loaded up with plywood and generators.

As soon as they had left the garage, Barty gave Persia her bottle and swaddled the blanket snuggly around her. She cooed and sucked the cold milk. Barty hadn't had time to warm it so he'd hugged the bottle under his jacket and armpit to warm it the best he could before he gave it to her. She didn't seem to mind. Her cheeks and nose were red, her baby eyes teardrop shaped like Barty's sparkled.

Barty slowed when he found himself near the closed school. He checked the baby. Persia had fallen asleep. Her long lashes splayed over plump cheeks, the bottle had slipped to the side. Barty re-tucked the blanket and pulled her knit hat tighter down around her head, golden curls peeped out the sides.

Satisfied she was protected from the elements, the thin boy shoved his hands in his pockets, he'd forgotten his mittens. No matter. At least his fine sandy hair protected his head and floppy ears.

He looked around. The school yard was deserted. He thought about the day the kids had chased the foster kid out of the gym. Jessy. Poor little guy was missing.

Barty had wanted to be his friend, but he had enough on his plate trying to keep the bullies off his own skinny back. The chicken that he was, he'd gotten good at darting from door to door and bush to bush. He was lucky he didn't have to take the bus where he would have been trapped getting on and off.

But Jessy U had a big target on his chest. First of all, being a foster kid made the other kids see him as weak and different for some reason, and therefore easier to bully, and he lived far enough away that he had to take the bus. Jessy was too kind and sweet and brave to hide away, he never stood a chance.

"Hey, boy…"

Barty swiveled on his heel. He'd been near a shrubby trail that ran alongside the back of the schoolyard, and hadn't heard the person exit the woods and approach quickly and silently by bicycle. At first he regarded the person with suspicion. But immediately he grinned.

"Hey, I know you!"

Chapter Twenty-Four

With help from the gardai, the profilers had set up their equipment pretty quickly. They had poster boards, black boards, books, laptops, scanner, maps, etc. spread around the large room inside the Town Hall.

The room bustled with busyness and chatter as the profilers mingled with the police.

Gardai had brought in several tables that were now covered with charts and notebooks, pens, various other office supplies, and strewn with Styrofoam coffee cups and take-out boxes, sodas, napkins and paper plates.

Scrawled notes, more graphs and maps of every part of Halo Valley, and pictures of the missing kids were taped or tacked on the walls.

Although it was quite warm inside the room, Micky Lam still wore his long leather coat like a king's mantle. He strode back and forth and up and down directing here and instructing there, his coat tails flapping.

Ignoring him, sunglasses on top of his braided head, Corporal Lamar Morlock stood at one of the blackboards. A file open in one brown palm, he wrote names and places of the missing children on the blackboard in the order they went missing like a family tree type of graph.

Leather jackets removed and hung on a coat rack, shirt sleeves rolled up, Corporal Lyell Gilroy and Corporal Raveena LaLinn deep in conversation with two gardai, leaned over a series of maps and texts scattered on one of the tables. Other police moved around the room carrying tables and files, books, school records, tax info, etc.

Michael entered the mild chaos carrying a steaming cup of coffee. Micky Lam bee-lined straight to him before Michael barely had a foot in the door.

"Mr. uh, Kelly is it?" Micky's eyes flickered to Michael's nametag. Everyone wore a tag to alleviate confusion. The dark wrap-arounds hung from a black cord around Lam's neck.

Michael nodded, glad his coffee still had the lid on it with only the mouth hole partially open as it would have likely spilled from Lam's rushed approach.

"I want that girl, the skirt, you know the one, the babe with the hot blue eyes and dynamite body. I want to see her now. I understand she has the entire records of all the residents of both Halo Hilltop and Clearsy Valley. I want to see those records immediately."

Lam was standing with legs spread, one hand on his waist holding back the leather coat, the other hand held colored pieces of candy tarts which he tossed one by one into his mouth. When his hand emptied, he reached into a pocket in his coat and pulled out another handful, repeating the movements, crunching while he spoke.

Michael pushed back the tab on his coffee and calmly sipped. He closed the tab then regarded Micky. "Sergeant Lam, I will be unable to take anything you or your team do seriously if you can't get the name of the town you're in correct, or mine or anyone else's names involved in this investigation. Clearly, you know that I am a sergeant, like you. I am heading this investigation. You and your team were sent in to *assist* us."

"Listen here, boy-"

"The towns are Halo *Valley* and *Cleasai*, and the *lady*'s name is Ms. Sylvester." Michael dismissed the profiler turning away before Lam could close his gaping mouth and respond, and moved towards one of his garda standing in front of a map with pins pointing the locations where each missing child had been snatched.

Setting his coffee on a table, Michael addressed one of the garda, "Floyd, do you see any patterns emerging?"

The officer shook his head. "No sir. I don't see any pattern regarding the missing kids. The pins are peppered hodge-podge all over the county. See," he gestured for Michael to see for himself.

"All right, Sergeant. You win," Lam said, following Michael, the sunglasses bouncing on his chest. "I will attempt to recall all the important names of the players, especially yours as it's so important for you to be recognized as an equal."

Michael's lips pulled in tight in his hardened face, his brows cut down. Arms bowed and fists clenched, he pivoted to face the profiler. Forcing himself to take a deep breath, he unclenched his fists and he forced his broad shoulders back.

Keeping his tone even, he said, "Sergeant Lam, this is not a pissing contest. This is about children that have been abducted and there will likely be more taken. The only *important* issue at hand is that we stop any more kids from being taken and find the ones that were, absolutely as fast as possible. And I will not have my police staff or anyone else in this town treated disrespectfully. Do I make myself clear?"

One of Lam's dark green eyes twitched, his hand stopped halfway to tossing candy into his open mouth. The corner of his mouth pulled in, throwing in the rest of the pieces and chewing he crossed his arms in front of his chest.

"Okay, okay, *Sergeant*, don't get your panties in a twist. We're on your side, remember? Anyway, I need to see the girl-" Michael's eyes narrowed, Lam continued, "uh, the *lady*, as soon as is convenient for everyone." The sarcasm was light, but there, crunch crunch.

At that moment, Cat came through the open door carrying a Tupperware. Hair pulled back in a swinging pony tail she smiled around the room, calling out greetings here and there. She set the container on a tiny empty space on a table and peeled off the lid. Layered inside was an assortment of homemade cookies.

Cat was allotted a suite at the Creafog Arms because she needed the extra space to do the work she was sent by the Region to do, moving an entire town into another one. Happily, with a kitchenette she was able to do one of her favorite things and that was to cook.

"Everyone, please help yourself." Cat spotted Michael and made her way over to him.

"Sergeant Lam, are you and your team settling in nicely?" Cat greeted Leatherman standing with Kelly.

Stiff-faced, Micky gave a curt nod. "We are as comfortable as can be expected in this one-mule remote hovel-" he cut off when he felt Michael stiffen beside him.

"Uh, we are fine, thank you. Miss, um, I'm sorry, I can't recall your name?" If he had listened to her, or read her tag instead of just staring at her breasts he might have remembered.

Cat's electric smile exposed a mouthful of pristinely beautiful teeth, just crooked enough to make her more interesting to look at. "Please call me Cat, Sergeant Lam. How can I help?"

Warm inside the huge room she unzipped her jacket and pulled it off. She held the jacket over one arm while pushing up the sleeves of her pink, angel hair sweater.

"Here." Michael took her jacket from her. "I'll hang it on the rack." He motioned to Lam. "I believe the sergeant requires some assistance," he bit back a grin and went over to hang up Cat's jacket.

Cat watched Michael walk away then gave Lam her full attention with a friendly smile, ponytail bounced to a stop. "Yes? What can I do for you, Sergeant?"

Lam looked down at the beauty, cleared his throat. "Ahem. Uh," suddenly he couldn't remember what he wanted from her, at this moment anyway.

He shook his head to clear it. "Uh…" realizing he had Cat's attention all to himself, his Popeye face settled into a grin. "Ah, yes, *mi aingeal*, uh, Miss Cat, that brooding sergeant of yours fears we lack proper respect for the people of this little town.

"But, please, I beg to differ, we have the utmost reverence for Halo, hmm, Halo Township, and, but mostly *I* have high esteem for the lovely residents of the town." He scooped up her hand and kissed the back.

Cat hoped it didn't show how her skin crawled from his touch. She gracefully drew her hand back forcing herself to not wipe it on her jeans. Slipping the fingertips of both hands into her jean's pockets, she said again, "So, Sergeant Lam, what is it that I can do for you?"

An oily smile smeared his squished face, Lam smoothed his short dark hair with a knurly hand. As he had before, he put one hand on his waist, holding back the open long coat, dipped into one of his trouser pockets with the other hand, gathering up a handful of colorful candies he tossed one at a time into his mouth.

"Ah," crunch crunch, "yes *mi aingeal*, I'd like to tell you what you can do for me, but that'll have to keep for later. But for now, I understand you have a vast and detailed record of all of the residents of both villages." The pupils in his dark jade eyes flared as they roved down her body, again lingering on her chest.

An imperceptible shiver rolled across her slender shoulders, Cat pulled the sleeves of her pink sweater back down and crossed her arms. It was suddenly chilly in the room.

"Sure, yes I do. The gathering of information was imperative in moving residents from one town into another. We had to organize jobs and schools, homes, doctors, bank info-"

"Yes, yes, I got it, whatever," Lam interrupted impatiently. "I got it pumpkin. The point is, I need it. Immediately. Where is this information?"

Cat struggled to maintain a polite smile. She looked around to see where Michael had put her jacket. "The gardai already have most of it, I see that some of the information has been added to the charts," she gestured to the wall of papers.

"However, I'll go get all my paperwork and laptop and give you what I have. I'm staying at the Creafog, the records are in my room. It'll take only a moment for me to retrieve them. I'll be right back."

Leatherman caught her arm to stop her. "Wait. I'll have one of my people go with you."

Cat frowned, her eyes shifted down to his hand clasping her arm. "I can carry the box of paperwork, everything is in notebooks and also on my laptop, I can easi-"

Lam trusted no one to possibly destroy, hide, or run off with important documents. He would have liked to go with her, maybe get some alone time with the dazzling babe, but he wanted to stay where the action was, he wasn't about to let Kelly get the upper hand. He was determined to show the people that *he* was in charge, not some young meshugana. He shook his head and called over to his people, "Lyell- come here."

The pasty skinned corporal with a muss of carrot hair skittered right over. "Yes, Mick?"

"Lyell, go with the girl, ah, lady, and help her retrieve her books," Lam instructed.

From a corner of the room, Michael discreetly watched Lam and Cat. Michael and several gardai were studying a wall covered with photos and papers to see if there were any patterns to which child was taken first then next, to see what the common denominator could be.

Ascertain if there might be a rhyme or reason why each particular child was chosen, the order taken, or if it was something particular to the child such as their school, friends, activities.

Or, relating to a parent such as their job, or something they might have done, perhaps an illegal act, adultery, extortion, or an episode in the town that occurred, or maybe the location was the deciding factor.

If they could find a pattern they may be able to determine who might be taken next and set up a trap to catch the perp. Or, best scenario, would be discovering who the offender was, put a face on the unsub, ID him, capture him and quickly rescue the children-alive.

They had tacked up a picture of each missing child, including Matty, with information such as their age, family members and what jobs their parents had, where they shop, go to the gym, church, etc. and theories on where and how the children were taken.

Such as, Matty, it seemed, opened a window and climbed out. There were a couple of instances where a bicycle may have been involved, and in police work, Michael believed there were no such things as coincidences.

While studying the papered wall, Michael kept one eye on Cat and Lam. A line formed between his brows when he saw Lam take a hold of Cat's arm to keep her from walking away. Half turning from an officer that was speaking to him, Michael started to go over when Lam released Cat's arm and the funky redheaded profiler joined the two. Michael stayed where he was when Cat and the carrot-top left the room without Lam.

The profilers and the gardai worked through the rest of the day. They broke for thirty minutes for a dinner of meatloaf, mashed potatoes, buttered corn, bread pudding and strong tea with infinite refills, then worked late into the night.

Except for a menu change the next day was a repeat. And so was the day after that.

Chapter Twenty-Five

The fourth day after a few short hours of sleep, a quick shower and a breakfast of a slice of folded bread spread with peanut butter eaten on the run, Michael entered the profiler room.

He was surprised to find others already at work because usually he was the first to arrive. When not with the group studying and comparing notes, maps, patterns, Michael brought copies of everything home to pour over again and again.

Every night he fell asleep on his couch with papers scattered all over him, the couch, floor and coffee table.

Grammy Zinny had given up trying to get him to go to bed. The hammering and sawing throughout their neighborhood going on late into the night and starting again with the dawn didn't allow anyone to get much sleep anyway.

She just kept bringing him fresh coffee and sandwiches until he passed out from exhaustion and then she would go to her own bed. She and Michael and Korey didn't share their nightmares of what had or could be happening to their precious Matty.

The L's were already busy at work when he got there. Michael had pretty much gotten used to their constant bickering and arguing. They seemed to only agree to disagree.

Micky Lam lorded over the others and that trickled down. Corporal Raveena had a difficult time sitting with that stick up her butt so she constantly paced going over to belittle Corporal Lamar who then tormented the pasty Corporal Lyell.

If Michael had to choose one of them to cover his back, he shuddered at the thought, it would be the female. The *bangharda*. She was narrow but muscled and sustained an ascetic demeanor, she was the only one that continuously wore her red RMP cap. And she wore it with pride. The team dressed in a non-uniform of long sleeved white shirts, black pants and black shoes. Raveena had a gun in a holster strapped across her chest.

The RMP, unlike the regular gardai, were allowed to carry firearms. Michael assumed the others carried as well, only because he figured the three men considered themselves *really bad* good guys. Of course he couldn't complain, even though frowned upon by the gardai, Michael was armed at all times with his Sig Sauer P226. He did a lot of police work alone in the woods and felt it was foolish to be unprotected.

Raveena was the only one to acknowledge his presence. "Good morning, Michael," she mewed, a very peculiar behavior for the austere corporal. Her crush on him was obvious to everyone. That surprised her co-workers as they had all surmised she was a lesbian.

Although Raveena was muscular, had short-short hair, a very serious countenance and an obvious contempt for the male species, their pigeon hole of her was evidently erroneous. Unless she played on both teams.

"Good morning everyone," Michael tossed out a general greeting to all. The others barely mumbled a greeting as they continued with whatever piece of the puzzle they were working on. Michael strode over to Lam, who did not look up at his approach. "Sergeant," Michael said to him, "can I speak with you privately for a moment?"

Lam didn't hide his annoyance. "What, Kelly? We are working here. Can't it wait?"

"Please give me a moment of your time, Sergeant." Michael's face stony, his stare implacable, he turned on his heel and left the room.

Waiting until Michael was gone, Lam slammed down the papers he was reviewing with a burdensome sigh then followed him.

Kelly waited for Lam in a small office they had been using for interviewing people. It was faster to add to their profiling boards than running information back and forth from the police station to the Hall. Michael sat down on one of the office chairs.

Lam entered but didn't sit showing he only had a second to spare for Michael. "What is it that's so dammed urgent, Kelly?" His hands as usual on his waist holding back the long leather coat, his legs spread rigid, like a cowboy in a dusty street still hungering for a gunfight.

Michael sat back in the chair and crossed an ankle over a knee. The phone on the desk had many buttons for different extensions. All of the buttons were lit or blinking drawing Michael's attention.

He pictured the citizens calling the crime stopper lines continuously with what they thought were clues, ideas, sightings of strange people or missing children. Normally, before the children started going missing, the usual crime stopper team was comprised of volunteers headed by Babby Bianchi.

Uncomfortable with the silence, Lam pretended interest in the phone that apparently Kelly considered more important than him. "So…wow, look at all those blinking buttons. Someone around here is certainly popular."

Michael dragged his attention from the phone to Lam, one brow quirked as he recalled Lucas' description of Lam as Popeye. "It's the crime stoppers hotline," he explained. "Normally crime is quite low in our small village." Lam crossed his arms, trying to look interested in what Michael was droning on about.

"However," Michael continued ignoring Lam's bored look, "due to the current emergency, a group of volunteers is needed 24/7 to field the constant stream of calls. Calls are triaged by Mrs. O'Reilly, Babby Bianchi and Dee Troicasi. The most enticing information given, those appearing to be the most real are brought to Lucas Bregg.

"He reviews them, weeds out the crazies, then the ones he thinks are legitimate he brings to Corporal LaLinn who then incorporates them into the investigation. If she deems them to be compelling, she doles them out to officers to check out for further validity. But," he said, "you know that, don't you?"

Lam jiggled his hand in his trouser pocket. Michael could hear the candies Lam kept in there tacking against each other as he fished around to grab a handful. "What about all those people breaking down the doors hullabalooing to help?" Lam asked

Michael nodded. "Parents and other family members of missing children flock to the station wanting to be of some help. But we decided that it was better that families of missing kids aren't involved in any fact finding. Their minds might not at this time be in the best frame for determining false or real information.

"We certainly don't need a desperate mother or father taking something they heard to be real and go running off in a frenzy to do their own vigilante investigation. They or someone innocent can get hurt. Plus we don't know if it's one of us, a resident, doing the taking.

"Mrs. O'Reilly has no children, Babby Bianchi's kids are too old to fit the profile of snatched kids, and Dee Troicasi's teenagers were also too old to fit the profile, at least as far as the legend goes. So they're considered to be safe enough to have a vital part in the crime stopper calls."

Michael leaned forward covering his face with his hands. No one said that he or Justin shouldn't be involved because Matty and Simone were missing. Wouldn't have stopped them anyway.

"Sergeant…"

Stroking his palms over his face, Michael realized he'd forgotten to shave this morning. Too many other things were on his mind. He blinked, remembering the man standing stiffly in front of him.

Lam pulled a handful of candy out of his pocket tossing a couple at a time into his mouth. Crunch, crunch, crunch.

Michael resisted the urge to slap the candy from his hand. He sat up straight, clasped his hands together on the desk.

"Sergeant Lam, your team has been here for over four days. Do you have a handle on our situation yet? So far all you've come up with is that it's only Halo kids taken, none from Cleasaí, but we already knew that. You haven't offered any theories or profiles or anything that can be of help."

"Huh," Lam grunted. He pressed his knuckles on the desk and leaned over to get in Michael's face. "Listen here, Kelly, we are a trained, professional team of – of officers. We have to examine every detail, review our literature, reference texts, prior like cases, incorporate all the missing children's data, find patterns, map out-"

Michael leaned forward so they were almost nose to nose. His eyes flared. "Yes, yes, Sergeant, I know the drill, I am a policeman too. You're duplicating the same work we've already done. But damn, man," he pushed off the desk, "we have kids going missing almost every day now. Time is wasting away, do you have any clue, an idea, anything? Who should be on our radar? You profile, what is the perpetrator like that we are looking for? We need-"

Banging a fist on the desk, Lam interrupted him, "Get a grip, boy, we'll give you what we've discovered when we're ready. This can't be rushed. There are procedures to follow and-"

Michael chair scraped back, he shoved himself to his feet. "I've had training too. And I know that you should have developed a profile by now. We need something other than nonsense calls to go on. Sitting around waiting for the unsub to drop into our laps isn't going to happen. We-"

"Simmer down, boy, simmer down. Now I know you want to run out like a cowboy and lasso up the bad guy, but we're doing this the smart way, we're saving our strength. We're not going to run around willy nilly looking under rocks." Lam crossed his arms in front of his chest then dropped his hands back down at his waist.

Rifling both front trouser pockets for candy he grabbed another handful. Holding the candy in one closed hand he perched his fists back on his hips.

Michael was thunderous, he shouted, "Save our strength? These are missing *children*!" His hands held out palms up, eyes narrowed to furious missiles, he demanded, "We have to take some action. Enough studying, reviewing, researching. I want something concrete and I want it now!" pounding a fist into his hand, he paced two steps in one direction then in the other. He stopped in front of Lam and mirrored him, his hands on his hips.

Lam threw the entire handful of candies into his mouth and chewed vigorously, his Adam's apple jumping like a boy on a trampoline. "All right, all right sonny, chill, we're almost ready anyway. We'll have a press conference tomorrow and we'll reveal our profile then."

Michael crossed his arms in front of his chest so he wouldn't punch the smug look right off Lam's scrunched face. His brows arched. "Press conference? What're you talking about Lam? Are you trying to use this tragedy as a catapult to stardom? This is not a reality show about profilers for crying out loud. You tell me right now what you have. *Right now,* " he pointed his finger rigidly at the floor.

Lam's shiny Popeye cheeks bulged with his smirk, "You don't hold top rank here, boy, you don't call the shots. You can't tell me what to do. We'll say when we're ready. Lamar already called that steamy reporter of yours, Madeleine or Mary or something. I'm not big on redheads, but Lamar is hot for them. She's ready to set up the stage. It's," he glanced at his watch, "almost one now. We'll have a relaxing lunch, maybe a nap,

"Raveena wants to hit the gym. We still have to review more of the information your girl Kitty Kat has about the residents. Then a nice dinner and early to bed, we need to be well rested for our press conference. You know, you look like shit, you could use some rest too, boy."

"Stage? Are you kidding me? This is not a dammed play, Lam, there are-"

"I know, I know," Lam held up his hands, "it's all about the children. Well, we'll get 'em. Don't you worry now, son. We got it all under control. Besides, you look like you could really use some sleep. Maybe you should-"

Michael turned and stalked out of the room and down the hall to the men's room. Shoving the door open so hard it banged against the wall, he stormed through the restroom checking each stall to see if he was alone.

Then, he couldn't help it- he punched the wall, *blam-blam-blam.* Shaking the pain from his hand, he moved to one of the sinks, leaned over, his arms rigid, back hunched, he cupped the side edges of the sink and looked into the mirror.

It was true what Lam said, he did look tired. Dark shadows rimmed his red-weary eyes, his skin ashy. Turning the faucets on, he ducked his head and splashed water on his face and over his hair. Grimacing at his image in the mirror, he pulled his comb through the thick wet locks. Averaging only two hours of sleep a night for the past weeks was taking its toll.

He rubbed his eyes, shook his head. Hair slapped him in the eyes, and a tiny, self-deprecating chuckle escaped. Sure, and he wanted to take clippers to Korey's hair. He had no room to talk.

His hair had already been in need of a haircut before all this happened, now the back waved over his collar and the front swung in his eyes. His five o'clock shadow more scrub now, made him look menacing. He felt damned menacing.

He slapped the hair out of the way. *There was no room for complaining about being tired, who knows what hell his Matty was enduring*, he chose the word *enduring*, because he didn't dare let him think about the worst that could have or be happening. A picture of his pigtailed little niece pleading for him to come get her swirled in front of his eyes, he rubbed them, blinking the image away.

Lack of sleep, haircut, shave, the rudeness and condensation from the RMP staff were nothing compared to what Matty and the other kids were likely going through.

"Buck up- boy," he ordered himself. His lip curled at the *boy*. Only a few years older than Michael, it made Lam feel the bigger man when he called Michael 'boy.' It was such a juvenile shot that Michael easily let it slide.

Smoothing his hair back once more, trying to flatten the damp waves, he pulled some paper towels to wipe his face and hands, balled the towels up and tossed them in the trash.

Feeling calmer he headed back to the profile room. Pushing open the door, he could tell by the horrified looks on the occupants' faces, another child was gone.

Chapter Twenty-Six

In a staggering daze of disbelief, Michael left the Hall around three o'clock. The sounds of sawing and drilling and hammering rang all around from people still working at boarding up their houses.

Already the town looked empty, doomed, like the beginnings of a ghost town. Aluminum shutters covered windows, those that didn't have those nailed boards across the windows.

Until the storm passed, every house would be like a dark tomb inside. Every candle, flashlight and battery in town had been bought up in case the electric didn't hold. Steadily growing huge piles of trash buried the streets.

Feeling the phone's vibration, Michael pulled it out said, "Kelly." Listening for less than a minute, he said only, "Okay." He stood at his car door with one hand in his trouser pocket holding his keys.

Another child missing. Eight-year-old Jamie Ming. The Mings had moved from Cleasaí to Halo Valley years ago. They'd opened the Party Pooper on Main Street where folks picked up favors and decorations for all kinds of parties. That meant that the kids from Cleasaí were not safe either as they'd thought.

The Mings had other kids, Michael tried to remember their names. *Why was Jamie chosen? His siblings were also close in the age group the legend decreed. Lin-Lin was around Matty's age, and there was another sister, an odd name, what was it- Xia or Xin or something.*

He sank back against his cruiser. *A nightmare, it has to be a bloody nightmare, soon, soon he'll wake up and it will all have been a dastardly dream. Matty will be safe at home with Gram and all the other kids will be where they're supposed to be, at home, at school, at-*

"Michael."

A soft voice whispered behind him. He recognized the melodic voice. He turned very slowly, very wearily murmured, "Cataleigh."

Her face wrought with concern, Cat touched him gently on his arm. "Are you all right?" She took in the tired eyes, mussed hair, strong face that now shone with a hint of vulnerability.

It was like he had pulled in all the missing children, tucked their souls under his wings until he could find them and bring them all home safely.

"Listen," she said quietly, "you need some exercise to keep up your strength and a good home cooked dinner instead of that greasy food from the Slippery Egg. I have a gym bag in my car.

"What do you say we dash over to your house, I'll get something started for you and Gram and Korey, then maybe you and I could go for a short run? Clear our heads, revive our vitality. What do you say?" She brushed the side of his rough face with her hand without realizing it.

Michael hesitated, his hand still in his pocket. Who could resist those stunning blue eyes? He smiled, it was bleak but it was a smile. He said nothing about her tender touch on his cheek. "Sure. That really sounds like a good idea. But you know Gram's been feeding me at night so I'm okay. Anyway, why don't you follow me to my place?"

He was rewarded with a big grin filled with lots of pearlies. "Okay! I'll go get my jeep and meet you around front, all right?" Cat took off jogging to get her jeep.

In his cruiser, surprised, Michael found himself smiling. His hands felt light on the wheel where only moments ago he was clutching the cruiser keys in his pocket so hard from stress he had imprints from them on his fingers.

Thirty minutes later, Cat and Michael parked at his antiquated mausoleum and met on the stone walk leading to the side door. "Honestly Sergeant, what on God's green earth possessed you to buy this- this miniature castle?" Cat stood shaking her head at the house recalling Korey's tale of Viktor Henrick and his lost bride.

His hands warming in his jacket pockets, Michael shrugged, his hair in need of combing again brushed his collar.

He looked up at the three story mansion and said, "Well, I look at this- this place, and I see history, not just Korey's storytelling history. Check out those eaves, the gingerbreading around the windows, the old leaded crisscrossed mullioned windows. The yard," he made a sweeping motion with one hand.

"Can you believe these beautiful oak, maple, chestnut trees," he gestured at them, "someone with dreams and pride planted so many years ago? The rose bushes, sure, they haven't had love and care in a long, long time, but they can be brought back to flourish again. I think with care and hard work, the whole place can return to its former grandeur.

"You saw that the original chandeliers are still there, the marble and hardwood only need a good polish to bring back their luster. Can't you see it, its beauty and history? A family could live here again someday and bring back its glory."

Cat listened thoughtfully while Michael described what he hoped the house could become. Right now it could have been featured in a haunted house horror film, but listening to his words she could see his vision.

She could actually picture the house evolving back into a grand home. Nodding, "I can see what you're saying. It would take a lot of refurbishing but it can be done. What are you waiting for?" she asked simply.

He laughed short. "Well, for one thing I haven't owned it for that long. And, well, there's been some issues, which, I really can't, uh, don't want to go into, at least not now. I've gotten a few rooms up to par like the kitchen, most of the den, library and a couple of the bedrooms are livable. Let's go in. I saw Gram peeking out the window and she'll be wondering what's keeping us." Cat grabbed her gym bag and followed Michael inside.

Gramma Zinny greeted them both warmly. She couldn't hide the worry and fear though, it oozed out of her pores like water through holes in a dyke. "Hello again, Miss Cat, it is so nice to see you. I didn't expect company or even Michael for that matter, he hasn't gotten home before midnight all week..." She trailed off uncomfortably as the reason he hasn't been home is because Matty and the other children were missing.

Cat hugged Zinny. "It is lovely to see you too, Miss Zinny. I hope the next time will be under better circumstances. But, for now, Michael, uh, I mean the sergeant and I thought it would be a good idea to go for a short run to rev up our energy and stimulate our depleted brain cells. I promised I'd cook everyone something nice for dinner too, he said there's a ton of food in the freezer."

Gram shook her head vehemently. "Oh no you don't, honey. You two have been working way too hard and long. You just go ahead on your little jaunt and I will prepare dinner. If I had known you were coming I could have had something hot and filling waiting for you."

Cat was distressed. "Oh no, Miss Zinny, it was my idea to take care of you-"

Zinny gave her a little push towards the hall. "I'll not hear of it, not another word. Now, you can change in my room, come, I'll show you." Climbing the stairs with Cat following, as they entered the bedroom, Zinny confided, "I swear, I don't know what got into that boy to up and buy this- this humongous, monstrous manor! It's not like he has a ton of family to put here after all. There's just me and Matty..."

Her face fell like a balloon when the air whooshes out of it. "Our dear Matty, he couldn't bring her here because-"

"*Gram-*" Michael stood in the doorway. Streaming through dusty windows the sun brightened the room lighting the lace bedspread and wooden floor. He glanced around taking in the antique white fringed lamp glowing on the polished rosewood Victorian dresser and vanity.

The heirloom silver backed brush and comb set out for decoration waiting to be used, begging to be brought to life again. "Oh, this room isn't that bad, huh Gram?" But the warning hung in the air. Gramma Zinny's cheeks reddened as if she had been gently scolded.

Michael said to Cat, "The rooms on the third floor need a lot of work and can be considerably dangerous as are some floors downstairs like the parlor, which is one reason why I didn't want Matty or Banny here. Anyway, go ahead and change and I'll meet you in the kitchen."

Cat nodded. She had hoped Gramma Zinny would elaborate on Michael and Matty. There were hints and rumors that something awful, sinister, tragic had happened, that Michael had gotten into some trouble.

The people in town were all a-twitter when they learned of Matty's disappearance as they hadn't known about her existence.

The reporter, Mallory O'Leary, gossips every chance she gets about Michael. She alludes to a murder, and hints there's something about little Matty. There was some big mystery as to who she actually is and why he worked so hard to keep her a secret. Now with Matty's getting snatched the cat was out of the bag. But the mystery remained.

Was Michael Matty's father? She didn't dare ask him, he got all closed up and shut down whenever conversation veered in that direction. Cat didn't even know if Michael had been married, divorced, widowed…not that it had anything to do with her.

Cat quickly leaped out of her jeans and sweater and pulled on tights, a long sleeved cotton shirt and braided her thick hair. Inside her bag she had stuffed socks and sneakers. Ready in a snap she left the room and started down the hall.

The staircase was located in the center of the hall sweeping wide and grandly down to the foyer. Cat took a quick second to snoop, she couldn't help herself. There were three bedrooms and at least three bathrooms on both sides of the staircase.

"Whew, big place!" she muttered. And there was still a third floor and on the first floor there was at least as far as she heard, a kitchen, living room, formal dining room, parlor, family room, den even a library and a bathroom or two.

She didn't want to exhibit too much curiosity and ask for a tour, they might think she was just plain nosey. Which, if she had to admit it, she was!

She couldn't believe that the handsome sergeant was embroiled in something bad, he appeared to be very serious but filled with integrity. Cat wished she had a decent girlfriend to fix him up with. She didn't consider him for herself, she was much too busy for a relationship even if he was interested in her which she knew he wasn't, and as soon as this storm business was over and the folks moved back to Cleasaí, she would be on her way back home.

Home. She sighed. Home is where the heart is. Not just an empty apartment. She should have gotten a cat. Or a dog. Even a fish. But then, what would she do with them while she was away on jobs such as this?

Something nudged her leg, she looked down. Banny bumped her leg with his nose, the snippy tail wagging a mile a minute. Cat bent down and picked him up.

Nuzzling him she grinned at the friendly pup. "Hey little guy, what are you up to? You missing your mistress?" He slathered her face with wet tongue kisses. Giggling, she hugged him tight then held him up in front of her face. "Listen little fella, your daddy and I are doing our best to find Matty. We-"

"Hey, what's going on up there?" Michael called out as he bounded up the stairs, stopping half way up, he set one hand on the railing the other on his hip and looked up at Cat and Banny on the landing.

"Hey, I thought we were going out for a quick run and here you are, stealing my dog's heart right out from under me!"

Cat laughed and set Banny down on the worn carpet. "He just needs some lovin' he's not too particular about who he gets it from!" She skipped down the stairs stopping one step above, almost eye-level with him. "I'm ready."

Michael took her hand linking their fingers loosely and grinned. "Okay jogger-girl, let's hit it. Gram's making meatballs for some spaghetti. I hope it's ready by time we get back, I am starving. Look," he held out his other hand. "I grabbed us a couple of apples to tide us over. Here." He handed her an apple. "Matches those red apples in your cheeks."

"The hunger is going to your head, Sergeant." Cat laughed, tugging her hand from his she took the offered apple. "Anyway," she grinned sideways at him, "isn't it supposed to be me that gives the sinful apple to you?"

Leaning an arm on the railing, Michael lowered his head to her with a smile. "If you're going to give me an apple of sin, you should call me Michael. Sin and sergeant have a funny sound, right?"

She grinned, tilted her face up to his. "Michael, I think-"

"Hey, you two! What's going on up there?" Gramma Zinny called from the bottom of the stairs. "You two better get a move on. The spaghetti and meatballs will be ready and waiting for you when you get back. Korey took the opportunity while you are here to run to the convenience market for some garlic bread. So, get hoppin'!"

"Don't have to tell me twice, let's go." Michael led Cat down the stairs. Grabbing sweatshirts, hats and gloves they were out the door.

Running in camaraderie silence, the only sound their shoes drumming the pavement and birds peeping from the trees and a bit of hammering way in the distance.

Cold but clear, the sky a crisp blue, the wind had died down, snow still floured the grass, trees and housetops. Smoke streamed out of chimneys from every house they passed. The comforting familiar fall smell of burning wood permeated the area.

Her mouth wide open Cat sucked in the cool air. "Oh my gosh, Michael, this air tastes so good! Clean and fresh, oh, it's wonderful! The smell of fireplaces burning makes me think of sitting around a campfire as a kid and toasting marshmallows. We learned to canoe, shoot a bow and arrow ..." She smiled over at him. "Anyway, it was great fun."

Their running steps in cadence, Michael grinned beside her. "You need to have a couple of little ones yourself and treat them to the same happy memories. It must have been those sugary marshmallows that made you so sweet."

"What! You're being silly!" Cat laughed.

"Anyway, it's nice to feel the cold air on my face, clean my thoughts, clear my head," he exclaimed, keeping a moderate pace. "This is exactly what I needed to get my engine roaring again. The kids aren't out of my mind but it's good to get a relaxing feeling inside my brain if just for a few minutes. The run, the air, it feels reinvigorating, you know what I mean?"

Cat nodded. "I feel energized too, yet oddly relaxed. And hungry. Let's head back, I can't wait for some spaghetti!"

Showered and changed, they eagerly devoured spaghetti and meatballs with a tossed salad and toasted garlic bread in the huge dining room. Zinny had cleaned the glass chandelier that hung over the table, it was now so bright it glistened rainbows on the polished wood.

Zinny pressed her fingertips on the table then ran a finger along the grain. "It's nice that this old table is still here. It seats 20 people easily. It's probably still here because it's too big and heavy to move. Besides, what normal person would have room in their home for it?" She got up and hustled into the kitchen and back with the tea pot then buzzed around the table pouring tea and passing out more bread.

"Hey, I'm normal!" Michael pretended to be offended reaching for the bread basket.

"Gram, have a seat, eat for cryin' out loud, quit hopping around us! We're adults, we can take care of ourselves, you don't have to serve us," Korey admonished Zinny while shoveling a huge bunch of noodles dripping in red sauce into his mouth.

He barely chewed and swallowed the spaghetti before cutting a meatball in half, forking it and stuffing it into his mouth, his glasses steamy from the hot pasta.

Zinny ignored him and flew off into the kitchen.

Michael made fast work of a hunk of hot buttered garlic bread. "Let her be, Korey. She likes fussing over people, it's the way she relaxes. Plus it takes her mind off of Matty." Banny sat quietly next to his chair gobbling pieces of bread and meatball Michael slipped him.

Bowed over his plate, Korey's long hair flopped in his face as he nodded. Another giant forkful plowed in, he talked while he chewed. "Yeah, I get it. All I think about is our baby." He nonchalantly slid a look at Michael, to Cat then cut back to Michael, asked casually, "Has anyone gone to see Kayleen?" He shoveled in another forkful.

Michael shot him a glare. "Shut up, Korey." He glanced at Cat.

Korey kept eating. He shrugged one shoulder. Without looking at Michael he said, "Somebody needs to tell Kayleen. She has a right to know. What if someone tells her about Matty or she sees it on the news? She may be secreted away in that place in the Western Region but this has got to make the news at some point.

"The way Mallory O'Leary is blabbing it all over, eventually the rest of the country will realize the children really are missing and it's not just an elaborate hoax. And she should hear it first from one of us, not the news."

"Korey-" Michael slammed his fork down and shoved his plate away.

His cheeks plumped with food, Korey shook his head, twirling up another glob of pasta. "No, Michael, someone has to see her. That bitch-" he sent a short grin to Cat, "sorry."

Back to Michael he said, "That Mallory, she's keeping this whole- whole- *thing*- blasting around the country. We'll be lucky if we don't get deluged by rubbernecking paparazzi and media from all around Ireland.

"So far they're just looking at us as a laughingstock. A tiny village, frightened to death of an impending wicked storm that gets freaked out and dredges up an old legend. Make-believe, fairy tales, leprechauns.

"They're dismissing the facts of the missing children. The word is that we've created this huge hoax for some screwy reason that the kids aren't really missing. So far the rest of the world isn't paying much attention to a bunch of wacko bumpkins making up stories. But eventually it will get to Kayleen and we must tell her about Matty before someone else does."

Michael crossed his arms and leaned back in his chair, his legs crossed at the ankles stretched out in front of him, he stared at Korey.

Korey kept eating as if there was no tension in the room. He ate all his pasta and meatballs and was running his bread across the plate sopping up the remnants of sauce.

Dying to know what the men were talking about, Cat ate steadily, keeping quiet, hoping they would spill the beans. Who the heck was Kayleen? What was Kayleen's relationship to Michael, and what was Matty's relationship to Michael? And who was Matty's mother- the mysterious Kayleen?

The sergeant had been very closed-mouthed about the little girl, only alluding that she was very important to him. Was she maybe really his daughter, not his niece as someone had said?

Cat had studied some photographs of the two on the mantle over the fireplace in the den. There seemed to be a resemblance, but if she's his niece there would be anyway.

"Here we go!" Gramma Zinny zipped into the room laden with a pie in one hand and a pie server and plates in the other. She set the pie on the table then proceeded to slice pieces of still steaming apple pie and deposited each piece onto a plate.

Cat got up to gather the empty plates. Michael got up too and picked up the big serving bowl that had contained the pasta and the saucer with one last piece of garlic bread.

As Michael passed Korey, Korey snaked a hand out and plucked the last piece of bread. Wolfing it down, Korey eyeballed the hot piece of pie Gramma Zinny placed in front of him. Picking up a dessert fork he said, "Gram, don't we have any ice cream?"

Zinny cut the fourth piece, frowned. "Oh yes, of course, I forgot. Be a dear, Korey, and get the vanilla ice cream."

Cat followed Michael into the kitchen.

Korey set his fork down and got up.

"Oh honey," Gram said, laying the pie server down and set a piece of pie where Cat had been sitting, "don't forget the scoop."

"Okay." Korey disappeared into the kitchen.

In seconds, Cat came out but the two men remained in the kitchen. Cat had the ice cream container and scoop. She set them on the table, peeled off the lid and scooped out the vanilla ice cream placing a spoonful onto each piece of warm pie.

Gram looked to the doorway where she could hear the men's voices down the hall to the kitchen. "Dear," she sounded puzzled, "where are the boys?"

Cat smoothed her long hair, still damp from a quick shower, she pushed it back behind her ears to wave down her back. She picked up a spoon and carved off a tiny bit of ice cream and piece of pie. "Oh, they just started talking and lingering, so I took the ice cream. Mmmm, oh Miss Zinny, dinner was delicious! Much better than I could have done."

Zinny smiled and ate her own pie. "Thank you, dear. I love to cook. It's seldom that I have more than just me and Matty to cook for-" swift intake of breath, she swallowed hard.

Cat set down her spoon. Resting her forearms on the table, she looked levelly at the older woman. "Miss Zinny, you know we're doing everything we can to find her, everything. The RMP's are set to deliver their profile to the media tomorrow, maybe then we can physically go do something rather than just sitting around looking at maps and texts and people's family histories."

Zinny dabbed at her eyes, but smiled warmly at Cat. "You are such a dear, Miss Cat. I mean, you're not the police, and these are not your kids, or even your town. But you are doing everything you can to help. You've jumped in with both feet. You just said, 'at least *we* can physically do something.'

"It shows you truly care. I appreciate that. With folks like you and Michael and Lucas Bregg, I just know you'll find our kids."

Cat leaned over and patted Zinny's hand, she said softly, "We just need to pray and keep working."

Zinny sat back. She looked thoughtful for a moment, studying Cat's lovely heart- shaped face while the girl finished her pie and ice cream. She leaned forward towards Cat. "You know dear, that I can't tell you about Matty, or Kayleen, Michael will have to do that. Which I'm sure he will do in time. It's been hard for him to trust anyone for a long time.

"Some really terrible things happened to- well," she hesitated, "well, I am not at liberty to say. I know when Michael finally reveals the tragic past that you will be there for him. You'll understand and be there for him, supporting, nonjudgmental, caring and-"

Cat cut in, shaking her head, "Oh Miss Zinny, you've got it wrong! Michael, uh the sergeant and I are not- not involved, uh, romantically." She gulped. "I mean, we are just colleagues, working together to solve this horrible mystery. There's no, uh, you know, there's no *relationship* between us, we're just working together to uh..."

Smiling, Zinny nodded. "Yes dear, of course honey, you two are just- work partners, nothing more, uh huh. You just happened to be a beautiful young woman that my handsome grandson just happens to bring home to check on our missing Matty, then out for a friendly jog, and then joins us for a family dinner..."

Cat nodded with a bald smile. "That's right, we're just, you know, colleagues, that's all. I'm sure Michael, um, the sergeant has brought home his best friend, Lucas Bregg, for dinner and maybe a run. They are both athletic."

Slicing off a piece of her pie, Zinny grinned. "Listen dear, no good looking man brings home a gorgeous woman just because they're working on a case together. He never has before and there is obviously-"

The men suddenly returned. They weren't talking but they didn't seem to be angry, more like they had resolved their issue.

"Here now, boys, eat your pie. Come along then," Zinny ordered cheerfully.

Michael and Korey sat back down at the table. "Yeah," Michael said, "but as soon as we've finished we've got to go. There's more work to do before the L's showcase their- media event..." His sentence trailed off sarcastically.

His views on the profilers choosing to put their findings out in the media format rather than only with the trained gardai steamed him. He had tried to call the Chief to get it stopped but was told to just work peacefully with the profilers, *'Don't make waves'* he'd said.

"The L's?" Zinny asked, with a cocked grey brow.

Cat cleared her throat, bit back a smile. "That's what Lucas has dubbed the profilers. It's nicer than what others have called them." She half-smirked at Zinny.

"Oh. I guess it's better I don't know then." Zinny hopped up and bustled around the table gathering up empty dessert plates. She stacked the plates and cutlery. "I'll clean up. You kids go right on and get going. Korey honey, can you help me take the dishes into the kitchen."

"Sure." Korey got up.

Michael and Cat rose as well. Michael retrieved their hats and coats and Cat's gym bag. Zinny and Korey met them at the kitchen door. Gram kissed Michael on the cheek and then Cat. "You two take care. Call me every couple of hours, Michael, keep me posted. So nice to see you, dear," she said to Cat, "please come back soon, you are always welcome."

"Thank you, Miss Zinny. Thanks for dinner, like I said, it was really, really good! I'm sure I gained five pounds already!" Cat rubbed her belly.

Checking the younger woman's figure Zinny said, "That's okay dear, you can certainly use a couple of extra pounds. You girls these days," she clucked, "just skin and bones. Men like a little something to hold onto you know. Right Michael?" She smiled innocently at her grandson.

"Here." Michael awkwardly thrust Cat's coat at her. "I am not responding to that comment, Gram, it's always a no win situation." He opened the door.

"Brrr." Korey shivered as the cold night air rushed in.

Michael turned to Korey, brows drawn down, his tone serious he said, "Like always, until this is over, you stay with Gram. All doors and windows locked, she's not to be in a room alone and she's not to go anywhere or open the door to anyone."

Korey leaned his lanky frame against the door, crossed one foot over the other, and straightened his wire-rimmed glasses. Pulling in a corner of his mouth, he said with the same serious tone as his cousin, "I will, of course, but really, Michael, the demon is not after old ladies, no offense Gram, he, or it, is after children."

Michael swung his head at Korey. "I know the basic criteria for the body snatchings, but since we really don't know what or whom we are dealing with, no one is safe. I don't know if this is an action against just one of us and the other kids are collateral damage, or a smokescreen or some other devious scheme. Someone could be after me. I'm not being egotistical, I'm being pragmatic. I've already let them get Matty-"

"Exactly why you should see Kayleen. Tell her what's happened and make sure she's safe too," Korey said, waving his piano player's hand at Michael.

Michael stood staring at Korey, his mouth hard shut, one hand on the door knob. Cat and Zinny waited nervously. Michael let out a heavy whoosh of air.

"Okay," he sighed, taking one step out the door. "You're right. I should have already done it. I'll take Cataleigh to her hotel and then I'll go see Kayleen. I wanted to make sure she'll be safe during the storm anyway. Gram, if you'll call the, uh, place..." he glanced at Cat, who seemed to not be listening, rustled around in her purse like she was searching for something.

His eyes sad, Michael set a hand on Korey's shoulder. He smiled bleakly at Zinny. Struggling to stand strong and hold back imminent tears, Zinny clutched at her apron then smoothed it back out, veined hands trembling against the white material, she assured him, "I will, dear."

Michael hugged her tightly but careful not to crush the elderly grandmother. "Just call and let them know I'm coming. Don't tell them why, just say I need to see her. It'll be all right, Gram, I'll call you after I've seen Kayleen. Please," he turned seriously towards Korey then Cat then Zinny, "not a word of any of this to anyone. Understand? No one. Trust no one."

The three of them nodded. "And," Michael wrapped his arm across his chest and scratched his shoulder. "Remember they're testing the siren again tomorrow at noon."

"Oh my, that horrible, horrible wailing thing. Loud enough to wake the dead!" Zinny shuddered.

Korey reached past Michael to flip on the outside porch light in the garage. "Well, Gram, it's necessary to make sure it works and that virtually everyone, even people closed in their cellars can hear it. It's the last one on the schedule. Any after this, the bill boards, news, TV, newspapers all broadcasted that when the siren goes off again it'll be because the storm is imminent to strike.

"It will be the time to get off the streets and get inside, and stay there until the all clear signal of short blasts of the siren for an hour."

Wringing her hands, Zinny agreed. "Yes, they've made sure that there won't be a soul that isn't aware that the siren had three practice runs scheduled and that everyone could hear it and take shelter. I heard that they've pretty much moved all of the hospital patients and the elderly in the nursing home up to Glenfall."

"Thank goodness," Korey said. "It's going to be hard enough to take care of ourselves much less the seriously ill or infirm."

Michael gestured to Cat to follow him. "Come on, Cataleigh, let's go." He held the door open for her. "I'll be in touch. Take care," he said to Zinny and Korey as they stood in the doorway watching them leave.

Chapter Twenty-Seven

The profilers secreted themselves in the interview room connected to the big chamber in the Hall they and the gardai had been using for their work. The connecting door was closed and locked, they refused to let anyone in, including Michael, except to take in food.

Like a fuse to a bomb and a match looming, struggling to hold in his anger and frustration, Michael paced drinking one cup of coffee after the other. He stuffed the craving for a cigarette he'd given up years ago and left to take a call on his cell.

Cat, Lucas, and Justin stood in front of the wall where they had arranged each child's picture and name. Juan and Santiago Trueno were added this morning.

Under each child they had attached the child's history such as teacher and grade. There was only one grammar, middle and two high schools in Halo Valley so it was easy to gather pertinent information such as each child's after school curriculum, scouts, sports, music.

Then each child's family history was included, parent's job, social life, etc. They still had found no common link between the kids or their families that was any way relevant or different from kids that hadn't been taken. They'd run records checks on residents, but nothing popped out at them. There have been no witnesses to any of the abductions.

Justin sniffed loudly, scratched his red head then muttered, glaring angrily at the closed door. "Those profilers ever coming out again? What the hell are they doing in there?"

Lucas grunted his feelings. "Stupid L's, it's probably for the better they're in there and not out here annoying us with their ridiculous theories. First they came out with that grand theory that it's a precursor diversion to stage a big bank robbery, except we have no really big banks here, then they decide it's a revenge act but with nothing to back that up.

"Then the nuts suggest that maybe the government wants this land to do experiments on, or hide foreign prisoners on, or contact aliens from outer space, or one of their other myriad of stupid hypotheses." He wanted to comfort his friend Justin but didn't know how.

Cat laughed at Lucas' derision, but Justin sniffed, staring blankly at the papered wall. Cat and Lucas shared a look at Justin's continuous snuffling.

Lucas gave Justin a light jab. "Hey, buddy, you know, you don't have to be here. We're working on every angle."

Justin wiped at red eyes that matched his red hair. Shoulders hunched, his hands deep in his pockets, instead of his uniform today he wore a sweater over a long sleeved shirt and jeans. A spotty red beard dotted his jaw, obviously he hadn't shaved in days.

He wiped his eyes again then jammed his hands back in his pockets. "I've done all I can do in the field. I've interviewed and re-interviewed. The only good news is… that if the legend is correct the last child has been taken this morning," grief suffocated words.

His gaze crisscrossing the information on the wall, Lucas said for the hundredth time, "There has to be a commonality between the missing kids."

Justin stared blindly at the wall, his eyes misted again. "There's just no goddamned common factor that I can discern about the missing kids, including my Simone." He choked, wiped an eye. Lucas patted him on the shoulder. Justin ran his hands over his coily hair scratching his scalp as if that would distract him from his pain.

"I can't just keep driving around in circles looking for- my baby. I feel I can at least help brainstorm or whatever here. I can't sit home and do nothing, waiting for her pretty blonde head to pop in the door, those big blue-" Justin choked off.

Lucas put his arm around his friend's shoulder. Justin shrugged him off. "No man, I'm okay, seriously. What's up with those profilers anyway?" He thrust the attention off himself and back onto the profilers holding up in the other room.

"Huh. Those bleedin' buggers." Lucas' lips twisted like he had bitten a sour lemon.

"So far they've done absolutely no good in this investigation whatsoever. Nothing. In fact, like I said about their stupid theories, I think they've more gotten in our way and mucked up the business rather than figuring something out." He stretched his long arms out then over his head and yawned.

"Yes," Cat agreed. "They've secluded themselves in the interview room all day. We've had to use one of the meeting rooms down the hall to continue our interviews. People are still coming in with sightings and suggestions. It's like some want to help so badly they come in and blab useless information, and others seem to just want to interject themselves into the investigation. I don't get it," she shook her head. Lustrous hair shimmered around her head and shoulders.

His hands on his hips, Lucas nodded at her words. He tugged at his midget blonde goatee with his finger and thumb thoughtfully. The husky blond garda said, "Well, let's just keep working as if they aren't even there."

Justin sniffed his agreement.

Cat stepped closer to the wall, walked back and forth peering at each name. "I agree, let's keep…" hesitating, her brow wrinkled, lips pursed, eyes narrowed. Shuffling side to side she scanned the pictures like a video camera.

"There's something nagging me at the back of my mind but I can't see it. There's some link in the chain. Something about the children's initial paperwork, their birth certificates I think, something…I just can't pull it out…I think we should put together all the information we have on the legend and compare it to what we have here. Maybe comparing the past to the present will indicate a pattern, a clue."

Lucas and Justin stepped forward, all three stood silently perusing the wall.

"If only it would jump off the wall and bite us on the nose," Michael said, joining them.

"I don't know if it's a help or a hindrance that you gardai are involved. Is it something familiar that one of you can recognize? Or is it something only a stranger might see, like a funny shaped piece that doesn't fit into the puzzle," Cat sighed.

"That's what the profilers are supposed to be doing," Lucas groused. The others nodded grimly. Michael left the room again.

The rest walked back and forth studying the wall for hours jotting notes, comparing them. They tuned out Justin's constant sniffing and ignored the other staff wandering in and out adding new info sometimes to the wall.

Unrelenting, they reviewed every new bit added, shaking their heads when they still saw no pattern. The profilers didn't emerge all day. They ordered food delivered and used the bathroom in the interview room.

At three o'clock, the four RMP profilers finally emerged from their secretive cave.

Lucas nudged Michael, Cat was already biting her lip, they all struggled to keep a straight face. Justin was too wrapped up in his pain to notice anything.

The profilers came out dolled up like they were hitting the red carpet. Their hair moussed and sprayed, all four wore makeup, and they were wearing their leather jackets as when they had arrived. Micky Lam in his long, black leather coat sported his dark wrap-arounds and slicked back black hair.

Raveena's short cap of hair was also greased back so tightly it might as well have been painted on, she wore her short red leather jacket, starched white blouse and razor pressed black trousers.

Lamar and Lyell were dressed in short black leather jackets, black pants and white shirts. They could have been twins except Lamar was dark skinned, his head covered with rows of tight braids.

Lyell, the shortest of the four, had skin so white sunlight could have reflected off it. He would have disappeared against the white wall except for the spray of kinky orange hair, and the mass of freckles that marched across his cheeks and nose.

Holding a hand over his mouth, Lucas muttered, "Can you say circus clowns?"

Justin finally noticed, he snorted his laughter, saliva burst from his mouth. "Where's the little clown car?" He started choking. Lucas smacked him on the back. Justin sputtered to Lucas, "The Circus L's! They should have their own show with tiny cars, big feet, red ball noses and balloons!"

Lucas clamped his big hand over his own mouth to stifle his guffaw.

Micky Lam scowled at the pair, he couldn't hear what they were saying but could tell they were laughing at his team. He tugged at the collar of his white shirt to pull it out and up around his neck like a tunic top rather than letting the collar lay flat, and smoothed the sleeves of his leather coat. He narrowed a look at Lucas. "What's up? What's so funny, bro?"

Lucas almost lost it hearing Justin choke back a giggle. "Uh, yeah, uh, well, you guys certainly look ready for, uh…"

Ever the mediator, Cat stepped forward smiling. She reached out and flattened the lapel of Lam's leather coat, half of it was caught folded under. "Your team looks ready to take on the media." She shot a warning glance at Lucas. "Come, let's go. I hear the stage is set downstairs in the auditorium. They're all there waiting for your presentation."

Lam leaned over Cat, his face hovered close to hers. He took her hand and kissed her palm. "When this is over, *mi aingeal*, there'll be some time for you and me to get to know one another better before I have to leave. I have some cat tricks up my sleeve…" he licked her palm.

Suppressing her involuntary recoil and *eeyeuw* response, Cat tugged to free her hand.

Lucas' chest puffed, he growled, "Hey Lam, we don't manhandle our womenfolk here, let her go-"

Lam didn't take his eyes or hands off Cat. "Off with ya then, boy, this is men's business. This is between me and the lovely *aingeal*. Right, doll?"

The tension in the room was tangible. Cat pulled her hand again but Lam held onto her. Lucas' shoulders drew up, his chest puffed bigger, hands balled into fists the size of melons, he moved within inches of Lam. "Listen here, you skeletal Pop-eyed son of a-"

"Luke."

Everyone in the room turned to the doorway. In Guardian uniform, Michael entered calmly. His gaze went from Lam's squished face to his hand that still held Cat's.

It was obvious she was trying to delicately extract herself from his grip without insulting the Leatherman, however, her face flushed as her professional manner was rapidly dissipating.

Michael approached the group. "Lucas, they're ready downstairs. Why don't you escort the L- uh, the team down to the auditorium? We'll be right behind you."

His gaze dropped to Lam's hand holding Cat's arm, and darkened as they rose back up to Lam's squinty eyes. Lam let her go then quickly reached into his pocket for his colored candies acting as if he wasn't threatened by Michael.

Lucas dropped his block of shoulders and straightened his back, clipping a nod to his boss, "Yessir." He winked at Michael then pivoted towards Lam and his team. "If you'll follow me?" He turned his back to the profilers pretending to play a flute like he was the Pied Piper. Fortunately they couldn't see him but everyone else could.

Michael tried to frown at him but couldn't quite pull it off. Lucas piped out the door.

Lam's team took a second to adjust jackets and check themselves in a mirror by the door. Then, noses high, they followed Lucas out the door.

Chapter Twenty-Eight

The second they left, Justin bent over bursting in laughter.

Cat giggled with him.

Michael stood straight-faced. Holding a hand against his stomach, Justin straightened then looked at Cat's struggle to tame her mirth and burst out laughing again. Michael's stern face dissolved into a crooked smile.

"Justin, as soon as you get a hold of yourself, go on down and help Lucas with-"

Justin cackled, "With the L's- you said it, Sarg, you bit it back, but we all heard you, it was hilarious! I don't know how Luke controlled himself. I had to bite my tongue."

A corner of his mouth nicked up, Michael endeavored to maintain his composure. "It's your imagination, Justin. Go on then, go help Lucas, you know he'll need it."

Justin grinned then in only a second he wilted, his mouth compressed, his shoulders slumped. Behind Michael's head Justin could see his beautiful young daughter, Simone's picture tacked to the wall with the other kids that were missing.

His face puckered, struggling to keep his tears at bay. Crying like a baby wasn't going to bring his little girl back. His head dropped, he scrubbed his eyes with the heels of his palms.

Michael stepped close beside the smaller, wiry man. "Listen Justin, we'll find-"

Pain screamed from Justin's blue eyes. "Will we, Michael? Will we?" The garda's ruddy skin grew ruddier. The freckles staining his anguished face spread like a family of ants on a mission. Hands deep in his pockets, his shoulders closed in around his ears.

"Justin," Michael said softly, "I'm there with you, you know that. My Matty is-" his voice caught, he kept going. "Being one of the few people besides Lucas and Hollis, you know what Matty means to me. And you know I love little Simone as if she were my own."

Justin sniffed, nodding, he swiped at his tears.

Michael touched his garda's shoulder. "You know that every muscle, every nerve in my body screams for me to drop everything and run everywhere, search every house, basement, barn, garage, shed, whatever, to find Matty.

"But I have to constrain myself to stay here and painfully, methodically figure out what is happening and who is to blame, to find out where the kids are. Slow and steady study will help better than reckless frantic running in all crazy directions.

"There's not enough of us to search everywhere. Besides, this is such a vast, forested place with outbuildings cashed in crannies all over the mountains. We don't even know if the kids are being held all together or if they've been separated and kept in different places. We will do everything we can to find those kids, J, you know that. We have to trust, believe, have- have faith that we will find them."

His head still down, Justin nodded, short red hair sprung in tiny springs. Wiping his eyes with the back of a hand he peered up at his sergeant. Coughing, his Adam's apple bobbed in his skinny white neck, clearing his throat he took a breath.

"I guess, Michael, I guess what is sticking in my craw and jabbing at me is- is, I was mad at her, at Simone that morning. You know," he gulped, another deep breath, red tinged the tips of his oversized elf ears.

"The morning she dis- disappeared, well, I, she- she wouldn't obey Emmy. They were fighting and Simone was being such a little brat. You know, back talking, she even cursed at Emmy. For the likes of me, I don't know where she got that from, we don't swear in our house."

"They pick it up in school from the older kids," Michael said. He remembered when Gram Zinny almost washed out little Matty's mouth with soap one day when she was around five and burst in from school blurting a profane word that even embarrassed Korey.

Realizing the young girl had no idea the meaning of the word she'd uttered, Michael sat with her and used the incident as a learning lesson for Matty.

He discussed how different words can have dual meanings and how people would judge her on her behavior and language. He asked Matty what kind of person she wanted to portray, who she wanted to be when she grew up.

Her perky face had screwed up as she thought hard. Cheeks still plump with baby fat she sucked on the tip of her index finger. Her lips pulled in then she said very seriously, "I plan to be a famous ice skating Prime Minister." Michael had bitten back a smile.

Indeed, Matty spent two hours every day after school and 3-4 hours on the weekends skating either at the local rink or in one of the frozen ponds in the fields nearby in the winter. Michael had asked her, "So, would you vote for a Prime Minister that curses?"

The little girl thought hard again, then shook her head, fat strawberry pigtails slapped back and forth. "No, Uncle Mike, I sure wouldn't. My teacher, Miss Perireed says that no one respects a potty-mouth. She says people who swear have no vacabablarry. She made Caspar Smythe sit in the dunce chair when he said a bad word."

Her lips turned down looking about to cry. Climbing off her chair she had gone over and stood in front of Michael with her head down. Bright blue eyes glittering with sudden tears, she peeped up at him through long red lashes.

She set a small hand on his thigh, "Uncle Mike," her voice had wavered, "I'm so sorry. I didn't mean to be bad. I didn't know. I don't want to be a potty-mouthed Prime Minister!" Ponytails flew back and forth with her shaking head. Twin globby tears rolled over round cheeks.

Michael's heart had almost burst right then and there. He grabbed her up and pulled her onto his lap and hugged her hard then kissed the top of her head. It was hard to keep his voice from cracking as he told her she was forgiven and very loved. Matty had never said a bad word since and she was quick to call others on their language choices.

Michael mashed his thumbs over his eyelids to dispel the image from the past. Wearily, he said, "Kids do stuff, J, they test us and themselves, it's just growing up."

Justin shrugged. "Yeah, well, whatever. The point is that I got really mad and yelled at her, at Simone, I took her cell phone and laptop and sent her to her room." His hands covered his eyes but he couldn't stop the leakage.

Michael patted his shoulder, "Justin, it's not your fault. Kids push their parents to see how far they can go. Really, they appreciate the discipline; you know that, they need it to feel that you care about their wellbeing. She's just being a kid."

Justin pushed the heels of his palms hard at his eyes, sniffed, wiped his eyes with his hands. Clearing his throat he shot a half-baked grin at Michael, "I know, Mike. My head understands she was just being a self-absorbed brat, but she's my brat, my baby. I hate that our last time together was strident. I-"

"Justin, stop beating yourself up. Let's put our effort into figuring this mess out and save our recriminations for later. Let's keep our faith and hold onto our hope. Listen, why don't you go take a walk, clear your head, lose some of the toxins building in your body from the damned stress and fear.

"I don't think you're going to miss anything from the L's presentation to the media. In fact," his wry smile pulled up one side of his mouth. "I think you'll be lucky not to have to suffer through it."

Justin's lips compressed, blinking back an errant tear he choked out a tiny laugh. "Yeah, I've had just about enough of the L's. I really could use an excuse to keep their foolish crap outta my head!"

"Okay, go on and take a long walk. Maybe go out to the foothills, it's wild yet peaceful out there. You'll feel ten times better. We'll all meet back here in," he looked at his watch, "like two hours? The L's will be done, the press will have their question time and we'll come back here to regroup and decide how to proceed after the presentation. All right?"

Justin breathed deeply, smiled slightly. "Sure. That's great. I'll head for the mountains, the cool air will help refresh me I think. All right," he fist-bumped with Michael and nodded to Cat who had waited quietly while the men talked about their families. "I'll catch you all later." He plucked his jacket and hat off the hat stand and with a jaunty wave closed the door behind him.

Their arms folded in front of their chests, Michael and Cat stood side by side.

"I know how scared he is. It's good to hear him laugh," Michael murmured, his eyes unblinking on the closed door.

Cat pulled her long hair to one side in front of her chest and ran her fingers through the waves, a calming gesture.

She rolled her eyes up to Michael's, said softly, "It's okay to laugh even though your heart is breaking, Michael. It helps relieve the tension. Letting the fear gnaw at your guts won't help find the kids, it'll only make you sick. Relieving some of your anxiety might even help you think more clearly."

Michael nodded with a slight huff, "Yeah." He scrubbed his fingertips over his stubble then smoothed the hair back off his face. "I see your beautiful long hair and I realize mine is badly in need of a haircut. Things will have to wait, I need to get to my stables today to move my animals to the cement feed stalls and seal them down.

"The horses should be safe in the storm, the cement building is solid and I've boarded up the windows. I need to make sure there's enough water and feed for a while in case I can't get out to them.

"The couple of older horses and a sickly goat I've already taken up country to Max Master's Stables & Feed. The storm is predicted to steamroll over the bottom of the peninsula, not up it. I'll hustle on that as soon as the L's- uh, the *profilers* are done. Anyway, you ready?"

Eyes sparkled at him like sapphire earrings, she said, "Sure. But," her face sobered. "I have a feeling we're not going to be prepared for what the L Team has to say."

Michael gallantly took her arm and guided her to the door. He looked glum as he admitted, "Me too."

Chapter Twenty-Nine

Downstairs the auditorium swarmed with bodies jammed packed wall to wall with men, women, and their children that they were too scared to leave alone at home.

Gathered tightly in front of the stage everyone that worked for a news venue; local TV, radio and newspaper jostled and elbowed to gain space and the best spot. Cameras swung on shoulders working for the best view, uncaring if some poor chump got smacked in the side of the head by an extended lens.

Half the people in the crowd held up cell phones at the ready to take pictures. Sprinkled throughout the throng, reporters from towns up country fought for space along with gardai interspaced throughout for crowd control.

The room writhed like a belly that had eaten something bad, erupting, rumbling, whining, groaning and gurgling. The din of voices and spurts of nervous laughter or exclamations of irritation grew as more people squeezed through the door into the crammed room.

Collectively, the audience's conversations bounced schizophrenically from the tip of the iceberg of still having hope of rescue, down to the grievous giving in to helplessness and fear that the stolen children were never coming home.

Outside the window, the sky grew unnaturally dark, a brisk wind pushed the piles of debris into bigger piles, smaller loose pieces blew like chunks of hail bouncing and rattling down the streets and clattering against buildings.

Halo Valley

Surrounded by a semi-circle of microphones and a select group of reporters, the profilers held court center stage.

Gardai stood on either side of them, most had notebooks out ready to record the profilers' findings. They planned on hitting the streets the second they had an idea of a viable perpetrator to look for.

Michael grasped Cat's hand, so tall he easily pushed his way through the crowd pulling her behind him. They made their way to one side of the stage to stand with some gardai. Lowering his head Michael spoke in Cat's ear, "I can feel the tension seething in here with nerves and anticipation, it feels as if the walls are squeezing and breathing like an asthmatic."

On stage, Micky Lam buttoned the two middle buttons on his long leather coat, coughed behind one hand to clear his throat and raised a brow signaling his teammates. Raveena, her face taut as a mask, snapped a nod- *ready.*

Lam took his place in front of one of the microphones on a stand. He tapped the microphone, leaned in and spoke loudly into it, "Hello? Hello? Is this thing on?" He blew into it couple of times then tapped it again. The whooshing noise and squealing feedback jarred the room, hands clapped over ears.

A tech guy with earphones hanging around his neck and holding a clip board stepped from the side of the stage and hurried over to Lam.

He put his hand over the mike and whispered in Lam's ear, "Sir, the mike is working. It's very sensitive, you don't need to yell into it. And we never tap or blow on it, you'll break eardrums and you can damage the mike." Rolling his eyes he quickly returned to his place at the side of the stage.

Lam deigned not to acknowledge the tech. He rotated his shoulders, moved them up and down like he was preparing for a race and cleared his throat. Plucking the mike off the stand he held it close to his mouth and cleared his throat again, it sounded like a train crash, the audience cringed.

"Alrighty then. Good afternoon ladies and gentlemen, *céad míle fáilte*, a hundred thousand welcomes. I am Sergeant Micky Lam. I have been sent here from the RMP Command to assist your local police force." His eyes flicked to Michael. Pulling his lips in he shook his head ever so slightly indicating what he thought of the expertise of the local gardai.

Michael's brows drew down at Micky's subtle slur, but he stood silently with his arms crossed. His attention scattered to the anxious and angry faces of the audience, he felt hearts straining with fear throbbing in the room like drums in the jungle.

At his side, Cat's polite smile was pasted so stringently on her face it did little to hide the fact that she doubted she was going to trust what the L team was about to impart.

Her eyes glazed with faux interest as she was really running the children's pictures and family info through her head like she was trying to put a puzzle together or find a missing link in a chain. Sugar and spice hair soft against her dark blue suit jacket and skirt, her feet were growing tired in the four-inch high booties.

Lam set one hand on his waist in his usual stance of holding back his long leather coat, his legs shoulder-width apart as if ready to draw that old west gun. He caught the tech guy gesturing madly for Lam to move the mike a little further from his mouth.

Clearing his throat again, he continued loudly, "I am sure by now you all know who we are and that we were sent here to utilize our invaluable skills and prodigious experience in profiling to assist your- *police*- with finding the cruel villain that is responsible for kidnapping your children."

Michael shook his head with a sour smile. Every time Lam mentioned the gardai he made them sound more like they were a Boy Scout troop than a police force.

"Let me introduce you to my team." Lam motioned for his colleagues to come forward. "This is Corporal Raveena LaLinn, Corporal Lamar Morlock and Corporal Lyell Gilroy."

Raveena stood so rigid she would have made the Queen's Guard proud. Lamar and Lyell bowed like they were celebrities receiving an Emmy. Lam stopped and waited for the audience to applause. They didn't. The entire auditorium stood silent, unusual for such a huge group.

Dressed in an emerald green dress and high heeled boots even Mallory O'Leary who had kicked and shoved to get her and her cameraman the best position right in front center of the stage couldn't hide her annoyance at Lam's blatant posturing.

"C'mon ya damn red monkeys- get to the point! This ain't no award show, we don't give a hoot who the hell you are- tell us who has our children!" A furious Zebedee Trueno, father of sons Juan and Santiago snatched yesterday yelled from the crowd.

Others from the audience called out for Lam to stop stalling.

In the next instant before anyone could take a breath, a fierce gust of wind bashed the windows so hard the glass rattled, unnerving the crowd, causing gasps and shocked spurts of screams from the surprised crowd, a startled Lam looked ready to bolt.

A man closest to a window took off his glasses and pressed his nose against the glass. Slowly he put his glasses back on then faced the crowd, his skin ashen. "The snow has stopped. The storm is on its way."

A peanut hitting the floor could have been heard in the room, silent except for the wind bustling around the building making old pipes creak and moan and howl through cracks. Then the murmurings grew, a few hundred people turned frightened eyes up to Lam.

Perplexed at their sudden intensified fear, he turned his palms up and said, "What?"

Mallory saw her chance to be involved. "Film me," she uttered under her breath to her cameraman. Authority rang in her tone as she spoke out bold and clearly, "Hello everyone, Mallory O'Leary here with station WAKT." Preening to the audience and then the cameras, she then focused on Lam speaking to him as if he were a bit slow.

"The snow stopping and the gustier wind is the precursor, according to the weather people, to the calamitous storm expected. Once the storm hits there'll be no chance to save the children, if they're still ali-" the redhead broke off her words.

Chewing a corner of her lip, some red lipstick flaked off. Holding her own microphone, she turned and faced the audience. Her tone grim, she continued, "Uh, according to the legend, shortly after the twelfth child is taken, the storm hits. It'll be too perilous for us to be outside to continue the search. The children's bodies uh…" Mallory paused.

The audience moaned, squirmed. Mallory went on, "Uh, the bodies aren't found until the spring. The storm is expected to chop off the end of the winter with a sudden, sharp, and extremely rare blasting wind- they call it *te mhor*, a hot high wind. This unusual wind breaks the winter and then oddly, probably from the intense hot wind, the spring hits in a week."

She swept her hand towards a window that was shaking violently from the burgeoning wrath of the wind. "The twelfth child, young Pilly," her chest puffed, she paused dramatically, "Pil Philo, went missing this morning."

"And?" Lam could barely contain his impatience, he pushed his sunglasses up on his head, dark hair spiked and feathered around them.

Lucas Bregg's voice deep with anger, impatience, and profound fear, cut through the growing murmurings of the crowd. "It means according to the legend, the storm is about to hit, once it hits, it'll be too late. The children will be lost forever."

The windows shook harder, each gust harsher than the last. The force of the wind came wilder, colder, without pity.

Michael moved to stand directly in front of the stage. He held a finger up to Lam and beckoned to him. Miffed, Lam warily crouched down so he could hear the sergeant. His face impassive, Michael put a heavy hand on Lam's shoulder subtly forcing the Leatherman to lean over further.

Annoyed, Lam let him because he didn't want to look foolish in front of the crowd by trying to resist, he was squatting in an awkward position it could only end badly for him if he resisted Michael's pull. But he made sure the audience could see him roll his eyes heavenward at Michael's antics. "All right, boy, what the hell do you-"

Michael's large strong hand clamped over Lam's shoulder. Pressing his fingers into his neck, he whispered through clenched teeth, "Lam, you have exactly three seconds to provide your profile. If you don't produce information immediately I will personally throw your scraggy ass out of here and send you straight back to your commander with a note pinned to your collar. I have no fear of any penalties I might incur. Am I clear?" Glaring eyeball to eyeball, he waited a beat, dug his fingers in harder then abruptly let Lam go.

Lam rocked back on his heels, flailing his arms like an ungainly duck trying to keep his balance. He scrambled to his feet, his face as red as the finger marks on his neck, the sunglasses flopped down on his nose.

Flushing angry and embarrassed, he jerked at his coat to straighten it, pushed the glasses back up on his head, ran his fingers through his short hair. His mouth hung open, he'd gone blank on his presentation. Baffled, he stared awkwardly at the crowd.

Quickly, Raveena snapped her fingers at Lyell, gesturing to their board. The two of them picked up their poster board and carried it to the front of the stage giving Lam a moment to regain his composure.

Eyes rounded wide, the audience could only guess at what Michael had whispered to Lam. But, judging by Lam's red face and Michael's irate expression they could figure it out pretty well. Tittering from some of the people in the crowd drew a stern frown from Raveena. Her hands on her boyish square hips she addressed the room like a schoolmarm.

"Now then," She started. The people attended to the corporal's deep almost manly voice. Arms rigid behind her back, her body erect, a dictator without a moustache, short hair slicked tight against her head.

Swiveling on the balls of her feet, she stretched out her hand like she was Vanna White and motioned to Lam like he was door number 3. She announced, "Sergeant Lam is now ready to reveal our profile of the offender in question," and stepped back as if she were yanking aside a curtain.

Straightening his shoulders, an emboldened smile rounded his popping cheeks, Lam nodded to Raveena and took his place in front of the show board. Facing the audience he waited a few seconds for the murmuring to die down. His eyes drifted for a millisecond down to Michael then flashed to the audience. Back to his cowboy stance of one hand on his hip holding back the leather coat, legs akimbo, he gave Raveena the go-ahead to flip the cover paper back off the front of the board.

The first page was covered with 8 X 10 papers with writing on them. Raveena handed Lam a laser pointer and a folder containing a sheaf of notes. She marched over to the opposite side of the board almost clicking her heels together like a soldier when she took her place.

Seeing he had everyone's attention and the cameras were rolling, Lam read his notes then tapped the pointer against the board. "After innumerable hours of analyzing the data," he knuckled an eye so the audience could see how weary he was from his days and hours of hard work.

"We have drawn some conclusions as to what kind of person the police should be channeling their resources towards to finding. We can only give you the information, it will be up to the gardai to utilize it to actually track down and capture the miscreant. Hopefully they can handle the job."

Michael opened his mouth to retort at the constant insinuations that his force was incompetent, Cat laid a hand on his arm. His expression hardened, eyes narrowed, but he kept his peace.

"Now," Lam continued, "we have determined that the perpetrator is not a local or even from Cleasaí. He is a foreigner, maybe from Russia, a married white collar worker with children of his own. He doubts that his kids are really his, he thinks his wife cheated on him and all of children were fathered by other men which is why he wants to hurt the children. He doesn't dare hurt his own because he's in fear of his wife. He is between the ages of 30 and 50 and-"

"Micky." Lamar came over to stand in front of the board. "I thought we had decided on the profile of the unknown subject was that he's a she, a Caucasian employed in manual labor, is a Halo Valley local that is under 30, single and wants kids which is why she kidnaps-"

"No, no, no!" Lyell hopped up and down joining the pair. "No, we chose the theory that he is a foreign criminal that had a lousy childhood so he wants to hurt children, he's black and over 40 and employed in an upscale-"

Raveena stalked over, stomping to a halt by her colleagues. "No, you fools, we had decided to go with the idea that there's a team of thugs that are going to hold up the town for money, demanding ransom for the children. We needed to find the person that started the whole legend fiasco to know who the lead criminal is. We decided they came from-"

Lam vigorously shaking his head interrupted, "No, no, you forget Raveena, we ditched that idea because there's been no ransom note, remember? We made up our minds to go with the rich white guy that wants to punish other families because he thinks his is flawed be-"

Lamar raised his clenched fists pounding them in the air up and down like a child having a tantrum. "You're wrong, Micky, you guys too," he pointed at the other two corporals. "The last thing we made up our minds last night on was the young woman that wishes for kids but is ugly or deformed and can't get a guy so she-"

Lyell kept hopping like a red-haired bunny. "No! You're both wrong, I wrote everything down, you were falling asleep, you don't remember we ended with-'"

"Oh shut up you bloody muppets, we will go with *my* idea!" Raveena bellowed.

Lyell's red eyebrows rose until they just about disappeared into his red fuzzy hair, he stopped hopping, grabbed his belt and pulled his pants up until the waist was under his armpits. Glowering at the manly woman he said, "No you shut up you *scanger* wagon- stupid female, you're thick as a ditch and don't know-"

Raveena crossed her arms and stared hard at the little man until he whimpered off and his head dropped.

"*My* idea's the best, we'll go with mine!" Lamar broke in, his fists balled on his hips.

Lam banged the board with his pointer, "Hey! I am the Johnny ray here- I am the boss, we will go with *my* profile-"

"No mine!" Raveena quacked.

"Mine!" Lyell squeaked stepping out of Raveena's long armed reach.

"Mine!" Lamar screamed pounding his fists in the air.

"You sons of bitches-" Lam slammed the pointer again.

Michael jumped onto the stage. He held his arms out, palms out, barked, "*Enough!* Stop this right now. Shut off those damned cameras-" he glared over his shoulder at the press then faced the profilers.

He slashed his hands out, repeated, "*Enough!* Lam, take your team and go over to the Creafog. *Now.* You will all stay there until I come over. That's an order." The RMP's stood like deer in the headlights, their mouths agape.

"Michael Kelly you- you- you *murderer*, you have no authority- you can't tell us what to-" Lam blustered but Michael ignored him and picked up the microphone.

"Please everyone, can I have your attention." Michael waited while the stunned crowd quieted down. "I want everyone, no, I'm ordering everyone to leave here now and go home. It's time to secure ourselves and our families. Anyone on the street after the storm hits does so at their own peril. The hospitals and stores are closed. If you are injured there will be no one to come to your aid.

"We'll be lucky if we don't lose the electricity. Gas up your generators, get flashlights primed, you know what to do, we've been preparing for this moment for a while now. Most of you have made rooms in your cellars so I say start heading there now. This is martial law I'm activating, no one is to be on the streets.

"Everyone has a place to go, Miss Sylvester has seen to that. So, please," he gestured towards the door, "go now." He set the mike on the stand and motioned for half a dozen of his gardai to come close.

"Sir," several officers said together.

Kelly tugged the knees of his uniform trousers up then crouched down to their level. His arms propped on his knees he said, "Floyd, I want you and Sammy to go up to the room we've been using and take down all the pictures and papers, and take them and all the files and box them up and take them over to my place. When you knock on the door you need to call out-" he looked embarrassed, "you need to call out the words, yellow flower."

"Yes, sir." Without question, the two gardai struck right out to do his bidding.

"And Timmins, I want you and Shelley and Sean to keep the crowd moving out, completely out to their cars and gone. Then check the building, every room, closet, bathroom, to make sure no one is here then secure the Hall and then go to your homes."

"Yes, sir," the officers responded in unison. They immediately started to gently jostle people aside making their way through the crowd to the sides of the room and slowly urge people like cattle to the door.

Michael turned some of the remaining gardai. "Robin, I need you to call dispatch, tell them to contact all the police including those that came down to assist us from Glenfall and Strowell to clear the streets, and the rest of you make sure all the businesses are closed and locked and then everyone is to go to their homes and stay there until Darrin the weatherman tells the mayor to give the all clear siren. Okay? Got it?"

"Yes, sir." Pulling out his cell phone to call dispatch, Robin hustled with the other officers to the side door to exit quickly.

As soon as they left, Michael jumped down from the stage and said something in Lucas' ear. Lucas responded with a sharp nod. Then Michael took Cat's hand and pulled her through the crowd and followed the other officers out the side door.

Lam's Popeye cheeks puffed in and out, his face a burning tomato he started to call out to Michael but Lucas and several other gardai jogged up the few stairs on each side of the stage and circled the RMP's. Lucas stood with his hands on his hips in front of Lam.

"Now listen here, boy-" Lam opened his mouth,

"No- be quiet," Lucas commanded, his voice harsh, his face a stony mask.

"My men are taking you back to the hotel where you will collect your belongings. A car will be there waiting to take you to the airstrip where you will get on the plane and go home. I have orders to escort you there with or without your cooperation. You get me?"

The thick blond officer motioned to several of the gardai surrounding them.

Lam sputtered, "Who the fuck do you-"

Lucas cranked back to the sergeant, face impassive but a steel edge to his words said, "Just have your people call our people. Don't embarrass yourselves by resisting. Now," he swept his hand towards the back stage, "let's go quietly."

Raveena made as if to stalk around Lucas to stage front, her fists clenched, eyebrows like crossed swords. Lam held his arm out in front of her to stop her. Raveena halted abruptly, tiny beady eyes shifting to Lam's hand in front of her red leather jacket to his pinched face.

Lam said to Lucas, "All right, officer, you have your instructions, it will do us no good to try to fight you. But," he thrust a bony finger with a rounded end like a gecko in front of Bregg's face, his small niblet teeth grit, "as soon as we get home I'm calling our command, and your boss' life in the Guard will be over, and you won't be able to get hired as a goddamned doorstop. You fucking mark my words. C'mon guys, let's go."

He turned his back and marched with his head high to the back stage where Lucas still pointed with his open hand.

Unaware he crushed a tiny pink candy under his boot, Lucas and his gardai escorted the profilers from the stage going out the back way to avoid the crowd that was just realizing what had occurred and were blistering with anger.

A sharp primeval wind like an animal on the hunt penetrated the room through the open front door.

Chapter Thirty

Michael dropped Cat at her hotel and disappeared for a couple of hours. She assumed he was visiting the mysterious Kayleen to discuss the enigmatic Matty.

Later he picked Cat up and she went with him while he organized the moving of his animals.

Hours passed before they returned to the police station, they dropped themselves onto cushioned chairs in the cozy blue and white lounge.

Cat kicked off her booties, removed her jacket and set it on the chair beside her, unbuttoned the top two buttons on the silk blouse. She splayed back with her head against the pillow on the chair, her arms dangling over the sides, feet stretched out on the rug.

Tossing his Guardian cap on the table, Michael took off his jacket and hung it on the doorknob then pretty much mirrored her. They sat in weary silence, just breathing, and thinking, trying to ignore the wail of the wind rummaging around outside of the building.

They sat quite a while in companionable silence. Then they traded thoughts on the profilers' inanity before moving on to their endless dissecting of the missing children. Michael compartmentalized Matty to a portion of his brain where she was always present but out of the way of the cognitions his brain needed to study the case.

They paced, made calls, Michael checked on the progress of the instructions he'd given his officers, and updated Gram and the mayor who hadn't been at the presentation as he was facilitating his grandmother's safe move.

Cat checked in with various volunteers around town she had set up to oversee the transporting of the homeless for whom they had found temporary safe residency until the wrath of the storm had passed.

Dacia poked her head in the door, her face a dark thumbprint against the light colored wall. "Hey Sergeant, you want me to make you guys some fresh coffee?"

Michael twisted his tired head at her, flashed a weary grin. "That'd be really great, Dacia, we could sure use some. Thanks. Hey, Dacia," he said as she disappeared.

Her head popped back in the doorway, bright teeth gleamed helpfulness. "Yes?"

"Can you give Lucas a buzz and see if the L's got on that plane?"

A little giggle erupted, Dacia chirped, "I'll call him right away. Goodbye to ridiculous rubbish I say, the sooner gone the better. I'll confirm their evacuation ASAP."

Michael and Cat sat quietly again, each letting their own thoughts swirl in the ten minutes Dacia was gone. When she returned she had a tray with a coffee pot, mugs, cream, sugar, spoons and a plate filled with thick chewy brownies crusted with walnuts.

She set the tray on a table then mentioned wryly, "I'll bet you two have had nothing to eat since breakfast. Dee Troicasi brought in the brownies, help yourself. I'll be out at the dispatch if you need anything, okay?" She waited.

"Thanks Dace." Michael pushed himself to sit up in the chair. He picked a brownie off the top of the pile. It was gone in two bites. He reached for another. "I don't know what we'd do without you, you have a heart of gold."

Dacia beamed. She fluffed a side of brown twists then clasped her hands behind her back turning side to side. "Oh Sarg, you know I'd do anything for you, all you need to do is ask…" without taking her eyes off Michael she walked out the door.

Cat groaned. "For cryin' out loud, Sergeant, is there not one female in all of Halo Valley that isn't in love with you?"

He leaned forward, his forearms on his knees. Black hair waving forward, absently he brushed it back, his muscled arms bulged even through the long sleeved shirt. A corner of his lip turned up, he sidled a look at her. "There's only one whose opinion matters to me."

Cat abruptly sat up. To hide the pink suddenly tingling her face, she got up and poured two mugs of coffee, handing one to Michael. "Well, so," stuttering, she put a spoon in her coffee and whacked a few stirs around the mug.

"Well, so," he parroted with a chuckle. "Do you always stir your coffee with nothing in it?"

"Huh?" Cat looked down at her mug. The coffee was black as she liked it, she had no idea why she was stirring it. Blue eyes narrowed at him. "You're trying to embarrass me."

He shook his head, picking up his coffee he looked down in it. "Gee, not everyone likes their coffee black. No cream and sugar for me?" he teased as he reached for the pitcher of cream.

Choking back a snort, she gulped her coffee then had a choking fit. "No, stop-" holding up a hand to Michael as he rose to help her. Coughing, she held the mug with one hand pressing it hard on her lap, held the other over her mouth as she fought the liquid that went down the wrong pipe.

Watching her, the sergeant sipped his coffee almost delicately, teasing, like he was showing her the proper way to drink a beverage.

The brief case of choking finally subsiding, her head dropped forward, her long hair fell forward hiding her flaming cheeks. Cat pressed a napkin to her lips then dotted her eyes that teared during her episode.

Crossly, she said, "That was your fault. I am not one of your little harem girls dying to wait on you hand and foot, fawning all over you."

She laid the back of her hand to her forehead, pretending to swoon. Her thick hair swept back and forth over her back as she drawled, "Oh, Sergeant *sah*, ah declare, ah ahm just so in love with you, please, please, smile upon me, make mah day and let me serve you, mah darling. Just let me melt into those big, black beautiful pools of eyes and ah am yours…"

Michael grinned, his brows arched. "Big beautiful eyes?"

Cat pursed her lips, squinted. "Don't be ridiculous, you are so vain. I was merely mocking your groupies." Carefully finishing her coffee, she set the mug on the tray and grabbed a brownie.

"I don't know." He shook his head laughing, swigged some coffee. "I kinda like that dark pools thing."

Cat plopped back down in her chair, chewing, crossed her legs femininely and sat back. "Mmm, these brownies, in a word- rich, delish!" Licking her fingers she said, "Seriously, Sergeant, what are you going to do about the profilers? The Superintendent ordered you to use them."

With a heavy sigh Michael stood up. He pointed out, "That's two words." Legging over to a window he set his palms on the window sill and looked out.

The sun was starting to set, a blurry blaze of orange behind grey clouds. The snow started again doubling in mass and size. The wind blew the heavier flakes in an angled flow. He turned and half sat on the sill.

"What a silly pot of quare hawks those L's were, odd bit of fools. I'm sure I've done it this time." He sighed again. "But, that's me, *amach as na muineacha is isteach sna driseacha*, out of the thickets and into the thorn bushes."

"Don't you mean out of the frying pan into the fire?"

Shrugging he said, "Sure, tomato tomahto-"

"No, that's different, that's a-"

"Hey." Justin Zeall entered the room. Bundled from head to toe he was swathed in scarves, hat with ear flaps, mittens, and a puffy down jacket.

In his stocking feet because he left his wet boots at the door he began unraveling the wool scarf from his neck. He walked and unraveled into the room.

"Ooh, brownies!" He yanked off a mitten to get a brownie. Stuffing the brownie half in his mouth he continued undressing dropping his outerwear on a chair. Relieved of the heavy winter clothes, he looked so boyishly thin he could have been mistaken for a teenager.

Justin had a small thin nose like his daughter's, 80% of his body was covered in freckles with a sharp chin to match his wiry body. His light blue eyes were bright and gleaming, red hair stood up in fuzzy squiggles from the electricity of the wool hat he'd pulled off. "Listen," he started, then picked up Cat's discarded mug and poured himself a cup then sat down.

Michael chuckled. "Hey, J, make yourself comfortable. Just pretend you're in your own home."

Justin chewed, his cheek bulging. "Yeah, so listen, Mike. I hiked out to the foothills to clear my cobwebs. I painstakingly kept a watch of everything around me, you know, in case there was any indication of the- the kids."

Justin picked up another brownie. Michael prompted him to continue, "And?" It was obvious the redheaded garda had something to say.

Cat sat forward in interest, her hair falling over her shoulders like a warm russet shawl. Glancing at her nails she wondered when she'd ever get a manicure again. Shrugging, she chewed a nail.

"Well," Justin said, chomping. Talking through a mouthful of brownie he told Michael, "I made my way across Fand's Trail up to the foothills on the east side of the mountains. You know where the recess is in the mountain, where the Faoi Cairn is?"

Michael nodded. "Yeah, sure, the cairn at the end of the old sheep's trail."

"What's a cairn?" Cat asked.

Justin swallowed and reached for yet another brownie.

"Man, you keep eating those and soon you'll be a coppernobbed beach ball," Michael warned him.

"*Is cuma liom,* I don't care, boss." Justin wolfed the brownie down as fast as the first. Licking his fingers and wiping them on his pants he swigged some coffee. "I hiked for a long time across snow covered shrubbery, I'm starving! Besides, my metabolism is really high, I've always been wiry. I'm like me da, he was always a skinny runt!"

"What's a cairn?" Cat asked again.

Justin's mouth was full, so sitting back down, Michael told her. "A cairn, or carn as it's usually called in Ireland but cairn in other parts of the world is kind of a man-made pile of stones. The pile is usually shaped like a cone or a roundish pyramid.

"They can denote many things, like, anything from a landmark, or marking a grave, marking a trail. Some commemorate events like war sites or an historical event, some were created for astrological purposes. Many, believe it or not, are even made for the superstitious, to stop the dead from rising."

"Yeah," Justin interjected, "my uncle in Wales had one he called it a carnedd. His developed just because he had cleared a field for farming and they just made a pile out of the rocks they dug out."

"But," Michael said, "I believe the cairn, at the foothills, the Faoi Cairn as Hollis has called it, I think it was just a general kind that was created by travelers picking up a rock at the foot of the hill and placing it atop the other rocks other hikers had placed. The bigger rocks are kept towards the bottom and the smaller ones go on top. It's just kind of a tradition."

"It sounds interesting, I hope I can see it before I- uh, leave." Cat looked down at her hands clasped in her lap. She twisted her twined fingers like she was studying her fragmenting nail polish. It struck her, it sounded so gloomy, her leaving. It would mean her job was over.

She had been successful in her task of moving the Cleasaí residents from their homes from their side of the mountain merging them comfortably into the neighborhoods of Halo Valley.

It had been quite an undertaking transferring children's schools including teachers and fitting people into existing businesses, churches, schools and the general community.

Sadly, the undertaking had been made harder by the animosity between the two villages. Yes, her job had been successful, but she felt no cheer. The horror of the missing children would always blacken her time in Halo Valley. It tugged so at her heart, she dreaded leaving without knowing what happened to the children.

She wanted to stay and help fight to find them- alive, and bring each one home to their family. Especially... she nonchalantly peered at Michael, ah, then there was the sergeant... she lifted her head, wound her hair behind her ears and pushed the bulk behind her back then settled her gaze on Justin.

Jumping to his feet, Justin talked while waving a brownie in the air. Very animated like a Howdy Doody doll, he chattered, "Yes, but the Faoi Cairn for years has always been only around three and half feet high, give or take. Yet, when I was there today it had grown, Mike, like a lot."

Michael's brows drew down, forehead furrowed. "What do you mean?"

"Yeah." Justin broke the last brownie in two, popped one half in his mouth, chewed twice then tossed in the other half, munching with relish.

"It's grown like three feet higher and it's wider. There's no way in this weather and the harsh location that people have been doing that much hiking to make the cairn grow that much."

Michael stood up, his hands on his hips he paced a few steps then sat back down. His brow creased, he conjured up the uneven conical cairn made up of all sizes and colors of rocks in his mind.

Picturing the craggy cairn and the rugged surrounding area, he said thoughtfully, "That's weird. It's a fairly remote area now, off the beaten track. The old dirt trails were made long ago before it grew so troublesome to get to.

"The terrain is so dense with scrub brush and the trails have been mostly grown over with bush and wild sharp grass it's difficult to navigate through. I don't think really a lot of people pass by there anymore."

Sitting back, Michael crossed his arms and laid an ankle over one knee trying to recall the last time he'd been in that area. It'd been some time.

"The cairn has been unchanged that I know of since I came here years ago. Periodically of course, I, and you policemen cross the area by horseback but I haven't noticed any changes myself, however it has been awhile since I've been out that way."

He put a thumb and forefinger to his chin, massaging as he pondered. "Did you, could you move any, I don't know, did you look around it, are any of the stones, I mean," he didn't know what to ask. "That's pretty strange."

Justin nodded fast in agreement. "Man, it was really strange. I did try to move some rocks just out of curiosity, but I couldn't. I don't know if the pressure was so strong from them being pressed against one another for so long or, or I don't know. I couldn't budge one rock, it's like they'd been cemented or something. Plus, it looked to me that the trails have been used recently. It's hard to tell of course because of the frozen earth and snow. The whole thing's a mystery."

Cat asked, "What does Faoi mean"

Justin shot a questioning look at Michael. "I'm not sure."

"It means under," Michael replied.

"Under? What's it under?" Justin asked. "There's nothing over it, it's just out in the open mostly, just backs up to the mountainside."

Michael shrugged one shoulder. "Dunno, maybe because it's under a, well I don't know maybe under the mountain's view, or maybe a tree used to be there. Under the sky? A shadow from an outcropped rock maybe, really, it could mean anything or nothing. Anyway, we need to go and check-"

Dacia rushed in the door, panic struck her face turning her black skin pale, eyes popping wild.

The three people turned at her entrance. "What is it, Dace?" Michael asked. Then they could hear the siren.

The uniformed Dacia put a hand on either side of the doorway to brace herself, her legs wavered like water. "It's here!" she shrieked. Letting go of the doorway she wrapped her arms around her body and bobbed her head up and down, up and down, eyes wide like white wall tires. Twisty hair bounced all over her head.

"Who's here?" Michael asked coming to his feet. Her distress so palpable the room filled with her urgency.

Dacia yelled, "The storm! It's hit- it's here- the storm is striking!

The siren warning to take shelter is wailing. Can't you hear it? They said on the radio that it's not a test, that everyone, even the police should all go home right away and stay there until it passes. Go down in your root cellars those that have them they advised.

"The siren started just seconds ago. They're battening down the hospital, everyone else is leaving." Pulling her coat and hat on, she turned in the doorway then looked back, "I'm outta here. Take care everyone and don't forget to lock the door!" She was gone.

The ominous wailing siren was truly loud enough to penetrate the building. Justin grabbed up the outerwear he'd dumped on the chair and shoved his arms into the jacket while trying to put his hat and gloves on all at the same time.

He looked like a redheaded silly doll that you wind up and it hops and does back flips. Wrapping the woolen scarf around his neck, he blinked agitated blue eyes at Michael, "Sarg, what are we- I mean, Emmy and-"

Michael moved quickly but calmly, left his cap and uniform jacket on the table but grabbed their outerwear off the coat rack and handed Cat hers while slipping on his own.

He said, "Okay Justin, calm down. We've planned for this, the entire town has practiced for this event for a year. We'll proceed according to our rehearsed plan. Right?"

Justin nodded fervently, but his mouth kept opening and closing with no sound coming out. His eyes darted to the door to Michael to the door. All three jumped when something banged the side of the building so hard it sounded like a cannonball hit the wall.

"What was-" Cat halted zipping her jacket, wide eyes looked to Michael.

Michael slapped his winter hat on his head then grasped Justin and Cat's arms ushering them to the door. "I think it's the wind strengthening, probably hurling things. Come on. Justin, you go home and take care of your family. Just go," he ordered.

Justin moved through the doorway, turned back. "Sarg, you-"

Michael waved him. "Go, I'll catch the lights and the doors. The station will be locked up as will every other business in town. The citizens are well aware that no one will be on the streets and no one will be risking their life to come to rescue anyone who's foolish enough to venture outside until the storm is over. Our instructions were clear.

"I'm going home to be with Gram and Korey, Cataleigh's coming with me. We'll stop on the way for her to pack her things." He didn't check to see if she agreed.

Justin's voice cracking he swore, "Mike, as soon as the storm is over..."

Michael nodded, turning out the lights. "Yeah, you know it. The second the storm lessens we're out looking for the kids. I'll contact everyone when I feel it's safe to emerge. Now go."

"You guys take care, you hear?" Justin's light blue eyes welled, his freckles brightened, he hugged them both quickly then turned and fled.

Chapter Thirty-One

Michael checked the station, secured anything not locked up or bolted down, made sure everything was turned off then he and Cat stopped by the front door.

With the lights off and the windows covered with storm shutters it was pitch black inside.

Michael took Cat's mittened hand, wailing siren abounding they stood momentarily in the dark, held by a bit of trepidation to leave the security of the station. "It's kind of spooky, huh?" he murmured near Cat's ear.

Shivers of fear tingled over Cat's shoulders and down her back, pinpricks raised along her arms and across her tightening belly. Michael's husky voice and warm breath on her ear melted the pinpricks.

The tight band around her stomach relaxed. A soft smile stroked her lips. Thankful he couldn't see her fear, or her smile, she couldn't see him at all but was comforted by his strength and calm.

He waited until he felt the nerves quiet in her hand, her rapid breaths calm. "You ready?" he squeezed her hand.

She nodded, then realized he couldn't see her. "Yes."

"Let's roll." Michael opened the door and nearly lost his arm as the ferocious wind snatched it out of his hand slamming it against the building. Sleet howled past the building so fast it sounded like tires screeching.

Lurching back inside, he almost stepped on Cat right behind him. The wind forced the door wide open. Yelling over the roar of the wind and the ear-splitting siren, Michael shoved his hat in his pocket and gripped Cat's hand. "I won't let you go, Cataleigh-" the ends of his words were cut away by the wind and noise.

"Keep your head down," he shouted, "stay directly behind me so I can block some of the wind. We'll move as fast as we can to my cruiser. I want you to hold onto my belt while I get the door closed, then I'm gonna grab your hand and as soon as I get it closed we move. Don't stop. Okay, you ready?"

Cat didn't trust herself to speak so she nodded. She looked like a nun, only her sea eyes were visible from her hat and scarf wrapped around her head. He pulled her out the door, the wind blasted them immediately thrusting Cat away-

Michael reached out and snatched her wrist. With a grip of steel, he pulled her back and behind him until she could wrap her arms around him and stick her hands under his jacket to grab ahold of his belt.

There was no point in talking, the wind slapped the words away. It took all of his strength to get behind the door and push it closed. Fumbling the key out of his pocket, he forced it in the lock then managed to drop the key back in his pocket.

The violent wind and the bullets of hail striking their faces, they kept their heads bent against the brunt of the wind, trudging as quickly as they could through the barraging storm to the cruiser.

Bombastic gusts forced tears from their eyes, knocking them about like drunks, the thick wall of snow trying to crush them as they struggled blindly to the cruiser.

The wind struck so hard and cruel it burned their ears. As loud as the freakish weather was, the wailing siren could be heard above the storm's clamor. A cold lump of terror grew in Cat's stomach. Squinting through blurred eyes, she could see the blizzard, a fully enveloping moving mass thick with snow bulldoze down the street, buildings were barely visible in the sheet of solid white.

Michael pulled off a glove and pitched frozen fingers into his pocket to get his car keys. His fingers rigid with cold couldn't hold the keys and the wind tore them from his hands dropping them in a bank of snow next to the cruiser.

Not able to see what was going on, Cat strained to hold onto Michael's belt while he bent to get the keys.

He fished in the bank, his numb fingers managing to find them and with effort he pushed the remote button, relief warmed him when he heard the 'beep beep'.

Finally, he got them inside and shut the doors. His frozen fingers shoved the key in the ignition, turning it, grateful when the engine caught. He flicked the heat and headlights on.

Already they were cocooned in snow rapidly freezing to ice, the cruiser rocked by escalating gusts. They sat in the dark car, catching their breaths, letting the cold air blow at them until the engine warmed and the heat finally came out.

The ride out of town was laborious and unreal. Her hands engulfed in mittens, Cat held them tightly in her lap to still the tremors. She smoothed her skirt then forced herself to set her hands calmly back in her lap, take a couple of deep breaths and relax.

It was an effort to see out the window. The wind blew the snow in viscid sheets, eclipsing any fingers of light from an all but invisible sun that might have clawed through the heaving black clouds.

Michael turned the radio on, checked all stations but as expected there was nothing but the crackling of static. The metronome whoosh-whoosh of wipers brushed back and forth hypnotically, the snow re-covering the window just as fast as the wipers cleared it. Crackle crackle, swish-swish, crackle crackle. He shut the radio off.

Almost impossible to see out her side window, Cat nonetheless wiped circles on the glass to clear the milky condensation. Straining to see out, she could barely make out filmy buildings that looked more like fudgy shadows than solid constructions, as the car travelled steadily down the street clotted with growing drifts of snow.

"Normally I find the pristine white snow flowing softly and powdering the land so pretty, you know, sparkling and downy as an angel hair blanket," a childlike wonderment in Cat's words and tone, then she shuddered. "But now I feel so secluded, with virtually every window in every structure boarded or shuttered, even if anyone was inside and had the lights on they wouldn't be visible through the covered windows."

Michael nodded, grunted.

Her nose closer to the window she said musingly, "It's spooky really, in this curtain of blinding horrid weather moving through the center of town in the car covered with snow, makes me feel more like we're travelling through a tunneled lightless crypt.

The buildings cloaked cubes and rectangles like dark watchmen guarding the abandoned Main Street, eyeless windows watching us trudge past."

"You have an interesting imagination," Michael said with a smile. Leaning over the steering wheel to see better, he occasionally wiped the windshield with his gloved fist. He saw Cat clutching her hands together in her lap to calm herself.

"You okay?" He sounded weird inside the muffled cruiser with the storm bashing at them.

Peering out her window she tried not to get too close or her breath would fog it up worse she replied, "Uh, yeah, I'm fine."

"You don't sound fine..." He took his eyes off the road to shoot a quick glance at her. "What's on your mind, besides this interminable drive home?" Their bodies jerked and bumped and swayed from the wind rocking the car.

She said, "Nothing, really, I'm just trying to be quiet so you can concentrate. I'm not a gabby woman you know." She swung her head at him. "Don't answer that! To men every woman is gabby!"

He chuckled. "You got me, I wasn't going to let that pass. But," his eyes darted over, "I can tell you're really worried about something other than getting out of this storm." He raised his voice slightly to be heard over the howling wind.

Broken tree limbs, trash, awnings, fences, chairs, even a bicycle that someone forgot to bring inside blew by. Like they were in a pin ball machine, things banged and crashed and scraped as they hit the car on their way down the street to oblivion.

Michael smiled wryly. "I'm glad this isn't my car 'cause it's not gonna be pretty by time we get home. I hate to sound hokey, but I really feel as if Dorothy and her dog are going to fly by any second."

Cat's lips curved up in amusement. "As long as there's no evil witches or creepy flying monkeys. I wouldn't mind seeing the singing munchkins, and I always liked the Scarecrow." The smile drooped.

He glanced quickly at her again. "Come on, tell me what's up doc?"

Cat sighed. She turned in her seat to face him. It was dim in the car but she could see him. He appeared so unperturbed and in control, even smiling at her here and there seeming unaffected by their dangerous position.

They had been the first ones to tell others to go home and not be out in the heart of the storm that was predicted to last over a week, and here they were.

The severity of the after effect of flooding was undeterminable. The projection of when it would be safe to venture outside would be a wait and see. Hopefully everyone's shelter would stay the damaging effects of the killer storm. Cat felt safe with him, her stomach unclenched. "I didn't want to bring it up, because of...of Matty." She hesitated watching his expression. It didn't waver.

"And?" he prompted.

She stared out the front window then back at him. "I'm so worried about the children. I can't help thinking, where are they? Are they safe inside? Are they out in the elements? I mean, they couldn't survive if they were- that's if they're still a-" she couldn't bear to say it.

Michael glanced at her, even with her face knit with concern she was still phenomenally gorgeous. To describe her as beautiful was almost too bland of a word for her. He patted her knee then put both hands back on the wheel. The wheel shrunk in his confidant strong hands.

"We can't go there, Cataleigh. We're running on faith. And we'll stick with the faith that the kids are safe and sound until we discover otherwise. So," he patted her knee again then held the wheel against the wrenching wind. "We're not even going to think about it or consider that we aren't going to find them. Now, tell me something about yourself; your family, your town, your best friend growing up."

She could hear the confident strength in his voice. If he had that strong of faith this was not the time for her to let her own faith wither. She promised herself she was not going to go there again until- until everything was resolved. She also promised herself she was not leaving Halo Valley until the children were found, whatever the outcome was.

Drawing in a deep breath, Cat regaled Michael with stories of the trouble she and her best friend, Ela had managed to get into when young teenagers.

His laughter rang in her ears at her antics as they finally saw his ancient oasis of a home half covered in the sterile white snow. The Victorian-ish house was still decorated with colored lights that burned hazy through the snow Michael had put up more than a month ago for Christmas even though few people in town had felt like celebrating the holiday. He hadn't had the time to take them down.

The cruiser burrowed up the long snow covered driveway. Michael had electric shutters installed in anticipation of the normally extreme weather that blew in off the mountains in the winter. Part of a shutter was open a few inches. Distorted through the misted kitchen window, Gram's anxious face appeared, a pale cellophane moon.

Michael parked in the drive because Korey's and Gram's cars were in the garage. They had offered earlier to move but Michael said he was fine in the driveway. No one would be leaving until the brunt of the storm wore out.

The bundled pair slogged through the snow deepening in the driveway. It seemed they moved in slow motion like they were plodding through knee deep white mud until they finally made it into the warm haven. Inside the enclosed porch they removed their boots before entering the foyer. The floor gleamed so brightly it was obvious Gram had been busy.

"Mmmm, I smell Gram's roast pork and blue cheese mashed potatoes. Can you hear my stomach rumbling?" Michael asked with a hungry grin.

"I am so hungry I could eat the smell alone! It's so toasty and cozy in here I feel like I've come home for Christmas, where's the eggnog?" Cat giggled. The couple shared a grin. Their relief making it home safe and sound, where it was dry and warm was palpable.

Before they could leave the foyer, Korey came down the hall with Banny jumping at his heels, he handed Michael a glass containing two fingers of whiskey.

"There ya go, Mike, that'll settle your nerves and warm your cockles. We were getting concerned, it took a long time since your call that you were on your way. Gram's finishing up in the kitchen."

"Yeah, it's a beast out there, you have no idea," Michael said grimly, still in the doorway removing his jacket. He shook his hair to get some of the moisture off.

Cat pouted. "Hey, what about me?" She bent to pick up the excited dog all wagging tail and licking tongue.

Korey laughed at her trying to nuzzle the excited dog as he lapped her sodden face. "I figured you as a tea person. The kettle's just gone on, but I'll get you a drink right away, I'm switching to Guinness for dinner. Gram has a hot meal waiting for us already on the table. There's some towels in the bathroom there for you to dry off a little with." He headed back to the kitchen.

Cat let the dog down who immediately gleefully attacked Michael. Michael handed Cat his whiskey. "Here, take mine, I'll get the one Korey brings." Crouching, he rubbed the dog's ears and scratched his head.

Cat eyed the amber liquid suspiciously. Reluctant now, she accepted the glass from him and took a tiny sip. "Ugh, that's awful. Tastes like burnt medicine, here," her tongue stuck out in a grimace, she thrust the glass back at him, her nose wrinkling.

Michael laughed taking the glass back, he downed it in one swallow. "Yeah, ahh," he sighed happily, "that'll warm your belly. What the hell's a cockle anyway?" he asked while leading the way to the kitchen.

Chapter Thirty-Two

Finishing the warm, chocolate bread pudding and a second cup of strong tea, Gram got up from the table.

"Okay you two," she said, "Korey will help me with the cleanup. I know you kids are itching to get into that cavern of a library and put up your boards and pictures and such your men brought to continue working the investigation. Korey put wood and kindling in the fireplace for you."

She moved to the tallboy where she went to pick up empty platters. "Korey, come along, dearie." The feisty bespectacled grandmother waved her hand at Korey to get up and help her.

Shaking his head like he was loathe to rise, hippie ponytail a loose cord down his back, the young man gulped down the last inch of his pint of molasses-colored Guinness before following the cheerful, tut-tutting grandmother.

Michael grinned at their backs and pushed back his chair. Tossing his napkin beside his plate, cradling the remnants of another whiskey, he gestured for Cat to go with him. He led her to a hall.

Flicking a light switch, he crossed his fingers that the electric would work well, it was the latest room wired. There was a hesitation, the lights flickered then came on fully.

He showed her a bathroom where she could change into dry jeans and a sweater she'd stowed in a bag at the station in the event she was snowed in. The officers had dropped it off with their other items. "I'll meet you right here," he told her, "I'll be back after I change out of this itchy uniform I wore for that ridiculous show today."

Ten minutes later he was standing outside the door when she came out, both more comfortable in casual clothes. He held his hand out directing to a hall. "We'll go this way, Cataleigh."

Antique gold lamps lined the walls as the pair strolled down the long, newly plush carpeted corridor to the library.

He opened one of the French doors adorned with old fashioned glass door knobs, standing aside for her to go in first. The roundish room with cathedral ceilings like the rest of the house was walled with books, thirsty carpets and large cushiony chairs. Michael closed the door behind them.

Cat moved into the room, taking in the sturdy teak tables, paintings on the walls, and the white marbled fireplace encircled in slate seating that dominated the far end of the room. "Oh my," she exclaimed, obviously impressed with the grandeur of the masculine room.

Stopping in front of a painting, it was striking even though awash with the dark red and brown hues typical of the time period.

She clasped her hands behind her back and gazed up in interest. "Magnificent, Sergeant, it's magnificent." She studied the work of art. The latter part of the Dark Ages, men dressed in hunting attire of the time lounged around a room that almost mirrored the one she was standing in.

"Ahh," she inhaled deeply. "I can practically smell the cigar smoke and the honey clove of the mead swirling in those intricately carved silver steins, and the heat radiating off the dogs warming by the fire. It's like we could hear the men talking, like their ghosts are in this room, but in a comforting way, not in a scary way.

"What a time to live, the world still a mystery, myths and fairy tales still believed in, amazing discoveries to be made, treasure to find..."

"Baths only once in a while, uneducated dentists, quack doctors, someone goading you into a duel at the drop of a hat, and don't even talk about bathrooms..." Michael joined in coming to stand beside her.

"Hey, you're ruining the romanticism of the painting. By the way," she said, swiveling to take in the rest of the room. "I thought this place was in disrepair, practically condemned. But this room…"

Michael moved to the fireplace and picked up a long, golden fireplace lighter. Kneeling, he sat back on his heels and used an iron poker to move the wood and kindling around, it took him only a few moments to get a small fire going.

Stoking it until flames lapped the wood; he stood back and placed the screen in front of it.

Satisfied, he went over to a long teak table the officers had set their boxes on. "It'll do. Well? Shall we get started?" Soft light from lamps and the fire made the room comfortable and warm.

One last longing look at the painting, and Cat joined him. They pulled out the stacks of pictures, papers, files, and started organizing them and taping some to the walls, the fire crackling in the background. Cat stopped shuffling papers and looked around.

"What are you looking for?" Michael asked.

"I don't see my laptop," she muttered, rummaging through the remaining boxes.

Michael glanced around, shrugged. "We must have left it in the cruiser. We'll have to work without it for now."

They worked steadily for several hours reviewing and re-reviewing all the paperwork they had been studying for weeks. One of the glass French doors cracked open. Gram poked her silver head in. Seeing them sitting bent over the papers and files scattered but in organized bunches on the teak table, she came in.

"Here then," the elderly lady said, still wearing her latticed apron she entered the room. Carrying a tray containing a bottle of red wine, two goblets, a corkscrew and a plate of sugar cookies she set it on the table where there was a bit of empty space. "You kids look like you're just about done in."

Leaning forward on his elbows on the table, Michael sighed then sat back yawning, rubbing an eye. "Yeah, Gram, I think we can't do much more tonight, everything is starting to look blurry to me."

Cat set down a file and closed it. She delicately covered a yawn. "I can hardly think anymore. I couldn't even tell you what 2 plus 2 is I'm so exhausted." Like water, she oozed back in her chair.

Taking a stance, Gram set her hands on her plump hips, her face stern. "Well, that's that then. You two enjoy a glass or two of wine to wind down then it's off to bed with you. I've made up the room Michael put the satiny bed and blonde dresser in for you honey, the new carpet is so plush your bare feet will love it!

"Michael will show you where it is. There are plenty of extra toiletries in the adjoining bath and since you weren't able to stop at your place to get some extra clothes I put in some of- of- Kayleen's clothes for you to use. You're a tad smaller than her, but they should fit well enough."

Before Michael could make a comment, Gram turned to him with a broad smile. "I am so impressed, Michael, you have really done a lot of work on this place. The rooms that are finished are lovely, especially for a man!"

Eyes crinkling, with a hue of abashment tingeing his cheeks, Michael replied, "Thanks. I used some of the money Granddaddy left me to hire a decorator to come in and she's been working with my contractor to get this place livable. I'm glad you like the parts that are done. This place is so grand and you keep telling me it needs a woman's touch."

Gram shook her head, silver curls bounced around her head. "Tsk tsk, dear, you know that is not what I meant. I meant that you needed to get a nice young la-"

Michael abruptly shoved his chair back and stood up, he moved hastily to Gram took her arm and gently pulled her to the door. "Never mind that now, Gram. Thanks for the wine. We'll go to bed in a few-" his head jerked to Cat when she stifled a cough.

"Uh, I mean I'll show Cataleigh to her room then I'll be off to mine." His forehead suddenly shiny, the tips of his ears reddened he ordered, "Now, out you go," and gave Gram a little push out the door.

"All right, well…" Gram said through the doorway, "I'll be in that little drawing room off the kitchen reading for a little while, so if you need anything…"

Michael closed the door and waved at her through the glass. "Bye now." He ambled back to the table and picked up the wine bottle.

Cat stood up. "She is such a doll, you are so lucky to have her." She trod over to stand near him.

"Yeah," he chuckled, sticking the corkscrew in the bottle. Twisting it until it was fully in, he pushed the levers down and pulled out the cork. He poured the robust wine into the two goblets. "She can be a handful sometimes but I could not do without her. She's a blessing."

He handed a goblet to Cat then started towards the fireplace. "Come on, let's unwind a little before hitting the sack."

Cat eyed the white bear rug spread out in front of the fireplace. "Oh Sergeant, that is so corny." Padding in her socks, she followed him over to the fire.

He laughed, slightly embarrassed. Setting his wine glass on the slate seat that semi-circled the fireplace, he knelt on the rug. "Yeah, I know. Actually, believe or not it's Korey's. He brought it over from his place."

Her brows rose in surprise.

"Yup. He may appear a bit hippie-ish, my farmboy veterinarian cousin, but apparently he's quite the ladies' man. He tells me when he brings a girl home, the rug pretty much clinches it. They claim it's so romantic and…sexy."

He lay down on his stomach and reached for his wine. "Come on, you can trust me," he said, wiggling his eyebrows at her and patting the rug then laughed.

Cat shyly knelt down on the soft fur rug squirming to sit sideways on her hip, her legs curled back. She sipped the wine. "Oh, this is nice, it tastes rich and soft at the same time."

She sniffed the glass. "It has a robust woodsy scent. It sure beats that whiskey." Relaxing more, she shifted down to her side and braced on her forearm.

Michael shifted onto his side close to her, then propped himself up on one elbow. Their faces only inches apart, he said, "Cataleigh," a slight smile curved his full mouth, "stop with the sergeant stuff, you're reverting. It's Michael."

Cat blushed, turned her head to take a sip then turned back to him, her lips dewy from the wine, he seemed to be even closer. She whispered, "Okay, Michael…" She felt herself pulled, drawn into his dark glowing eyes. The orange flames of the dancing fire reflected in them.

The wine and the warm room tugged Cat's lids half closed, her head tipped back, shiny lips parted. The room was still, the only sound embracing them was the crackling fire, the storm a muffled backdrop.

He was so close she could feel his breath caress her cheek, then—a coolness, a forlorn draft as he turned his head, took a drink and rolled back on his stomach, she couldn't see his fingers gripping the glass to still his shaking hand.

Cat fully opened her eyes, took a sip and sat up cross-legged cupping the goblet in her lap with both hands. Her long hair drifted over her shoulders, the den's diffused lighting and bright flames lit the highlights in the wavy tresses, shining like the morning sun rippling across a shaded lagoon.

Uncomfortable now, she unconsciously fluffed her hair and gazed around the room feeling awkward to look at him.

"Sooo…" Michael sat up too and crossed his legs. "Tell me some more of your childhood stories, you were quite the pistol when you were a kid. My da would have called you a little lady chit."

Cradling the wine glass between her legs, Cat set her palms on the deliciously furry rug behind her and leaned back, cocked her head sideways and rested it on her shoulder. "No, let's talk about you."

She sat up straight, took a huge sip of wine. "Can, um, will you tell me about, you know…" her words dropped off to nothing.

Brushing her hair back off her shoulders she said, "I mean, Serg-er, Michael, you have to know there's rumors swirling around out there about…you. I've ignored them, refused to listen or engage in the gossip, but…" she tucked the stem of the goblet between her crossed legs and leaned back on her arms again.

"Gosh, I don't know if I'm curious or nosy, or self-protective…or…I don't know. But," she looked at him but he was staring at the fire and sipping his wine.

He turned to her. His stubble, growing out dark from his early morning shave chiseled his already rugged face making him look a more dangerous man, half-shuttered eyes darkened to burning coals. The pulse beating at his temple contradicted his cool demeanor.

"But, you know, of course if you don't want to talk about it, that's fine," Cat said hurriedly. "I would never pressure you to, in fact, I really never should have brought it up. It's so none of my business. Please forgive me for prying. Forget I opened my big nosy mouth." She stood up in one motion went to the teak table and set her glass down.

His lips pulled in, Michael sat silent for a minute. Then he rose to his feet, walked over and put his glass on the table next to hers, matching remnant pools of burgundy nestled in the bottom of the goblets.

Cat stuffed her hands in her pockets, her head down, she stood awkwardly, feeling a fool.

Michael faced her. He slowly reached out and gently held her upper arms. His thumbs caressed her over the blouse, he said softly, "Listen, Cataleigh, I feel I know you so well now that I would trust you with my life."

His hands tightened, pulling her slightly to him. "But, right now, I need to see this tragedy behind us before I can think of opening my soul to anyone. It's not you, I- I," he released her arms and stepped back.

"I just can't right now. Can you understand?" His tormented expression contorted from internal pain, shards of suffering bled in the miserable coal eyes.

Feeling the burn of his distress, Cat nodded gently. "Let's pretend I didn't mention it, okay?"

He wound one arm around her shoulders and pulled her in for a brief hug. Closing his eyes, Michael brushed his face against the silky hair, breathing in its fragrance, then slowly let her go.

Clearing his throat, his voice deep, husky, he said, "Come on, I'll show you your room. I hope we can sleep with that crazy racket out there. Let's pray the town holds up to it." They walked around the table, he turned off the lights and closed the door on the way out.

After Michael showed Cat to her room, he went back downstairs to where Gram was. He found her as she said she'd be, curled cozy on the couch, her feet up, a book in her hand and a tiny glass of brandy at her side.

When Michael came in she set down the book and pushed her round wire spectacles back up her nose. Not seeing Cat behind him, unabashedly nosy, Gram asked, "Well, how did things go?"

Michael inched into the room and sat on a corner of the ottoman in front of her. "We still can't figure this wretched mystery out. But we'll keep trying until, well, until a resolution. It's-"

Gram cut him off. "I wasn't asking about the children. If you'd come up with anything you would have blown in here with the news." Slow with age, she swung her legs around and set them on the floor.

Bending forward closer to him, she said, "I was asking how things are going with you and that darling girl." Her grey brows high half-moons over her questioning eyes enlarged behind the round glasses.

Shaking his head, Michael eased off the couch to stand and picked up Zinny's empty brandy glass. He stated formally, "There is nothing between Miss Sylvester and me."

Gram slipped her puffy feet into her fuzzy slippers. She dropped a bookmark in her book and slapped it closed. She regarded Michael seriously. "Now you hear me, grandson. You need a woman in your life and she is perfect for you. Have you told her about Kayleen yet?"

His lips bunched, he shook his head, "No. This is not the time. There's too much going on."

234

Zinny stood up on wobbly legs brushing her skirt down. "The timing isn't important, Michael. The feeling of the heart is. You can't carry this burden forever. She's a good woman, she'll understand what you had to-"

"No." He shook his head again. "I can't lay my fractured past on her. She deserves better, she's too good for me. And I don't want to lose her trust. Besides, after this turmoil is over she'll go back to where she came from. Anyway," he headed for the door.

"I don't need a woman in my life. I'm fine the way I am. I'm happy with my life. I'm not going to brabble with you about this. I have all the company I need with you guys and Banny, speaking of," he looked around. "Where is the little bundle of furry mischief?"

Gram followed his footprints to the door. "Korey has him in his room. Banny has been terribly skittish with the noise outside and the trees banging against the house, and the lights flickering. Korey was afraid he'd hurt himself dashing about the halls in terror."

She gently patted the side of his unshaven rugged face. "I'm not *brabbling*- arguing with you, but I do think thou dost protest too much. Listen, why don't we have Miss Cat-"

Michael turned out the lights and stood in the darkened doorway. The hall lamps splattered light on his black hair like a firecracker splashing on ink. "Let's leave Miss Cat alone and go to bed. I want you to promise me you'll drop this subject. Please?"

Gram brushed her plump figure past him and traipsed down the hall saying nothing.

He followed her closing the door. "Is that a yes?" he called down the hall.

Chapter Thirty-Three

The warm bath made Cat so sleepy she couldn't keep her eyes open. Her hair blown dry she climbed into borrowed shorts and a t-shirt and slipped gratefully between the cool, fresh smelling sheets.

While braiding her hair into one long braid, the Bible on the nightstand caught her eye. She picked it up and set it on her lap.

The book was old, so old the cover was peeling and the pages yellowed. Gingerly she opened it, flipping bunches of pages at a time through the Old Testament to the New Testament.

Snuggling back onto the fluffy pillows she pulled her legs up and rested the Bible against her thighs. While scanning Matthew and parts of Mark she drifted off.

In her fitful dreams, the faces of the missing children kaleidoscoped around inside her head. Flashes of children being snatched off the street cut in and revolved with pictures of the kids they'd tacked to the wall, while voices of the young ones crying, begging to be saved cried in the background.

Way in the recess of her mind the Bible floated, it slid onto the hunter's painting in Michael's den landing open on a table. The men in the painting stood around the table, pointing to it like there was something important in it.

Squinting in her dream, Cat tried hard to read which page it was open to, but try as she might she couldn't make it out. The words swam in and out of focus. The children's cries grew louder and louder. She covered her ears with her hands struggling harder and harder to read the open page of the Bible-

Thump. The noise broke her dream. Bolting upright her braid swung around slapping her back. "What the-" the room was dark but Michael had switched on a nightlight for her before he left.

Loathing to leave the comfort of the heavy quilt and now warm sheets, she scooched to the side of the bed and slid to her feet. But she stepped on something.

Bending over she realized it was the Bible. It must have fallen off the bed when she'd rolled over and fidgeted in her dream, *nightmare* she corrected herself. Picking up the book she sat on the edge of the bed. It was open to Matthew.

No longer tired, she scanned the lines trying to find whatever it was the Book was trying to tell her. After a few minutes, frustrated at not being able to discern what the message was, as she believed someone or something was trying to tell her, she closed the book and set it back on the nightstand.

Wide awake, she shuffled to the bathroom. Moments later, switching the light off as she left the bathroom, her thoughts wandered. Her laptop popped into her head. She had been so annoyed when she had realized she'd left it in Michael's cruiser. There was something nagging at her to review her notes.

Moving to the window, she pushed the curtain aside to look out. "Darn," she grumbled. She'd forgotten the hurricane shutters, she couldn't see out at all. Standing still she listened. It sounded like the storm had lessened.

"I'm sure I can get to the car and back with no trouble," she said out loud while pulling her clothes off the back of the chair she'd draped them over.

Changing out of the shorts and T, climbing hastily into her jeans and sweater, she left her room and tip-toed down the cushioned stairs in her socks to the kitchen.

Retrieving Michael's keys off the kitchen counter, she headed to the mud room.

Everyone was dog-tired, she didn't want to wake anyone. She carefully opened the door to the garage so it wouldn't squeak, grabbed her coat and hat, pulled on her mittens and stepped into her boots at the door. Still unable to see out the window from inside the dark garage, she bit her lip and pulled the sturdy garage door open.

Remembering the wind tearing the door of the station out of Michael's hand, she was careful to hold the knob with both hands, which was harder to do than she thought.

Although the wind had decreased slightly, it was still forceful enough to make it difficult to hold onto the door, it was easily snatched away and flung open, the wind pressing it into the wall kept it glued it open.

Taking a nervous step outside, she got behind the door and pushed it, it was like trying to push a car up a driveway. Finally she got it shut and leaned back against it to catch her breath.

There was zero color, just black and white. White dazzling snow against the black night.

Wishing she'd grabbed her sun glasses to protect her eyes from the sleeting snow that stung, blasting her like shooting icy gravel. She held a hand over her brows to shield her eyes the best she could then pushed off from the door into the vortex of the storm.

Immediately the strength of the turbulent wind struck her, almost knocking her off her feet. Doubling over, she had to work to move each leg like she was wading through a river rushing against her.

She huddled over, wrapped her arms around her chest and lumbered on with the wind screaming at her, slapping snow at her face and tearing tears out of her eyes.

In the sudden total white-out she could barely make out the cruiser already molded in snow. Because of the height of the snowdrifts near the house, Michael had been forced to park the cruiser farther down the drive.

After what seemed like hours of getting bashed back and forth, she managed to reach the car.

Exhausted from her struggle to get to it, legs shaking from the effort, she brushed snow off the sides to find the door handle.

Then she grabbed the handle to pull herself to the car until she was hugged tight against the cruiser to keep from being blown away in the wind, she had to take a moment to catch her breath again.

Louise Furley

But instead of regaining her strength, her heart beat faster thumping like paddles on a fan inside her chest. The wind whipping through the trees had magnified and if possible, grew even more deafening like a train speeding and roaring through a subway. Without realizing it she must have started out in the eye of the cyclone that was normally the quietest part, and now the eye was passing and the storm was rapidly growing fiercer.

Desperately she thought, *I need to move quickly or I'm not going to make it back to the house.* Frantically, she pulled Michael's keys from her pocket.

Holding the keys tightly in her trembling hand scared to death she would drop them and never find them again in the deep snow, she painstakingly turned them in her clumsy mittens to face them up.

Snow laced her lashes so heavily she had to keep blinking to see the open button on the remote. Thumbing the button, her shoulders relaxed a bit when she heard the comforting 'beep beep.'

As soon as she unlatched the door- it flung back, bounced against its hinges then stayed pressed open by the wind. The key popped out falling into the deep snow. Leaning inside, "There!" she pronounced. The laptop had fallen to the floor, that's why they had missed it.

She caught up the strap to the bag her laptop was in, and pulled it out hustling it up on one shoulder, then dragged it around her neck to cross over her chest. If she fell the last thing she needed was to drop the computer in a snow bank.

For a split second, the thought of facing the daunting storm to get back to the house scared the hell out of her. She considered only for a heartbeat of climbing inside the cruiser closing the door, rolling up in a ball and trying to outlast the wrath of the blizzard. But the news said the gale would last for days.

Taking a deep breath, the frigid air filled her lungs, freezing her belly. Her fingers, nose, lips and ears were numb. It was stupid to waste time standing there.

Every second the violence of the storm increased, her chances of making it back to the house decreased. Now she kind of wished

239

she'd awakened Michael to tell him she was going out to brave the storm.

But, she shook her head ruefully he certainly would have stopped her. She was just going to have to forge ahead and do it. After all, with the fear about the missing children the last thing the family needed was to find her missing too. Her heart beat faster as her panic rose, the way the snow was packing in they would never find her, not until the snow melted and her frozen body- *good God, get a grip girl*!

Resolute, she held onto the top of the door for balance. Out loud she said through gnashing, trembling teeth, "Michael's going to kill me when he sees his cruiser." The wind tore off her words.

There was no way she would be able to close the door, the storm was way too powerful. There was going to be a wet mess inside the car.

"Oh my gosh." Her eyes widened fearfully when she looked around from the protection of the car door. The wrath of the storm seemed to have doubled in the few minutes she'd been out.

The snow rained horizontally, a solid wall of white and it was piling up fast, already past her knees. The house stood so heavy with a blanket of snow it looked like a bloated snowman.

Outside lights lit up the white snow at least making it easier to see in the night.

Bending her head, Cat sucked her lips in then thrust her body from behind the door and out into the core of the storm, and was instantly blinded and blown uncontrollably several feet from the car then slammed to the ground.

She scrambled to stand back up but the wind's mighty fist forced her to her hands and knees, in seconds she was blanketed with snow.

Her strenuous efforts to get back to her feet were to no avail. The gale kept her hammered down. On her hands and knees with only her head and shoulders above the snow, she crawled like an infant back to the car.

The wind came at her face like a surging locomotive, she could only make it to a few feet in front of the car when the wind strong-armed her flat to the ground.

Louise Furley

Taking one big adrenaline breath, she pushed up and threw herself at the cruiser's grill, hit it then slid down into the snow. Leaning back to brace herself against the bumper and block the fierce wind, she slumped over, her strength spent. In minutes she was buried to her shoulders. No way could she find the car keys and push the alarm button.

The snow weighed on her like creamy cement. A potent adversary, the storm had overpowered her, it won.

The last ebbs of energy drained from her limbs until they were empty pipes. Succumbing to the inevitability of death, a wry smile pulled a side of her mouth when she pictured herself as the filling of a pie with a snowy crust hardening over her, like the bluebirds baked in a pie.

Cat's eyes grew heavy like weights tugged on them. Her mind drifted until it was shrouded in darkness, she was slowly sliding through a long, dark, tunnel, with no brilliant white light at the end.

Chapter Thirty-Four

Was she delirious? She thought she heard a voice. Was an angel calling her to come home to Heaven?

Painfully, she pulled her swollen head back, it felt like it was filled with lead, she peered up with bleary eyes through snow lashes.

Like a warrior to the rescue standing over her, her angel was Michael. He appeared as a dark angel in a black jacket and hood covering most of his face, and rapidly about to become a loaf of bread so floured by the falling snow.

A rope tied around his waist and looped over his shoulder trailed tautly back through the door inside the garage where it was secured.

He leaned over, grasped her arms and pulled. Unfortunately, she was not only dead weight but she was bound by a heavy carpet of snow. He crouched and wrapped his arms around her and heaved her to her feet. The wind forced her head back, she hadn't the strength to bend it forward.

Michael folded her under his arm, and holding the rope with both hands, he pulled them forward painfully slowly, like a torturous tug-of-war back to the house.

Just a foot from the house, the impact of the gale bashed them bodily into the side of the building. The wind clawed Cat from Michael's arms tugging her like a fish on a hook.

A gust knocked her from his grasp flinging her back down the drive. The wind captured her screams. Wrapping the rope around his arm, Michael ponderously made his way back to her. Fighting the wind, she struggled to walk to him but then a gust punched her hard into a deep drift.

His head down, Michael inched his way to her. He grabbed the front of her coat, dragged her out of the snow bank and back into his arms. They plodded back to the house. Prepared this time for the gusts, he made sure they didn't get thrown at the house.

Michael tussled with the garage door, pulled it open, pushed Cat inside and jerked the door closed behind them. He threw his back at the door in respite, his gloved hands splayed against the cold steel, breathing heavy as if he'd been in a bullfight.

Cat stood trembling, panting loudly, surprisingly the bag containing the laptop was still strapped around her shoulder. She clamped the bag to her chest, wrapping her arms around it.

So scared, she couldn't speak, just stared unblinking at Michael. Her soaked lashes dripped down her cheeks.

Fuzzy ice crystals fringed his own dark lashes. With stiff fingers he untied the rope from his waist and dropped it on the floor then tramped up the few steps to the door to the house and opened it.

Untying the hood of his jacket, he slipped it back off his head and pulled off the wool hat that was under it. Shaking the hat, water drops sprayed pelting the door. "Come on," he said, a tiny shake in his flat tone betrayed his calm stance.

Cat couldn't move, her feet seemed glued to the floor. She stood clutching the bag, her legs buckling. Tears slipped out rolling over the frozen hills of reddened cheeks, hands too cold to lift to wipe away the tears.

His boots thumped back down the steps and over to where she stood quivering. "I've got you, Cataleigh," he whispered. "You're safe now. I won't let anything happen to you." Winding an arm behind her back he half carried her up the stairs.

Inside, Cat stood like a toddler while Michael unbuttoned her coat, pulling it off he tossed it on a chair, her hat, scarf and mittens followed.

"Here," he said, his voice gruff, emotion choking the words in his throat. He pulled out a chair guided her to it then gently pushed her down. Bending over her, he lifted one of her legs and pulled off each boot.

After taking off his own coat and hat and boots, he slipped out of the kitchen for a second and returned with a tumbler of scotch and a blanket. Wrapping the blanket over her shoulders, he poured a rock glass of scotch and handed it to her.

Dazed, she just stared down at the glass. He took her hands and wrapped them around the glass then guided it to her mouth.

When she went to take a tiny sip, he pushed the glass up so a big mouthful burned her lips, sliding a fiery trail down her throat where it spread its heat, filling her belly with delicious warmth. Then the coarse tongue of the fiery liquid scraped her throat-

Cat sputtered, mouth wide open, she hissed and coughed, eyes blew water. Gasping, she cried, "Why did you-" throwing off the blanket, her lungs on fire she hacked and wheezed, eyes popping spasmodically.

Michael put a foot on a chair, rolled his sleeves up to his elbows then leaned over and rested his arm on his leg. "Do you feel better?" he asked politely, not smiling.

He had shaved, the light played off the rugged planes of his face, the damp ends of his hair curled. He was close enough to her that she breathed in his musky aftershave. A pulse at his temple beat like a drum.

Gulping fast shallow breaths the harsh alcohol now coursed like a sedative through her veins, smoothing the tremors in her hands, soothing the panic in her stomach, spreading a fluid comfort through her limbs.

Her teeth unclenched, her jaw slacked, relaxed, her muscles loosened until she melted in the chair like Raggedy Ann.

A partial smile raised her ears like a sprite's, the tips tinged red from the cold and liquor. The single light from over the sink lit one side of her face making one wind-burned rosy cheek shine. Against the stark white of her face, eyes the color of the winter sea sparkled.

Pinching her nose, she took a smaller sip, made a face, then "Ahhh..." A slightly giddy grin puffed her eyes into crescents. Easing back, she laid her arm across the back of her chair smiling into the glass. The whiskey burned her face from inside until it glowed, lips reddened like spring poppies.

Setting the glass on the table, she drew her legs up on the chair seat then wrapped her arms around her knees. A giggle gurgled, she looked over at him. "Yeah, I feel better. Thank you so-"

Dropping his foot from the chair he stood in front of her, leaned over and gripped the arms of her chair. His arms rigid, his face thunderous, his tightly controlled demeanor cracked like thin ice on a dark pond.

He leaned in so close to her black brows slashed down over boiling slits of his furiously burning eyes, she backed away.

"You feel better? I'm glad you feel better," Michael snarled savagely through grinding teeth. He jerked the chair- she jumped, her feet fell off the rung.

Jaw dropping, her arms stiffened on the arms of the chair. "Michael, I, what-"

He jerked the chair again. "No, *what* were *you* thinking? What the hell were you thinking? Do you have a death wish? With all the warnings, and our fear for the children, and you- you go out *there*," he jabbed a finger at the door then grabbed the arms of her chair again. Violently shaking the chair, he leaned his enraged face in so close they almost touched noses.

Eyes wide as blue bouncing balls, her mouth opened and closed and opened. "I- I- I didn't mean anything. It looked okay, the wind had died, it looked safe-"

He jerked the chair again then let it go and paced away, his hand roughing through his hair. He paced back, stopped in front of her grabbing the chair arms again. She drew her knees back up again in defense.

"Safe?" His sarcasm scissor sharp, cutting her, "You think it was safe? Don't you remember all of our preparation these months for the storm, the cataclysmic storm that would strike for at least a week? We spent days, weeks, months advising, teaching, training the people how to protect themselves, *stay inside* until the all clear siren goes off. Are you bloody addled-brained? Of all the foolhardy, reckless, stupid-"

Cat ducked under his arm and slid off the chair to stand a foot away. Wiping the back of her hand across her forehead, she said, "Stop it! Stop yelling at me! I had to get my computer, I had-"

He threw his head back in a fake guffaw. His hands on his hips, he glared black rockets at her, his mouth a hard line. "Had to? Had to what- get yourself killed?" He shook his head. "I can't believe you would do such a goddamned foolish-"

"Stop it!" Cat slashed her hand down, the other planted on her hip. "I had to get the computer, there's something there, something…"

"What? Something what?" he bellowed. "Something important enough to risk your bloody life, what could be so goddamned important?"

Cat's face deflated. Tears brimmed in her eyes, she put a hand to her head covering one side of her face. Shrugging, she looked up at him, the tears slipped out and ran down her face. "I- I- I just don't know, I was reading the Bible and something-"

"The Bible!" he thundered. "The Bible told you to go outside in the middle of a goddamned killer blizzard to-" he stepped towards her, his fists clenched.

"Children!"

The pair turned to see Grandma Zinny standing in the doorway, her hands on her plump hips. "Michael, what is going on here? You know I don't allow cursing in my home. You're loud enough to wake the lechuzas! You may not be superstitious but I don't need witches haunting this house!"

Cat stared puzzled at Gram. Michael picked up a chair by its back, lifting it off the floor and banged it back down. Cat backed away from the muscled man so broiling mad she feared he might explode.

Astonished, Gram hurried over to Cat and laid a motherly arm around her shoulders and frowned at her grandson. "Michael! What's the matter with you? You're frightening this poor child." She hugged Cat assuring her, "Honey, he would never raise his hand to a woman, his bark is way worse than his bite!"

"Oh for the love of-" Michael stalked across the kitchen dragging his hands through his hair. He snatched up the bottle of scotch took a glass out of the dish drainer poured a healthy bit, drained the drink in one gulp then slammed the glass on the kitchen table, both women jumped.

He stalked back over to them. "*She-*" he pointed at Cat, "for some stupid godforsaken reason she felt compelled to leave the sanctuary of this house and risk her life to go out in that- that- hellstorm hurricane-"

Cat drew in a sharp sob cupped her hand over her mouth and ran from the room.

"Cataleigh, dear! Don't leave-" Gram called out but she was gone. Angry, Zinny glared an accusation at her grandson. "Michael, for heaven's sake, what has gotten into you? It's not like you to treat a lady like that!

"I've never seen you behave this way before. Except that time Matty disappeared that day in the park when she was three, gave us such a terrible scare. I still remember the horrible fear in your voice as you ran helter-skelter through the park screaming her name. Boy, when you found her, you-"

Michael sat down in the chair Cat had vacated, his shoulders slumped. The color and fury dissolved from his face and body like sand down an hourglass.

Gram shook her head, clicking her tongue. "Oh yes, I remember that day, it was all you could do to hold yourself back from spanking her little butt when you found her safe and sound near the pond chasing the ducks. Oh yes," she smiled at the memory that had turned out okay.

"You were fit to be tied. You chewed out that little girl so loudly the ducks fled. Matty cried, you picked her up in your strong arms and hugged the stuffing out of her.

"You tried to explain that you were only so mad because you were so scared because you loved her so much-" she stopped in mid-word, her lips parted, then she nodded, curly silver hair bobbing around her head. A wide grin split her face plumping her cheeks and deepening her wrinkles, she waggled a finger at him. "Oh Michael..."

Michael jumped to his feet. "Stop it, Gram, don't make something out of nothing. I was just concerned as I would have been if a dog was out in the storm."

Gram nodded, the grin widened. "Uh huh, but in this case, it was a cat."

He ducked his head to look into her face at her level with warning. "I mean it Gram, let it alone. There's nothing between us and there isn't going to be. Stop trying to fix me up. I'm damaged goods, you know that. No decent woman deserves a man with my past. Cataleigh is too good of a woman to get wrapped up with the likes of me."

Michael straightened, stuffed his hands in his jean's pockets, said wearily, sadly, forcefully, "Let it go."

Gram reached a finger under her glasses and wiped an eye. "Honey, you know that's just not true. Is that why you only go with one-time wicked girls like that O'Leary trite? Oh yes, I know that red-headed harlot would like to get her hooks in you, and she thinks because you only go with bad girls she has a chance. Stay clear of that trash.

"Someday the truth will come out and you'll be cleared with the public like you were with the authorities. Your friends look the other way and don't talk about it, the wrong women, one night stands, you're afraid to let your heart out there because you don't think you're worth it. But you're wrong, Michael. You are a good man, you deserve a good woman, a loving home, children-"

"Exactly. The children. Right now the only thing I care about is getting the children, Matty, back. Don't bring this up again, Gram," his face softened, "please."

"But honey-"

"No buts, Gram. Let's go back to bed. There's been enough drama for the night."

They strolled to the door, Gram turned to Michael. "What made you go looking for her anyway?" He turned out the light, she couldn't see his expression.

A quiet moment, then, his voice haggard, "I honestly don't know, Gram. I couldn't sleep, I was tossing and turning. I thought I heard a noise downstairs but figured it was that damned wind. But something bugged me, I had to get up and check it out."

He tried for levity to ease the strain of the night. "So I got dressed and soundlessly went downstairs."

"You mean you slinked down the stairs," she laughed.

"Yeah. Anyway, I checked the rooms and found nothing. I was ready to go upstairs and back to bed when, I don't know," he shook his head in wonder.

"The back of my neck crawled. All of the windows are shuttered, the only movable one is the kitchen window. So I rolled it open and looked out. It was so nasty out there all I could think was that I'm glad we shut the town down. Outside was no place for man or beast.

"Then, I saw something move, something red. Even through the blurry window and the sleeting sheets of snow I recognized the pattern of Cataleigh's scarf flapping out of a bank of snow in front of the car. I remember her taking it off when we got inside. Oh my God, Gram," he bit his lip.

She set a reassuring hand on his arm. As if the weather knew it was being talked about it cranked up a notch. The trees whipped back and forth, thrashing the house, it would be a miracle if there was a limb left in the yard when it was over.

"Gram, my heart caught in my throat, I thought I would suffocate. I could hardly think I just ran for my jacket and boots, stopping only long enough to get a rope and tie it to me and the door. I probably should have enlisted Korey's help, but he sleeps like the dead. Besides, there's no way a person could move ten feet in that blizzard or survive ten minutes.

"Hell, the strength of the wind- my God, I saw it pluck trees out of the ground like they were dandelions and hurl them away or pulverized them to sawdust in a nanosecond. I, damn, I thought of her out there, Gram. I was so goddamned scared that I wouldn't be able to get her back here."

Mauling his words through clenched teeth, Michael realized he was holding his breath. He let the air out in a slow trembling whoosh. Wiping his palms on his shirt he straightened his spine.

Her face wrought with concern, Gram could see the terror that still gripped him, squeezing the color out of his complexion, his eyes stark and bright. Wringing her hands she twisted her apron smoothed it out then twisted it again. "Michael, honey-"

He pinched his eyes to vanquish the nightmare. "Anyway, it's over. We're all safe. I guess I came down pretty hard on her, but she used such colossally poor judgment, such a foolish thing to do. Hell, I had a stronger urge to paddle her behind than I had with Matty's escapade. Anyway, what's done is done."

Yawning now that the tension was released he said, "I'm going to bed, Gram, I'll see you in the morning, which," he looked at his watch but his wrist was bare. "It'll be morning soon enough. Let's go."

"You go ahead, dear, I'm going to go check on Cat. I think she was pretty courageous to do what she did for the sake of the children. And you, my dear," she stood on tip-toe gently touching his broad shoulders, kissed his chin. "You are my valiant hero. You took an equally humongous chance going out there and getting her.

"Foolhardiness is pressing against the walls in this house for sure. Maybe it's haunted, it's certainly old enough to have seen many trials and tribulations, and happiness. Maybe Viktor and Chersina have returned… " Deep dimples beside her mouth creased.

Chuckling, Michael scratched his head. "Gram, please don't share your fancies with Cataleigh or Korey, they can be whimsical enough without listening to you."

"Anyway," Gram said, "unfortunately, I don't think your *rescuee* is too enamored of you right now. Good luck trying to fix that rift! Nighty night, baby, sweet dreams." Slippers slip-slapped down the hall.

Chapter Thirty-Five

Pil Philo flew down the chute on his back- hitting the curved bottom- he shot off the slide, hurtled a few feet in the air then slammed on the ground like an egg flipping into a pan and splat, the ten-year-old lay inert on his back, his round chest still.

Like ghosts barely visible in the gloom, the children shuffled guardedly to the body.

Inching across the muddy interior, shoes scraping the dirt floor, shallow breaths, each child came one by one to stand in a circle around the boy.

Eleven pairs of eyes stared down at him.

"It's Pil Philo." His Italian heritage evident in his olive skin and dark eyes, twelve-year-old Drew Artzi dressed like Rembrandt in a shirt of wide black and white stripes, black jacket and black pants, ran his hand over the top of his head.

He whispered to Juan Trueno next to him, "Falcon, he's the twelfth one."

Juan grimaced at the childhood nickname. "I can count." He pushed his ball cap facing backwards, hair sprung out through the hole.

Teddy Keegan, baby fat still clinging to her cinnamon round cheeks contrasting her petite frame, pulled her sweater tighter and wrapped her thin brown arms around her little chest. Brand new sneakers, the bottoms caked with dirt but the toes still white, fanned from the bottoms of flared blue jeans.

Even her braids quivered from her knees knocking in fright, her eight-year-old voice shook, "You- you know what that means…"

On the verge of tears, Simone Zeall stroked her long blonde hair nonstop with both hands. A bedraggled Cinderella, the luster of her all pink outfit; jeans, jacket, sneakers, even the twinkling pink earrings dulled from a layer of dusty dirt. Hardly able to get words out through chattering teeth, she stuttered, "It means- it means- it means-"

"We're fucked. It means we're fucked," Rocky Artzi exclaimed. He stood so close to his older brother Drew they appeared as one in the dim, dank room. Except short Rocky with his square bulldog frame and pug nose was the total opposite of his brother's more elegant features and long artist's frame in black and white.

Matty pushed between the other kids and knelt down beside Pil.

"Please, Rocky," she said gently, "we're in a bad place, but there's no need for us to become animals using bad language."

She lightly touched Pil's doughy face with her fingertips, his pale skin was cold, he didn't move. Tenderly she brushed his dark hair off his face and leaned her ear against his lips, she announced with relief, "He's breathing."

Balling his hands into tight fists, Rocky bent over Matty. Separating a stubby finger from a fist he stabbed it like a miniature sawed-off shotgun in her face. "Don't you tell me what to do you little bitch, I'll-" he broke off when someone touched his arm.

Square lips twisting crossly he shoved Jessy U's hand off his arm. "What do you think you're doing, you half-breed foster punk? Don't you touch me, I'll break your face!"

Unflinching, Jessy's smile kind, he said softly, "We're all scared, Rocky. We need to stick together, be a team, we're all we have. We have to try to stand united against-"

"Against what?" Furious, Santiago Trueno stepped in jamming two knuckles against Jessy's chest, he poked the younger boy twice more emphasizing his words. A litany of Spanish burst from the boy then he switched to English.

"You little *bicho*, freak, we don't know what the hell is against us! We don't know who or what brought us here- we were all unconscious when we were dumped in this room just like Pil. So, don't you-" he hesitated when someone tugged at his arm.

"Come on Santy, until we know who or what is keeping us here, like Jessy says, we need to stick together." Barty's timid voice belied his brave stance. He stood solidly on skinny legs next to Jessy linking them as new brothers, a strengthening chain against overwhelming fear, and the unknown.

"You little shit-" Santiago bared coyote teeth reaching for Barty's collar- Barty side-stepped him causing Santiago to have to hop to keep his balance.

"Stop it you guys, stop right now," Matty lightly ordered. "We all know who brought us here, but he- they- can't be the monster. I'm sure they must have been tricked or forced to or something to do it." Still kneeling next to Pil, she patted the boy's face gently. "Here you go, Pil, it's okay."

Craning her neck up at the other boys, freckles popping against china white skin, she said, "Pil's coming to. You know how you felt when it happened to you, so let's gather together and comfort him."

She turned back to Pil, her fat red ponytails flopped on his small barrel-chest. She patted his face again. "Here you go, Pil, you're okay, we're here for you."

Moaning, Pil rolled his burly head back and forth, thick eyelids fluttered. He had inherited his father's Latin coloring, the thick skin and lips he got from his mother. Paroxysms of blinking to clear his vision before he could finally make out Matty's concerned, round blue eyes smiled reassuringly down at him.

"What the- where am I?" Pil's head jerked as he took in the other kids standing in a circle around him. "Juan? Drew? Santiago? What the heck is going on? Where am I?" He struggled to sit up.

Matty pulled his husky shoulders to help him.

Sitting cross-legged, he rubbed his eyes, dirt shook off the back of his head. He kept blinking hard looking around like he couldn't believe what he was seeing, barely able make out the parameters of the dark room. Still stunned, he climbed to his wobbly knees and leaned back on his heels, his mouth gaping.

The children stood silent, shrouded in the murky haze. Everywhere Pil looked all he saw was rock. Walls, ceiling, floor, all rock. No wonder his body was bruised and hurting. Meager light flickered from a single bulb dangling from a wire hooked to the ceiling. The wire from the bulb trailed across the ceiling and down a wall where it disappeared into a crack.

Pil cringed at the kids' creepy hunching shadows wavering across the rocky walls.

Light from the bulb glinted off the children's eyes like they were animals in hiding. They didn't move around as much as nervously jittered in one spot, huddling together.

Pil clamored to his feet, backing fearfully away from the other children, his crazed eyes flying back and forth and all around. Scratching his head with one trembling hand, he kept looking around trying to grasp where he was and how he got there.

Jessy took a half a step towards him, his hand outstretched. "Pil, the same thing happened to us. We're all in the same predicament. We need to work together to figure out how to get out of-"

"Don't touch me!" Pil screamed holding both thick hands up, he stepped back. Tears burst from his thick-lidded eyes and stormed down his petrified face.

"You!" He pointed a finger at Jessy. "You're one of them- the monster- you stay away from me!" Trembling, the tears pouring, he wrapped his arms protectively around his chunky chest.

Matty stood up, brushed off her jeans, red ponytails flipping. Calmly, she pushed her bangs out of her eyes, set her hands schoolmarm-like on her hips and said sternly, "Listen here, Pil. None of us is the monster. We were all snatched off the street or tricked out of our homes and brought here just like you. We need to work this out together if we have a chance of getting out of here."

She turned to the group and said, "Now, let's search the room again."

"Oh for Pete's sake, we've looked and looked until our hands have blistered and we've found nothing," Juan chided. He pulled his ball cap off, slapped it twice against his thigh then shoved it back on his head, bill facing backwards, and crossed his arms.

"Yeah," Simone cried, "there's no way out! We're trapped! We're gonna die here! Momma and Da will never find us, never!" Teddy ran over and threw her arms around Simone, the girls hugged, weeping and crying, "No way out! No way out!"

Jessy leaped over and quickly embraced both girls. "Come on, guys. We're gonna get out. You'll see. We'll find a way. We got in we must be able to get out."

Matty came over to the trio. "Yeah," she said very determined. "We'll find a way, we're going to go home." She wriggled in and embraced the other kids. Barty shuffled over to awkwardly join the group hug.

"You guy are wacked," Santiago said. "We all came in from the chute- and as you knuckleheads can see," he gestured to the almost vertical slide that attached to the hole in the wall. The slide ended about ten feet up in the air.

"We have no idea how far up that chute goes. It's dark and Falcon and Drew being the tallest already tried to boost each other up it.

"We even tried throwing Rocky up it since he's like a square ball, to see if he could grab onto something maybe and climb out. But if you jerks remember, it was too steep and slippery to climb. It seems to only be there to dump us and food down with no way back up. So, just get it, we're screwed. Don't get everyone's hopes up that there's a way out," Santiago sneered, but his words were shaky. He darted a fearful glance at his brother, Juan.

Juan stared silently at his shoes, shoulders hunched, hands in his pockets. Juan was always the adventurous one.

Their parents predicted Juan would grow up to be an adventurer, maybe a treasure hunter, while Santiago seemed more like a future vineyard owner, making wine, lounging on a wicker chair with a goblet of wine and a thin European cigar tossing out orders to his migrant workers like a lord of his kingdom, and a bevy of giggling, buxom barefoot grape stompers.

One hand on a slim hip, Drew gestured with the other. Dirt ringed the bottoms of his black pants and the sleeves of his jacket that partially covered the black and white striped shirt. He offered his thoughts, "According to the legend, the monster is gonna throw the kids, uh, us now I guess, off the cliffs in the spring.

"This, according to the weather lady is soon because that super-hot wind comes and in only days the snow is supposed to melt, and as soon as the floods stop the grass and trees and stuff start growing right away in the extreme heat like they were super fertilized." He hesitated for the group to get his drift.

"That's nice," Juan scoffed. The oldest at 12, turning 13 next month, if he lives that long. "Scare everyone further, you dope."

Only a month younger than Juan, Drew turned to his friend since they were in diapers. Shaking his head, he pulled a crumpled pack of cigarettes and matches from his jacket pocket and tapped one out.

"No, Falcon, sorry, Juan, what I mean is, if the legend is true, then the monster must be able to get in here and get us out. So there has to be a door or something."

Lighting the cigarette, he pulled hard on it. The end flickered red in his eyes. Blowing out a steam of smoke, he caught Matty's disapproving frown. He dropped the cigarette on the dirt floor and ground it out with the toe of his boot.

"Not if he's a monster that can fly or something so he can get up and down the chute," Rocky joined in. A grin sliced his face like a square pumpkin. "Maybe he's got sticky feet like a lizard, or super long, creepy scaly arms that he can stick down the chute and stab us like we're a shrimp or something then yanks us up the chute and-"

Annoyed, Drew held his hands up, spreading tapered fingers that spent hours daily with a paintbrush. "Knock it off, Rocky, you're scaring everybody more."

He said to brothers Juan and Santiago Trueno, "There's got to be a way out, we need to search again."

The brothers, almost twins with olive skin, patrician features, dark brown hair and eyes, tall for their ages with long limbs shook their heads. Angrily Santiago said, "You're crazy, Drew, there's no way out." Santiago was barely a year younger than Juan.

Matty broke from the little pack she huddled with, her small hands palm up. "Guys," smiling gently, her voice low, almost cheerful, two front teeth like white chicklets protruded slightly. "Buck up. We can do it."

Jessy came to stand beside her. "First," he said, "we need to pray. Come on everybody come over and hold hands." He stretched his arms out for the kids to gather together.

His arms crossed, Drew Artzi shrugged. He nudged his ten-year-old brother, Rocky with an elbow. "C'mon kid, it can't hurt." Surprised, Rocky sputtered, "Huh?" But Drew was already moving so Rocky trailed him.

Teddy took up Drew's hand. Drew held Simone's who held Rocky's hand who then held Matty's hand who was holding Barty's hand. Jessy took Teddy's other hand and held out his free hand beckoning to the rest of the children to join them.

Jamie Ming's almond eyes closed to mere slits barely visible beneath arrow straight black bangs. "But Jessy, what if, well, you know, maybe some of us aren't Christian. Some of us might be like Jewish or Buddhist or-"

"That's no problem," Jessy reassured him. "I'll say the words and each person can say out loud or in their mind who or what they want to direct the words to. Okay?"

"It's no good, it'll do us no good," Jamie Ming said miserably not moving an inch, shaking his head. "It's just words, prayers are just words. Words aren't gonna blast a hole in that rock wall and rescue us. Our parents don't have a clue as to where we are. And we're only guessing that we're in a cave or something. We really don't know where we are, we could be underground even, how is anyone gonna find us?"

"You'll see, Jamie. Come on, you'll feel better. I promise." Matty beckoned, smiling at him, the two prominent chicklet teeth gleaming, ponytails flipping.

As petite and small boned as a girl, eight-year-old Jamie dug a hole in the dirt with the toe of his shoe thinking, mulling over his belief in prayer.

Then, with a sigh, he wandered over without looking up and took Jessy's outstretched hand. Jessy encouraged the others to join them.

"Come on guys, all for one and one for all you know. My mom says there's always strength in numbers."

Juan elbowed his brother to go ahead and join in. They did reluctantly.

Tom-tom Two-Feathers approached husky Pil, the school's most notorious bully. One front tooth missing in a mouth that stayed perpetually opened in an O, Tom-tom grinned at the scared newcomer. That tooth had earned him 5 dollars from the tooth fairy.

"Let's go, Pil," he sputtered through his teeth, twitching his round glasses back up an aquiline nose he inherited from his Native American father, a stark contrast to his pudgy figure making him the image of a sundial.

He chose for the time being to forget all the mean pranks Pil had perpetrated on him over the years. Locking him in his locker, flushing his head in the toilet, and just last month Pil had tied Tom-tom to the flag pole and pantsed him, exposing his Spiderman briefs for all the schoolyard to jeer over. Their mocking laughter still rang in his ears.

Still in shock, Pil's eyes bulged, sweat marbled his forehead and over his thick lip. Petrified, he held his breath trying to staunch the tears. But he allowed Tom-tom to take his tremulous arm and pull him to the group.

The kids linked hands like they were going to play 'ring around the rosy.'

"Okay." Jessy's tranquil, confident voice travelled the dirt covered interior with no echo. Pil wasn't the only child crying, sniffling see-sawed around the circle. Without dropping their entwined hands, the children wiped their eyes and noses with sleeves and shoulders.

Dark curly hair framed Jessy's cherubic face. Anchoring the group with an uplifting smile, his bold eyes lingered on each child as if he could inject courage into each one. "Now, everyone, close your eyes," he said, dropping his head forward.

The girls, Matty, Teddy and Simone, trustingly mirrored him, closing their eyes and bowing their heads. Barty, Tom-tom and

Jamie shot anxious glances around at the others then clamped their lids shut.

Juan slew a look at his brother Santiago and then Drew silently asking, '*Is this a joke? Should we laugh out loud at the little priest-kid then punch him out, or…*' the boys noticed that the girls suddenly seemed at peace, relaxed. Soft trusting smiles drew across the girls' dirty faces. Juan shrugged, and imperceptibly nodded his head.

Squeezing the hand he held like a vise, fear unraveled through Rocky's body, uncontrollable shaking started in his hands to his legs. The metallic taste of blood on his tongue he bit so hard rather than show his brother Drew or the other boys that he was scared.

His small bug eyes shifted back and forth to each of the older boys to see what they were going to do before he made up his mind. Drew and Santiago and Juan had closed their eyes.

Struggling like a leaf in the wind, Rocky tried to curb his terror. His scared brain, a spewing volcano of panic buzzed so intensely he couldn't think. Tremors berated his body, shudders of a thousand kangaroos kicking inside trying to get out.

Scared to shut his eyes, who knew what kind of hideous monster was waiting to seize them and rip them apart, hack them to pieces, eat them…then he saw how calm each kid had become as they joined in, clasping hands, closing eyes, dropping their heads.

Jessy's words flowed like ice melting slowly, pooling around the children in a comforting, hugging cloud.

Rocky gripped each kid's hand he held and plunged his eyes shut, trying to block out the visions of hideous monsters with bloody fangs ready to fling from the shadows and- he shoved the scary thoughts away and waited impatiently for the reassuring peace to chill him, calm his tremors so he'd feel safe and positive as the other children appeared now.

Pil stood frozen except for his shaking knees, sniffing like an old car huffing up a hill. His face a picture of a *Scream* painting but with the mouth clenched, studied the other children.

In the faint light they appeared as dolls, hardly moving except to wipe an eye or nose. Just moments ago they all had seemed to be just as frightened and bewildered as Pil was.

Without moving his head, Pil took in their dirty clothes, shoes covered in mud, dirt streaked faces. Tears made trails through the filth on every child's face. The longer they'd been missing, the more raggedly they looked.

Jessy's clothes were the dirtiest; holes had already worked through his jeans and his jacket. He had tried to finger-comb the knots out of his curly hair that by now reached past his collar. The grubby black hair matched his mud-caked shoes.

The image of a tiny, black Pocahontas, Teddy blended into the dimness with her cinnamon skin except for the occasional flash of dazzling brilliant teeth and luminous brown eyes. Simone and Barty's faces hung like pale saucers in the dark.

Still without moving, Pil held his comrade's hands, watchful. His eyes adjusting to the dark, roamed the room behind the linked children. Actually, it seemed more a cavern than a room. Walls made up of chiseled rock, and they were standing on rock and dirt.

The ceiling was at least twenty feet high, the entire enclosed space maybe thirty feet in circumference.

The only contents besides the children were boxes of food and water, and toothbrushes. A small flowered screen, and a shovel to bury the waste in the rocky dirt the best they could was their make-do bathroom.

No outside sounds were audible, only the kids' breathing, occasional weeping and scuffing feet. No cars, planes, birds, nothing. Not even the howls of the voracious wind penetrated the thick craggy walls of wherever they were imprisoned. An absolute absence of any sound, as if they were sealed like a clam, or like a coffin. Maybe they were in a mine.

Pil's heart quickened when the word *sealed* reverberated in his brain. For it appeared they were indeed solidly enclosed by rock. There was no natural light, just the lone light-bulb, no window no doors…nothing, an impenetrable stone cage.

A glint caught his eye. Squinting, Pil could make out something like a TV monitor or something burrowed about five feet up and into the wall. Shudders of fear ran up and down Pil's arms, he gulped air faster afraid he'd run out of it, his heart beat like spokes rounding a wheel- faster, faster, he couldn't catch his breath, he couldn't feel his arms, his face was so hot it felt on fire, dizzy, he swayed, he was gonna pass out from terror.

Each child on either side of him reassuringly squeezed his hands. He drew a big wobbly breath then let the air and panic flow out. The boy forced himself to tune into Jessy's peaceful voice.

"Okay," Jessy said. "Everyone take a really deep breath." He waited. A cadence of audible breaths butterflied around the circle. He began, "Dear Father in Heaven, hear our words. We are scared and lost and in terrible danger."

A sob broke near him. He continued, his voice soothing yet unwavering, "We really need your help, God. Please guide us to a way out of here for all of us. Protect every single one of us Lord, and- and give us strength to face whatever is ahead with courage. Thank you." He waited a beat then said, "Does anyone want to add anything?"

"Send my daddy," Teddy murmured.

"And my da, too. Quick." Simone sniffed.

Matty added, "Send my Uncle Mike, he'll know what to do."

"Anyone else?" Jessy asked.

"Send us a gun," Tom-tom bleated.

"A *big* gun," Rocky said. The kids laughed breaking the tension.

Waiting a second, Jessy then said, "Amen."

Echoes of 'amen' skirted the circle of scared children like saying the word made it a promise.

Chapter Thirty-Six

A good hour before daybreak, in the dark, Michael trod quietly down the carpeted stairs. Yawning, comfortably dressed in jeans and a long sleeved shirt, he rubbed his hands through his tussle of thick black hair, trying to rustle his body into waking up faster.

Ambling down the hall, his footsteps silent in wool socks, he heard noise coming from the kitchen. Assuming it was Gram fussing around getting breakfast ready, he was surprised because even industrious Gram didn't usually rise this early.

The cheery kitchen was somewhat subdued due to the shutters. He noticed the glaring absence of sound, of the storm. It no longer rattled and beat at the house.

Flipping the light switch next to the door, Michael jumped when a short yelp corked from the other side of the kitchen. "Good morning, Gram, I didn't mean to startle you-" he broke off when a head poked out from behind the refrigerator door.

"You scared the daylights out of me! I almost dropped the eggs!" Cat scolded. Closing the door with an elbow, her hands full with eggs, cheese, milk and butter, she moved to the counter next to the stove and set them down.

In a skillet on a hot burner, thick strips of bacon sizzled. The campfire aroma of the crisping bacon drew Michael like a fly to a horse further into the kitchen. Two pieces of bread sat half in a toaster at the ready to be toasted, more piled on a plate waiting their turn. Until Michael hit the light switch, only the light over the stove had been barely illuminating the small area.

Michael approached the island in the center of the kitchen, he spied the coffee pot, red light lit indicating it was on and he could see the canister was full. Scooping a mug out of the sink strainer, he picked up the canister and poured a steaming cupful.

He crossed a foot over an ankle and leaned his forearm on the counter before blowing across the top of the mug to cool the brew. Taking in the view of Cat, also in jeans but cozy in a borrowed sweater bustling about, he said somewhat stiffly, "I'm sorry. I thought you were Gram getting an early start on the day. Why didn't you turn the lights on?"

Using tongs, Cat plucked each piece of bacon out of the cast iron skillet, placed them on a plate then put the plate in the pre-heated oven to keep warm. She slid a pat of butter into the pan adding it to the bacon grease, it melted immediately releasing a savory buttery smell melding with the smoky bacon.

Michael sniffed then breathed in deeply. "It smells in here like we're smack in the middle of the woods searching the darkening sky for that first shooting star and cooking dinner over a crackling campfire." He took a sip, craned his head towards the counter Cat worked at. "You got any marshmallows over there- I can find a couple of twigs..." Michael pretended to look for an aberrant branch lying around.

Cat cracked several eggs into a bowl, poured in a measure of milk added some salt and pepper then whisked it altogether, the metal whisk scraping the sides of the ceramic bowl. Pouring the mixture into the skillet, she reached for a spatula and pushed the eggs around, scrambling them until they were fluffy yellow.

Her lips pulled in, she kept her attention on the eggs. "Now who has the crazy imagination?"

Michael smiled, breathing in deeply. "Ahhh," he sniffed the air dramatically. "I love the smell of bacon and eggs and coffee. Makes me feel so..."

"Safe? At home? Rustic?" Cat offered. She lifted the heavy cast iron pan and pushed the eggs out of the pan and into a shallow bowl. Slipping the bowl into the oven to join the warming bacon, she pushed the lever on the toaster to get the bread started. Another dollop of oil into the sizzling pan and she cracked a few eggs in it for fried eggs.

"Hungry," Michael finished, sipping his coffee pretending he didn't see Cat roll her eyes.

"You know," Cat said stiffly, "you can make yourself useful and maybe put the butter and orange juice on the table. It's already set. And can you turn on the plate warmer on the sideboard? Everything is pretty much ready, but I don't know how long it'll be before Gram and Korey are down."

Michael noticed the table set for four. Drinking his coffee, he thoughtfully watched Cat expertly butter the toast that was ready while popping two more pieces in. Irony tinging his words, he said, "I'm glad you can ask for help instead of flightily doing things on your own."

Cat swung around, mouth open, hands on her hips, the tail of her apron swatted back and forth, her hair swung over one eye. "Are you serious?" Irritated, she shoved her hair back.

"I can't believe you're nagging on me about my tiny, uh, mishap. I mean really! I felt it was vitally important that I retrieve the laptop, I-"

"Mishap! You call that deadly fiasco a tiny mishap? And what good did it do you? Did you glean anything more than we already know? You put your life at risk," slamming the mug on the counter coffee sloshed out spilling on the counter. Black eyes flashed barely visible beneath hard brows.

Mirroring her with his hands on his hips, bridling his rage he pressed his lips closed and glared at her. Then he snatched up the mug again, gulped some, swallowing fast like he was trying to mask a bad taste then slammed the mug back down.

"Are you going to throttle me for the rest of my life about this-this incident? I admit I was foolish to go out in the storm. I- I admit I was scared to death. I admit seeing you magically appear in that blinding hailstorm of snow was-"

"Incident!" Michael blurted, about spewing his coffee out of his mouth. Swiping the back of his hand across his mouth he took a step closer to her. He was a good intimidating foot taller than her, she didn't lean away or cringe but stood firm, refusing to be cowed.

"Throttle is the word for it- yeah- I coulda throttled you when I saw you out there in the midst of that butchering storm!" His fingers curled into claws hovered scant inches around her neck. Now she did shrink back. He snarled, "I damn well could have wailed on that ass-"

"Hey! I smell *bacon*!" Pulling a hooded sweatshirt down over his head, Korey materialized in the doorway. By the time he got the sweatshirt pulled down, his grin framed in the hood, Michael had dropped his hands, Cat cast her eyes to the floor.

Korey pushed the hood back, ran his hand over the top of his head flicking the ponytail out from under the sweatshirt, he entered the room with Banny bounding at his heels.

Making a loud smacking sound, Korey licked his lips and rubbed his palms together. "Oh boy am I hungry! All that stress over the storm has made me totally famished. We having eggs?" He kept moving towards the tea kettle warming on a burner. He didn't notice Michael and Cat awkwardly sidle away from each other.

Keeping her eyes down, Cat hazily swept her eyes from the floor to the counter as if she was trying to remember what she had been doing. Wiping her palms on the front of her apron, she moistened her lips then opened the oven door, staring blankly inside as if she didn't know what she was looking for.

Banny hopped around the room barking and running from person to person. Gleefully, Korey grabbed up the tea kettle, dropped a teabag in a mug and poured in the boiling water, the vapor steaming his glasses.

Michael scowled at Cat's back but said to Korey, "Damn, Korey, you act like Gram never feeds you. Or you," he growled down at Banny. Unabashed, the dog sat back on his hind legs, his paws begging in the air, tongue lapping at both sides of his mouth and tail wagging flop-flop on the tiled floor. Michael ruffled the dog's head.

Snagging a piece of toast from the pile on the plate, Korey tore off a corner and tossed it in his mouth. "I love breakfast, Mike. After a night of fasting, the odor of eggs and bacon wafting up the stairs, down the hall and into my room, sifting up my nostrils, luring me awake making my mouth water before my eyes were even open, I-"

"Ooh Korey me boy, you are so fanciful. You just had eggs sunny side up yesterday with a slab of smoked ham, you're hardly starving! So kids," bustling into the kitchen, Granny Zinny turned her attention to Michael and Cat. "The wind and snow have stopped so abruptly it's like a loud radio has just been turned off leaving a vacuum in my ears."

She unrolled the shutter over the kitchen window. The budding sun blazed through the window panes painting a brilliant swath of gold across her gardener's face. "What's on the agenda today?" Cheery grandmotherly cheeks swelled with her happy smile. Behind round glasses, blue eyes twinkled like sun flashing off silvery scales of a leaping fish in the sea.

Setting a hand on the counter, Gram observed a vein throbbing at Michael's temple and his clenched mouth, and Cat hadn't even turned around, just tossed a hiya over her shoulder.

"Is everything all right?" the sweet old lady asked. Her worried faced rotated from Michael who still frowned at Cat's back and Cat with her head stuck in the oven like she was building a science experiment that needed her complete attention.

Korey shoved a hunk of toast to one side of his mouth making his cheek bulge while gulping tea through the other. He wiped his hand on baggy, frayed jeans that he had since before college. The scuffed deck shoes and long-sleeved plaid shirt over a t-shirt didn't look any better with the elbows worn and patches covering holes. It only had one button left.

Talking through his stuffed mouth Korey said, "You bet somethin's brewin' Gram, when I got here they looked like a pair of sparring boxers against the ropes, ready to pounce. Lover's quarrel." As if he hadn't just dragged the elephant right into the center of the room, leaning against the counter, Korey imperturbably broke off pieces of toast and tossed them in his mouth.

"We aren't-" Cat sputtered.

Gram's eyes widened then settled. She bustled over to Cat, she could see the young woman's red neck from where she was, and

Michael looked steamed. "You boys go to the table, Miss Cat and I will get the food. Michael, please bring the coffee pot and kettle."

Korey smirked at Michael. Michael's eyes darkened, the pupils grew huge. He snatched the remains of the toast out of Korey's hands and held it down for the dog. Banny jumped, snagging the toast in one swoop, gulped it, landed and waited for more.

"Hey!" Korey squawked. "That was mine!"

Heading towards the table, Michael grinned short over his shoulder, "Grab the pots, would ya, Cuz?"

Thirty minutes later, sopping up the remains of her eggs with a piece of toast, Cat's ears pricked. The toast dripping with yellow yolk hesitated near her waiting lips. She was eating the fried eggs while the others gobbled the scrambled. "What's that sound?"

Everyone halted, forks in midair as ears cocked to listen. A strange sound, like water running, dripping, sucking, surrounded the house.

Michael resumed eating. Through a bite of bacon, he said, "That's the snow melting super rapidly. The floods will start in a few hours." He nodded to Korey. "Lucas told me you worked for days stacking the sand bags along the city's perimeter to hopefully hold off any flooding from the lakes and rivers. The fence of forest should help too."

Cat laid her fork carefully on her plate. Her long hair had escaped the elastic that she had wound around it first thing this morning. She pulled the elastic off. Raking her fingers through her hair she dragged it back into a neat ponytail and re-secured the band then ran a finger across first one eyelid then the other.

She clasped her fidgeting hands in her lap to still their sudden shaking. She didn't look at Michael but said, "It- it sounds so... uh... weird. Like the very earth is- is-"

"Being sucked down a gigantic drain?" Korey offered cheerfully.

Cat shivered. "Um, yeah, or like we were going to get washed away. I, uh, it's really kind of scary..." she hated to sound like a nervous Nellie, but she wanted reassurance.

"That's why we sandbagged. It could happen. Especially once the *te mhor* comes. It's so powerful who knows what kind of deliverance it can bring, total destruction or the wonderment of spring," Korey said.

Michael shot Korey an annoyed glance. He had taken in the women's fearful expressions. Gram hadn't said a word, just kept eating but the lines around her eyes tightened, her papery skin was as white as the melting snow outside. He took a deep breath then set his knife and fork on his plate and pushed the plate away. Resting his forearms on the table in front of his plate, he folded his hands together.

"Okay, listen to me," Michael said calmly.

Cat sat across from him keeping her eyes on her plate. Gram stared in constrained panic back at Michael, Korey ate with gusto.

"We've done everything we can do to protect ourselves. So far, it's all good. We haven't even needed to retreat to the cellar to withstand the storm. We've prayed," he leaned over and picked up Gram's hand and squeezed it.

Blue eyes blinked through round lenses at him. Her lips pressed into a tight line wavered then turned into a shaky trusting smile.

He squeezed her gardener's hand that so lovingly planted and nourished flowers and vegetables and trees, the hands that fed the birds and rescued injured fowl and animals and nursed them back to health.

"It should crest at its worse today then start to recede, hopefully, by tomorrow. How fast it recedes will determine how soon we can safely get out and start searching again."

A muted roar, something like a slow plane in the clouds sounded far off growing louder bit by bit as it surged closer and closer. The sound of water sloshing against the side of the house quieted the table. They listened, and waited, and prayed.

For the next days the *te mhor* came broiling in with the rising sun. Flowing in waves of burning white heat, the rare blazing wind scorched the land as it covered it like a stifling blanket. So intense, it was if you could hear the blistering grass scream, hear the paint peeling off the houses, the ground burning up.

The heat sucked out every sliver of water from every crevice of every tree, the hiss of steam evaporating then the cracking of limbs as pieces of bark stripped and curled right off the trees. Not a bird dared to fly in the sky. The region turned into a carbon copy Death Valley. The hostile heat burned like the sun through a magnifying glass heating the land until it was a boil about to burst.

They were forced to stay inside while the land boiled. The more time Cat spent in Michael's company the more she was irritated with him. He moved his work into the den leaving her to use the library as a workplace. Dropping a box of paperwork onto the teak table she let her breath out as it landed.

Pulling out a sheaf of paper, she slammed it on the table, muttering, "He treats me like a child." Mimicking him she snipped, "'*Stay inside where it's safe, don't go near the windows, what were you thinking?*' I'm not an idiot," she growled, "I won't stand for it."

She snapped out another folder of paper and slammed that down too. Mimicking Michael again, she whined, "*I can't tell you about my life, I don't trust you with my secrets.*"

Grabbing her laptop she yanked the top open and angrily pressed the on button. Still mimicking Michael, "'"Incident*! You call it an incident?*' Talks to me like I'm a toddler for Pete's sake. Just let it go Sergeant, move on, give it a rest, put it to bed." A picture of her and Michael in bed together flashed in her mind. With a huff, she shook her head to vanquish it.

Picking up the laptop, she went over to a stuffed chair in soft tweed material and flopped down with the computer in her lap. Thankfully, although it went off and on, they were lucky to currently have electricity.

Tossing her hair tied in a long braid behind her; she wilted back against the cushiony chair and reviewed all of the notes and information they'd recorded, again.

Chapter Thirty-Seven

For days, Michael worked in his den. Korey hung upstairs in his room reading and watching DVD's. Banny went from room to room to room searching for Matty. Cat mustered in the library, and Gram baked pies, cookies, brownies. Anything to keep busy while waiting for the flood to dry and the land to nourish itself.

After a quiet lunch of turkey and Swiss sandwiches with pickles, chips and sodas, Cat settled again in the library with the computer on her lap. Yawning, she rumbled through the names of the missing children for the hundredth time when her eye caught the Bible setting on an end table next to her chair.

She turned her attention back to her computer, but then something drew her back to the Bible. Her lips pulled in, she reached for the big book. With a grunt she moved the computer to one knee and opened the Bible on her other knee. The book opened to Matthew 10.

Leaning over closer to the book, a line furrowed between her brows. Her eyes flicked to the laptop then back to the Bible, back to the laptop. Her thumb and forefinger twiddled a pale yellow earring that matched the borrowed, soft yellow sweater she wore. Pushing her sleeves up, her eyes continued their back and forth. Scratching the side of her head, the furrow deepened.

Suddenly, like a light bulb popped over her head, she grabbed up a pen and started writing. Hours later she closed the lid of the computer without turning it off, stuck a finger in the Bible and picked it up. Her hands full, she squirmed off the thick cushions to her feet. Tucking the computer under one arm and cradling the Bible in the other she left the library and trod down the hall to the den.

Hesitating on the threshold, she clutched the Bible to her chest. Michael was a duplicate to the way she had been in the library. His long sleeves rolled up, he was ensconced in a plush leather chair, his feet propped on an ottoman, a computer in his lap, a pencil and notebook filled with scribbles on the table next to him. His forehead wrinkled in deep concentration, hair spiky from his obvious scratching it in frustration.

Cat cleared her throat delicately to get his attention but his eyes were glued to the screen.

A faint glow from the monitor lit the planes of his face, angling the normal oval cheeks and straight nose and emphasizing the strong jaw, it also emphasized the shadows under his eyes dabbed like brown cotton ball prints from long hours of study and worry. The light dramatized his fading tan. His love of the outdoors apparent in his perennial tan, even in the winter he was outside so much he retained color year round.

His head looked like a lawnmower had run over it. He had declined Gram's offer to trim his hair that was now waving wild well past the bottom of his collar. Korey called him Samson. Gram had told him he looked like he belonged on the cover of one of those romance novels, a warrior on a horse, his long black hair flowing in the wind, the horse's front hooves punching the air, Michael holding up a sword ready to forge into battle.

Korey and Michael had burst out laughing at her description. "Uh, you need to write books, Gram," Michael had said, shaking his head. Self-consciously he had smoothed the hair back, out of sight out of mind.

"Ahem. Um, Sergeant," Cat murmured, one foot over the threshold, she still waited as if asking permission to enter the room. The pair had spoken only a few necessary words in the past weeks.

Frowning at the interruption, he didn't look up. "What?" his voice short.

Cat stepped gingerly into the room, her socks made small prints in the lush carpeting Michael had installed himself. "Sergeant," her voice soft, trying to gently get his attention.

Impatiently he turned his eyes up. Seeing Cat standing unsure a few feet inside the doorway, he waved her in. "Come in, Cataleigh." Taking in the computer and Bible clutched in her arms, one brow arched. Curious, not unfriendly, he asked, "What is it?"

She moved towards the varnished mahogany table in the middle of the room. Setting the computer and Bible down on the table, she awkwardly set a hand on her hip. "I…" her tongue clicked, "I found, I think, a kind of pattern to the children. I know it'll sound quite odd, but nonetheless I thought I'd run it past you."

Michael closed his computer and set it on a matching mahogany table next to the leather chair, alongside a glass of soda and a bowl of mixed nuts. Tiny specks of salt dusted the part of the table between the bowl and the chair from him munching while working. He got up and came to stand in front of her. He looked interested but not hopeful considering her choice of wording.

"Odd pattern?" he asked.

"Uh, yeah, kind of. I mean it might be just fanciful and nothing at all. But," Cat paused, pulling her long braid in front of her chest she pawed it nervously. The room reflected in her clear sea eyes. She pushed the braid behind her back and turned to the table, opening the computer and then the Bible. She slid the Bible next to the computer so they could both be easily viewed. "Here," she said, pulling out a chair, "let me show you."

When they were sitting comfortably on the wooden chairs with the leather seats, Michael folded his hands together and waited patiently.

Cat shifted in her chair. Then she pulled the computer closer. "Well," she stopped. Shaking her head, the braid swung around flopping over one breast. Pushing a few wisps of hair off her face she took a deep breath. "Well, now that I think about it, I really think it was a silly idea. I'm sorry I bothered you." She went to close her laptop but Michael set a hand on hers to stop her. They both stared at his hand covering hers.

"No. Go ahead and tell me. It doesn't matter if it's foolish or not, we have to investigate every avenue no matter how insignificant or preposterous. We don't know what we might stumble onto while checking out trivial or absurd or weird but compelling stuff that might not make any sense at this time. Besides," a corner of his mouth pulled up in a brief smile. "I trust you, Cataleigh. You're not a frivolous thinker. Normally. Go ahead." He moved his hand away.

She took in the earnest eyes, serious mouth, he appeared sincere. Her smile unsure, she pointed at the screen that was up on her laptop.

Michael leaned in. Frowned. He tipped his head slightly sideways. "Uh huh, the missing children's names..." A slight question in his tone.

Cat pushed her sleeves up, pursed her lips, let out a breath. "Yes. Well, I noticed that none of the children really have regular, well, English, Irish, or American names." One hand on the keyboard the other trailed down the monitor.

Michael sat back. Both brows rose. "So? I don't see where a couple of unusual names can mean anything pertinent."

Cat nodded. "Okay, I know, but wait. There's a method to my madness. I told you it was a bit crazy. Let me tell you and then you can tell me I'm insane. All right?"

Michael's palms faced up, he shrugged, gave her a quick smile. "Sure. Go ahead, I'm game for anything at this point." Clasping his hands in his lap, he faced the monitor again to show his interest in what she was trying to tell him.

She stared at his profile for a moment. She had agreed with Gram but hadn't said it out loud. Michael did resemble a warrior of ancient times. A rugged profile, wild black hair flowing, strong and tall and brave, fierce aggression held in check.

Cat had seen a dangerous side to him when he dealt with the L's and when he found her in the snow. Brought to her mind that he had been in such a rage, cursing at her over the wail of the wind, he had practically crushed her arms after he roughly pulled her out of the snow. But he rescued her at his own risk.

Yet it seemed he struggled to keep his temper under control. Then there were those eyes, so dark, almost black. In the low light they looked black as the night sky with refracting twinkles of stars. She could see herself in them they were so clear but they seemed to pull her in, so mysterious, haunting secrets held back behind round, shiny black walls. Blinking rapidly she turned to the computer.

"So uh, I looked up each of the children's birth certificates, the ones I could find that is, and I wrote down all the interviews we did with the parents. First, let's see," she peered at the computer skimming down to the notes she'd made. "There's Juan and Santiago, Zeb Trueno's boys. Juan is Spanish for John and Santiago is actually a version of James. Then, there's Drew for Andrew. His father, John Artzi said Drew's brother Simon is called by his nickname of Rocky."

She pushed the down arrow for her notes to move up to be visible. "Um, then there's Jamie Ming, Jamie is another form of James. Then, little Teddy, her mother, Quineisha Fady, said her given name is, get this, Thaddus. For some crazy reason, I think Quineisha said it was her family's name and that naming her that had something to do with a promise to her dying mother or a nutty bet or something. It's a derivative of Thaddaeus."

Michael sat back in his chair and crossed his arms. "I don't see what any of this means."

"I know, I know. Just hear me out." Cat pushed the down arrow to view the rest of her notes. "So then, young Pil is Paul Philo's son Philip. Apparently when his little brother Cody first started talking he couldn't say the Ph sound for Phil, it came out Pill and that stuck, however when young Phil tried to write his nickname it came out Pil, apparently he wasn't the Einstein of the family. Okay, then there's Barty Solomon, Barty for Bartholomew per his mother. And next we have, uh, oh- Tom-tom." She giggled. "Poor little guy."

Michael's face creased into a smile. He watched Cat's lips when she laughed. Korey had rhapsodized for an hour after he met Cat for the first time. "Man, Cuz, how do you keep your hands off that amazing body when you work so closely together? And those lips, honey from a bumblebee couldn't be sweeter or richer!"

Calling him a dork, Michael had blown him off, telling his cousin that he was a professional, their work was grave and he barely found the young woman attractive. Korey's unbelieving guffaws had followed Michael, his ears tinged with red, down the hall, out of Korey's sight and digs, and his own untamed thoughts.

"Tom-tom, yeah." Michael grinned shaking his head. "He got that handle when he was a little guy not even in long pants yet. His name, Thomas, and being a Native American, well the monocle fit and stuck."

Cat's own lips curved up, blue eyes sparkled. "I think you mean moniker."

He slapped his forehead and rolled his eyes. "Great. I've been hanging around Hollis too much. I'm picking up his goofy habit of saying things incorrectly. Anyway," he said soberly, "they also called Thomas 'Tom-tom dumb-dumb.' He's not the fastest ant in the hill."

Nodding, Cat said, "Kids can be cruel. And bullies. The word is that the kids were brutally mean to young Jessy. Anyway, Justin's girl, Simone, isn't that unusual of a name, but it can be if it fits my profile. That leads me to," she hesitated, watching Michael.

He was staring intently at the monitor, brows pulled down and furrowed between his eyes. Like he was struggling to see what she saw. After a moment of silence, he glanced at her then back to the computer. Then back to her.

"Leads to what?" he asked.

Resting her elbow on the table, she tapped her fingers against her lips. Then twined her fingers and set them in her lap. She peeped at him through her lashes, hesitated, then plunged right in. "What is Matty's real name? Matilda?"

He swung his head at her, night eyes snapped, then clouded. A corner of his mouth twitched. "I don't see what-" he crossed his arms over his chest.

"It's important, I wouldn't intrude otherwise."

"Harrumph." He tightened his arms as if to block her question, glaring at her. But then, she seemed so sincere, kind. His arms loosened, relaxing slightly he dropped his hands on the table. "Her name is unusual too. It's Mathieu."

When Cat made no response or even a flicker at the oddity of Matty's true name, he said, "Her mother, my sister Kayleen," he winced, saddened. Mouth drooping and eyes now vacant. "Kayleen, was a romantic. She fell in love at an early age. The guy, he uh, he-he was murdered. Kayleen was pregnant."

Michael took a deep breath, expelling it slowly. The pain in his eyes like a strobe light poured out so strong Cat winced.

In a voice teeming with emotion he said, "The young guy's parents were from France although he was born here. His name was Mathieu." His shoulders stiffened, he looked away blankly at the computer.

Softly, Cat whispered, "I'm guessing Mathieu is French for Matthew?"

Michael nodded wordlessly. There was a space of silence between them.

Her voice hushed, compassionate, "You must have cared deeply for him."

His eyes welled, making them look like pools of oil. He sat back and crossed his legs. "No. I hardly knew him." He pushed the heel of his palms against his eyes. "Well? What else? What's the big deal with the names?"

Confused at his emotion without an explanation, Cat stood up and set her palms on the corner of the table. She picked up a piece of paper and a pen, setting the paper next to where Michael's right hand rested on the table. She started writing:

Santiago-   James
Juan-   John
Pil-   Philip
Drew-   Andrew
Jamie-   James
Tom-tom-   Thomas
Simone-   Simon
Rocky-   Peter
Teddy-   Thaddaeus
Matty-   Matthew
Barty-   Bartholomew

Michael's back rounded over the paper. His eyes widened up to his hairline. His mouth agape he looked at Cat then back at the names. "They're the names of the Apostles…"

His back straightened, he leaned back then gazed confused at Cat. "It's peculiar, but," he held his palms up, "they are really very common names. And, hey wait a second," he ran his finger down the names. "There's only eleven names here. So…?"

Her lips curled. "Yup, eleven."

He shook his head trying to get her point. "I'm sure you're going somewhere with this?" He snapped his fingers. "Wait, Jessy is one of the missing kids, the first in fact. How does he fit into your schematic?"

Without answering, she picked up the pen again and wrote under the last name.

Jessy U.

His brow arched. "And?"

She smiled and wrote, Jessy u - Jesus.

"It's like an anagram," he said, "but what about the y?"

Setting the pen down she turned in her chair to face him. "First, the U. According to Mary Montebello his adoptive mother, the U was written on his paperwork, it stood for 'Unknown.' Sad, huh?"

He nodded. She continued, "Mary said his papers stated his name as Jess U. She was not informed of where he had come from or why he didn't have a last name. Furthermore, when she asked him where he came from, his family, his last name, he claimed to have no memory of anything. He must know, he was 5 when he came to stay with her. She didn't force it. The kids called him Jessy."

Michael's tone grim, he said, "Probably his life had been hell, abusive maybe, maybe he just missed his parents so much or they were in prison or dead, who knows. He might really have pushed his memories so deep to forget."

He went on, "So, that makes 12. But Jesus wasn't an Apostle. Your math is flawed." He got up and went over to a cooler on a table by the door. Taking out two sodas, he popped the tabs came back over, sat down and handed one to Cat.

"What difference does this all make? Like I said, they are common names. And so what if they were called something else but their true names were the names of the Apostles?" He swigged his soda. Then he said, "So what good does all this do? I don't see how it can help us find the children." They drank for a minute in unison, in silence.

"Ahh," Cat licked her lips and set the half empty can down. "That was good. I was feeling parched." Crossing her legs, she tugged the bottom of her sweater down, it had gotten hunched up from sitting for so long.

Relaxing back in her chair, she smiled slyly at him. "I think the children were taken specifically because of their names. If we had seen their true names right away we would have seen the Apostle pattern and started looking at that and trying to figure out what it meant. It could have led us right away to the kidnapper and to the children." She picked up her soda and sipped.

Michael grasped the arm of her chair and turned the chair and her in it to face him. "Well? Are you going to keep me in suspense? What does it all mean, how will it lead us to the kids?"

She wrapped both hands around her soda and set it on her lap, like it was a small shield to keep between them. "Once I realized Jessy U was an anagram, I started looking at the adults and playing with their names too. Then it came to me that someone had to know all of the kids' real names. Someone had to have access to our records and notes."

Michael took a hold of both arms of her chair and pulled her closer to him. So close that her knees were snug between his legs.

Cat twitched but stayed where she was. She said, "The records were only available to a select few, that would be…"

His eyes shifted up as he recalled the people that were in the room at the hotel. "Uh, the few gardai allowed in the room, not Jason or Lucas, I trust them with my life. You and me," he flashed a brief grin.

"And uh, let's see, there was Babby Bianchi, and," he rubbed his chin, raked a hand through his hair. "Oh, yeah, and Mrs. O'Rielly. Once the first two kids were taken, the records were right out there.

Of course people came and went and papers could have been picked up. I doubt your computer was hacked but that's a possibility, wait," he snapped his fingers, "there also was," he shook his head.

Peering up at her under a flop of hair, he said, "No, no way. It couldn't have been them. Maybe it was one of them..." he laid his arms along the arms of Cat's chair and leaned in. He leaned so close his face was an inch from hers.

"Sergeant," Cat whispered.

He leaned closer, his eyes dropped to her lips then rose to her eyes. "You have the most beautiful eyes I've ever seen, Cataleigh...like the wild Irish Sea..." his lids hooded, half-covering his own dark orbs. He leaned in so close she could feel his breath, could feel herself being drawn. He murmured, "I know you're mad at me, but it's still Michael."

Cat lifted her soda can higher, to keep something, anything between them. She averted her eyes. They were too close, she was afraid he could see her soul, her feelings in them. She shivered, she felt drawn into his own dark pools.

They were like magnets pulling her, pulling her from her chair to, she pushed her chair back, still holding the can in front of her. "Michael, you're-"

"Those damned RMP's! It was them, or one of them. My money's on Lam, that *amadan*- idiot. I knew there was something hinky about that Popeye- or- or wait- he doesn't have the brains, but the female, Raveena, oh yeah, she's a bright one. I don't know how she extracted the information on Matty.

"That wasn't easily obtainable. She must have gotten into my records. Maybe it was the two of them together. That would make more sense. That way they could take turns being present when a child went missing so suspicion wouldn't fall on them." He jumped up. 'We've got to go, I've got to call the-"

Cat held up a hand. "No, Michael, no, it wasn't them! It's-"

A pounding at the front door so loud they could hear it from the den snatched their attention. Michael shot out of the room- Cat yelled, "No! Michael, wait!"

Chapter Thirty-Eight

"Isn't that *precious,*" a sarcastic voice sounded in the cavern.

Their eyes shut so tightly in prayer the children hadn't see the monitor carved into the wall light up. Lids flew open at the unfamiliar sneering voice.

All heads turned to the monitor. They tightened their grip on each hand they held, their chain made stronger by linking them together.

The monitor, 3 feet by 3 feet, a little over five feet up from the ground commanded attention from its encasement in the rocky wall. The milky eerie glow of the screen made the face appearing waver in and out and almost too opaque to make out at all. Finally, a figure grew steadily into view.

"My dear children, please come closer. Come now, don't be afraid." The crackly voice bade the kids to move nearer to the monitor. Their feet remained planted. Not a child blinked or moved or breathed.

The face wiggled as if under water, flickering and rolling like waves from the top to the bottom. It wormed closer so that the face took up most of the screen.

The face scrunched, brows drawn hard over the eyes, the mouth a snarl, he barked, "I said move in closer! Do you want me to come in there and pull you closer, because I can and I will, and I promise you won't like it. Not one bit. *Move now.*"

Stiff as multi colored crayons, some short nubs, some long and thin, the children still linked together moved as if wading through a thick swamp, barely a foot closer to the monitor.

"Closer."

They inched closer.

"Closer!" the voice bellowed.

The children jumped and hurried so close to the screen they had to look up to see it.

"There, that's much better, I hate to shout." The malevolent face grinned. It appeared he enjoyed the children's palpable fear, as if he thrived on it.

Not a child wasn't trembling, most had tears sliding over still round baby cheeks. Even Juan the oldest struggled to hold back tears that stuck in his throat making him choke. They all stood silent, too scared to talk.

The face rolled as it spoke. "Now then. You wonder why you're here. I'm going to tell you. I'm going to tell you what's going to happen to each and every one of you. Let's get this straight right now," the face swayed even closer.

"There is nothing anyone of you or your family or the police can do to help you now. This is your fate, accept it, it'll be so much easier for you than if you try to fight it."

"Uh, sir, can we like maybe make a phone call?" Pil asked. The other kids looked at him aghast that he had the nerve to speak.

Drew leaned over and angrily whispered, "Shut up you idiot, are you trying to get us killed? Don't piss him off dude."

Annoyed, Pil said, "Don't tell me what to do, all I did was ask if-" As one, the children shifted back leaving him standing alone.

"You!" the voice roared. "Yes, you," a gnarly finger pointed at Pil, he ordered, "portly Pil Philo, come over here."

Pil's hair stood on end, his face a white sheet, liquid trickled from his pant leg. He shook his head. "No- no- please, I didn't mean anything-"

"Now!" it screamed.

Pil leaped in the air flying to directly in front of the screen, a tiny puddle stayed behind turning the dirt to mud. Like an undammed river, tears sprung from Pil's eyes, his body quivered like a plucked violin string. He locked his fingers tightly together and clutched them hard against his thick chest.

"You," the figure said, "you will be the very first to go, I promise you. I want you to remember that. All of your friends can watch you go and anticipate how they will meet their own demise. If you faint, boy, you'll go now, get me? Now step back. And no baby mewling from any of you," he eyed each child individually.

Each dropped their eyes petrified to be signaled out.

Stepping back, Pil nodded so vigorously it looked like his head would snap right off.

"Now then, where was I?" The creature smiled. "Oh yes, what's going to happen to you. Well, of course you've all heard the story, the *legend*. The legend about the lost children. Well, the good news is, you will no longer have to wonder if the fable is true. You will be living the legend; you are the legend.

"Also, you won't have to wonder what happened to the other children, you know, the missing ones that were found crushed and mangled at the base of the cliffs over the past eons. The bad news is, the way you'll learn this is by being up front and personal, you know, by it happening to you!"

The children gasped, horrified eyes bulged. Teddy and Simone whimpered like new born puppies. Simone cried in a whisper, "I want my da…"

Matty let go of Rocky's and Barty's hands and laid her arm around Simone's shoulders and moved her head so it was just barely touching Simone's. "Hush, Simmy," she whispered.

"Yes, hush little girl, Simone is it? Your daddy is Garda Justin Zeall, right?"

Simone didn't answer, tears rushed down her face. The dirt enabled her pink barrette to still cling to a few strands of tangled blonde hair. Matty hugged her shoulder. Their eyes glued to the monitor like frightened dolls.

He continued, "Oh I know your papa pretty well." His face filled the screen, sharp teeth gleamed, eyes pointed and mean.

"The next time he sees you he will be stroking that silky blonde hair of yours as he's kneeling over your dead body lying crushed, twisted and broken on the blood-stained, rock-hard ground at the foot of the cliffs, unless of course you're washed out to the sea and lost forever. Anyway honey, don't count on him coming for you. He doesn't know where you are, no one knows where any of you are. If they ever do figure this place out, and they won't, but if they do, it'll be too late!"

Teddy screamed through her hands pressed tight against her mouth. Jessy unlinked and came to comfort her. The children quaked as one, and waited.

Like he was telling a bedtime story, the man in the monitor put a finger to his chin. "Now, where was I, you kids keep distracting me. It won't work, you're all gonna die anyway."

He ignored the wrenching sobs and muffled screams and continued on matter-of-factly. "Okay then. This is our agenda. By tomorrow I think we'll begin. The *te mhor* has done its job. It's cooled the region, the land is about dry and the grass and wildflowers have already sprung. You should see the daisies, so pretty.

"Anyway, when dusk arrives, I will take each one of you and fling you off the cliffs into the sea. In a few days your families or the police might find some of your bodies."

Juan clenched his fists and stepped forward. "You and what army, Mister? Me and my brother and buddies, we'll give you a fight that's for sure!"

Drew and Santy joined in, "Yeah, yeah we'll fight you!" Their jeers died in their throats like they hit a brick wall when the face burst out laughing maniacally, great sinister guffaws, razor blade teeth gleaming.

"Oh you little boys think you can take me on? Just for fun I should let you take a try. But," he sighed, "I want your parents to find your bodies intact. You know, with your arms and legs and-heads still attached to your torsos." He roared with hideous laughter at their terrified faces.

He sneered, "But go ahead and give it a try. You don't even know if you'll be awake when I take you. I could gas the room and knock you out. I wouldn't want to gas and kill you because I want you aware when you're going over the cliffs. Ha ha ha ha," he laughed at their petrified expressions.

"Besides my little friends, what makes you think that I am alone, or that I don't have powers you could not even imagine?"

Matty bit her lip red, her voice quivering, she asked, "Please, sir, is there anything we can do, to say, to change your mind?"

"Yes." Jessy moved next to her. "We'll do anything you want if you let us go. Let us all go."

"Oh really," through the murky wavering screen the eyes appeared a sick green, they seemed to enlarge and aim straight at Matty then at Jessy.

"You'll do anything my pets? Hmm. That gives me something to think about. I love a game. Especially if it's a no win challenge, uh, for you that is." He grinned, the corners of the mouth curving up into points, the nose lengthened and dipped so far it almost covered the middle of the mouth.

The face and eyes a sickly grey-greenish glow. "I'll get back to you on that." The screen flickered, crackled then the image fractured into fragments and the screen blinked off.

Dead silence. No one dared move, breathe, cry. They stared at the monitor, scared it would come back on, scared the man could reach out of the screen grab them around the neck and yank them into the monitor to disappear forever.

Drew turned to Jessy, jabbing a finger at him. "Way to go you little *muzzy*, brat. It's bad enough with him saying he's going to toss us over the cliffs but now you give him the idea to think of other ways to torture us first? What if he wants like, sex or something?"

Barty and Jamie's faces reddened at the suggestion. Simone and Teddy clutched each other and moaned not really sure what he meant but it sounded awful.

"Yeah," Pil joined in. "What if he like wants us to fight each other, or-"

"Or cut off each other's head, or-" Rocky said making a slashing motion with his hand.

Juan held his hands up to the boys. "Knock it off, guys. Jessy was just trying to help, buy us time. Maybe the freak will come up with something that we can beat him at, we don't know. Let's just chill until he comes back. Let's not let our imaginations go crazy."

Santiago's laugh was harsh. "Imaginations? Could we ever imagine anything worse than the horrible nightmare we're in right now?" The others nodded with him.

Matty broke from the group and went over and sat down on the dirt ground, her back against the wall.

The others joined her, to sit and wait, and ponder, what horrors could this demon come up with?

Chapter Thirty-Nine

Michael pulled open the front door and almost fell back as the scorching heat from outside rushed in like steam from a kettle. "Lucas," he said, surprised to see his garda standing there he gestured for him to enter. He stood aside as Lucas Bregg came into the house.

Lucas pulled off his hat gazing all around in awe. "Wow, Mike, I like what you've done with the place," he laughed at his platitude. His boots clunked across the tiled foyer. "No really, bro, this looks great. Now I see why you were absent from our softball games on Saturdays. It looks great!"

Smiling, Michael said, "Thanks. Come on into the kitchen, you must need something to drink. It's hot as hades out there. What are you doing here? I looked out first thing this morning and it still looked pretty flooded except up here near the house the water has greatly receded but the road still looked under."

Lucas followed him into the kitchen where Michael took two beers out of the refrigerator and handed one to the officer.

"Thanks," the ex-football player said accepting the drink. He set his keys on the kitchen table then pulled the tab off the can and downed most of it. He wiped the back of his hand across his mouth then hooked a thumb over his belt standing with his legs akimbo.

He was ready to go, ball cap on his head holding down some of his moppy blonde hair, dressed in jeans, gloves sticking out a back pocket, sturdy work boots with steel tips and a short sleeved t-shirt.

It was hot outside and they would be roughing it where they were going so he skipped the tie and uniform.

"Your street is still pretty deep but much of the water has withdrawn to a safe distance especially near the mountains and the wooded areas. I got here with the jeep. The all-clear siren hasn't gone off yet, but it looks good enough for us to go out. It's still hot, but really it's bearable. I think we can go-" Lucas stopped mid-word when another knock pounded the door.

"What the- did I plan a party and forget to tell myself?" Michael strode out of the kitchen down the hall to the front door with Lucas at his heels.

Throwing open the door Michael smirked. "I should have known. Come on in, Justin. What, do I live in the lowest lying area of the whole damned region?" He stepped aside to let the red-headed garda in.

Justin nodded, bumping fists with Lucas, dressed pretty much the same as the officer. They followed Michael back to the kitchen where Michael offered Justin a beer, which he eagerly accepted. "Yeah, Sarg, your freakin' neighborhood is still under water but the forested area is drying fast with the burning sun."

"Yeah, even though I knew it would be crazy hot, I never expected to open the door and practically get cremated on the spot." Michael finished his beer. He crushed the can in one hand and set it on the table. "I'm assuming you guys are here because you think it's safe enough to get out and start the search?" Both gardai nodded.

"Yes. I got a cooler packed as I'm sure Luke does too. I'm ready as soon as you are." Justin said. Lucas nodded his agreement, "Yeah, me too. Ready when you are, Mike."

Michael said, "I'll be right back." He opened the cellar door and disappeared down the stairs.

He reappeared in seconds with a cooler in his hands. "I've been ready since before the storm started. I just need to grab my keys. I think we need to go straight to the mountains.

"I've got a feeling that the cairn holds the key. But I think you two," he motioned to Lucas and Justin, "should go around the foothills to the south where the mountains are more traversable where you might be more likely to find some kind of entrance. Check where they closed up the mine. It always seemed impassable to me, but you never know what some enterprising person might have done."

At his friends' eager expressions, Michael said, "Let's roll. You guys are all packed so go ahead. I'll be right behind you, I need to tell Gram I'm going." Lucas and Justin finished their drinks, tossed the empty cans into the trash, grabbed their hats and headed out the door.

After telling Zinny his plans, sweating the second he stepped into the sandblasting sun, Michael set the cooler on the backseat of his cruiser. He opened the driver's side door, as he slid in, the passenger door opened. Surprised, he hesitated as he was shoving the key into the ignition.

Cat climbed in the cruiser tossing a backpack into the backseat. She closed the door and hooked the seatbelt on. Staring ahead, she said, "Don't bother trying to dissuade me, I'm coming and that's it. You need someone covering your back. You shouldn't go alone." She glanced at him, smiled, then turned to face straight ahead. "I'm ready when you are."

Perusing Cat's lovely profile, Michael knew when he saw that pert nose up in the air there would be no arguing with her, short of hauling her over his shoulder carrying her back in the house and locking her in a closet. She'd only get out and go out on her own, put her incorrigible self in danger again. That's why he hadn't told her he was leaving.

His lip twitched. He shrugged one shoulder then started the cruiser. "Okay, I don't have time to fight with you. I'm going to drive around back and pick up a couple of horses. We can only drive so far to the cairn then we'll need the horses to get closer. We could ride them from here but I don't want them to have to carry the coolers and shovels and stuff."

He looked back over his shoulder through the two Heckler & Koch MP7 sub-machine guns hanging in the rear window like an American cowboy, then backed out of the driveway and around to the stalls where he got his horse, Rossie, and another for Cat.

"Oh what a beautiful chestnut you are," Cat cried, running her palm down the horse's neck. "Did you name him Rossie for his lovely reddish color?" Cooing at the horse she combed his mane with her fingers. The horse snickered and stamped his front foot. All four feet had white socks.

"Uh, no," Michael said, saddling the horse. "Rossie means Brat. Aptly named when he was a colt, he's matured some with my expert handling." He grinned. Fitting the bit in, he handed the reins to Cat to hold the horse steady while he turned his attention to the other horse.

"This is Crionna, she'll be perfect for you." He straightened a blanket over the Palomino's back before throwing the saddle on.

Cat scratched Rossie between the ears. His ears twitched, he nudged her arm with his nose. "What does Crionna mean? It's a pretty name, probably means something like 'golden' because of her beautiful gold coat and white mane and tail, but knowing you it means loony bird or something, right?"

Michael held the reigns of both horses and pulled them to the truck. He handed Cat the keys. "Here, you drive and I'll lead you on horseback." Cat took the keys.

Michael hopped up on Rossie and held Crionna's reigns to pull her alongside. "Her name means 'wise.' Odd name for a female I admit, kind of an oxymoron. We named her that contrarily because she never comes in when it starts raining. Pretty apropos horse for *you*, don't you think?"

With a teasing smirk, he yanked the reins and kicked Rossie, they darted across the yard before Cat could respond to his remark. She stood shaking her head, smiling, then got in the truck to follow Michael and the horses.

Chapter Forty

Leaning against the rocky wall or curled up on the hard dirt floor, the children dozed off and on, waiting for hours, limbs jerking in fear, whimpering and moaning as a new terrifying thought of what the monster behind the screen was going to do to them flickered from one child to the next.

Static crackling woke them. Rubbing weary eyes they shifted slowly, some climbed to their feet, others too shaky to stand knelt or just sat. The monitor lit, lines rolled up the screen until the face wavered into view.

Jessy and Juan stood side by side, almost touching shoulders as if to garner strength and courage from each other. Matty scrambled to her feet to stand next to Jessy. She slipped her quivering hand into his. Her fat red pigtails so dirty she looked more like a brunette than a redhead, round blue eyes swam with tears. All three children locked their knees to keep them from knocking.

"Hello my darlings, did you enjoy your little nap?" The man grinned, evil seemed to ooze from his oily pores, dripping from his mocking eyes and dagger teeth. Then his eyes widened, he grinned cheerfully.

"Oh looky, I see three brave little Indians. The rest of you babies, too scared to stand, your shaking legs too rubbery to hold you up? Ha ha ha," he enjoyed the children's terror.

Sniffing, hiccupping, her chin quivering, Simone slowly struggled to her feet. On his knees, Rocky pushed himself up to stand beside her and took a hold of her dirty hand. She shot him a fragile crooked smile. One by one the kids got to their feet and held hands again like a human chain, they moved forward to link with Juan and Jessy.

Chortling, the man in the screen slapped his hands down in glee. "Oh this is too precious! You kiddies are brave now, but let's see how you are when I tell you what you need to do to escape…"

Swift intake of breaths, the children glanced around at each other, a way out- *he's going to let us go*! Eyeballs so wide the whites clearly showed around their irises, the children eagerly yet with trepidation, watched the screen, waiting to hear what they will have to do to save their lives.

****

It took over an hour to get to within eyesight of the Maru Mountains. Michael pulled the horses off to the side. Looking down in amazement, he couldn't believe the grass was already sprouting. The horses immediately bent to chomp.

Michael motioned for Cat to stop the truck. She hopped out pocketing the keys in her jean's pocket.

Leaving the truck's air conditioning the heat pressed against her like a soft hot wall. Her hair was tied up in a ponytail, she brushed wisps of curling tendrils off her heated face. "Whew, it's hotter than I recall it ever being!"

Seeing her hot pink cheeks, Michael said, "Actually, I can already feel a difference in the temperature. It's less humid here because there's no water left like there is at my house, and the mountains definitely keep things cooler. But I think the severe heat is finally going in abeyance. Look," he said, pointing, "wild flowers already in the fields. The speed of the growth spurt is incredible."

Cat followed his direction, her smile widened. "Oh, amazing they're growing extraordinarily fast. So pretty, like a meadow bouquet." Taking in the surrounding area, deeply breathing in she said, "Oh, smell the fragrant air." Rossie snorted breaking her revelry. She laughed and patted the mahogany horse's bulging side. "Okay, okay, I get it, let's go."

Michael slid off his horse and brought the other one over to her.

"We need to go by horseback from here, the furrows are too deep and boulders too big for the truck to maneuver through. On the right side over there around a mile or so there's a kind of drawbridge over the giant crevasse created when the mountain was first made from an earthquake, but it's controlled from inside the mine and that's been dynamited closed."

"Oh, here." Cat untied a bag from her waist. She handed him two wrapped sandwiches.

Opening a small cooler tied to the back of the saddle, he set the sandwiches inside. The cooler was already stuffed with bottled water, a loaf of bread and jar of peanut butter and candy bars. He held his hands together for her to step on and hiked her up onto the golden Palomino. Crionna's tail swished like a platinum blonde mop.

Michael led the way across the wildflower strewn meadow, bugs and moths fluttered up at their feet like stirred dust. He directed Rossie towards the north point of the mountains. The mountains were so far away they looked like pointy ant hills.

An hour of trotting through spring green, baby grass, the horses' hoofs clumped along the rocky pasture, the mountains seemed to grow bigger. They followed Fand's Trail, a worn path made by hikers and travelers from ages ago as a way around the mountain.

The path passed nearby the Faoi Cairn, but to get closer, travel would become more difficult as they would have to scuttle over rocks and shallow ravines and be mindful of peat bogs. Michael kept a rope tied to his belt just in case one of them stepped into a bog by accident, it would be like falling into quicksand.

Eventually they turned off the path and headed across the open field. Cat trotted up beside Michael. Craning her neck she studied the area in wonderment. "It's so bizarre, the way everything is growing so super-fast, I actually think I see leaves sprouting on limbs that were bare seconds ago."

Michael kept his attention on their destination. "Yeah, it's from the *te mhor* following the storm. The severely hot wind and powerful sun dried the area unusually fast, kind of like of like an immense blow dryer. The saturated ground and the brilliant sun combined created an outdoor hot house."

He slowed his horse. Picking through the weeds and pebbles carefully, he said, "We need to watch our step, there are bogs all around. I know where most of them are but with the weather we've had there might be new ones."

"Oh." Cat stared hard at the ground around her. "You said bogs are like quicksand?"

He nodded. "I have rope if we get stuck, but I'd hate to try to haul a horse out, so keep an eye peeled."

They travelled silently for another hour. "There," Michael said, pointing. "See it?"

Squinting, Cat held a hand to shade her eyes from the late afternoon sun. The leather squeaked as she squirmed in her saddle, her legs and butt were cramping from the long ride. She tried to follow his pointed finger across a hazy field of green.

Then, she crowed, "Oh, oh yes! I see it!" Grinning, "The cairn, I can see the cairn. Finally." She sighed wearily. Noticing Michael's hard study of the ground in front of him, she asked, "What is it?"

Frowning, lips pulled in, he scratched his chin and pushed back the black hair gliding over one eye. His hair had grown long enough he tucked it behind his ears.

"Hey, I have an extra rubber band, you want me to tie your hair back in a ponytail?" Cat offered. She picked up the end of her own pony tail and waved it at him.

"No thanks. I don't do girl stuff." He leaned over one side of his horse and studied the ground they passed.

"That's good. I see you don't do earrings or bracelets or necklaces and things like that, but I do see a tattoo on your forearm. Doesn't seem like you're the punky kind of guy that gets tats all over his body."

A corner of his lip pulled in. "No." He kept his eyes on the ground. "I'm not really into body art and the sort, but," he smiled sheepishly, "when I was in the service we guys went on the town on leave and got a little carried away, you know...."

"I know, guy bonding. You got smashed and turned maudlin then someone brought up how if you all got branded you'd be sort of hero brothers bound together forever. You wanted a tangible memory of what you went through together."

His head swung over to her, admiration in his expression. "Yeah, just like that, you got it. Boy, you're good." He turned his attention back down at the ground.

"I have brothers. What are you looking for?" she asked.

Holding the reins loosely in one hand on his thigh, he replied, "It's strange. Someone has been out here. There's grass beaten down in a path. Looks like a 4 wheeler. I can't believe anyone would be crazy enough to come out here, the weather only just broke a short time ago."

She shrugged. "So, someone had cabin fever. Had to get out."

"No." He shook his head, black hair sweeping across his shoulders. "This is hard land to go over. You'll see in a minute. According to the records, there was some minor mining on this side of the mountains around a hundred years ago or so but the opening was dynamited closed a long time ago causing a tremendous rock fall. No one goes this way anymore, it's too rough for average hikers.

"Even someone wanting to see the cairn would wait for the extreme weather to subside. There's danger of mudslides or avalanches, not counting the bogs here and there and the rocky terrain. It looks all fields and soft rolling green hills, but in this area it can be treacherous. You saw the posted warning signs when we left the tarred road and hit the dirt road. No, no one would come out here unless they had a specific reason."

Cat was silent, thinking. "But wait, we know Officer Justin came out here. He's the reason we know there's something strange about the cairn. Maybe it was him?"

"No." Michael shook his head again. "He only came out that one time and that was before the storm. This path has been driven over frequently. Look at the vibrant new green growth of grass, it's smashed down and that could have only been in the last couple of days. Let's go." He spurred his horse. Crionna followed at Rossie's heels.

About a half mile from the cairn, Michael stopped his horse and dismounted. Turning to Cat he held out a hand. "We need to walk from here."

Acquiescing, she drew one leg over her horse and slid down Crionna's side, into Michael's arms. He caught her around the waist then, slowly, gently, let her slide like silk down his rough body, both feeling every soft curve and hard muscle, belt buckles catching briefly then to the ground.

Enfolded loosely in his arms, she turned to face him. His hands stayed wrapped around her martini glass waist like he was holding a fragile flower with steel fingers. Stroking small circles on her back with his thumbs soon turned to bolder caresses.

They both seemed unaware that he was imperceptibly pulling her closer to him, until their bodies pressed together.

The horses snorted, tails swished, they moved a few yards away to munch the new baby grass. The couple didn't notice the horses drifting away.

Caught in the moment, Cat's heart shaped face turned up, the scorching heat of the morning had finally settled into a balmy breeze, tossing wispy strands of sun-kissed hair between them, tenderly tickling their faces.

His lacquered eyes captured hers like a pirate boarding a ship. Velvet orbs turning turbulent reflected a heated glow of arousal.

****

"Now then," the creepy voice crackled from the monitor. The ghastly grin leached such evil, the foul freak was every child's nightmare. He had the children's rapt attention, their feet glued to the floor they were so frozen with terror.

The grin broadened. "All right, my young friends. I want you to listen v e r y c a r e f u l l y. Are you listening?" Silence. "I said, ARE YOU LISTENING!" he thundered, brows slashed, spittle splattered the screen. The children jumped.

"Yes sir!" They responded in a unison cry.

The man smiled. "That's better. Now, after our earlier discussion, I gave your words some great thought. A slight change to the legend, maybe. A little twist that if it works out for you my little pets, everyone will know about it. But," leering, the pointed mouth widened, the nose lengthened sliding over his top lip.

"But if you don't win, you don't survive, and truth be told, you ain't gonna anyway, not a one of you. But, I digress, if you survive, then the world will learn of the twist and the legend will change. Maybe."

He waited for a response. Hearing none, the greenish face glowed with self-satisfaction. The children were riveted to the monitor. Preening from the children's fear and gripped attention, he continued. "Anyway, let me proceed with what you can do to save yourselves, well, at least some, or most of you to survive."

The children dared to shoot each other curious glances. *Only some*?

"As you can see, you are imprisoned in a stone cage. Really, there's no way out except up the chute which through your childish efforts you discovered you can't get back up it. So, this is all really ridiculous to even discuss, but, I promised," he sighed dramatically. His brows rose at the children's sudden fidgeting at his rambling.

"Fine, you kids are always so easily bored, or frightened. All right, this is what you need to do to survive." The grotesque face wavered closer to the monitor, eyes piercing through the milky screen stabbing each child in the heart.

"If you kids figure out how to get out of here, your rocky prison, I will let you go. I will not stop you or pursue you like little prey, although, I admit that would be fun. But, like I said, if you kids figure out how to get out of here, and maybe there is a way, a way I didn't share with you, and you haven't discovered, I will let you go free. Free to go home to your mamas and papas. But!"

Pointy mouth pulled back in a delighted grin, he pronounced, "There is one tiny catch."

Chapter Forty-One

Cat pulled from Michael's embrace. She needed to protect her heart. The man had too many secrets he didn't trust her with to share.

He hid his pained look quickly at her rejection but she saw it. She reached out to him, "Michael, I-"

He turned away. "I need to get the tools from the pack." Hands tucked in his jean's pockets he strode to the horses grazing in a fresh field of sprouting grass.

Cat's arm dropped to her side, she let out a slow breath watching the dejected man so handsome her heart quickened every time she saw him, walk away. Dejected, but with his back straight, black hair flowing in the breeze, again, the image of the ancient warrior of his ancestors.

Sighing, Cat knelt to one knee and plucked a daisy from the nest of lime blades. Standing in the unspoiled meadow waiting for Michael, she brushed the daisy across her cheek, it felt soft and tender, like Michael's breath on her lips.

Holding the daisy under her nose she breathed in the glorious smell of spring, her skin suddenly pricked, someone was behind her.

She turned, started to say, "Michael, I-" the daisy fell from her numb fingers, the sea eyes suddenly drained of color, goose bumps popped from shoulder to fingertip in heart strangling fear.

Surrounding Cat, three growling, wild dogs circled her. One snarled snapping huge sawing teeth at her. The others, their long vicious faces pulled back revealing teeth so sharp they could puncture a tire, eyed her like she was a real trapped cat they were relishing devouring. "M- M- M-" throat dry as a desert, Cat couldn't hack out a cry for help. Her hands instinctively covered the front of her neck.

"Don't move Cataleigh, I'm right here. Don't move," Michael's voice low, he crept slowly towards her from behind. The dogs growled, barked, teeth bared, each snapping at Cat as they circled her closer and closer.

Moving as slowly as possible to not attract attention, Michael slid his hand down his leg to get the small gun he usually kept strapped to his ankle.

He stifled a groan when his hand touched his bare ankle. He had left the gun in the cruiser's glove box. Cursing himself for leaving the pistol behind, and the shotguns were with the grazing horses.

He didn't dare call them to come, the dogs might attack the horses before he could get a gun off the saddle. Scanning the immediate area for a weapon he crept furtively closer to Cat.

One feral dog crouched, lowering his head snarling savagely preparing to leap at her, Cat screamed-

****

The screen cracked and rolled in waves over the face tinged green by the antique monitor. "I do love a good roiling game, don't you?" Nasty laughter broke through the screen, coating the stone room with guttural mirth.

Entrant tears drizzled down, nibbling through layers of dirt over their adolescent cheeks, the children held each other's hands so tightly their fingertips looked like they were dipped in white frosting.

Santiago opened his mouth to say something but his brother, Juan, nudged him ever so slightly with his elbow.

"Okay, here goes, this is the one and only rule," the man in the monitor said agreeably. "If you kids manage the unlikely event of escaping this granite cage the deal is… that you must leave one of you behind." He sat back immensely satisfied with his game.

The children that understood him gasped. The youngest ones, Simone and Teddy, Jamie and Tom-tom's expressions were confused.

"That's it. That's my catch. If you kids make it out of here and leave one child behind, doesn't matter to me who, I will allow you to run home free to your families." The triangular mouth, the lips pressed together drew back in a sly slash.

"So there you go. I'll leave you to draw straws or do whatever to decide who will be left behind. Remember," he leaned close to the monitor again, feral eyes gleaming. "If you choose to try to escape and don't leave someone behind, you will all fail. I will prevent you from leaving and you'll be fated to stay here forever. Ah, that is until I toss you off the cliff.

"Then you will *never* go home again. I promise you. So, the majority of you get to leave, or none of you at all. It's up to you. Anyway, gotta go, things to do! Ta ta for now my cursed disciples." Gales of inhuman laughter resounded around the room long after the image faded and the monitor turned off.

The air in the room was like lead, suffocating. Crushing fear anchored the miserable children standing motionless in silence. They struggled to draw a breath.

Juan dropped the hands he held, he stepped in front of the group. In despair, he looked at his friends, neighbors, school chums, his own little brother, kids he'd known his whole life.

Their small, tear-streaked dirty faces gazed back at him, hopeless, helpless, terrified. He could almost hear their bones clacking, teeth chattering they trembled so hard.

He drew a stammering shaky breath. "Well," he cleared his throat, the word had barely eked out. He started again, "Uh, we need to talk about what we're going to do."

"We're going to choose who to leave behind, that's what we're going to do," Santiago spouted.

"But, but who? How? How will we decide? I don't wanna stay here...please don't leave me!" Teddy wailed.

"Me neither! Don't leave me here!" Simone threw her arms around her friend, the girls sobbed together.

"Should we draw straws?" Jamie asked. "Where we gonna get straws? Maybe we can toss rocks, like, whoever gets the furthest rock from the wall or something like that."

Pil shook his head vehemently. "No way. I'm not throwing any rocks, unless it's at him," he pointed a rigid arm at Jessy. "This is his fault. We're here 'cause of him. He was the first taken, he did something to this monster guy, he's the one to stay!"

Matty plopped her hands on her hips and scowled at Pil, then the group. "It's no one's fault, Jessy didn't do anything. None of us did anything to deserve this." She reached for Jessy's hand and squeezed it tight. He shot her a thank you look, but he didn't really look reassured. His cherub face paled, shiny dark eyes dimmed.

"This- this- this is not a- a- witch hunt, I don't want to draw a straw, I don't want to leave Jessy behind. I-" Barty broke off, his skinny arms fell to his sides. Scared to make eye contact he stared at the floor.

Almond-shaped black eyes sparked, Jamie flared, "I say we leave the foster kid here. He's the only one that doesn't have real parents that'll- that'll cry for him, miss him..."

"I agree!" Tom-tom blurted. "Who else are we gonna leave? I want to see my mom and da, we should take a vote." He adjusted his round glasses leaving a pudgy thumbprint on one lens, he pushed them back up his red-tinged, native aquiline nose then wiped the tip of his nose with a finger.

"No." Simone shook her head. Sky blue eyes, shiny marbles of light in her tear riddled filthy face, the pink bow still clinging to her matted blonde hair. "I don't think we should leave anyone behind."

Teddy swiveled her own dirt streaked face to her friend, crossed her arms and nodded fiercely agreeing, "Yeah, no one."

"No, you heard the fiend, he said either one stays or none of us goes. I say we vote," Santiago grated.

His brother Juan, pulled his lips in, pulled off his baseball hat, studied the grimy cap in his hands, then said, "What if it's you, bro, or me? Then what?" He shoved the cap back on, the short hair stuck up through the hole in the fastener.

Santiago reddened, "It ain't gonna be me or you, it's gonna be him," he gestured again to Jessy. Jessy stood stoic.

Rocky sent his brother Drew a worried look. Drew shook his head. "Don't you worry little brother, I would never leave you behind." Rocky bowed his head, then raised his chin. "Me neither, Drew," he said solemnly, "I'm not going anywhere without you."

Drew winked at his brother then pulled out his crumpled pack of cigarettes. Feeling Matty's disapproving eyes on him he stuffed the pack back in his pocket. "I think we should find the way out first, then decide who stays and who goes."

The group stood in reflective silence contemplating his suggestion.

"But we've looked and looked and there's nothing, no way out," Pil whined.

The rest of the kids nodded, murmuring. They had looked and searched and scraped and banged the walls, floor, they had even dug as much as they could with the shovel trying to tunnel out. But, under a foot of dirt was solid rock. They were in an impenetrable room.

"Yeah," Rocky said derisively, "you guys even tossed me up that stupid chute."

Slowly, in the midst of the dissenting discussion, Jessy explored the room for the hundredth time with his eyes. Suddenly, those big dark eyes widened. He detached from the group and wandered over to the monitor.

Juan watched him. Curious, he stepped from the other kids. "What? What is it?" he asked. Before Jessy could answer, Juan strode over to join him. The other kids one by one grew quiet as they took in the two boys staring in heavy concentration at the monitor stuck in the wall.

Jessy moved closer, pointed to the monitor over five feet up in the wall. "We never checked that thing out." His forehead furrowed, finger across his mouth he studied the monitor. Dirt clung to his black curls from sleeping on the ground. Juan stood still behind him, his eyes glued to the screen.

The two boys then turned simultaneously to each other. "That's it!" they said in unison, cautiously, hopefully. They turned back and looked up at the monitor.

The rest of the kids ambled over, surrounding the boys in a semi-circle. "What?" Santiago asked, exasperated. "What do you see?" Rocky chimed in, "Yeah, whattya see? There ain't nothing there but that stupid TV."

Jessy gestured to the monitor. "It's stuck in there somehow. There's got to be cables or something attached to it because we're surrounded by rock that a satellite can't get through."

Juan nodded. "Yeah. And if it runs on a battery, well, that would be nuts, but it would have run down in the time we've been here, so that leaves only-"

"There has to be something behind it," Jessy said, "like a generator maybe. Or a connection to one somewhere."

"That's ridicu-" Tom-tom sputtered.

Drew cut in, "No wait, it could be, there could be a hole or something behind it."

"We need a tool, something to pry it out," Matty couldn't keep the excitement out of her voice. They all quickly scanned their prison for something strong enough to get a metal box out of a wall.

"Geez, I know!" Teddy gleefully announced, running over to the screened curtain that contained their make-shift bathroom, braids flapping behind her. She emerged from behind the screen triumphantly dragging the shovel. The shovel was almost as tall as the little cinnamon girl.

"Great thinking!" Juan darted over and took the heavy shovel from the tiny girl. He ran back to Jessy. "Ready?" he asked the foster boy. Jessy nodded and gave the older boy a thumbs up. Juan clamped his cap down tighter on his head and rubbed his palms together.

"Here goes." He lifted the shovel over his head and jammed the steel end of the shovel between the embedded monitor and the inch of space between it and the rock wall. Dirt and splinters of chipped rock sprayed out. The children stood holding their breaths, their hands clutched as if in prayer in front of their chests.

Wedging the shovel in, Juan jerked it back and forth trying to get it in as deep as possible. Jamie stuck his fingers in his ears to block out the grinding sound of steel against the metal box and the wall.

While moving the shovel, Juan said, "It feels like there's a lot of space behind this thing." Grunting with each motion he continued pushing and prying, but the monitor seemed not to move at all.

After a while, Drew stepped up and said, "Here, you're getting tired, let me have a whack at it." Juan let go of the shovel that was wedged hard between the monitor and the rock. He pulled his shirt up and used it to wipe the grimy sweat from his forehead; his chest rose and fell in rapid breaths.

Drew spat on his palms and smoothed the sides of his hair. Dropping his jacket to the ground, he rolled his shoulders in the black and white striped shirt then took over the shovel.

After a strenuous struggle pulling and pushing, levering the shovel back and forth, the monitor finally moved, but barely a hair's breadth. Drew let the shovel swing down to the floor, he leaned on it breathing heavy, needing a break.

Juan moved next to him and reached up to hold onto the rim of the ledge and jumped up and down to be able to see over the edge.

He exclaimed, "Hey, I think I see light, I swear to God I think I see light behind the dammed thing!" The kids stirred, feeling his enthusiasm but scared to be hopeful. Santiago came up, his hands held out. "Let me give it a try, then, Juan can give it a go again after me."

Simone and Teddy held hands, occasionally wiping away a fretful tear. Tom-tom whispered to Pil, "I don't see it moving. I don't see it moving at all." His words came out with a little whistle through his missing tooth. His glasses had fingerprints all over the lenses it was amazing he could see anything at all.

"Yeah," Pil agreed, nodding. He rubbed the side of his face. "It's a waste of time. Quit spitting on me Tom."

Matty smiled at the boys. "We need to keep the faith alive that we will get out of here. Right, Jess?" She came alongside the curly-haired boy. Jessy returned her smile. His cherubic face alight with a luminous glow, rosy cheeks, eyes glistening. "Yes, we have to have hope. We won't give up, we won't!"

Rocky, Tom-tom and Jamie, crossed their arms, with pessimistic expressions they silently watched the three oldest boys struggle with the shovel.

Barty, his hands clinched behind his back, dug a toe in the dirt, twisting it around. He asked shyly, "Juan, can I help? Can I try?"

Juan smiled kindly at the skinny child with the teardrop shaped eyes and patted him on the shoulder.

"You're a bit too short sport, to reach the shovel. But," he said quickly seeing the boy's fallen face, "when we get that thing out, and we will," he shot the other three boys a frown when they started muttering negatively, "you guys can help after we get it out."

Barty nodded emphatically, reassured he was not just a boney bump on a log.

"Okay guys, let me go again." Juan trotted back to the wall with his arms up to take over the task.

Just as the kids started growing restless, Juan whooped, "I got it! I got it loose! Help me Santy- Drew!" He kept jiggling the shovel, the monitor was indeed sliding back and forth now. Santiago and Drew rushed over, and standing on the balls of their feet they stretched up to get a hold of the opposite side that Juan was working on.

"Watch your fingers, Drew!" Santiago yelled, pulling his own hands back quickly as the monitor swiveled enough to come close to smashing his own fingers.

"Okay guys, I'm gonna pull with the shovel one last time and at the same time you guys pull, we can gouge this baby right out of there." Juan briefly let go of the shovel and wiped his sleeve across his forehead and his mouth.

He said, "You little kids need to step back. Get out of the way. That machine is gonna come down fast and hit the ground. Why don't you guys go over by the bathroom?"

Juan waited while the younger children scooted out of the way. He reached up and grasped the end of the shovel, took a deep breath and said, "All right bros, on the count of 3, ready?"

Drew and Santiago rubbed their palms on their pants to dry them, tongues sticking out the corners of their mouths in concentration, they nodded, "Ready."

"Here we go, one, two-" grunting, Juan pried the box a little closer to the edge, "three!" The three boys pulled at the same time, the monitor moved over the edge of the wall.

"Pull hard!" Juan shouted. "Now!" They pulled the box, it was heavy, scraping across the rock it finally tottered over the edge- "Look out! Get out of the way!" Juan yelled after one more mighty pull.

The three boys covered their heads and jumped back as the monitor toppled over the edge and waited for a big crash. But, there was only a couple of metal bangs and scraping and the shovel clanging on the ground.

The boys peeked out from the protection of their arms.

"Oh bloody hell," Drew groaned.

Chapter Forty-Two

With a warrior's roar, Michael raced over and dove in front of Cat slamming into the dog attacking her, knocking the surprised canine off its feet.

It immediately jumped back up but backed off snarling and yapping at Michael.

The two other dogs circled them growling and snapping and barking, saliva dripping over big teeth splattering wet spots on the ground. Michael stood in front of Cat with his arms up and out and his legs shoulder's width apart ready to spring into action. Then the dog made to lunge at Cat again.

Keeping Cat behind him Michael held his arm bent to block the dog, the dog backed off but one of the other dogs tried to attack from the side. Michael held his arms straight out to the sides and with his back an inch from Cat, he circled around her to face each canine as it charged.

The vicious dogs were trying to get at Cat as the smaller one, they knew they could easily take her down.

Michael suddenly reached out and tried to grab one of the hounds. "Michael!" Cat screamed. "What are you doing? Stop, they'll bite you!"

Ignoring her, he jostled back and forth trying to catch one of the dogs. The dogs barked and snarled and snapped at him, taking turns crouching then springing at him. He caught one of the mongrels around the neck but it shook out of his clutch.

Cat kept screaming, "Michael, stop it! What are you doing?"

He jumped with one foot forward to snatch the closest dog, it leaned back out of his reach. "I'm trying to get one and hurl it at the others," he panted, "it might run them off." Taking a swipe at another canine that crept closer, he tried to stay clear of the bared razor teeth that fought to seize Cat's neck and rip and maul it until it slaughtered the life out of her.

His efforts to catch one of the dogs caused them to back off a little, giving him a moment to look around. His eyes darted from the ground to the dogs to the ground.

In one fluid motion Michael crouched, snatched up some rocks in both hands then jumped back up as one of the dogs took that opportunity to pounce. He kicked out at the dog connecting with a shattering blow to the side of his head with his boot. He hit it so hard the dog yelped falling on its side but rolled in a flash and jumped back to his feet.

Michael kicked him again, jabbing him in his neck. The dog stumbled sideways, yelped, then ran off. The other two dogs struck-lashing out at the couple. Michael pivoted and hurled a rock at one of the dogs bashing him in the nose. The dog howled then ran away.

While Michael threw rocks at the fleeing canine to make sure he was really leaving, the last dog tried again to get at Cat.

The wild dog vaulted three feet in the air aiming for her neck- she screamed- Michael spun and his fist shot out punching the dog square in the head stopping him dead in midair. The dog dropped like a bag of cement.

The animal lay inert for seconds, then he staggered to his feet, shook his head and limped a few feet away.

Michael ran at the dog with his hand raised clutching a rock, the dog whimpered then weakly tripped away looking back only once before he disappeared behind the side of the mountain.

"Michael!" Cat rushed over and threw her arms around him. He wrapped his arms around her, holding her head to his chest, ran a shaky hand through her thick locks. She sobbed against his shirt.

Michael soothed, "It's okay baby, you're okay, we're okay." He patted her hair, resting his head tenderly against hers he held her until she stopped crying. Finally, gulping a breath she leaned back. He smiled down at her.

"Your eyes are all sparkly from your tears." His voice husky, he murmured, "Reminds me of the sea first thing in the morning with the sun shimmering off the mellow ripples. Here," he pulled his shirt out of his pants and held the bottom to her. "Dry your eyes, Cataleigh, we've got work to do."

Cat accepted the shirt and dabbed at her eyes. Holding the shirt against her eyes she breathed in the masculine scent, all natural, no cologne, just strength and grit.

Once composed, she stepped away, straightened her own shirt, shook out her long wavy hair then used her fingers to comb it. "What was with the dogs? There are no dangerous wild animals here except for badgers and foxes, small mammals."

He agreed, "There's never been a complaint of wild dogs that I know of. I think it was perpetrated by, whatever or whoever is responsible for taking the children. I think they were brought here deliberately to attack anyone that got too close. That means we're on the right track.

"So, let's go. I'm not going to tie up the horses I don't want them to be trapped if those dogs come back. Even if the dogs come back and chase after the horses, Rossie won't go far from me and Crionna won't leave Rossie so they will stay within hearing distance. I'll get the backpacks, let's get to the cairn."

****

The monitor had left its enclosed case but was hanging just over the edge of the wall held fast by cables.

"Oh crap, it's still blocking the hole. What the fuck are we gonna do now?" Rocky griped. The kids stared gloomily at the monitor, now free from its encasement but hanging by attached cords.

"Rocky, *please*," Matty implored. Her face was so dirty her freckles were barely visible. Her red bangs had grown past her eyelids and fluttered when she blinked. This morning she braided her long red hair into two flat plaits so they were dirty but neat.

Rocky sniffed, a sheepish urchin. "Sorry," he muttered.

Matty draped an arm around the square boy and hugged him. "T's okay, Rock. We're all scared," she grinned her chicklet front teeth at him, forgiving him his foul mouth.

"Doesn't matter." Juan tugged on the cables attached to the monitor. "Actually we can use it as a kind of ladder, it'll help us climb up the wall. I'm the only one that's tall enough to be able to reach the top of the wall anyway. We can use the boost."

"Look out!" Barty yelled. The monitor snapped off from one of its three cables, it dropped, swung, banging against the wall a few times before stopping, it now hung at an angle.

Juan jumped back so if it fell, the box wouldn't crush his feet. "Ow-" he winced as his elbow banged into the wall. Rubbing his arm, he moved back further when the second cable broke free, the metal box scraped the wall as it swung.

Now the monitor hung from only one thin stretched cable causing the box to swing a couple of feet from the ground.

"I don't know about standing on that thing, if that last cable breaks one of us could fall and get really hurt," Drew said.

Santiago spoke up, "I can fix that. Stand back." He picked up the shovel and jabbed it at the glass screen. The glass broke spewing shards everywhere.

The children stood in consternation waiting to see what he planned. Santiago picked up a big piece of glass, wrapped the bottom of his shirt around his hand then went to the monitor and sawed at the remaining cable covering then used the shovel to cut the wire inside.

It took a few minutes for him to cut through. He hopped back as the metal box crashed to the ground.

"Yeah bro! Let's go!" Juan waved the others over. He pushed the monitor against the wall and stepped on top of it. He placed his palms on the edge of the wall in the hole that the monitor left ready to get up in it. "A little help guys," he called out grinning.

"This is where all those kip-ups and pull-ups you've done for so long will finally pay off!" Santiago teased his brother, then he and Drew linked their hands making a stirrup for Juan to boost him up.

They pushed him up until he pulled with his arms and jumped from their hands, he was able to get his waist over the edge. Clawing and scrambling with his feet, he managed to get up the wall and rolled into the hole.

The kids stood still waiting for him to reappear.

After several minutes, Drew impatiently called out, "Falcon! Tell us what's going on! Is there a way out?"

Santiago cupped his hands around his mouth and yelled, "Juan, bro, are you okay?" He climbed up on the broken monitor grabbed the edge of the wall, stood on his toes and tried to peer into the hole. "Hey Juan! Where the hell are you?"

Jamie giggled nervously. "This," he said, "is where one person disappears and   another goes to look for him and then another goes to look for that one until everyone disappears and you find out some killer has-"

"Geez James, shut the heck up! What's the matter with you," Santiago scolded the small-boned delicate Asian boy.

Jamie held a hand over his mouth. Then said, "I- I'm sorry Santy, I didn't mean to scare everyone, I was just trying to take our minds off of-"

"Hey!" Juan's head poked out the hole. His gleeful grin told them there was good news. He crawled to the edge of the hole and smiled widely down at them.

"It looks really good, dudes and dudettes! It's not just some cables strung through a tiny hole and the monitor just crammed into a small space carved out just for it, the wires disappear into the rocks, but, there's a big old tunnel up there.

"At first I had to crawl on my hands and knees for like a few yards, then I was able to crouch then finally I could walk straight up. It goes for a ways. It's dark but there's a dim kind of light. Let's go, I think it's a way out. Who's first?"

Drew said, "I think me and Santy should help the littler ones up first, we can hike 'em up then you can pull them up."

"Yeah, that's a good idea. Barty, you go first bro, I can use your help up here." Wanting the boy to feel worthy, Juan motioned for the spindly lad to come forward.

Barty's head jerked when he realized they wanted him to go up in that big dark maybe never ending hole. Biting his lip, he gulped hard. *Be brave*, he told himself, show the young girls there's nothing to be afraid of. He hurried over to Drew and Santiago.

The two older boys cupped their hands together. Barty stepped one foot on their linked hands and they pushed him up to where Juan could reach his hands.

Juan grabbed Barty's bony wrists and hauled him fast up the wall over the edge into the hole where he landed on his stomach.

Barty sat up and surveyed his new surroundings. It was even narrower and smaller than he had thought. He swallowed the claustrophobic feeling climbing up his throat, his belly churned. He would pretend he was safe in his closet where he hid in the dark when his mum and da were fighting.

Juan smiled knowingly at him. "It's okay kid. It gets bigger back there. The miners must have dug this small arm of a tunnel. Let's get the others. Help me, all right?"

Barty's lopsided grin showed he knew the boy was trying to be considerate, and he sure wasn't going to show the older boy he practically wet his pants on the way up the wall. "Yeah," Barty replied. The boys crawled to the edge.

"Next!" Juan called down.

Santiago and Drew helped each of the kids up the wall. First the girls then Jamie, Jessy, Rocky, and Tom-tom who cried all the way up the wall fogging up his glasses, it was like pushing a squirming bean bag chair. Santiago and Drew stood with their hands on their hips perusing the bulky Pil.

"What?" Pil asked. "I'm ready, let's go."

"Yeah, good luck getting that ol' heifer up here!" Jamie scoffed.

"Shut up you saucebox," Pil yelled at Jamie. "You wait 'til I get up there, I'll knock your block off-"

Santiago and Drew looked at each other, sighed heavily then linked their hands. Drew said, "Come on, Pil, let's hit it." Pil stepped on their hands, the boys grunted as they tried to shove the husky kid up the wall, "Grab him, Juan, a little help here!" Drew yelled.

Juan hung over the edge of the wall grasped one of Pil's thick wrists and Barty grabbed the other.

Santy and Drew shoved Pil's butt, the four boys pushed and pulled and groaned, Pil scrabbled at the wall with his shoes trying to dig a toe in. Finally, after pulverizing his hammy knees, Pil finally flopped on his stomach inside the hole.

"Whew," Juan, huffed. Sitting back on his heels, he pulled his cap off, wiped his forehead then shoved the hat back on. Back on his knees he leaned over the edge. "Drew, you're the next tallest after me so Santy, you go first."

They got Santiago up. "Okay," Juan instructed Santiago, you hold my legs while me and Barty pull Drew up."

It was a struggle, but finally all of the kids were up in the hole. "All right then," Juan said cheerfully, "follow me. Everyone stay close to the person in front of you. Not that you have room to wander but I think down a ways it'll really widen and there might be other branches to the tunnel. We don't want to lose anyone. Let's hit it."

On their hands and knees the children crawled in a raggedy line over the dirty rocky ground into the dark unknown.

Chapter Forty-Three

"There's the cairn, see it over there?" Michael pointed at the tower, cradled in a crevasse like a rocky fist in an outcropping foot of the mountain.

Cat draped a hand over her eyes to shade the sun. Nodding. "I see it. It's like a tall pile of rocks."

"Yeah." Michael chuckled. "A big pile of rocks. Come on." They headed across the last part of the field. When they reached the cairn, Michael slipped the backpack off his shoulder he'd untied from his horse and let it drop to the ground. Cat followed suit. After she dropped her pack she rubbed her lower back.

"You doin' all right? Do you need to take a break?" Michael asked her.

She pushed a lock of hair off her sweaty face and shook her head. "I'm fine. Let's find those kids, we can rest after we find them." She strode over to the cairn.

Stopping in front of the tower of rocks, she set her hands on her hips, studying it with interest. Michael pulled an ax out of his pack and a fold-up shovel and joined her.

A shade of uncertainty in her soft voice, Cat said, "You think there's a way in? It looks pretty solid to me."

"Yup. I think this cairn is the key to finding the children. Every house, building, shed, deserted building, the woods have all been searched thoroughly. There's nowhere else someone could have hidden those kids. We even considered a boat, but a boat wouldn't have withstood the storm and the creep that took them would certainly be smart enough to know that. That leaves the mountain.

"Since the only entrance was dynamited closed years and years ago it never dawned on us that the children could have been secreted inside. But it makes sense. I think the cairn is the door in, or *a* door in. We just need to get it open." He walked slowly around three quarters of the cairn, the back of it bunched right up against the foot of the mountain.

He touched the rocks, feeling up and down and around. He pushed and pulled and tapped, then stood back. "It's been cemented together. Someone did that for a reason because the whole point to a cairn is that people add a stone to it as they pass by, so it should be loose. But it isn't."

"Maybe it has like a spring, you know, a stone we can push or lift up or something and a door will open," Cat suggested.

Michael shrugged one shoulder. "Like in the movies? Like a pyramid or something?"

"Yeah."

"Well, I just tried, but let's really work at it." Michael started pulling and prodding the rocks. He worked the top part of the cairn, and Cat bent over and worked the bottom.

After over an hour of trying to find a lever or something, they stopped. Cat sat down on the ground exhausted. Michael flopped down next to her. Cat said, "Maybe we should try 'open sesame.' " Wearily she crossed her legs resting her elbows on her knees, her chin propped in her hands.

"Why not?" Michael leaned over and dragged her pack over. "We've tried everything else." Opening it, he pulled out the sandwiches and a bottle of water. He handed a sandwich and a bottle to Cat. Drained from the travel there and working at the cairn, they ate and drank in silence.

Chewing his last bite of sandwich, Michael turned to Cat and said, "Hey, as we were leaving the house you said I was wrong about it being one of the L's that took the kids. I realize now that makes no sense anyway, the first few kids were taken before the RMP's were even sent here. You said you knew it was someone else. Who is it?"

Cat pushed in the last of her sandwich and held up a hand while she chewed. Swallowing, she twisted the top off her bottle and drank a third of it down, put the cap back on and set the water down. She wiped her mouth with a napkin then took the napkin and balled it up with the sandwich wrapper, took Michael's too and stuffed them in her pack. Standing up she brushed off her jeans.

She explained, "Like I said, I had figured out all of the children's names were variations of the Apostles,' which seemed like a deliberate attempt to choose kids with the Apostles' names but altered to avoid detection of a pattern. I mean, if we saw a list of the children's names in the Apostle form we would have been suspicious right off the bat if there were no Carols or Roberts etc.

"So I thought maybe the perpetrator had disguised his name. I thought he would have a…a, oh I don't know, I thought with all the secrecy and sneakiness he might have disguised his true name with an anagram just to be wacky clever, showing off, creating a puzzle. Hiding in plain sight as it were.

"My brothers and I used to compete as kids to see who could figure out the daily Jumble in the paper. You know, where they print a word with the letters all mixed up and you have to figure out what the words are then you guess the cute little phrase."

A corner of Michael's lip pulled in. "I wasn't too good at word puzzles. My brothers and I were more into wrestling and playing ball and stuff. Anyway, what'd you figure out?"

"Well, after sifting through hundreds of names, starting with the kids and their families, and the police closest to the investigation and us, I eventually hit on a name that was, well I felt it had meaning."

"Keep talking," Michael said as he got up and started hitting the cairn with his ax. He decided to try to cut the cairn off the mountain. He struck and struck and struck.

He managed to finally chip away enough rocks so there was a space between the cairn and the mountain. Frowning, he studied the back of the cairn and the mountain. He set the ax on the ground and leaned on the handle.

"What is it?" Cat asked.

"I can't believe it, there's no opening. I thought for sure the cairn was a door into the mountain. I- don't know what to do next..." He sounded deflated, hopeless for the first time.

He turned a sad face to Cat. "We need to do some more brainstorming. You haven't said yet who you think the kidnapper is, maybe that'll help me figure something else out. I can call some officers and have them go look for him maybe we'll get lucky. So, who is it?"

"It's-" Cat stopped mid word. Her face scrunched up, she scratched her head squinting at the pile of rocks. "What did you say the name of this cairn is?"

Frustrated, Michael swung the ax and struck the rocky tower. "Faoi Cairn." He struck the tower again. Only bits of rocks broke off. There was nothing inside the cairn, only more rocks under the rocks he was breaking.

"What does Faoi mean again?" she asked.

"It means 'under.'"

They stared at each other then their eyes shot to the bottom of the cairn.

Chapter Forty-Four

"How we doing?" Juan called out. The oldest at almost 13 he was the appointed leader. T

he kids had been pretty quiet while snaking their way through the tunnel. They weren't sure if there was anyone else around to hear them. There could be monsters lurking around corners, in the dark.

After yards of crouching, they were now able to stand up straight. Feet shuffling and scraping the dirt, labored breathing, small rocks and pebbles kicked, rolling and bouncing along the dirty rocky trail and a quiet word occasionally warning of a turn in the tunnel or a jutting rock or hole to avoid, they were otherwise silent. They rested every half hour or so.

Hushed fragmented mumbles traveled through the tunnel. No complaining, too scared to talked, they just wanted to get out and go home.

Trepidatious anxiety kept adrenaline pumping, giving them the energy to continue moving forward. After what seemed like hours, they made their way into a larger area.

Visibility was murky but they could make out their surroundings. A faint light had been guiding them. The further they went the brighter it became. But it was still very, very faint, like a pinch of quarter moon beaming through.

Juan stopped. The kids came up next to him one at a time as they entered the cavern.

"Why are we stopping? We just took a break a few minutes ago?" Drew questioned. He tried to follow Juan's line of sight to see what made him stop.

"It's another wall. This one's higher," Juan answered him, sounding thoughtful.

"Another wall? So what, we got over the other one with no problem," Pil remarked, rubbing his belly. "I'm hungry."

"We're all hungry, Pil, there's nothing we can do about it. You have plenty to live off anyway," Jamie snickered.

"Shut up you scrawny runt. I don't eat rice and sushi crap like you, I eat manly food. That's why I'm husky and big-boned, not a pansy like you." Pil faced off against the smaller Asian boy.

"Husky? Ha!" Jamie chortled. "You're plain fat." He backed up when Pil raised a fist and started towards him.

"Fat?" Pil threatened. "You'll take that back when I shove my big muscled arm down your scaggy throat you little shrimp-" He swung at Jamie but Jamie ducked behind Drew.

"Maybe we shoulda stayed where we were," Tom-tom whined. His filthy white shirt hung out of his belt wrinkled and torn from the climb up the wall. "At least the freak fed us and we had toilet paper... maybe we should go back."

"You go back, stupid. We're getting out," Jamie said from behind Drew's back. The boys started bickering.

"Okay everybody shut up, none of us is going back. We're staying together," Juan told them.

Jessy added, "Forward, we need to keep going forward. There's light somewhere so we can't be just going deeper and deeper."

"An- and no name calling, that's mean," Barty whispered.

The older boys hustled over to the wall to look for a way over or around it. Saying, "The wall melds right into both sides of the tunnel," Santiago followed the wall from end to end pushing at it here and there. "There's no way but over."

"We- we, can we go back?" Teddy asked with a whimper. There was absolute silence. All eyes turned to Juan.

Santiago shook his head. "No. We were trapped in that room, that asshole creep could gas us or whatever and we would be screwed. There were no other tunnels except for this one."

"Yeah but," Drew interjected, "we don't know what's on the other side of that wall. That freak could be over there just waiting for us. Who knows if he's alone either, we haven't seen the rest of his skanky family that helped lure us here in the first place."

"No." Juan crossed his arms over his torn sweatshirt. Perspiration gleamed across his forehead and over his upper lip. The sides of his short hair were damp.

Almost a teenager he was the oldest, he needed to keep up a strong front so the younger ones wouldn't see that he was scared out of his mind, and run off in a panic back through the tunnel to the cage they had escaped from. That would surely be a fatal mistake.

He said, "This is the only way."

Santiago shrugged. "Fine, Falcon, let's give it a go. How're we gonna get over?"

Juan turned and scrutinized the wall. "There's only one way, the same way we got over the other one. It'll just be harder. Who's first?"

"Let's do like we did the first one; Barty, the girls, then Jamie, Tom, Rocky, Pil, Santy and so on," Drew said.

"Swift on then," Juan ordered the group. He and Santiago and Drew moved to the wall and looked up, way up.

"Sure is high," apprehension lay heavy in Drew's voice. The other two nodded in agreement.

Reaching into a pocket in his rumpled jacket, Drew pulled out his pack of cigarettes and tapped one out. He tucked the cigarette over his ear and shoved the pack back in his pocket. Then he bent over and he and Santiago linked their hands into a stirrup.

Juan put a foot in their hands, hesitated then called over his shoulder to Jessy, "Hey kid, pray for there to be freedom on the other side of the wall."

Unable to speak past the lump in his throat, Jessy nodded wordlessly. He'd been praying nonstop anyway, it has always been his way to pray unceasing.

"Santy," with an apologetic gesture to Barty, Juan said, "you're going to have to be next, Barty's arms are too short."

At Santy's nod, Juan's voice heavily serious, he said, "On the count of three, guys, you're going to have to really push, pretty much throw me up the wall, you ready?" He looked at Drew then Santiago.

"Love you bro," Santiago blinked back tears. Then the boys chanted, "One, two, three!" They threw Juan up as hard as they could. Juan was able to grab onto the rim of the wall, and scrambling his feet frantically against the rocks, he was finally able to climb over the top.

After taking a big breath to calm his racing heart, he leaned over the edge. "All right, just come up, I'm not gonna check the place out, it's the only way we have, it's gotta be good." He hung over the wall as far as he could to grab the kids on their way up.

Santiago went up next so he could hang over the wall to help pull up the kids. It was much harder and more exhausting than going over the first wall, but after some time everyone was up except for Drew, Rocky and Jessy.

The children up on the wall lay on their stomachs to watch from the top of the wall.

Santiago called down, "Come on Drew, toss Rocky up then Jessy can get on all fours and you can use his back as a step up."

Everyone took in his words complacently then they realized what he was saying.

Matty cried out, "No! No! You're going to leave Jessy there! No! Juan, please-" she clutched at Juan's torn sweatshirt. "Tell them Juan, tell them they can't leave Jessy there, tell them!" Juan didn't say anything.

Pil said, "Someone has to stay, Mat, there's no way to get everyone up, and besides, you know what the guy said, we have to leave someone behind."

"No!" Matty screamed, climbing up on her knees and looked over the edge. "No Drew, don't leave him!" Simone crawled next to her and joined her in her pleas, "No Drew, don't leave him behind, please!" The other kids cried but said nothing.

Drew said to Rocky, "Okay champ, let's go." He leaned over with his hands linked for Rocky to step onto. Rocky looked at Jessy.

White as a sheet, his lip quivering, Jessy nodded, "Go Rocky. It's fine. I'll be uh, I'll be just fine, don't worry." He glanced up at the kids hanging their heads over the wall.

"Really, everyone, Matty," he smiled weakly, "I'll be fine. God will watch over me, I promise. Go on," he said to Drew and Rocky then stepped back.

"No! No Jessy! We're not leaving you!" Matty screamed, tears flooded her eyes then cascaded down her cheeks.

Rocky put a foot into Drew's hands. Drew said, "Okay kid, ready? On the count of three, I'll toss you as hard as I can and Juan and Santy will catch you and pull you up. A little square ball like you should shoot up like a rocket, easy. All right, one, two-"

"No." Rocky pulled his foot from his brother's hands.

Confused, Drew's brown brows rose in question. He smiled, coaxing, "It'll be easy Rocky, don't be afraid, I'll be right up after you, bro. Come on," he reached a hand out to pull Rocky back to the wall.

But Rocky stepped back further to stand next to Jessy and emphatically shook his head. "No. We're not leaving Jess behind."

Drew's patrician features darkened, he frowned at his little brother. He pushed the sleeves of his tattered jacket up to reveal bruises from throwing kids up and climbing the other wall.

"Well, you are not staying, and I am not staying and someone needs to get us up the wall, so," he reached for Rocky again but Rocky moved away.

"No Drew. We all go or we all stay. That's it." He crossed his arms, mouth a drawn line in his square filthy face. Brown hair spilled over his eyes so dirty he blended into the dark cave. He swung an arm around Jessy's shoulder. Jessy held his breath.

"Yeah, he's right, we can't leave anyone behind," Juan said wearily from the top of the wall.

Matty let out a loud laborious sigh, patted Juan's shoulder and smiled at him through a veil of tears, her blue eyes swimming. "Thank you, Falcon."

Juan patted her hand on his shoulder. "Don't worry, Mat. As we brought each of you up I was brainstorming what to do to get all of us up. We're just going to have to go for it."

Leaning over the edge, Juan said, "Drew, in school, you were always the best runner and jumper."

Drew looked up at him perplexed, nodded.

Juan told him, "Throw Rocky and Jessy up, then, move back, then run as fast as you can and try to literally run up the wall. I'm gonna hold Santy over the edge and Santy's gonna try to grab your hands and we'll- we'll pull you up. What do you say?"

Pondering this, Drew bit the inside of his cheek then shrugged one shoulder. "I'm game. I didn't want to leave the kid here either." Taking a deep breath he scratched both sides of his head then smoothed the hair off his forehead. He turned to Rocky and Jessy. "So, Rocky and me will link our hands and toss you up, Jessy, then I'll toss up Rocky, then, I go."

Jessy hugged Rocky, said tearfully, "Thanks, Rocky, thank you."

"Yeah." Rocky pressed the heels of his hands into his eyes to stop his tears. Drew got Jessy then Rocky up the wall.

Juan leaned over to see him. "Okay buddy, rest for a second, get your strength up, say a prayer, then just go. Whatever happens, we're not leaving without you, count on that." He waited while Drew leaned his back against the wall for a second to prepare.

After several deep breaths, Drew wiped his sweaty palms on his dirty pants, started to pull his jacket off then decided to leave it on, zipping it up over his striped shirt.

Combing his hair back with his fingers, the cigarette still lodged over his ear, he grinned feebly at the faces of the frightened kids peering over the edge of the wall down at him. Pulling his bottom lip in, he snapped his head once, "I'm ready."

"Santy," Juan said to his brother, "you hold my legs and I'll lean over as far as I can. Pil and Jessy, you guys have the longest arms and are probably the strongest. I want you guys on either side of me, hang over the edge and try to grab him when he comes up. You other kids, well, just grab onto anyone of us that's moving and hold onto us for dear life."

He looked around at each of them and asked, "Everyone ready?" A trill of frightened, "Ready," murmured all around and behind him. Juan crawled on his belly to the edge of the wall, then hung over as far as he could.

Santiago took hold of Juan's legs, he could feel other small hands clutching at his pants and shirt to anchor him.

"Wow," Jamie uttered, "this is kind like when that guy reached into that hole at the festival last fall and rescued little Stormie Dodge after Champ Clyde fell in trying to save her. Remember?"

"Yeah, hey, you guys remember who that guy that rescued Stormie was?" Pil laughed ironically when he heard the gasps of remembrance from the other kids.

"Oh my gosh, I remember!" Barty said.

"Go- go- go Drew!" Juan yelled at the top of his lungs, he squirmed as far over and down the wall as he could. He heard Santiago grunt as he struggled to hold onto him. Pebbles and dirt flew as the kids all scrambled to hold each other from tumbling over the wall.

Below, Drew sucked in a deep breath, counted to three in his head, with the children's screams of encouragement ringing in his ears, the twelve-year-old boy ran as fast as he could towards the wall.

Chapter Forty-Five

Michael picked up the shovel, swinging it as hard as he could, he slammed it into the bottom of the cairn.

Nothing happened so he swung again and again, hitting different rocks around the bottom. In the meantime, Cat knelt down and punched and jabbed at rocks all over the lower part of the cairn with the ax.

Suddenly, a rock Cat pushed at gave way, moving inward. "I got it!" she cried.

Michael threw the shovel down and knelt beside Cat and pushed with her. Two of the largest foundation rocks moved as if on a hinge.

Once they moved rocks beside them, together they pushed at several stones above them, and the rocks swung opened like a miniature door.

The pair sat back on their heels and stared at the cairn in wonderment. "I can't believe it. I didn't really think it really-" Cat dropped off.

Shaking his head in disbelief, Michael exhaled a ponderous breath. "Yeah. I'll go first. I wish I could have brought the guns but I figured without straps on them it'd be too hard to get inside, climb and crawl around with them. It seems like I was right to leave them, but still... Anyway, you wait here until I tell you it's okay. Got it? Seriously, Cataleigh, please do as I say, we don't want to endanger either of us."

His head cocked sideways he regarded the beautiful woman next to him. He'd never met anyone like her before. *Lovely, yes, but a hot body encased a kind, caring, intelligent and courageous woman. And funny, she so easily made him laugh. If only he wasn't dogged by his past, if only-* His thoughts broke as Cat said, "You're the boss, Sarg, your wish is my command." She smiled earnestly, indicating with a gesture for him to go first.

"Hmm," he smirked and said, "maybe later I'll take you up on that. But for now, I'll tell you when it's safe to come." Shooting her a wink, he laughed at her expression then crawled on hands and knees into the hollow bottom of the cairn. Inside he could feel something under his hands. It was a trap door.

The door lifted out easily by a metal ring. Michael opened the door, it wasn't attached to anything, he set the door on the ground. The hatch had covered a hole large enough for him to climb down into. He pulled a tiny flashlight out of his pocket and shined it inside.

He couldn't see anything but rock and dirt. And a ladder attached to the side of the wall. Without hesitation, he swung his legs into the hole and climbed down the ladder.

The hole was so narrow, he more dropped down by his hands on the rungs than his feet because he couldn't bend his knees much.

Cat paced impatiently in front of the cairn worried that the wild dogs might return. She rubbed her arms, the sun was setting and it was cooling down. It had been so hot they'd left their jackets tied on the horses.

As she paced, she looked back and forth and behind her. Waiting alone in the darkening fields, she heard birds cawing as they started roosting. She didn't know if the twigs snapping and footsteps she heard were real or imagined. Her flesh crawled as she pictured those snarling vicious dogs stalking her, ready to pounce when night fell, and she was alone.

Cat was just about to toss Michael's orders to the wind and go in the cairn and down the hole after him, when his head suddenly popped out of the hole.

He motioned to her to follow him. "Come on, it's clear as far as I can see." He crawled back in. Cat dropped to her knees in relief and followed him into the hole and down the ladder.

Reaching the bottom of the ladder, they stepped off onto hard earth. Michael turned on his flashlight and pointed it around. His voice eerie in the dark, insulated by rock, he said quietly, "This seems to be a leg of tunnel some of the miners must have used. I think somehow someone came across this leg while exploring the mines in the mountain.

"Maybe the tunnel ended near where the cairn was, and they dug the rest up to it and put in the ladder and door then proceeded to concoct the way to spring open the hollow bottom."

He started walking, leading with the light of the flashlight. The light bobbed and wobbled along the ground and rocky walls.

"Michael," Cat said at his heels, "I don't understand, how did he get the children down the ladder?" Their footsteps scuffed the dirt ground, echoing down the tunnel.

"Ah, I think there's another way in, this wouldn't be accessible or easy to bring the children through. He might have designed this to be an escape hatch, or just another entrance."

Cat pondered, "Still, he had to somehow get the kids inside."

Rubbing his chin with a squint, Michael nodded, "I'm thinking they were knocked out somehow, I hope by some mild medication, and carried in another way. As dreadful as it sounds, according to the legend the children were killed when they were tossed off the cliffs, so he has to keep them alive until the time was right to throw them.

"Anyway, the other way that I know of, is up the side where there's a deep dangerous ravine. There used to be a drawbridge to drop down over it, but there's a story that the ravine can be flooded suddenly from a mechanism inside. The word is though, that the drawbridge and all have been sealed up. Stay close."

He didn't have to tell her twice. She kept as close to him as she could get without stepping on his heels.

They travelled following the coiling tunnel without speaking and making as little noise as possible. They didn't want to announce their presence to whomever, if anyone, or any*thing*, might be ahead.

They lost track of time, trucking along in the bowels of the earth. Their noses wrinkled from the pungent smell of the earthy soil, they tripped over loose stones. Cat could feel the damp cool air prodding goose bumps along her arms, sticking her shirt to her back. The dusty air coated her throat, she struggled not to cough. Her eyes grew dry; she blinked continuously, reminding her of windshield wipers to keep them moist, and swallowed frequently to keep her throat clear. Thankfully the flashlight's beam remained strong.

After some time they noticed the tunnel widened and eventually they came to forks, bringing them to a halt.

"Which way?" Cat asked.

"Damned if I know. Let's go this-" Michael cut off when they heard something. There was a noise down one of the branches, far off, but they could definitely hear something. Michael swung the flashlight to shine down the tunnel but then switched it off.

"It'll be easier for them to see us than for us to see them. I prefer to spot them, whoever they are, first. We'll have to plod along in the dark. You game?" he whispered. He couldn't see her nod but he knew she would. He stepped forward into the tunnel the noise was emanating from, she didn't hesitate to follow close behind.

Treading slowly they moved quietly, picking their way carefully over fallen rocks and clumps of uneven ground. Fearing her pounding heart could be heard a mile away, Cat's own breathing sounded like she was under water, a muffled pounding in her ears. Her eyes strained staring at Michael's boots. She could barely see a meter ahead.

Michael stopped so suddenly Cat ran right into his back. He threw out a hand to catch her from stumbling.

"Shh." He held a finger to his lips. Holding onto her shoulder, he pointed.

Puzzled, Cat tried to peer through the length of dark corridor. She could make out nothing but more rocks and darkness. Blinking hard, she gazed up at him in question.

Michael looked down at her, she looked so serious. He gently pushed back a curl of hair off her face, the golden highlights dimmed in the shadows. His knuckles hovered beside her face, he rubbed his thumb gently to erase a smudge of dirt from her cheek.

Then, cradling her face in his hand he bent and kissed her, softly at first, then tasting her sweetness he forced her mouth open, exploring her with urgency. Her hands curled up around his neck- the sound of muffled voices and banging pulled them apart.

"Stay here." Michael paused for a second before turning from her then trekked stealthily down the tunnel. He left so abruptly Cat just stood in confusion.

When he didn't return for several minutes Cat muttered, "I'm not staying here alone in the dark," then she tiptoed down the corridor following the noise. As she crept closer, she could hear Michael talking. Catching up to him she scuttled up beside him. "What are you-"

"Wait," he said to her, "listen."

A second passed, and then she could hear. Muffled voices penetrated from the other side of a slew of piled rocks. She looked at Michael in question. He held up a hand for her to wait. Surprise struck her when she realized she recognized the voices on the other side of the wall of fallen rocks.

Michael grinned, called out, "Yellow Flower!" The voices stopped on the other side. Then they could hear rocks hitting rocks like a door knocker, and the voices started yelling, "Yellow Flower! Yellow Flower! Michael!"

Laughing, Michael leaned an ear next to the wall. He could hear Lucas shouting from the other side.

He said to Cat, "It's Lucas and Justin. I could hear them better than they could hear me. They apparently found another way in but were sabotaged. They got this far when someone blew up an entrance to this branch of the tunnel. They got lucky, the blast was relatively small so they weren't hurt but they're trapped. We're going to dig out the stones on both sides to get to them."

Cat's hand went to her throat, the danger they were in hit home. She pressed her lips together, leaned over and grabbed a rock and tossed it aside.

Michael quickly joined her. They worked steadily for 20-30 minutes, hearing the duo on the other side of the wall matching their efforts.

Louise Furley

Then Cat leaned back against a wall to catch her breath. Splotches of dirt smeared her face like she had madly painted on cosmetics with a brown blush. Michael took a break coming to lean beside her.

He stroked the side of her face tenderly, murmured with a smile, "You're beautiful even with your face looking like you lost a mud pie contest."

He laughed out loud when horrified she rubbed at her face with both hands, then realizing she was making it worse, she dropped her hands wiping them on her jeans. Who cared anyway, they were all in a perilous position and still needed to find the children. It sounded like the officers on the other side were taking a break too.

"Cataleigh," Michael said, then stopped. He dropped his head to study his feet.

"What?"

He waited a beat, then faced her and said, "Have you considered staying here after this is all over? You said there's nothing much keeping you where you live now, you have no relatives in that area, and, well, this town could really use someone of your caliber and talents."

He turned away quickly, then, faced her again. He aimed his flashlight to just below her chin, his eyes roamed her pretty face of sea blue eyes, plush lips, and creamy Irish complexion under the smeared dirt.

She didn't answer, her mind started racing, her heart quickened. She slanted her face slightly at him, unsure. "The town? The town needs… there's enough people here to work-"

"I want you to stay," he said flatly.

Her eyes flew to his face, the dark eyes, mysterious midnight pools made her heart palpitate faster. Sincerity etched in his hard face, his mouth bone-straight serious. She felt her soul floating to him like a tugging undertow of a pulsing ocean, then, she jerked herself back. "We can't have any kind of a…a…relationship until you trust me with your- your secrets, your past."

Leaning against the wall, one hand casually stuffed in his pocket, he lifted her ponytail with the other, letting the hair drift down like a fan as he held the tip. "You have the most unusual colored hair, brown with gold leafing, the prettiest that I've ever seen."

"Michael…"

He dropped her hair and took his hand out of his pocket to take both of her hands in his. He pulled her closer to him. "I do trust you, Cataleigh. I trust you with my life. You wouldn't be here if I didn't trust you to have my back. I could have made you stay home. I wouldn't have hesitated to lock you in the room in the back that has no window for escape if I really wanted to.

"But I have to be honest with myself. I wanted you by my side. It wasn't really fair to you to put you in this hazardous position, but I find when you're around all my good sense flies right out the window." He drew her to his chest, cupped her nape pulling her to his lips-

Cat's fingers of their own volition wound into Michael's wild black mane, she pulled him closer, pressed her lips against his, their mouths meshed into a mindless, passionate deepening kiss. Winding her tresses tightly around his fingers, he pulled her head back, his lips on her neck kissing her softness then moved up until he ground his mouth against hers.

His other hand stroked down her back to the curve of her waist drawing her tight against his aroused body. His lips and hands grew more amorous, more intense, it took all of Cat's will to shift back and put both hands up, pressing her splayed fingers against his chest she pushed him back an inch. Under heavy lids he blinked at her with dazed eyes.

Feeling his muscles flex under her hands like a warhorse about to surge into battle, not taking her eyes off his, she shook her head. "Your past first."

His arms tensed around her, like a vise holding her, but carefully like she was made of delicate crystal. She could feel the strength, the steel fencing her in. Holding her breath, she forced herself to stay enclosed in his arms, trusting him to be the man she believed in her heart that he was.

Slowly, he relaxed his arms letting her lean away.

Shaking his head he laughed wryly then set his hands gently on her shoulders. Several minutes passed in silence with the pair just gazing at each other, sea eyes trying to fathom what secrets the dark orbs held. His gaze dropped to her slightly parted lush lips, puffy and red from their passion. He was drawn to those lips like a moth to a flame, he bent- she pressed a hand against his chest.

Now his eyes glittered dangerously, he didn't try mask his desire for her. Squeezing her shoulders, "Cataleigh," his voice husky, "aren't you afraid to be here, in this place, alone with me? There's nowhere to run."

She didn't move or answer him. They both stayed still for a few long, quiet moments.

He sighed, "All right." Yielding, he let go of her then rolled back and leaned against the wall, took a deep breath, let it out slow, turned towards her.

"Since we all need to rest for a few minutes I'll tell you." Still ravaging her with his eyes he crossed his arms. Another deep breath, he said, "Only my truly closest friends know. Others, scaremongers, having only part of the information made up spurious rumors, but-"

"I know, I've heard them," she said softly.

He ducked his head then said, "It's not a long story, but it is a...devastating one. My sister, Kayleen, was pregnant with Matty when she was 16. Matty's father was a, I hate to say it, he was a thug. A small time thief and drug addict. For some reason she was nuts about him. He was handsome and devilish I guess. He was also seeing Ceire, my girlfriend at the time."

Cat gasped.

Chapter Forty-Six

Reaching her hand out to touch him, comfort him, Cat stopped, letting her arm fall back.

His head down, Michael gazed up at her, then his eyes cast down. A few seconds passed. Raising his head he stared blankly straight ahead, eyes glazed remembering the past.

He said, "Apparently, Dyago, that was his name, Dyago the Devil, the patrons of the Slurp and Burp Saloon called him. He ate it up. Stupid name for a gang bar, but the devil was an appropriate name for him.

"Anyway, he wanted to marry my Ceire because her family was quite wealthy. Of course, I didn't know anything about it. I was away with the military police, and then I came back and was stationed in Glenfall for a long time before I moved to Halo Valley. Our home was in Maryshire. Ceire and I are very distant cousins actually, cousins by marriage, not blood."

"That's nice, I guess." Cat smiled lightly.

"Uh huh." He leaned against the wall. "Anyway, Dyago used to beat my sister Kayleen on a regular basis, again, I wasn't aware of it, yet it was no secret, the entire town knew about it but no one saw fit to tell me. Everyone also knew Ceire was two-timing me while I was away."

"I'm so sorry," Cat whispered.

He smiled sadly at her. "Yeah. Anyway, Dyago didn't beat Ceire because she was his golden egg. So, Dyago finds out Kayleen is pregnant and he tells some of his punk friends from the pub that he needed to get rid of Kayleen and the baby before Ceire found out and dumped him. And when I say 'get rid of' he told plenty of people he was going to take her out on his little boat and throw her into the sea and watch her drown."

Michael's eyes closed in painful reminder of his fear for his sister. Shifting his position against the wall, he collected himself and continued.

"Then, one of his friends tells Ceire, and another friend lets it out to others and eventually the whole sordid story gets back to me. As soon as I heard about my sister, I hightailed it out there as fast as Dyago could down a damned beer. Foolish of me, I was in such a rage, I let it show. I hit every saloon, strip joint and drug den in town looking for the son of a bitch."

Michael's face darkened, his fists clenched so hard his knuckles were white.

Cat drew away slightly, she could see the rage burning off him even now, years later, she couldn't bear to picture how mad he was then.

He pinched between his eyes with his finger and thumb as if squeezing away the pain then crossed his arms settling back against the stony wall. "Everyone in town knew I was there and what I was doing. I was going after that bastard. There was no doubt that when I found him I would-" he hesitated.

He shot a blank glance at her then stared straight ahead. "He was beating my sister for God's sake. I hope I wouldn't have killed him, to this day I don't know what I would have, if I would have stopped..." He took a deep breath, his chest swelled with it.

"At the very least I would have beaten him to within an inch of his wretched useless life. Hurt him enough that there'd be no chance of him being able to get her." He looked down at his fists.

Cat wanted to touch him, comfort him, but he was beyond livid still, reliving the past.

His shoulders hunched he clasped his hands around the back of his head. "At first I tried to go after him with the law but all the damned witnesses clammed up, refused to cooperate. Then, I got word from a con at one of the pubs that Dyago was hiding out on his boat. He had called Kayleen there to lure her to her death. I raced to the marina. I was too late. When I got there…" his eyes closed as he flashed back to that time.

His voice slow, plodding, remembering, "I climbed on board, I'd left my revolver in my car, I didn't quite trust myself to not use it, even though it went against my very grain not to keep it with me but I didn't want an accident." He stopped talking.

"So," Cat prompted, "you went on board…"

He breathed deeply, composing himself again. Glancing at her then away down the tunnel, then at the pile of rocks, there was no sound on the other side, the officers were resting from hours of digging.

"Yeah, I got on board, found my way to the cabin. Inside I found," his voice caught, "inside, Dyago was lying on top of Ceire. They were both dead, lying in a pool of their mixed blood. Kayleen, she was sitting on a small couch, a pistol in her hand."

He covered his eyes with his hand. He spoke slowly, his voice rough, "She didn't even look up when I came in. She was…catatonic. She has really never come out of it. Permanently anyway." He fell silent.

"How devastating," Cat said softly, gently touching his arm.

He pushed from the wall, paced a few steps then turned to her. "There's more."

Cat's concerned face prompted him. "I got Kayleen out of there, carried her to my car and drove her to my place and," he shot her a glance, "I know it was wrong, I was a law officer after all. But, I hid her with Gram Zinny then made an anonymous call to the local police. Since the entire town knew I was gunning for Dyago, no pun intended, the police came straight after me. I was arrested. There was a trial. I was convicted."

Cat slapped a hand over her mouth at her swift intake of breath. "What? You were convicted? But you're out, you're here- why didn't you tell them the truth?"

He shook his head. "The truth? I didn't know what the truth was. We had to put Kayleen in a hospital, she wouldn't talk or eat. She was so traumatized she couldn't tell what happened. The police thought I killed them both for two-timing me and my sister, and with Dyago's threats to kill Kayleen that pretty much sealed it." His face hardened like the rocks around him.

"What happened was, I was not going to give up my sister. I was convicted and sent to prison. I should have been separated from the general pop as a law enforcement officer, but I wasn't, I don't know why, a glitch," his voice trailed off. He shuddered, his eyes closed tight, remembering… "Every day was a brawl."

Shaking his head, lids rose over bleak eyes. "Let's just say it took everything I had to keep myself alive while in there. During this time, the doctors medicated Kayleen to a point where she had some lucid moments.

"While in the hospital rec room one day, she saw an old newscast of my trial. She told the doctor and he helped her contact the police, and, well it's a long, long story, but, she told them what happened. After she had the baby, Matty, and the stress, depression, whatever, drew her back behind her catatonic wall where she's pretty much been since." He stopped talking, shook his head and paced again.

Cat waited silently, her heart went out to him, the pain in his eyes was heartrending. She couldn't help herself, she asked, "What? What happened?"

Wiping his eyes, he blinked, turned to her with a grim smile. "It took an eternity before I was released, this went on over a couple of years."

He raked his fingers through his hair, scraped them down his face then twisted his head side to side to release the tension in his neck. It obviously pained him to continue but he needed to finish the horrible story for them to move on. He leaned back against the wall.

Cat realized now where that hard, dangerous side of him came from. Violent, lethal years in prison.

He went on, "Kayleen had told the police that she went to the boat because Dyago had called her. Ceire was there too. He hadn't expected her, she just showed up. The girls confronted Dyago. He admitted everything. Then, he attacked Kayleen and started beating her. Ceire screamed for him to stop- he was killing her- killing the baby.

"Ceire ran to a drawer where she knew Dyago kept a gun. She aimed it at him and told him to stop or she'd shoot. He sweet talked her to get close to her, she was scared, too scared to shoot."

Cat clapped a hand over her mouth to stifle her gasp, unnerved eyes stared wide over her hand at him.

Michael's voice rushed now, low, unemotional, get it over with like ripping off a Band-Aid. "He grabbed the gun, they tussled, the gun fell out of Ceire's hand and slid across the floor. Kayleen was half lying on the floor, disoriented from the beating. She saw the gun, grabbed it, she held it up to scare Dyago, to stop him, but in her shaking hands the gun went off- at that split second Ceire leaped in front of him, she really did love him, and the bullet hit her.

"She dropped to the ground, dead. Alarmed and furious, Dyago lunged at Kayleen- and she shot him. That's it. Kayleen couldn't handle that she killed her beloved and that he had wanted her dead. She has always been…fragile, she lapsed into an awake coma-like state and other than that brief lucid time she has been that way since." He set his head in his hands, trying to erase the horrible memories.

Cat let the silence sift for a minute. Michael just leaned against the wall with his head in his hands. After a moment or so, confused, Cat said, "But you were convicted, how did you get this job?"

A sad half-smile drew his handsome face down. "Since it was a wrongful conviction, I was only guilty of accessory after the fact. The superintendent, a longtime friend of mine, he understood, he had a sister too…unfortunately even with the conviction dropped there was still a stigma around me, around the entire, uh, episode.

"People always want to believe the worst, the whispers still grow with the years. Most people think I actually killed Dyago and Ceire from jealousy, and Kayleen covered for me. That's why I moved us up here taking the sergeant position and kept Matty a secret."

Lips pursed, Michael crossed his arms over his chest and stared blankly down the tunnel. "I'm not saying I've never had to kill someone," the corners of his eyes twitched, "it comes with the territory, military and law enforcement."

He shook his head slowly. "I was quite young really though at the time, I truly don't know what I would have done if I came across that bastard with his hands on my little sister…"

"I see," Cat murmured. He sounded funny about that last bit of information, like he was leaving something unsaid, but she let it go.

"So you raised Matty? That explains a lot of things. The nasty rumors of you murdering someone, and you wanting to keep people from knowing about Matty, to keep her mother's history a secret from her, why you keep people at arm's length.

"I understand. I understand you feeling low and dirty from your time in prison, like spoiled goods having to fight and hurt other men to save yourself."

She moved in front of him. "But you're not. You're a decent man, uncle, grandson, cop, friend." Setting a hand tenderly on his arm, she smiled up at him through tear filled eyes. "Thank you for trusting me. I can't tell you how that makes me feel-"

Suddenly the wall of rocks tumbled down like a set of bowling pins hit by a ball.

Seconds after the dust settled, a face peeked out from behind the pile. "Hi!" Lucas grinned through a thick layer of grime. "Boy are we glad to see you!"

Chapter Forty-Seven

Like a fusion of variegated clothes pegs the children hung perilously over the edge of the wall, a volley of arms stretching and flailing to catch ahold of Drew who ran like the wind, and with a powerful flying leap left the ground- hitting the stone wall about halfway up.

Miraculously, the kids managed to grab his wrists and arms and jacket, anything they could hold onto and pulled him with all their might. Cries and grunts and groans prevailed as they pulled, his stomach cutting open on the rough wall, his feet bruising and banging while he kicked himself up.

The wall was only about six feet wide, the children had all put themselves in dire danger of falling off either side of it, but with everyone yanking him he finally made it up and onto the wall.

Drew lay on his stomach with his arms and legs stretched out gasping. Wiped out, their strength spent, the kids all flopped down around him.

After a few seconds, Pil sat up and grinned at the exhausted kids. "Hey, we did it! We're a hell of a team!"

The other kids looked at him like he's lost his mind. Ever the whiny pessimist, he seemed to always be the first one to throw someone else under the bus.

But this time his own flabby white hands were raw and bleeding. He had held onto Drew, trying to pull him up with everything he had. Instead of crying about his injuries he held them up as badges of honor.

"We needed every last one of us to get from that prison room to here. I'm proud of us!" Pil beamed. "I don't think any other group of kids could have done what we did. We're the best!"

The other kids laughed at the novel enthusiastic praise, releasing the terrifying tension that had built up for weeks, their morale rose several notches.

Drew rolled over and dropped an arm around Pil's thick shoulder. "You bet, Pil, you bet. We did it. Teamwork." The group enjoyed their moment of congratulating themselves for what they, even as only kids, were able to accomplish.

Santiago grinned and pointed at Drew. "And brilliant, you freakin' did it without losing that freakin' cigarette!"

Reaching up, Drew fingered the cigarette that was still lodged over his ear. "Oh yeah, cool." His tone was nonchalant but he smiled, his hands and face crisscrossed with scratches. This set the kids off laughing again.

Juan stood up, stretched and yawned. Reaching back for his ball cap he had tucked in his back pocket while trying to get them all up the wall, he pulled it out, shook it then plopped it on his head. He moved it back and forth to get it just right. His own hands were stinging from hitting and scraping against the sharp jutting pieces of the wall.

He stood in front of the lingering group and said, "Okay guys, we've had our break and celebration. We're not out of the woods yet. We still have to find our way out of this cave or mine or whatever. Plus, we don't know where that deranged maniac is. Let's go. I'll get down the wall first, then Drew next. You, Santiago help the other kids down to us. Got it?"

They nodded their acquiescence and then reluctantly, one by one climbed to their tired feet.

After each of the kids landed safely, last to go, Santiago clung from the wall by his fingers. He let go into Juan and Drew's waiting hands then dropped to his feet. Slapping his hands together to brush off some of the dirt, he said, "Well, that was ten times easier than getting up that damned thing!"

The group readily agreed with him. As before, Juan led the way through the dark tunnel. He didn't share that he was praying that there would be no more walls, or ravines, or whatever other barriers could befall them.

After what seemed like hours, the kids had grown so weary from walking, they hadn't eaten or drank anything since escaping earlier from their prison. Barely able to put one foot in front of the other, they straggled along the side like mice bracing themselves with their hands against the interior wall to help them from falling down.

Jamie tripped for what seemed the hundredth time, landing on his bare knees. When he had been enticed from inside his home where he had been watching TV in his room, he had been lounging comfortably in shorts and a shirt. He'd grabbed a jacket when he had decided to leave his house, which came in handy now in the cold damp cavern. His bare legs were banged up and freezing.

Staying down on his cut up knees, Jamie cried, "I wanna go home."

Barty tried to console him. He crouched down next to the delicate child. "We're going to get home. Jamie, really we are. We can do it. Look how far we've come so-" he broke off as he soberly took in his surroundings.

They were trapped inside what they figured was an old closed up mine tucked deep inside the cavity of the Maru mountains. They hadn't eaten or drank anything for hours; they seemed to just tramp from one dark tunnel to the next with no emergence in sight with God knows what kind of hideous fiend gnashing at their heels.

Worse, they were definitely traveling uphill. No one wanted to say it out loud, but it wasn't just that they were tiring that their legs dragged like they were cement filled, they could feel the upward incline of the ground.

"No." Jamie scowled, painfully climbing to his feet. Zipping his jacket up to his chin, he turned back towards the way they had come from. "I'm going back. At least we had food and water and- and toilet paper." He started trudging back down the tunnel.

"Come on, James, come back here. We can't go back. Come on," Juan called after him. The small boy kept going.

"We can't let him go," Matty cried.

Jessy took off in a jog after Jamie. He quickly caught up with him. His hands tucked in his jacket pockets, he walked beside the slight boy. His voice soft, Jessy said, "Jamie, to go back is certain death. To keep going further, I think we're heading towards the light, to life."

Fervently shaking his head, Jamie kept moving like a brittle china doll tripping over the rough ground in his haste to get back to what he considered safety.

Jessy maneuvered beside him. Then he stopped abruptly and caught Jamie's sleeve causing him to stop too. The young boys faced each other. Jessy's fluorescent smile glazing his porcelain face, cheeks rosy from exertion, he set his hands on Jamie's shoulders.

"James, we can't go back. You know that. You can't get over those walls on your own. We have to go on. At the very least we'll go down fighting. Our parents will be proud of us. If it's meant to be, we'll die a valiant death. But," he said quickly with conviction when Jamie's eyes welled, his lip quivered. "I swear we're gonna make it. I swear, James. Trust me, please."

He gently squeezed the slender boy's shoulders gazing at him with hope igniting like glorious candles in his eyes. "Come on, let's go, forward," Jessy turned slowly, and confidently started walking back to the fatigued gang.

Jamie stood unsure. He watched Jessy go back to the bosom of the other kids. Plucky Matty dislodged herself from the group and went to go meet Jessy half way. Jessy stopped and turned back to Jamie who still stood unsure which way to go, what to do.

Matty slipped her arm through Jessy's. She grinned at Jamie, her blue eyes like headlights in her pixie face streaked with grime, but the welcome shone through. She gestured for him to come back. The other kids waved and called out to the frightened youngster.

"Come on, Jamie, come on. Come with us," a harmony of young voices, flying like balloons suddenly freed, bobbing, floating up to the big blue sky, encouraging him to return to the fold.

Jamie ducked his head and stared at his shoes. Two shadows hovered in front of him, he looked up.

"C'mon James we gotta go and we ain't leaving without you," Pil said, his and Tom-tom's expressions grave, they waited.

Stuffing his hands in his jacket pockets and dragging his feet to display his reluctance, Jamie walked back with Pil and Tom-tom to where the rest of the kids waited. They enfolded around him as if a warm blanket over a chilled baby bird, embracing him to give him courage.

"Okay," Juan said disentangling himself from the others. "We've used up enough time. Let's get going." The children straggled back into a crooked line following Juan through the endless cold, dark tunnel.

Chapter Forty-Eight

Rocks toppling down, dust flying, Michael and Cat pulled at the rocks and stones, hastily dropping or rolling the bigger ones out of the way. From the other side, the trapped officers pushed loose rocks to spill forward, gravel flying everywhere Michael and Cat had to jump aside to avoid crushed toes.

When a hole big enough was dug out, first Lucas pushed through, Justin powered right behind him. If they hadn't recognized their voices, the two gardai would not have been recognizable. They looked like a couple of red and yellow traffic lights that had gone through a dust storm in a desert. Lucas' blond mop was dulled by dirt and Justin's short red springing curls were too soiled with earth and stone dust to spring. Their happy grins though, beamed through the soot.

"Boy are we glad to see you guys!" Gleefully, Lucas made to hug Michael, but the sergeant leaned back with his hands up.

"That's great, Luke, you don't need to show your appreciation." Michael grinned.

Justin laughed, dirt fell off him in dusty clumps. "Blimey Sarg, you two ain't looking all that much cleaner than us!"

Michael and Cat checked each other. "Do I look as bad as you do, Michael?" Cat asked, appalled at how dirty he was. He nodded wryly. They both immediately wiped their own faces with their sleeves, but it didn't help. Only a good long hot shower was going to get any of them clean again.

"Forget getting pretty you two. As far as we're concerned you guys are the most beautiful people we have ever seen!" Lucas flashed his teeth in a huge grin, like a white flag in a black sea.

"Yeah," Justin agreed, brushing at the dirt that layered him like a blanket. "We were starting to think we might be trapped forever. Someone caused the way we got through to cave in then did the same in front of us to trap us. I thought for sure we were goners."

"Nah." Lucas patted his friend's arm. "Come on J, we never lost faith. We knew you guys were out here somewhere and as soon as the civilians and the rest of the police realize the water has receded and the messages we left as to our destination, and the idea of where the kids were being kept, it would only be a matter of time before someone got to us. We hoped."

Justin parroted him, "You're right, we had our fingers crossed. Course the way is so rugged out here the only way the townsfolk can get to the mountain is across that old drawbridge but I think it's walled up inside."

"Well," Cat said, smiling broadly, she hugged both men. "I'm thrilled to see you guys! If I ever get to meet your girl Kenzi, Lucas, I want to be able to tell her what a brave man you are."

Grinning back at her, Lucas brushed at his shirt and pants. "Yeah, she's a nurse, she's been transporting the patients from the hospital up to Strowell. When we're out of here, and this whole- whole horrendous nightmare is over we'll have to get together. All of us..." he snuck a wink at Cat and grinned at Michael, who ignored him.

Michael ducked his head and shook it to get the bulk of the dirt out. Then he tossed his head back and tried to detangle his hair with his fingers. Deciding that wasn't going to do much, he brushed off his sleeves and jeans as best he could.

While they stood like a pack of bedraggled gophers that just climbed out of a hole in a farmer's field, Michael surveyed their immediate area. "We need to determine our next course of action. I say we keep heading in the direction Cataleigh and I were going when we heard you guys."

"As long as we don't go back the dead end way we came," Justin said. "I'll follow you anywhere." Michael started walking and the others fell in line behind him, Justin then Cat then Lucas.

Whenever they worked together, Michael and Lucas always operated like bookends. They were used to covering each other's back. Now they made sure Cat, who they thought was their weakest link, but would never tell her that, was kept between them where they felt they could protect her from- whatever.

They trudged for a while when they came to another fork, another opening. Michael shined his flashlight down it. "It looks like there's a couple of other tunnels spread out like tree branches." He stepped into the middle of the fork and shined his light around in an arc then around the ground.

"I think we should stay away from the one there on the left. It's a good thing we stopped when we did. In about three feet there's a big drop, like a crevasse, I can't see how deep it is. So that leaves these other two tunnels."

They checked around a little more thoroughly then decided to take a momentary break, stretch and share a candy bar that Justin had tucked in a pocket. After a moment of discussion they decided on the direction they would go.

As they started moving, Michael said to the two officers, "Cataleigh says she knows who the demon is that has the children. And wait until you hear how she puzzled it out. It's nutty but it makes sense. Go ahead, tell 'em," he smiled at Cat.

Lucas' face lit up behind the coat of dust. "You're kidding, you know who it is?" Then his face darkened, he clenched his fingers together in a tight fist like in an angry prayer. He said to Michael, "We need to go get him, force him to tell us exactly where he has the children imprisoned." He swung to Cat and asked, "Who is it?"

They stood in a huddle while Cat explained how she discerned how the children were taken, their names, eleven apostles, and Jessy U. Justin and Lucas stared at Cat first like she was joking, then in bewilderment. Then, like a lightbulb popped on over their heads, they nodded vigorously as they agreed with her figuring.

"Yeah, yeah," Lucas mumbled, "I can see what you're saying. It makes sense. He, or they, had a reason yet to be explained why they desired, needed to, or wanted to take only children that had the same names as the apostles, but different enough so no one would see it, see the pattern and look more in depth as to why."

"Yeah." Justin nodded agreeing with him

"But," Lucas said, turning questioning eyes to Cat. "You know who's responsible?"

Her hands twined behind her back, Cat nodded.

"Don't keep us in suspense Miss Cat, tell us!" Justin demanded. The sooner they knew who took his daughter, Simone, the sooner he could rescue her, take her home safe to her family. Grouped in front of Cat, the men waited on pins and needles, because the minute she uttered the name they would be off like a shot to go after the person, or persons.

Cat pushed her hair back off her shoulders and cleared her throat. Lucas and Justin's eyes were glued to her parted full lips ready to divulge the name of the monster that was terrorizing their village.

"It's Dusja Troicasi," she announced calmly.

Brows rose, faces still in question. "Who?" they asked in unison.

With a half grin, Michael said, "Don't worry, I had to think too. It's his first name that's confusing you." He crossed his arms in front of his chest, legs akimbo. "Remember just before the first dramatic television production of the legend by Mallory O'Leary the reporter, when little Stormie Dodge fell into that well?"

Still confused, the two gardais' faces screwed up, struggling to place the name. As he recalled the incident, Lucas' face smoothed out somewhat. "It wasn't that guy, Champ what's-his-name? I thought he died." He looked like a giant confused, blonde dust bowl. His brawny arms were streaked with dust and dirt.

"No, Luke. Champ did die. This was the guy who actually rescued Stormie. Remember the man from Cleasaí, or he said he was from there, for all we know he could have come from anywhere. You know his wife Dee, helped a lot with the phones with the Crimestoppers. The guy's name was Dusty. I could never remember his real name." Michael looked to Cat for help.

"Dusja Troicasi," Cat supplied.

"Who?" Justin asked.

"Dusja Troicasi," Cat repeated.

Michael nodded. "You weren't there at the time, Justin, I don't think. But you know him, Luke. He was the guy that ran up and laid down over the hole, he had those crazy double jointed legs where he could like 'frog them out' as he called it. I held his legs as he reached in and pulled Stormie out. His picture was in the paper the next day as the town hero. He disappeared before he could get interviewed."

With a small nod, Lucas said, "Oh yes, I remember Mallory pulled in every favor trying to find him. She stalked every bar and shop in town hoping to snag him."

Cat rubbed an eye the realized her hands were filthy so she pulled a corner of her shirt up and used the inside to wipe the dirt off her eyelid. "She never got to him, at least until the first search party for little Jessy. By then the excitement over the rescue had died down."

"His wife Dee, she said it was short for…" Michael's eyes turned up as he tried to recall her real name. "It was something from the Bible, not a nice figure either if I recall. You know, the one who had John's head cut off and served on a platter-"

"Herodias," Cat filled in.

His hands on his hips, Michael nodded. "Yes. That's it."

Frowning, Lucas spoke up, "Anyway, what's this got to do with Troi- Troisterosky or whatever?"

"Troicasi. Dusja Troicasi." Cat said. The three men faced her while she explained, still feeling not totally confident about her supposition of the villain. "I think his wife's name Herodias fits in with my picture."

The men looked confused but eager to hear what she had to say. She brushed at the dirt that was itching her arms then pulled her ponytail around the front of one shoulder and stroked it with both hands while she gathered her thoughts. The men followed her strokes, like long gentle caresses. Even under a layer of dust the golden highlights still gleamed in the dim light that made its way weakly from their flashlights.

"So," Cat started, "when I realized the children's names meant characters in the Bible, I pulled a list off the computer of the residents of Halo Valley and Cleasaí. I figured I'd start there and if I needed to research further I could check Glenfall and Strowell and on and on. But it wasn't necessary.

"I started with people involved with the search and the children's parents first. History says that a perpetrator likes to insinuate themselves into a crime scene like watching the firemen work on a burning building that he set on fire, or join a search party.

"I set aside the most normal common names and worked on the odder ones. I fooled around with switching letters like anagrams. Dusja Troicasi was only the fifth name I tried. Once I had his name, his wife's name only confirmed my idea." The words hesitant at first now spilled out as she tried to explain her madness.

She stopped to catch her breath. The men waited, eyes wide with interest. Michael already knew but she had only just told him as they entered the cairn.

"And it means?" Lucas asked, impatient.

"The anagram of Dusja Troicasi is Judas Iscariot. Put that together with the stolen children having names of the Apostles, and Herodias as his wife, that was too abnormal to not be part of it..." Cat left off, waiting for them to come to their own conclusions. As the information rambled around in their heads, their reactions registered on their faces.

"You mean-" Justin said with confusion.

"The guy responsible for this whole horror thinks he's Judas? Judas from the Bible? The betrayer Judas?" Disbelief coated Lucas' face. "Are you freaking kidding me?"

"Are you trying to say this guy *is* Judas or *thinks* he's Judas?" Justin's face reddened as he strained to comprehend.

Michael looked at Cat. She shrugged. "I have no idea."

"I- I mean that would be just ridiculous to think that this guy is the- the reincarnated Judas?" Justin's words were sodden with skepticism.

Lucas coughed out a sarcastic laugh. "Come on, there's no such thing as ghosts or- or- reincarnation or zombies or-" his palms up,

348

he glanced around at his friends in disbelief. Their faces pretty much mirrored his.

"We have no answers, only that it's too coincidental to not be right," Michael interjected. His arms crossed in front of his chest, he unconsciously pushed a hunk of black hair out of his eyes then set his hands on his hips.

Lucas jammed his hands in his pockets, his shoulders hunched he glared at Michael then Cat then Justin. They all had the same questioning expressions.

Justin balled his hands into fists and slammed them on his hips, his red brows drew down making him look an angry Howdy Doody. "Whatever he or it is, let's go get him. He has my daughter. I don't give a damn if he's bloody Frankenstein, I'm getting my daughter back. Who's with me?" His mouth set fiercely, he watched the others. The red crept up his leprechaun ears.

Everyone straightened. Michael said, "Oh, I'm there with you, I was just waiting for you two to take in what you just heard and decide if you were coming with us." He glanced quickly at Cat. She smiled back.

He said, "Our cells are of no use in here. We've already decided we're going all the way on our own. We believe the children are being held here inside this mountain somewhere. I'm going to find Matty and bring every last child safety."

Lucas didn't wait for Michael to finish before he said, "Oh count me in, I can't wait to get my hands on the monster. That bastard is going to be sorry the day he-"

"*The day I what?*" a snide voice calmly spoke in the dark.

The four friends turned their flashlights into the tunnel branching to the left.

"Oh shit," Justin said, "Troicasi."

Chapter Forty-Nine

Juan stopped so abruptly Jamie smashed into him. "Hey Falcon, what are you-"

"Shh," Juan whispered. "Wait." He motioned with his hands for the kids to stop. But they kept coming forward like yo-yo's. Juan held his arms out as deflections to stop them from going past him.

"What is it?" Drew asked coming alongside him. He tried to peer through the opaque tunnel to see what made Juan stop.

"Listen a sec," Juan said quietly. He shushed the children, they all listened.

Barty said, "I don't hear nothin'."

"Wait, wait," Santiago said, reaching the other side of Juan. Their voices were now echoing when before they were flat from the tunnel walls. "Is that," he gulped, "is that water?"

"Hey!" Pil chortled "I hear it too!" Then his expression waned. "Uh, is that good?"

"Or bad?" Jamie asked.

"Dunno." Juan got on his hands and knees and crept forward slowly. Drew and Santiago followed suit. The three boys crawled, following the sound of the dripping water which was growing louder. "Wait," Juan ordered. They slowed, their hands feeling the edge of the ground dropping.

"Can you see anything?" Matty called out.

There was quiet from the three boys. The other kids started fidgeting. Jessy tiptoed behind the older boys but they were coming back. They looked troubled. Santiago looked scared, even in the dim light his olive skin paled.

"What is it?" Rocky asked.

Santiago and Drew tucked their thumbs over their belts and waited for Juan to speak.

"Uh," he tried to sound positive. "Well, there's like a lake or underground kind of river or something. Maybe like a grotto."

Matty asked, "Can we get around it?"

Juan shook his head, biting his lip. "Nah, it looks like it's completely surrounded by solid stone wall. We have to decide whether to dare go in it or- or, the only other way is back." No one said anything, they bleakly considered their choices.

"We can't go in the water," Jamie cried, "I can't swim. I'm scared. We gotta go back." Some of the other kids agreed with him.

"It smells mucky, seaweedy and muddy," Rocky said, sniffing loudly, his nose crinkled.

Grimly, Drew faced the children. "We already decided that to go back would be certain death."

"Yeah but to go in a- a- lake or river or whatever, what if it has no end?" Pil bemoaned, rubbing his belly nervously.

"What are you worried about, you bean bag? Half of us could sit on you and we could float across like on a raft." Tom-tom said scornfully.

"Me? You're the tubbo, me da says I'm a fireplug like him!" Pil drew himself up, fists on his hips.

"Yeah, plug is right, you're a big fat butt plug," Tom-tom countered. Pil stomped over to the smaller pudgy boy, his fist raised. "You take that back you-"

Drew held his hands up. "Come on you guys, quit fighting for crying out loud. We have to get out of here, save your energy for the- swim."

Jamie swung his head at Drew in horror. "No! I can't! I can't swim! Don't leave me here!" he begged, pressing his hands together praying, tears flowed over his china doll cheeks sliding down his narrow chin.

Jessy went to him. "No one is leaving anyone. We made a pact, remember? We stick together no matter what."

"Right," Simone crowed. The other kids chimed in.

Juan waited for them to calm down. Then he sighed. "Listen. I know you guys are scared, but the water is the only way out. It looks like the light we've been seeing is coming from behind the water. But it's too far to tell if it's above or behind or what. We have to chance it."

"Noooo…" Jamie wailed. He put his hands over his face. Matty wrapped her arms around him. She looked over his shoulder at Juan and asked, "What are we going to do?"

Juan shrugged one shoulder, glancing back at the water. "Uh, I guess maybe me and Santy or Drew should try first. We're probably the best swimmers. We can check it out. Maybe it's not as far as it looks," he didn't sound too hopeful.

Drew moved forward, pulling on the hem of his jacket. "That sounds like a plan. We'll check it out first."

Concern straining his tone, Santy said very low, "Guys, the water is so low beneath us, that…" he trailed off.

Drew ran a hand through his hair. He slipped the cigarette from over his ear and stuck it in his mouth, but didn't light it. He finished Santy's sentence, "That once we're in, we can't get back out."

The children gasped, Jamie cried louder.

Rocky wiped at his eyes, he said to Drew, "You ain't going, bro, no way, let them go." He gestured to Juan and Santiago.

Drew shook his head. "I'm sorry kid. I think it should be me and Juan. If we don't-" he broke off at the frightened look on his little brother's face.

Taking a deep breath he went on, "If we don't make it, at least there still might be a chance for you and Santiago to, uh, if you guys survive at least our parents won't lose both their boys."

"No!" Rocky clutched at his brother. Drew hugged him back.

"Wait a minute-" Santiago didn't want his brother to go either.

"He's right, Santy," Juan agreed. "He's right. No more chattering about it. It's the only way." He hugged his brother. They each wiped tears from their eyes.

Louise Furley

Tucking his cap in his back pocket, Juan stepped forward before anyone could say anything to stop him, or he changes his mind, he leaped into the dark.

The kids stood frozen, stunned. They heard a splash and all ran forward to the edge and looked down. Juan's head was visible in the water. He treaded, then waved at them.

"Come on in- the water's fine!" he joked.

"Is it really?" Drew called down. He leaned over with his hands on his knees.

Juan's voice echoed in the rocky chamber, "Uh, you don't want to know."

Drew straightened up and turned to the other kids standing there aghast at what they had to now face. The unknown, in the dark, in the water. Not knowing if there was an escape beyond the water. Or if there were falls or cliffs, or just never ending deeper and deeper water.

"Can you tell how deep it is?" Drew called out. He waited while Juan took a deep breath then kicked his feet up with a little splash and disappeared headfirst into the murky depths. The kids held their breath with him.

It seemed like hours when Juan finally surfaced. His head popped up and he shook his head like a dog. Water slung around from his hair. He pushed the wet wad back. His buzz cut was growing out unruly.

"Well?" Drew asked.

Treading again, Juan shook his head grimly. "I can't see the bottom. I went down as far as I could but I couldn't see it or touch it."

Jamie screamed at the top of his lungs. Matty tried to console him but he screamed louder. Santiago went over to the hysterical boy. The other kids didn't make fun of him, they were just as scared to death as he was.

"Hey James," Santiago said to the screeching boy. He grasped the frail boy's shoulders shaking him gently. Jamie sobbed, gulping air. "No, Santy, nooooo…" he howled.

Santiago shook him gently again. "Come on, James, take a deep breath, I won't let anything happen to you. Do you trust me?" Jamie's face streaked in muddy trails, his sodden eyes gleamed, his nose ran, he kept crying but he listened to Santiago.

"Now, this is what we'll do. If we have to go in, you'll get on my back and hold on and I'll swim with you on my back like a frog on a turtle. What do you say to that?" Santiago asked the weeping child.

Jamie swiped his nose with the back of his hand. Hiccupping and shuddering, he nodded wordlessly. Santiago wrapped an arm around the boy's shoulder and addressed the other kids. "Does anyone else not know how to swim? Simone? Teddy?"

The two girls stood clinging to each other. They nodded. "Da taught me at the lake," Simone said, "and me and Teddy took lessons in school too." Teddy nodded in agreement.

Their eyes big and terrified. "But we don't wanna go in the icky water, Santy. There's no slide or steps or nuthin' an what if we can't get out? I want my daddy," Simone wailed, Teddy chimed in with her.

"I can swim really good too. I swim in the pond in the park every summer and it's really deep," the rail-thin Barty proudly announced.

Santiago scratched his head. He was used to terrorizing the younger kids, stealing their lunch and playing pranks, not trying to reassure them.

He held Jamie's hand then crouched in front of the girls, the three were the youngest ones there. "It'll be just fine. Just pretend you're at the lake, and when we get to the other side your da's will be there waiting for you, okay?"

Matty's chest puffed out. "I was on the junior swim team when I was seven," she said proudly, grinning chicklet teeth. "I can swim really good. I'll help you guys." Simone and Teddy smiled tremulously at the spunky redhead less than a year older than them. "K," Simone sniffed. Teddy laid her head on her friend's shoulder, her braids fell across Simone's chest like brown satin ribbons.

"Hey! What about it!" Juan yelled from below. His voice bounced around the cavern.

Drew jogged over to the side and peered down at his friend. Then he took his cigarette and stuffed it back into his crumpled pack of cigarettes and handed the pack and his lighter to Matty. She stared at them in dismay. "What?" she asked.

"Hold these for me. I don't want them to get wet. For when I return." He sounded scared yet determined. Matty smiled softly and took the pack and lighter. If he came back they were all going in the water anyway. He was trying to be hopeful, pretending they were all going to get out safely.

Drew muttered a quick prayer. A fast hug with Rocky then before Rocky could stop him, he took a deep breath and pushed off like a bird in flight, diving head first into the unknown. The kids ran to the side when they heard him splash. They looked over the side. Juan and Drew's heads bobbed together in the dark water.

"Damn it's cold you son of-" Drew sputtered.

Juan chuckled and slapped his friend lightly in the head. "If I'd told you that, you might not have come in!"

"Drew! C-c- come back for me- us…please…" Rocky cried. His little square face crumpled, lower lip trembling, he dropped to his hands and knees, then sat. His chin on his hands he looked down at his brother.

Treading water and biting back tears, Drew smiled as brave and as brilliant and as reassuring as he could. "I'll be back little brother. I promise. Don't you worry."

Tears streamed like a muddy rainfall down Rocky's grimy cheeks. He didn't wipe them away, more would follow.

"Listen guys," Juan called up to the children. "We're going to swim as far as we can to see what's there. If we're not back in, say, thirty minutes," he stopped, "then, then go back." He tried hard to keep the fear he felt from strangling him. He had to be brave.

Someone had to be strong for the littler ones. He took in his brother, Santiago's white face. He stared for a minute at Santy like he was trying to memorize every feature, as if he was never going to see him again.

Then he saluted his brother. Smiling tremulously, Santy returned a weak salute. He dashed at a tear.

Juan turned to Drew and said, "Ready?"

Not trusting himself to talk, Drew nodded, water dripped from his hair and the tip of his nose. Without another word, Juan turned and started swimming away from the wall, Drew followed right behind him. The lonely chords of their splashing, the only sound in the cavern, grew quieter and quieter until they fainted away. The children watched until the boys went out of sight.

His voice tear-clogged, Santiago said, "We need to keep track of the time. One, two, three…"

The children sat down, crossed their legs, set their elbows on their knees and their chins on their hands, counted out loud in a monotone chant, and waited.

Chapter Fifty

"Dusja Troicasi," Cat stated flatly.

The man she just named, the man they knew as Stormie Dodge's savior, amicably called Dusty, who had together with his kind wife Dee, helped search for the missing children and consoled their parents, stood in the mouth of the connecting tunnel, with a gun clenched in his hand. Smiling, he aimed the Sig Sauer straight at the group.

"Very good, Miss Cat." Troicasi leered with a sardonic bow. "You have brains and beauty. I thought you might be the one to watch out for. I've been listening. You are quite clever, my dear." He bowed again to the slender young woman.

It was hard to look dignified with disheveled hair, the rubber band long gone, it waved down her back like a brown and gold silk scarf. Feeling far from chic in grubby jeans and a form fitting t-shirt with rips in dangerous places, Cat folded her arms across her chest and glared at him. His praise meant nothing to her.

Setting her lips in a straight line, she leveled her gaze at Michael, dismissing Troicasi. Peripherally she caught his scowl when she dissed him.

Michael moved in front of Cat to shield her. Lucas and Justin stepped to either side of him. Pushing his long hair behind his ears, Michael set his hands squarely on his hips, lean legs locked in a strong akimbo.

Glittering black eyes seared through the gloom like an arrow at the man, not the gun. Michael appeared relaxed, but his stance indicated he was holding his powerful energy in check, ready for action. "That's my gun you bastard."

Troicasi laughed harshly. "Ha, yeah, God you rural people are so trusting. Nevertheless, I still had to break your truck window to get it. Couldn't get the shotguns though, the damned horses wouldn't let me get near them, but nonetheless this little pea shooter will do nicely."

Michael scowled, feeling so stupid for leaving the weapons. He really didn't think anyone else would be out in such a treacherous area where the cairn was. "What are you going to do, Troicasi?" he asked. "Murder the entire village? By now everyone knows the children are somewhere here in the mountain. As soon as the roads are more passable they'll be out in leagues coming here. You won't get away."

Troicasi frowned, then quickly shrugged. "Truth be told, I hadn't quite thought you people would figure any of this out. Maybe the children's names at their funerals when the paper came out with their real names, someone as canny as you, Miss Cat, would eventually have connected the dots. Frankly, I also didn't expect you all to figure out about the cairn.

"However, no one besides you knows about the cairn and they can't get in the entrance, the drawbridge is up and locked my friends. Anyone tries to get to the drawbridge I can open the dam holding back the water inside the mountain and drown the entire damned town. Surprisingly you two," he motioned his head toward Lucas and Justin.

"You found one of the other few entrances that I thought was quite well camouflaged. Fortunately, as clever as I am I had little warning systems set up all around for that happenstance. I found you two bunglers right away. Of course it was I who caused the cave in. You were supposed to be trapped and die there, a slow agonizing death. But alas," he sighed.

Michael took a step towards him, but Troicasi moved the Sig up and aimed it between Michael's eyes. "Oh no, my young man. You're going to die but perhaps not quite so fast. So, back off. Besides, I'm going to shoot her," he swung the gun briefly at Cat then back to Michael, "before I kill you so you can suffer watching her die in your arms, Romeo. Yeah, everyone except you two could see you had it big for each other."

He went on, his voice a mock, "I thought I might have a chance with her at first," he winked at Cat when she cringed. "But I knew she was only interested in you. Girls like you tall, rugged, 'I got a deep, dark, painful secret' hint of dangerous types."

"You piece of garbage, you have a wife-" Justin spat.

Troicasi laughed at him. "You haven't figured any of us out yet, have you, you fiery little pipsqueak?"

Justin burned red and made to lunge at him. Michael and Lucas grabbed him quickly, wrestling him still. "Take it easy, J, he's trying to goad us into going at him so he can pick us off without guilt," Lucas said through clenched teeth, his maplely eyes narrowed at the demon holding them hostage.

Troicasi shook his head, smirking. "Don't worry, folks. I have no qualms about killing you all in cold blood. In fact, that's exactly what I'm going to do. Then it's on to those squirmy wormy sniveling kids. Anyway," he swung back at Michael, "I thought the dogs would have gotten anyone that accidentally came near the cairn.

"It wasn't easy I tell you, to get their cages out here on a four-wheeler and setting them loose and booking before they made me mincemeat!" He said to Michael, "But yet again I underestimated you. However, here you are, trapped, eyeballing your demise."

"All right, Troicasi, enough preening. What are you going to do?" Michael growled at the man. He kept Cat stashed behind his back, he could feel her trying to look around him at Troicasi.

He latched onto Justin's arm to keep him from leaping at the demon holding them at bay. He clenched and unclenched his other hand trying to keep it limber, ready to spring when the opportunity presented itself.

One sarcastic brow rose. "Oh? In a hurry?" Troicasi asked. He rubbed the barrel of the gun against the side of his face. As soon as Michael moved a foot towards him he swept the gun back to aim at him. Michael stopped.

"Hmmm. Well, as much as I love toying with you people, I am busy, busy, busy, I do have children to hurl off the top of the mountain you know."

Cat cried out, quickly slapping her hand over her mouth.

Troicasi grinned drolly. "You know, you guys would be so proud of those youngsters. Industrious the lot of them. Futile though it is, they actually were able to get out of the prison I had them in, *never* expected it. I thought it was totally escape proof. Those kids are quite resourceful, and brave, and caring of each other.

"Even the thuggiest ones came through when the chips were down, so opposite of their lying, cheating, thieving parents. Working together they managed to figure a way out of the rocky prison and also were able to breach other incredible obstacles."

Sighing dramatically he said sadly, "But, the poor little darlings, out of the furnace and into the fire as it were, they're trying yet another dangerous escape, swimming a pretty wild fiord as it were. There's no way on earth they'll be able to cross the lake.

The silt bottom descends even while water continues to gush in from the melting snow run off. That makes for a killer current.

"Remember, the youngest are 8 and the oldest are only 12. They're just children, I'd say their chances are one in a million of surviving. Of course then there's the zenith at the titan falls where the lake pours out...I'd say your puny little girl, Simone is it? Has a snowball's chance in hell of-"

Justin suddenly lunged at him but like lightening Troicasi swung the gun out and slammed it into the side of his red head. Justin dropped to the ground like a duck on hunting day. Jumping back, Troicasi aimed the gun at Michael and Lucas daring them to move.

"You animal!" Cat screamed, stepped forward and dropped to her knees beside the fallen officer.

Groaning, Justin lay on his side, touched his head then looked at his fingers. The tips were bloody. He wiped them on his jeans, the dripping blood disappeared into the rest of the dirt and grit. Shuffling his feet back like a crab, his arms rigid on the ground behind him he pushed to wobbly stand up.

360

Cat slid his arm over her shoulder and helped him regain his balance. Shaking his head, red coils springing, he wiped his sleeve across his temple to stop the blood running down the side of his face. His head bobbed dizzily like a bobble-head doll on a dashboard.

Troicasi waved the gun at the wiry garda. "Just for that young man, if by some monumental chance your blondie girl makes it out of the rapacious lake, I'll be sure to throw her off the cliffs first. It'd be a kinder death if she drowns. Maybe." He laughed as Justin lunged for him again, Cat and Lucas held him back.

Justin's legs wobbled, he tilted to the right then dizzily forced himself to center. His face a beet, pained eyes blue slits, he swore at the man, "I'll kill you, you son of a bitch! You're a dead man, dead!" Justin struggled to free himself from his friends' hold, but his head was spinning, his legs like jelly, his voice hoarse, he dashed an angry hand at the blood sliding down the side of his head.

"Oh yeah," Troicasi laughed. "I'm real scared," he mocked. "Shut up or I'll slam you on the other side of the head and you won't be able to tell your hair from the blood you ruddy little runt!" He laughed harder at Justin's weak efforts to break free from his friends and lash out at the man.

They held him back with little effort, the redhead looking like an unsteady pipe cleaner figure with freckles swayed, his hand to his head trying to keep his balance.

"Who the hell *are* you, you deranged beast?" Lucas ground out.

Smiling nastily, Troicasi wrapped one arm around his waist and rested the gun on his arm. "Geez, I was wondering when you people would get around to that."

"So quit gloating you lame creep, tell us." Lucas, like Michael, was carefully watching the situation, waiting for an opportunity to strike. They planned to keep him talking as long as they could, eventually they'd find their moment.

Troicasi eyed the husky blond garda up and down. "Okay sport, simmer down. I'll speak slowly for you. The bigger they are the dumber they tend to be and the harder they fall. You're probably as soft and squishy as your waffles nickname, all yellow hair and brown sugar eyeballs," he goaded the officer. Lucas wasn't biting. His face remained impassive.

"Just spill it, Troicasi," Lucas demanded. "Tell us what a Brainiac you were to do all this. Hold an entire town hostage gripped in fear and panic, worried to death about their children. Just tell us who the hell you are, and how, *why*, you committed this- this abominable act."

Troicasi's smile spread viciously across his angular face. His hair, like Michael's had grown long in the months since the beginning, since the festival when Stormie Dodge fell into the well. It was slicked straight back.

Every time he smiled, his nose, already long, dipped over his upper lip, his chin strained to a dagger point until he resembled more a caricature than a man.

He tugged at one long ear then rubbed his unshaven face. Spreading his double-jointed legs he planted his boots solidly on the rocky ground, keeping the gun aimed at the four people in front of him. Surprisingly, even after moving about setting off cave-ins and such, he looked neat and clean in khaki pants and matching shirt.

"You got it, Mr. Patience, I'll tell you my story." Troicasi smirked. "Well, it goes back a little around 2,000 years ago when I was born."

Michael, Lucas and Cat's brows arched like incredulous boomerangs. It was all Justin could do to stay on his feet.

"Of course you don't believe me." Troicasi shrugged. "I don't really care what you think or believe." He said he didn't care but he obviously relished the attention and couldn't wait to tell them his story.

"So you were saying," Lucas urged him impatiently.

"Geesh, keep your pants on. As I was *trying* to tell you, a very, very long time ago I was created by, of course you won't believe this, but anyway, my parents were children of God. *Real* children of God, not *gods*. The real God, not those made up gods like those mythical gods and goddesses that did magical acts and rode on white flying stallions."

"Oh come on," rolling his eyes, Lucas dripped sarcasm.

Troicasi's dagger chin rose, his brown eyes hooded. Then he lowered his head spearing Lucas with a haughty look. "Do you want to hear or not?"

Michael held a hand up in front of Lucas. "Yes, Troicasi. We want to hear everything. Please continue." He heard Lucas grumble but he knew the officer was aware that time was their gift. The longer they kept Troicasi talking, the longer they lived and the better chance of rescuing the children.

Troicasi nodded royally. "Thank you, Sergeant. You are the only one with his head on his shoulders. As I was saying, God, yes, the Almighty Being up in Heaven, created my parents, as well as other children, from his, oh, it's hard to explain, but he created them from his spirit. But they were very real.

"And like any children, there was fighting of course. Father and Mother were created at different times- way too difficult for you to comprehend how they came about. Regardless, they met and fell in love and were sanctified to be as one. They had me and many other offspring. I was first born." He glanced proudly around the small group.

Michael held Justin up, his knees kept buckling but he refused to sit down. Lucas glowered through lowered blond brows and eyelashes but kept his tongue. Cat worked to keep the skepticism off her face, she struggled to hold up Justin on his other side.

Troicasi went on, "As first born, I was promised a kingdom. You are not aware of course, but there are other kingdoms out there," he waved his hand in an arc over his head.

"Out in what you people call galaxies. But I was promised *this* kingdom, the kingdom of Earth. We siblings were sent down to be raised, to learn and grow amongst the human people. When the time was right, as I said, I was to be made the ruler. Then," he scowled, the memories flooded darkening his face, he could hardly contain his anger.

The gun shook in his hand, his eyes blanked like brown nickels, vaporous, vacant. He stared over their heads, remembering, thoughts raining down like bitter needles piercing his essence. It was as if the life drained from him, emptying him as a bowl tips and water pours out. The barrel of the gun drifted down.

Lucas discreetly nudged Michael with his elbow. Michael stood stock still, however he blinked rapidly, acknowledging with Lucas that this may be their opportunity to overpower the monster and get the gun.

But, then, life flowed back into Troicasi's face, his eyes brightened, the dark color drained, his hand tightened on the gun, he raised it. The thin smile grew bigger, but it didn't reflect in his eyes.

"Pardon me for wallowing in remunerations," he sighed, shaking his head. "It was a different time then. Reality was vastly different from what you think you are experiencing now. However," he waved the gun. "That's for another day. Which, of course, you won't be seeing."

"It all sounds fascinating, Mr. Troicasi," Cat ventured. "Or should we call you Mr. Iscariot?"

Chapter Fifty-One

Troicasi grinned at Cat and inclined his head to her, "Oh you are the witty one. Please call me by my given name, Judas." Ignoring Lucas' rolled eyes he turned his full attention to Cat.

"I'm sure you, Miss Cat, have the intelligence and creative mind it requires to comprehend the truth. So, to continue with my story. Picture the world then. No electronics, nothing to hide behind, nothing to shield yourself. Everything was out there, primitive, fresh, raw, new, filthy, gritty, scary- cutthroat.

"People were straight up, no punches pulled. Humans were bought and sold and murdered every day for the most trifling of offenses like they were mere ants. Someone wanted your property or wife, they just killed you. Women were basically cattle, no offense, hon." His insincere apologetic smile didn't make it an inch from his lips.

Covered head to toe in dirt, a hole ripped across her t-shirt exposing a lot of skin, and another on the knee of one jean leg, Cat elegantly raised and lowered one shoulder blandly. She had no intention of letting him get her goat.

Head tipped slightly to one shoulder, she fluttered long lashes over sea blue eyes and smiled politely at his boorishness. Even the smudge of dirt on the swell of one cheek only added a contour to her extraordinary beauty.

His gaze travelled down her body revealing he appreciated her beauty. He let out a harsh breath. "That life was a whole different life. That's also a story for another time, again sadly you won't have any more time. Anyway, to make a long story short, *I* was to be the Prince. The Messiah, the Lamb. *I* was to be the beloved one to lead. The entire world was promised to *me*, it was to be mine!" he thundered, slamming a fist to his chest.

"But," he bent and shook his head, dingy hair swinging, smiling wryly. "That younger brother of mine, of course you've heard of him, Jesus. He kept getting in front, pushing me out of the way. People flocked to him, even when he was a child. He was, I hate to say it, charismatic.

"A magnetic golden voice, he could draw people in like they were listening to a vivid, hopeful dream. A fairytale come true, everlasting life- bunk! I fought him at every turn. When he was 12, we caravanned to Jerusalem for the feast of the Passover.

"When it was over, we left Jerusalem to go back home. I told my Earth mother, Mary, that he was in one of the clusters of groups travelling with us, when I knew we'd left him behind in a temple. I had hoped by the time we got home it would be too late to go back for him.

"I'd *prayed* someone would have tired of his constant yammering and have stoned him to death, or sold him, or jailed him, anything to get him out of *my* limelight. But no, just as we were arriving home, Mother Mary noticed he was missing and stopped the entire goddammed caravan to turn around and go back for him."

Troicasi's grimace twisted so macabre he could have been an ancient gargoyle perched atop a castle waiting to attack and destroy any misbegotten visitor. Resentment burned off him smelling like sewer steam.

The gun still in his hand, he dragged his sleeved arm across his face to clear the perspiration. His lank hair hung like wrinkled rope in the damp dungeon. He was no longer pin neat, he seemed to be wilting before their eyes.

Lucas whispered to Michael while the man ranted, "It's like he's dissolving Sarg, atom by atom, like in a while he'll slowly disintegrate, until he spirals into a nasty pile of dung, or ash, you know, like the wicked witch melting." Michael whispered back, "If only that were true. I think you're getting delusional, like him. Just stay ready...."

Troicasi went on, "It was to be my turn at that wedding. I had practiced and practiced the primeval Chinese trick of turning water to wine. I had been taught at the master's knee, secret pellets stuck to my palm to be surreptitiously dropped into the water to miraculously turn it to wine. That would have been my in, my start.

"It would have all been me after that because Mother Mary was the catalyst to the kingdom. Without her it couldn't be had. She would have been so proud of me, she would have put me first now, given me my legacy, my destiny..." he trailed off, again getting lost in the memories of time.

Lucas inched a toe, Michael shook his head faintly. *Not yet-*

Blinking himself back to the present, Troicasi continued without prodding, nothing like a captured audience. He finally had the attention he had always craved.

"It was bad timing. I was in one of the rooms way in the back at the wedding where the servant girls were kept, getting my fill of, well, of whatever I wanted. There was such an array to choose from, and as I said, women were nothing then. I was not exactly an aristocrat but we were friends of the groom so I could have any female I wanted, and I did, with their cooperation or not, who cared?"

"Geez, Troicasi, we don't want to hear about your exploitive exploits," Lucas furiously interrupted cutting him off.

"Fine, blondie, don't get your knickers in a twist. You men these days, whipped, all of you." He looked directly at Michael. Michael calmly gazed back, face impassive, he would not be provoked into doing anything rash.

"So," Troicasi ranted like a madman, "what would become a stinking rotten pattern, my little brother usurped me at the wedding and every time after that, again and again and again. I spent years plotting how to dispose of him.

"I paid thugs to murder him, but the clumsy fools bollixed it every time. I tried desperately to push the Jewish and Roman leaders to bring charges against him, but he always somehow managed to slip from their clutches.

"He had a silver tongue, eyes shining so bright they rivaled the very sun. Brilliant words flew like doves with angel wings from him." Frustrated fury filled his face, tremors shook his hands, he pounded the fist with the gun into his palm.

As blind rage threatened to unleash, he waved the gun at the group. Michael nudged Cat behind him with one hand and did the same with Justin. He and Lucas prepared to rush Troicasi, but Troicasi suddenly caught himself. Panting, he struggled to regain his composure.

He wiped the sweat off one hand on his khakis then switched the gun to that hand and wiped the other hand. He brought the gun up, aiming it steadily at the group. Coming to grips, he took a deep breath, sniffled noisily then laughed, a short ugly sound.

"It seems just like yesterday. Time, time really has no meaning, it's intangible, you can't see it or touch it or hold it or, stop it." His face hardened into cement, eyes became squeezed pinpoints stripped of light.

"Ahh, I finally resorted to bribing the town leaders into arresting him. Then, I had to obtain more money to keep them riled up to call for his head. It was a lucky thing I was the treasurer. Those trusting fools, I'd been robbing them blind for years, pretending to give money to the poor when it was really going into my pocket." He gently stomped his legs up and down, he was getting tired of standing, as they all were.

Troicasi looked from each of them to the other. Total disbelief rang in their faces but he was blind to it. He was finally getting the attention and adoration he'd always dreamed of. Soon, the entire village would be at his feet, then, little by little, the world would bow to him. He wasn't so self-absorbed that he didn't notice his hostages were getting edgy.

Justin swayed back and forth; he would have fallen if Michael and Lucas weren't holding him up. Cat, still behind Michael was leaning against a wall, bend forward at the waist, her hands on her thighs. The long luscious hair draped over half her face.

"I'll get on with it. Of course you know what happened. He was crucified. I waited for time to pass, for Mary to forget him, for my brothers and sisters to stop talking about him." He forked bony fingers through his greasy hair.

"I waited for the world to move on, for the Apostles to look to another leader, me." The gaunt face closed in remembered torment. The pain of being invisible, a nobody, ignored.

"Well," he paced a few steps. "It never happened. They threw me aside like I was a reviled serpent. Every time they saw me they turned their heads, crossed to the other side of the road. I was not invited to partake of even the evangelism. I was ostracized." Pacing again, he kept the gun up and his eyes on the men.

"You know," Troicasi spouted, "Irenaeus' summary indicated that Jesus set me up. These words my brother Jesus said to me, 'Truly I say to you, Judas, those who offer sacrifices to Saklas, the great fool, exemplifies that everything is evil.

"But you will exceed all of them. For you will sacrifice the man that clothes me. Already your horn is raised, your wrath has been kindled, your star has shone brightly, and your heart has been hardened.' So see, his plan was to make me look like the devil.

"He knew my rage burned against him. Really, I can rationalize my so called betrayal by saying I carried out my actions in order for Jesus to have died on the cross and hence fulfill the theological obligations, make all the prophecies come true. So, actually I was the good guy. But, nonetheless, I was tossed aside, slandered, exiled." He ran the back of his hand over his nose to wipe the fluid seeping from it.

Lucas, his hands fisted on his hips, snorted scornfully. "Listen you creep. In mythology I read that Judas was a demiurge, an inferior deity. He built the material world out of chaos, he never should have been born.

"The name itself, Judas Iscariot, Iscariot is a Hellenized transformation of Sicarius. The suffix '-ote' or 'ot' denotes membership or belonging to – in this case the Sicarii. And," Lucas crossed his arms across his football muscled chest, "the Sicarii were a cadre of assassins among Jewish rebels intent on driving the Romans out of Judea."

Michael tucked his hair behind his ears, his brows arched in mockery at his friend. "Wow Luke, I didn't know you read anything other than Sports Illustrated."

Lucas pretended he felt insulted. "Hey man, remember, I did go through four years of college."

"Uh huh, four years of football college you mean, doesn't mean you actually studied or anything..." Justin painfully raised his head to jeer his friend,

"Hey," Lucas said, "at least it was real football, not the English version-"

'Hey!" Troicasi waved the gun around. "Knock it off. This is about me, my story. So, as I was saying," he glared at the men for taking he spotlight off him. "Finally, I gave up. I moved far, far away. Away across the great sea, away to bide my time, make my plans for revenge. After years of plotting and gathering a group of, let's just say uh, nefarious friends to help me with my quest I started my plan." He smirked, paced a few steps.

"You do remember my delightful wife Dee? She told you her real name, which I strongly told her not to do, she said it was funny, an inside joke. She said you'd never catch on. But, my friends, she is the *real* Queen Herodias. Yes, the one who had John's head cut off and served on a platter.

"And my daughter, Belle, of course they're not really my family, my pretend daughter is, wait for it- Jezebel. Ha! You should see the looks on your faces, priceless!" Bending over in laughter he could hardly keep the gun steady on them.

Justin raised his head painfully. "You are not only a sick vile bastard, you are 100 percent insane- kookoo you-"

Troicasi wiggled the gun at the pale red headed garda. "Of course, there's always non-believers."

Cat pushed herself from the wall and crossed her arms, she grimaced at him, incredulous and horrified. "Are you saying that for the past hundreds of years you've come along every 150 years to kidnap 12 kids under the age of 13 with the names of the disciples albeit in different forms, and kill them, in a horrendous ghastly way, for- for what?"

Troicasi turned his attention to her. "For revenge, dammit, for revenge. Those sons of bitches Apostles dropped me, exiled me. I was supposed to be their *leader*. Some of them were my blood brothers. I tried to reason with them but they wouldn't even speak to me. Mary, well, she pretty much disowned me and father Joseph had passed on by then.

"So, for hundreds of years I did it for revenge. My brother Jesus would have been devastated. Then, after the last time I started to get bored. So I started thinking, how can I make this work for me?" His eyes shifted around as he spoke.

"I devised the plan that after the kids were found dead in the next week I would start snatching kids again. The town would freak out. I would sell each kid back at a price. Eventually I'd take it large scale and hold Ireland for hostage. After that?" He shrugged. "Who knows?"

"Troicasi," Michael said, "humor me. Tell me how you got the kids." He held his arms out and a couple of inches from his side, hands spread to appear harmless, that he was not about to launch an attack.

Troicasi's sneering sly grin creased deep, slicing his face like a malevolent jack-o-lantern. "Hah," he spat. "Easy as pie. You know, you can warn kids all day long about talking to strangers and taking candy, and stay away from the boogie man that wants to show you a puppy.

"What you don't warn your children is that the hero in the paper might not necessarily be good. But they think since I defeated death with bravery I could be trusted. Besides my rescuing that child from that hole, that was just good fortune. It gave me a respectable, raised platform, or pedestal if you will."

The villain snickered and went on, "You helped, Sergeant, I acted all embarrassed and humble and you played right into it. It all made me go immediately from a stranger to an old family friend in one fell swoop! That, what genius! I couldn't have written a better entrance in. Then, Dee and I threading ourselves into the search and the phone leads, well, we were accepted like we were the police or at the least, good neighbors, and all so we could follow the search and know what the police knew."

Michael responded, "You preyed on our good nature and that we taught our children to always go to the police when in trouble, that the police are safe. So, you as the town hero, hanging around with the search parties and us at the hall where we did our investigations made it look like you were one of us. Therefore you were trustworthy. Innocuous." His smile lopsided. He brushed back a wave of black hair, settled his hands on his hips and made a tiny indiscernible step towards Troicasi.

"Yep. That was my plan and you cops welcomed us with open arms. The kids were a snap. I built this incredible cool bicycle. It's totally unique. It's built especially for my crazy double jointed legs. It's funny," he laughed.

"The second those kids see me riding this spectacular bike they all beg to try it. All your parental warnings go right out the window. I got the two girls, Simone and Teddy to ride tandem. They loved it!"

Michael's head dipped sideways. "I remember, I saw bicycle tracks outside my niece's window. That's how you got her."

Troicasi nodded emphatically. "Oh yes. What a darling she is, your little Matty. Fat red pigtails, two front teeth like- oh what did I hear the other kids call them," he snapped his fingers.

"Chicklets! Yeah, she's a cutie pie all right. All freckles and rosy cheeks and indignant bravado. She's a courageous one. A mother hen at- what is she, nine? She's one to watch, I see President written all over her. Oh, but she's not going to have that chance now, is she?" he taunted.

Michael struggled to stand straight, loose, keep his shoulders from hunching, keep his hands open, not clenched in fists. He wanted to appear friendly, open, nonthreatening. But he couldn't control the vein throbbing at his temple.

He lowered his head, looked up at the tormentor through slit eyes but he didn't bite at the taunt.

Troicasi huffed, then smirked. He had already seen how much the child Matty meant to the man. "Anyway, I mostly used the bike to entice them away from their homes. There're two seats so we could ride away together.

"The girl, Jezebel, you know my faux daughter Belle, she used her girlish charms on the older boys. No matter what horror is out there you can depend on the male ego and testosterone to shut off their brains and to think only with their eyes, especially boys on the brink of manhood. She brought in the older boys like drawing hummingbirds to sugar water." He grinned triumphantly at the group.

"So what about then, your wife, daughter, and you have a son too, where are they? Who are they?" Cat asked from her perch against the wall.

Michael's eyes narrowed at the fiend, then they widened. "Wait," he hesitated, "I'm just getting it now, Troicasi."

Troicasi smirked at him. "Yes? What brilliant deduction has the fine sergeant come up with?"

Michael put a hand over his mouth and shook his head like he was trying to figure something out. Then he said, "It was you. The skull we found after the evacuation. It makes sense now." His friends turned their puzzled attention to him.

He crossed his arms. "I think you killed a man, and if I got it figured right, you murdered the whole family. A family of four. Am I right?"

Trying to hide his surprise, Troicasi nodded, "And?"

Michael looked down, thinking. Then he looked at Troicasi unable to hide the fury in his face. He pointed at the man and said, "You needed an in here, in Halo Valley, without anyone knowing your true identity. What better scheme than to kill a man and his wife and two kids, pretend you're them and move easily into Halo Valley without anyone being the wiser."

Cat gasped. Everyone looked sickened. Except Troicasi. He sneered. "Well, Sergeant, you're finally catching up with Beauty here in the brains department. Fortunately the family hadn't resided in Cleasaí very long. They lived in the most rural area and were not well known."

Lucas took a step forward, his arms curled like he was going into a fight, his face thunderous. Troicasi waved the gun at him. "Back up, Beefy. You're tough, but not as tough as a bullet. So keep back." He grinned at Michael. "So, the big brave officer finally figured something out."

Michael's anger amused him. "Yeah, me and mine needed to get in so I took out the whole family. Thought I had them pretty well cooked and dissolved as it were, but that damned boy, Red, he was to dispose of the rest of the bodies. I gave him explicit instructions, but you know how kids are, lazy. Still, I never thought you'd put 2 and 2 together, there wasn't enough left of him to-"

Her face a mask of pain and rage, Cat leaned forward, her arm shaking she was so mad, she thrust her finger at him in accusation, "You're nothing but an animal, a beast, a, a, you're nothing!"

One arm holding up Justin, Lucas wrapped the other around Cat's waist to hold her back. His expression perplexed, he asked their captor, "But the names, you're Troicasi, what was the other guy's name, how did you-"

Troicasi shrugged. "Eh, there was so much paperwork coming and going, Red's a whiz at computers, he easily hacked into the City Hall's computer and changed all of our names." He snapped his fingers saying, "Piece of cake. We only needed to have recorded that there were four bodies transferring to Halo Valley so we could take their places."

Holding the gun aimed at Michael, Troicasi turned his head to look at Cat. He eyed her up and down, his face an unashamed leer. "I do wish I could keep you around to play with after all this is done. But," he sighed heavily, "I need to get rid of all you loose ends as quickly as possible."

His eyes dropped to the tears in her blouse. Licking his lips he said, "Maybe I will keep you for a little while." He pushed his arm out straight, the gun aimed at Michael when he appeared to be about to run at him. "Back off, Sergeant, don't make me kill you sooner than I have to."

He looked back at Cat. She shook off Lucas' arm. "So, to answer your question my dear, I told you before that Dee is not really my wife. She is Herodias. She and Jezebel wanted revenge too. However, we had a little disagreement and we parted ways.

"I told them they are going to miss out on all the fun of throwing those kids off the cliffs, but they said they had other fish to fry. Now, the boy, Red, that played my son, you will not believe who he really is!"

Lucas held onto Justin with one arm and set the other on his hip. "Come on you slimebag. You expect us to believe any of this reincarnated or demi-god whatever bullshit? Give me a break."

Smugly, Troicasi's wide smile revealed a cropping of uneven teeth, the long nose dipped. "It doesn't matter what you idiots believe. You're going to die, and right after, I'm going to chuck those children off the cliffs to their deaths. And then, I will rule the world!" He held his arm out in a rigid line and moved the direction of the gun to aim straight at Justin.

"Enough of this. Officer Zeall first, as he's the weakest. I was going to shoot Miss Cat next so you boys can watch her die, but like I said, I may keep her around for a while. I need a toy to play with. So then, after I've disposed of you, I'm onward and upward to get the children." He gave Michael a squinty eye.

"Sergeant, you might as well let go of the puny redhead, a bullet between the eyes and he'll drop like a lead weight and pull you down. I am the king! The world will revere me! I am-"

"Sheep-dip," a wry voice drawled from dark.

Troicasi swiveled around. "What the-" his mouth dropped.

Chapter Fifty-Two

An hour went by, the children didn't stir. Time trudged so slowly they sat or laid down, each lost in his or her own desperate thoughts. There was such a cacophony of sniffing and weeping and sighing from the children it sounded like a hovering cloud of despondent mosquitoes.

They could hear the boys returning before they could see them. Slow, pattering splashing echoed around the chamber.

Tom-tom scrambled to his feet hurried to the edge got down on his knees and peered down. "They're here! They're back!" he cried out. The other kids all jumped up and ran to the edge of the wall and looked down.

Juan and Drew moved towards them slowly until they reached the wall. All that could be seen of them were their heads. Then they raised their drawn faces and wearily waved.

All of the children peered over the ledge. "Well?" Santy called down, the only one brave enough to ask. So relieved at seeing his brother return after such a long time his knees turned to butter. He would shriek joyfully if he wasn't so terrified of what was going to happen next. Juan didn't look happy.

Treading water, the boys' faces bobbed like twin pale balls in the weak light.

"Yeah," Juan called up to the kids, all lined up looking down they looked like a row of hopeful sunflowers. "There's really nothing to say. We went for a long time, the water just goes on and on. We figured if we went any further we'd be too tired to return. So we decided we're just going to have to chance it."

The row of sunflower faces fell. Jamie said, "But the water's got to end somewhere."

"Yeah but what if it's like a humongous waterfall," Tom-tom said, his voice rising as he pictured careening over a waterfall.

"Or what if it ends at a giant wall because the rain fell down and made the lake in a big hole? We won't be able to climb out," Pil wailed.

Rocky joined in, "What if we fall right into the monster's mouth and he chews us up and-"

"Rocky dude," Santiago murmured.

The kids stopped talking for a moment. They contemplated what else could be at the end of the lake. Ever the positive one, Matty endeavored to look on the optimistic avenue, she offered, "Maybe there will be an easy out that is just a little further than you went. Maybe our families will be there waiting for us...maybe..." Even she couldn't keep up her Pollyanna attitude, her hopefulness rang shallow in her own ears.

She had tried so hard not to give up, not to cry, but, a tear, crystalline against her dirty face oozed out and rolled like a dewdrop on a leaf over her cheek, it fell plop on the dirt.

Jessy ran to her and wrapped an arm around her shoulders, but said nothing. There was really nothing he could say.

"Guys," Juan's voice trailed up the wall. "We gotta decide what we're going to do."

Drew whispered to his friend, "Whatever they decide, we can't go back. There's no way we can get back up that wall. It's at least 20 feet up. And it's slick. I climbed a palm tree when we went on vacation in Florida, but there's no way I can get up that wall. I don't even think a lizard could do it." The boys swam over to hold onto the stone wall to help them rest, conserve their waning strength.

"I know," Juan nodded bleakly. Water dripped from his lashes and hair. They'd have to do something soon, the water was cold and they were tired. He could hear the children discussing their options.

It sounded like it was half and half. Half wanted to try the lake and half wanted to go back. One or two said they wanted to just stay where they were. Maybe someone would eventually find them. They talked for a few more minutes.

Squinting hard in thought behind his glasses, Tom-tom suggested, "What if we took off all our clothes, tied 'em together like a rope and pulled you guys back up here?"

Juan considered the idea, then shook his head. "The wall is too slimy for us to work our feet on, and it's too high for us to pull ourselves, climb up, and we're too heavy even if all of you pull one of us up at a time."

"It was a great idea though, Thomas," Drew gave the youngster a rewarding albeit weak grin.

The children talked some more, shoulders sagged with despair, heads dropped in resignation.

Finally, Santy said, "Okay," and leaned over the edge. "We've decided. We're coming in. Jessy convinced us to at least try, to go down fighting if that's what's to be. We're gonna jump down one at a time. Jamie's gonna hang onto my back, we'll go last so all of you can help us if he gets separated. The rest of the kids all say they can swim." He stood as tall and straight as he could and smiled confidently, stuffing his 'we ain't got a chance of ice cream in the oven of making it.' He asked, "Who's first?"

Panicking now that the chips were down, the kids all stared wide-eyed like frightened kewpie dolls at each other.

Then, Pil puffed his oxen shaped chest and stepped forward. "I'll go first. I float really good. I'm not scared." His pursed lips and creased brow belied his statement, but he decided it was time he started stepping up to the plate. There were kids younger than him that acted with more courage than him and it was embarrassing.

Pil trod with tiny steps to the edge of the wall and peered down. Juan and Drew's bodiless faces bobbed in the water next to the wall. The surface moved only with their treading efforts, otherwise it was like glass.

"It's okay, Pil, you can do it. We'll make sure you're safe!" Drew called up to Pil. Pil's eyes bulged with fear, the color fled from his stocky face. "On the count of three, Drew said. "One…" The other kids joined in with him in encouragement, "Two…" Pil flapped his arms back and forth to loosen them and bent his knees like he was about to fly off a diving board and sail like a graceful eagle into the water.

"Three!"

Pil froze. Rocky pushed him. Over the wall he went, an ungainly beach ball, arms and legs flailing, screaming at the top of his lungs- splash! Pil hit the water with a huge bellywacking splash then quickly disappeared under water. The kids held their breaths as if it was them plunging into the dark water with him, and waited, Juan and Drew immediately dove under to find him.

Seconds later, Pil popped up like a cork, sputtering and coughing and shaking his head, water sprayed in all directions. Juan and Drew emerged next to him.

"Yay! Way to go, Pil! You did it!" Drew high-fived the frightened boy. Pil panicked for a second, but then gathered himself when he heard all the kids cheering him like he was a hero. He grinned up at them.

"It's not so bad. Come on guys," he called up to the kids. His eyes narrowed at Rocky. The square kid's face split with a grin. "You wait Rocky, I'll get you back!" Pil threatened, but there was no malice. He was secretly grateful because he knew his bravery had died once he looked down, way down, at the water. He knew there was no way he was going to jump. Rocky did him a favor but he wasn't going to admit it.

After Pil made it safely, the rest of the kids jumped in one at a time. Drew and Juan were there to make sure they were all right and could swim. When it got to Jamie and Santiago, Jamie balked.

"I can't- I can't-" Jamie wailed, eyes scrunched up and mouth drawn so far his bottom teeth showed, he put his hands up to ward off Santiago.

Santiago spoke gently, "Listen dude, I know you're scared. We all are. But if you don't go you'll have to stay here alone."

He touched Jamie lightly on the shoulder then made his way to the edge of the wall. Jamie's sobbing broke his heart. If the kid didn't jump in on his own, Santiago had plans to grab him and throw him over. They couldn't leave him there alone. Pictures of Jamie's skeleton with cobwebs on it flashed in front of his eyes.

When it looked like Santiago was going to take the plunge, Jamie ran over to him- "No! Wait! I'll- I'll go. Don't leave me!"

"'S alright little guy." Santiago turned his back to the boy and bent over. "Hop on my back and hold onto my chest. Don't hold around my neck 'cause you'll strangle me and we'll both drow- uh, just hold on tight."

Jamie scrambled up on Santiago's back, wrapped his thin arms around his chest clutching his shirt and laid his head on his back. "Thank goodness you're a featherweight," Santiago told the delicately-boned child. He moved to the edge and said, "Hold your breath on 3-" then counted to 3 and jumped.

The boys made it safely. They joined the others treading around Juan and Drew.

"Let's roll. Everyone stay really close together," Juan instructed. "In fact, we should do like at Junior Lifesaving and everyone should have a buddy. So, buddy up and let's go. Drew, I'll take the front with Teddy and you buddy with Simone and take the rear.

"We're going to swim really, really slowly to conserve our energy. If we come across any ledges or boulders or anything we can rest on we'll stop and break. We'll take turns carrying Jamie. Ready? Swift on then gang." He slid into an easy sidestroke then pulled forward slowly in a crawl so the kids could fall in behind him.

The children treaded the water as they buddied up. Then with uneven strokes and splashing feet, they started their journey, having no idea where it would take them.

Chapter Fifty-Three

Hollis Hunter stood at the threshold of the tunnel behind the demon, with a pitchfork in his hands.

"What the bloody hell!" Troicasi spun around while backing up a foot to keep Michael and Lucas in his view. His eyes bulged like ping pong balls.

"No cheerio for me, Mr. Devil?" Hollis jeered. "Hey Michael, look what I found back at the entrance. Recognize it?" He waved the pitchfork at Troicasi. "Bleedin' lousy thief."

Troicasi's face blackened as dark as the cave. He backed up another step, aiming the gun at Hollis. Michael and Lucas half carried Justin to the wall near Cat and leaned him against it. Cat caught him under the shoulder to hold him up. Then they slowly maneuvered themselves so they were on opposite sides of Troicasi facing Hollis.

Troicasi swung the Sig Sauer at them then back at Hollis yelling, "Don't any of you move!"

Hollis held the pitchfork up in front of him and inched closer. "He's scared boys, he knows he only has 5 shots, maybe, *if* the gun was fully loaded. Oh?" One eyebrow arched at Troicasi when he chewed at his lower lip. "It seems maybe our thief here was in too much of a hurry or too stupid to check the gun. You used the gun before the storm Mikey boyo to scare away that vulture. That means he knows if we rush him he can't get us all," he smiled slowly at Troicasi.

Troicasi's eyes narrowed at the older man, he sucked his lips in and blew them out, one eye twitched. He swung the gun back and forth at the men. "Who wants to take a chance? Hmmm? Who wants to die? You going to gamble on how many bullets I have?"

He shifted his eyes from Hollis to Michael to Lucas to Hollis. "You, old man? You want to chance it?" He leveled the weapon at Hunter Hollis. Hunter didn't flinch.

"If you shoot me," Hollis said, motioning towards Michael and Lucas with his head. "They're gonna be on you like flies on a dead body before you can get another shot off."

"You want to chance it? You're just a big talker, Hollis. That cowboy moustache has gone to your brain," Troicasi sneered boldly, but his forehead wrinkled and sprouted beads of sweat, his arm shook ever so slightly.

Hollis shrugged, still holding the pitchfork out with both hands. "I've had a good long happy life. If I can trade my life for even one of my friends here or the children's," he shrugged one shoulder.

"Hollis, you-" Troicasi swung the gun back at Hunter.

Michael spoke loudly, "But Hunter, you old tramp, what about Lorielle? I mean, your third wife deserves a-"

"Dammit Mike, I told you she was my fourth-"

"No, no, I'm sure you said she was your-"

"No, number four I told you, she's the love of my life." Hollis dropped the pitchfork a hair.

Troicasi moved the gun back and forth commanding, "Knock it off, I will decide who-"

"No," Michael said with a frown, "I distinctly remember you saying she was your third mistake."

"Don't argue with me boy, I know which wife she is. There was number 1, Mabel, then 2 was Suzy, then 3-" at 3 Hollis rushed Troicasi shoving at him with the pitchfork held sideways- and Michael and Lucas sprung from the other side.

Troicasi backed into the wall, Hollis held him against the wall with the handle of the pitchfork, he let go of the fork with one hand and punched at Troicasi's hand holding the gun pushing his arm up, the gun went off, it was deafening- the bullet slammed into the ceiling showering them with rocks and dirt.

Troicasi rolled out of Hollis' reach, Hollis rammed at him with the pitchfork pushing him back over the threshold into the narrow tunnel.

Before Michael or Lucas could reach them, the gun fired again- the bullet hit the arched top of the tunnel, a rumble, then like shooting stars- chunks of rocks rained, the rumble turned to thunder. Michael and Lucas jumped back falling on their butts as a ceiling of boulders came crashing down. The cascade of boulders continued falling, piling rapidly into a solid mass.

"Hollis!" Michael yelled. "Hollis!" He could hear them grunting and scuffling on the other side of the avalanche of boulders. The gun went off again- the bullet ricocheted down the tunnel banging off stone after stone. Cat slammed her hands over her ears. Justin pushed himself off the wall and stumbled over to help the men.

The officers scuttled out of the path of more falling rocks, then scrambled quickly to their feet. Screams reverberated from the other side of the piled rocks, then cut off dead. Everyone stood still, not a sound came from the other side of the wall of rocks.

"Oh my God! Hollis!" Michael shouted. Shoving rocks and stones aside as fast as he could, he leaped over the rest and rushed into the tunnel, Lucas and Justin burst after him. He stopped so abruptly they almost ran into him.

"What the-" Lucas spurted, catching his balance. He drew up alongside Michael, Justin breathless lurched on the other side.

Michael held both arms out blocking them shouted, "Stop!"

The three officers peered through the dark, and down. They were at the edge of the crevice that Michael had mentioned earlier. There was not hide or hair or sound of Hollis or Troicasi.

Michael leaned over the gaping fissure. He put his hands around his mouth and called, "Hollis! Hollis can you hear me?" He waited. Nothing. Cat came running up behind the men. "Here." She handed Michael the flashlight he'd dropped in the skirmish.

Michael took the flashlight and pointed it into the hole yelling, "Hollis!" He moved the light around. Shaking his head, he wiped the back of his hand across his forehead. He rolled the light around again and then up and down the rest of the tunnel. The light ended about twenty feet away at a wall.

He aimed the light back down the ravine. "Hollis! Hollis!" he yelled again and again his alarm skyrocketing. Dropping to his hands and knees, then onto his stomach, he ducked his head in the opening still unable to see the bottom of the curved ravine. He called out again, turning his ear to listen.

"Can you see the bottom?" Justin asked in a fraught voice.

"No." Michael gravely shook his head, trying with all his might to hear a sound, see a glimmer of light, hope, anything suggesting life coming from the chasm. Nothing. He yelled until he was hoarse, but was met with silence.

He closed his eyes tight, tears bundled up behind his lids. Tipping his head back, he did the only other thing he could do, he prayed. Lifting his lids, he turned woefully to the others, tears shimmered in the dark eyes.

Clasping his hands he raised them to his forehead, then dropped them to his side. Aching despair bowed his shoulders in like an old man. Misery knit through his words, "It's deep. Too deep without a long dammed rope to get down. We left the rope back at the cave-in," his voice died off.

He turned from the crevasse, lips parted in disbelief. Torment burned through the black coals of his eyes, pain etched like a knife across his face. He dropped his head and draped his arm over his eyes. The other arm clutching the flashlight hung limply at his side.

He uttered the words he didn't want to say, to say them made it real, final, "He's gone."

Chapter Fifty-Four

What seemed like hours and hours and miles and miles, the exhausted children swam to a halt at a protruding ledge.

They formatted in front of it like mismatched bowling pins. What smidgen of strength they had was dismally fading.

Juan doggy-paddled close to the ledge. Drew who had taken Jamie from Santiago handed the boy back. Jamie climbed onto Santiago's tired back. Drew swam over to where Juan was examining the ledge.

"What do you think, Falcon? It looks like another rotten wall," Drew groaned.

Water slipping from Juan's short hair to his eyelashes dropped like tears into the water. Pinching his finger and thumb he squeezed the wet from his nose. "I don't know. We're going to have to see how deep it is. Maybe the water flows under it."

Juan said to the other kids, "We're gonna check it out under the water. Just hang in." The children were too tired to complain or even voice their fears.

Holding the wall for support, the boys took a moment to catch their breath then Juan dove under with Drew right behind him.

The children started counting the seconds out loud.

The boys were gone fifty seconds- then they burst back through the surface like dolphins leaping for fish, spewing water, gulping and hacking deep breaths. The other kids circled, little bobbing buoys.

"You guys all right?" Rocky asked, concerned small chocolate-drop eyes in the square of his face.

Juan wheezed and coughed. Drew's lungs rasped and squealed as he gasped for breath. Juan nodded, water droplets flying. "Yeah," he choked out, coughed then spit. He glanced at Drew, who was looking back at him trying to smooth the worry from his face.

"Uh, listen guys," Juan hesitated. The kids swam closer. Jamie clung to Santiago's back, his head lying on the bigger boy's shoulder. The soaked kids waited all spiky lashes and chattering teeth.

"The deal is…" Drew said louder than he meant to. The kids turned to him. "The uh, the good news is that the wall doesn't go all the way down. The water flows under it."

Silence.

"And? The bad news?" Barty dared to ask, fearing the worst.

"We tried to swim under it. We can't tell how far it goes. It could be just a few feet further than we went or…"

Blonde hair sticking to her face, Simone's voice squeaked out, "Or what? Like maybe it doesn't never ever end?" Her voice grew piercing to a wail. The lake and the bobbing kids reflected in her big clear blue eyes. So did the sudden horrifying panic.

They had moved beyond the fear of getting in the lake and swimming towards the unknown, they had still held some hope, but now…

Juan's forehead wrinkled. "We just don't know. We have to chance it. We just have to. There's *really* no going back now, we'd never make it."

The children were just too plain tired to cry. But Tom-tom whimpered, "God I'm so hungry…"

"Oh be quiet you big crybaby!" Teddy snapped at him. "We all are. It doesn't help to complain. Aren't you Injuns s'pposed to be brave?"

Squinting, Tom-tom had stuffed his glasses in his pocket, his mouth widened in its perpetual 'O' with only one front tooth. Surprised at the younger girl snipping at him, he stuttered, "Tha-that's not nice. That's called stereo-typing, and that's wrong."

"Come on guys, no name calling," Drew's weary voice gently scolded.

"What are we going to do?" Matty queried. Even her ever hopeful 'everything will turn out all right' disposition was wilting, sliding into desolation.

"We have to do what we've been doing," Jessy said determinedly. "Keep going forward."

"Oh shut up you freakin' gospel-loving, mixed-breed, foster jerk! I am so tired of your preaching hopeful crap, what's it gotten us? We're here in the middle of the freaking ocean in the middle of the freaking mountain, who knows where the heck we are? Maybe we're under the core of the whole freaking earth, maybe we're-" Pil rambled, obviously panicking, his strident voice echoing off the water and bouncing around the chamber.

"Calm down, Pil. Jessy's just trying to keep our spirits up. Lay off. We can't let ourselves panic. We need to stay solid as a team, not pick at each other," Juan said tiredly. He treaded over to the barrel-chested boy who floated easier than the rest.

Pil lowered his head and let the tears flow into the water like a miniature waterfall. Juan briefly set a hand on Pil's shoulder while treading. "We have to stay positive, Pil. We've gotten this far. Someone's on our side. Right?" He dipped his head so he could see into Pil's eyes.

Pil nodded and wiped his eyes and nose with one hand while treading with the other. "Yeah," he hiccupped. He shot Jessy a sheepish look, "I'm sorry Jess, I'm just scared."

Jessy sent him a sad smile, "'S okay Pil. Me too."

Juan swam back into the middle of the circle the children had formed. "We're just gonna go for it. We're gonna take a minute to gather our strength, take some deep breaths. I'm gonna count to 3, then when I say 3, everyone goes under and follows me. Got it?" An assembly of nods ran the circle.

"You guys ready?" he asked Santiago and Jamie who was still clinging to his back. Both nodded wordlessly. Juan swam to the ledge, Drew waited, he would bring up the rear as usual to keep the stragglers close.

"Okay now," Juan said, his own voice quivering. "Take a couple of deep breaths, then on the count of three we all go under at the same time and swim as fast as you can, don't stop, stay as close to the top of the water as you can. Try to use the wall to climb down. Hold your breath, we can rest when we're...safe."

He waited while the children got in formation as close to the ledge as they could.

Rocky sighed loudly, "I can't wait until we can count to further than 3." The kids giggled weakly, releasing a shred of anxiety.

"All right now, ready, one...two..." Juan counted, he could hear the children taking deep breaths like they were about to play a tuba. He shouted, "Three! Let's go!" Sucking a deep breath he dove under, the kids followed him, little fish going down the drain behind the pied piper.

Holding their breaths, cheeks puffed out, faces turning crimson, the kids swam underwater deeper and deeper until they reached the bottom of the ridge. Like a school of human fish they swam as fast as they could behind Juan.

Kicking his legs like scissors, Jamie held onto Santiago's belt as tightly as he could like a little pilot fish attaches to a shark swimming as one so Santiago could use his own arms and legs freely.

They swam and swam and swam, arms pulling and pulling and legs kicking for all they're worth, lungs compressing, about to explode- then Juan started heading upwards, surging head first straight up like a rocket, bubbles streaming from his mouth and nose. The train of kids followed little beads on a necklace. Then-

Pop! Juan burst through the surface gasping for air, pop-pop-pop-each child right behind him, flailing, gasping, choking. Finally, they all caught their breaths, treading water, laughing, crying with relief.

"We made it!" Rocky yelled. The children cheered.

Grinning joyfully, Jessy swung his head back and forth looking at each child, then he suddenly dove back down.

Drew had popped up next to Juan. He struggled to catch his breath. Just as he finally breathed easier, he saw Jessy go under. He looked at Juan in question.

"I don't know..." Juan murmured. He was so tired. Seconds ticked by and Jessy didn't appear.

"Come on," Juan said to Drew. The boys dove back down. Now the other kids waited, one, two three, four, the seconds kept marching- then, Juan and Drew burst through the surface again pulling Jessy up between them, Jessy was holding Pil. Pil was blue.

"Lay him out! Float him on the surface!" Santiago yelled. They maneuvered Pil to lie flat on his back, the kids treaded frantically with their feet trying to hold Pil afloat. Juan swam under the boy and pushed up under his back trying to make it as much like he was lying on solid ground as possible.

A surge of water and Rocky was beside him pushing on Pil's backside to help keep him rigidly afloat.

Kicking his legs like crazy, Santiago flung Jamie to Barty then pushed on Pil's chest. When he stopped pushing, Matty gave two rescue breaths. They repeated and repeated. Nothing happened. Pil was not breathing. Santiago pushed again, and again, and again.

"Come on Pil, come on Pil, breathe, breathe," the children chanted, teeth chattering from the cold and the penetrating fear that they'd lost one of their own.

Suddenly a geyser of water spurted from Pil's lips. He bent in half spitting and choking. Drew got behind him, wrapped his arms around his chest to hold him upright. The other kids tried to help hold Pil's head above water.

Wheezing like an old man, it took time before Pil's breathing smoothed. Eyes bulging, tongue hanging like a dog he blinked around at the other kids, embarrassed.

"You said you could swim well," Jamie accused the gasping pudgy boy while he clung to Barty's back like a baby monkey to its mama. The children had been holding their collective breaths, but then Pil laughed, they all laughed teeth, unclenched and air blew out releasing frayed nerves.

The kids treaded water and doggy-paddled gathering into a circle looking to Juan to get started, to lead them out of the watery grave.

Juan said, "Well, we made it!" His shaky grin worked into a steady wide smile. The relief of getting out from under that mountain wall almost overwhelmed him.

He had put on a brave front but in his gut he thought they'd never be able to swim under water long enough to get back out to open air. He wasn't about to tell them that he figured they would all perish trapped underwater in the subterranean lake. But, against all odds-

"Hey!" Simone yelped. "Lookit!" She pointed excitedly. The other kids turned to see what she was so frenzied about.

"Oh my gosh," Matty exclaimed.

Chapter Fifty-Five

Michael stepped back over to the other side of the tumbled rocks, his head down in misery.

Tripping over to him, Cat wrapped her arms around him. He laid his head against hers, black hair draping golden brown.

Cat couldn't hold back, she wept out loud. Fraught with incredulity and sorrow, Lucas and Justin unashamedly joined the pair. The four friends hung on each other, besieged with grief.

"What is this, some kind of kinky hugfest and I wasn't invited? What a shame, I happened to be a veritable expert at cuddling. Just ask my *fourth* wife." Hollis stood on the other side of the collapsed pile of rocks, the rocks mounded up to just past his knees.

His hands on his hips, he clicked his tongue and shook his head. It looked like he'd grown hair on his head from the dirt clinging to it. His khakis were torn and covered with dirt. A sliver of blood gleamed from a gash in his forehead and a bruise was swelling on his cheek.

Hollis coolly pulled out a cigar and a lighter and proceeded to light the cigar. He took a couple of puffs, held out the cigar, looked at the end then stuffed the front back in his mouth, twirled the tip of one long moustache and smiled like an innocent Snidely Whiplash at the astonished group gawking at him. He stepped over the rocks to the side where they were standing.

"Hunter!" Cat shrieked and ran to him, throwing her arms around him almost knocking him over.

Frozen in shock, Michael broke free and hurried over to his friend. He wound one arm around Hollis' back because Cat was hugging him like she'd never let him go, and gave his friend a hard hug then stood back and grinned like the man in the moon at him. Justin and Lucas did the same.

"You old son of a bitch," Michael spouted. "You scared the damned daylights out of us. I swear I thought I'd seen the last of your obstinate, reckless, bald-assed, old hide! I wasn't upset you know," he smiled, his watery eyes gleamed. "I just was worried about what to tell Lorielle."

"Hell man," Hollis chuckled. "She'd be calling the insurance company before you got out of the doorway!"

Lucas tugged his fingers through his unruly mop of grungy blond hair. "Hollis, man, we thought you were a goner."

"Yeah." Justin shook his head ruefully. "We couldn't see the bottom of that hole. How did you-"

"Yeah, what the hell are you, Houdini? How'd you get out?" Lucas questioned.

"Well," Hunter drawled. The cigar went out and he stuck it back in his pocket.

Cat let go of the tanned brawler and stepped back clasping her hands behind her back like a schoolgirl, smiling broadly at the rugged older man.

"It seems this mountain is chock full of caves and tunnels. I originally got in by finding a shoddily concealed hole about halfway up this side of the mountain. Just nosing around I discovered a boulder blocking a tiny cave. That's how I got in."

"What about the dogs?" Michael asked.

A corner of Hollis' mouth tugged in. "Those pups? I come prepared son. I always bring a dart gun tipped with a sedative in case I come across an irate animal like a mama bear protecting her cubs that I don't want to kill. Bap- Bap- Bap- a few darts and those fellas slowed immediately, the surprised, confused look in their eyes as they slunk to the ground was funny, then- out like lights."

"How long does the sedative last?" Lucas asked. He was propping Justin up, the young garda was sinking.

Hollis pulled a handkerchief from his pocket and wiped his eyes then his tanned, bald pate, shook it out then shoved it back in his pocket. "I gave them enough to keep them out for half an hour or so. I'm sure they will awaken and drowsily stumble off forgetting that they were ever here."

"Anyway, you-" Lucas pressed him.

"Oh yes. How I survived the fall. As I was saying, this mountain is sketched with tons of tunnels, half-tunnels, crevasses, huge bodies of water on different levels. When we tumbled into that chasm there were spider tunnels branching off. It's so dark you can't see them.

"I didn't know I'd hit one until I was skittering down it like on a kid's slide. I went fifty feet or so. What was amazing was that the skinny tunnel I slid down led back here like a loop. It was a steep incline to get back up here but obviously I managed."

"What happened to Judas?" Cat asked.

"Judas my foot," Hollis spat. "That creep is no more a Biblical reincarnation or immortal or god or whatever he deigns to think he is than you or me. He's just a whack-job with delusions of insane grandeur."

"Whatever he is, what happened to him?" Michael asked.

Hollis shrugged one shoulder. "Dunno. He might have hit bottom and smashed into a billion little pieces, that would be the ideal scenario, or he might have shifted onto a slide like I did. The actual hole really narrowed the further down I got. I have cuts and bruises from banging against the stones."

"So," Lucas said, "we don't know if he's dead or alive."

They stood silently for a minute, glancing around in case he snuck up on them like he did the last time.

Michael turned to Hunter. "So he could be going after the children right now."

Hollis nodded.

"We still don't know where he's keeping them," Michael observed.

"No," Hollis agreed, shaking his head. "I didn't come across anything that could look like a cage or big room with a door or wherever he's got them, even if they're all held together or are separated."

"Let's roll," Michael said, turned on his heel and started jogging back the way they had come.

Hollis jogged up behind him. "Where're we going?"

Over his shoulder, Michael told him, "The way you came in has been blown and blocked. The way Lucas came in has been blown and blocked. This tunnel Cat and I came in ends here. We need to follow the tunnel back to the cairn, and get out of the mountain and find the way in that Troicasi has been using instead of the cairn. If we can get out. Hopefully that fool didn't block that way too."

"Gotcha," Hollis uttered, right at Michael's heels.

Cat followed closely behind Hollis. Lucas was helping Justin walk as he was dizzy from the whack in the head, they followed as fast as they could manage.

The group had traveled deep into the mountain, it took a long time to get back out. Finally they climbed out of the cairn.

They stood in front of the mountain, studying every craggy nook and cranny they could see. There were few trees, but a lot of shrubs and boulders. Night had long fallen and was almost over while they had been traversing the cavern.

All traces of the storm had gone leaving a clear night. Stars twinkled like sterling thumbtacks in a black felt sky, the moon hung bright as a silver dollar.

The warm air had cooled to a pleasant temperature; a wisp of a breeze gently strummed the humidity away. The mountain loomed dark and foreboding, a rocky pyramid, but as they had learned, not a solid one; it was crocheted like a wool sweater with tunnels and caves and great pools of water.

"Where to start?" Michael pondered out loud.

"Well," thumb to his chin, Hollis said thoughtfully, "the entrance probably isn't any of the ones we used. It's probably opposite to where we all came in. You and Miss Cat came in the front. Luke and Justin came in on the left, as did I but I went in way higher up. It takes over a day to get around to the Cleasaí side. So," he ran a palm over his dirty tanned head.

"To the right," Michael agreed. He said to Cat, "I can move more quickly without you, Cataleigh. You stay here with Justin. If more cavalry come, tell them where to go."

Cat nodded. He approached her slowly. Reaching out a roughened hand he let a curl of her hair wind around his finger. Michael said, "In case we don't make it back," he took Cat's hand drawing it behind her back at her waist and pulled her close, hip to hip.

Wrapping his hand around the back of her neck, he tilted her head up. Midnight eyes swallowed up the air of her uncertainty, his pupils flared to black saucers.

He pulled her up on her toes, bent his head, ebony waves caressed her face as he kissed her gently. She didn't resist. His body hardened, his mouth thrust against hers, savage, brutal, bruising, demanding she respond.

Cat couldn't stop her response if she wanted to. Her hand wound up around him grasping his head, pressing against his powerful physique she burned into him.

Michael's entire being throbbed like a tuning fork for a fleeting second, then he pulled his head back. His eyes dropped to her swollen lips kindled red then scrolled up to her limpid sea eyes. "If we were alone…"

"Woowee! You go Sarg!" Justin crowed and Lucas whistled. Hollis chuckled, "Yeah, get a room!"

Michael smiled. "I would if she'd let me." He brushed her lips with his thumb, then her cheek softly as if it was gossamer and could tear. Cat shivered, her skin tingling from his touch. They melted apart.

Not taking his eyes off hers, Michael pushed a lock of brandy colored hair off her shoulder letting it swirl down her back, then turned to the men. "Come on Lucas, Hollis, let's hit it." He shot Cat one more quick glance, night eyes of promise, then headed briskly towards the right side of the mountain with Hollis and Lucas beside him.

Chapter Fifty-Six

"It's land! It's land!" Rocky shouted.

Seeing what Simone was pointing at, the rest of the children's cheers resonated off the curved stone grotto like chiming hand bells.

As if in a race, the children's weariness dissolved instantly. They swam as fast as they could, mini propellers churning through the swampy liquid straight at the solid earth ahead, hoping to escape what they each thought was going to be their watery graves.

Juan and Drew reached the dry land first. Rocky was next, he stared up in wonderment at the ridge of land only inches above his head. "Guys! It's not rock, it's dirt, land, and it's low, it's low enough we can get out!"

"Thank God," Juan's voice heavy with relief. "I was so worried if we did reach land it'd be too high for us to get out or it would pour out to a waterfall."

Pil swam up and touched the earth. "Oh wow," he exclaimed as tears sprung when the dirt turned his fingertips brown. "I thought for sure we were gonna wash over some ginormous killer falls and get crushed on rocks or smushed in the falls, or get sucked down in a whirlpool, or go fleeting down a rushing river that never ever ends and drown or-"

"Okay, okay, okay Pil," Juan said gently. "It's all good now, we're here."

"So what are we waiting for? Let's get the hell out of this freakin' pool!" Santiago swam up with Jamie holding onto his belt. Juan scrambled up onto the low ledge. He knelt and kissed the ground.

"You're sick, dude." Drew laughed at him.

"Yeah, wait until you're up here. Start handing up the little ones." Kneeling at the edge of the ledge, Juan wasn't the least bit ashamed of the tear that fell from his eye.

"Let go of Santy, kid," Drew said to Jamie. His feet braced against the wall Drew caught the slender child around the waist and swung him up to Juan.

Santiago climbed up on the ledge to help Juan haul the children up. Up went Teddy, Simone, Barty, Rocky, Jessy, Matty, then Tom-tom. Kicking his legs to keep afloat, Drew wiped his hair back off his forehead with both hands and stared at Pil. Pil treaded water smiling eagerly at Drew, waiting for him to push him up to Juan.

"Well?" Pil asked holding his arms out to Drew.

Drew ran his palm up his face from his chin over his nose off his forehead. "Hold on a sec, Pil, I gotta catch my breath."

Pil frowned at him. "What's the matter?"

Jamie poked his head over the ledge. "He needs to get his strength up because you're fat." Some of the kids giggled.

Pil shot Jamie a fierce look. "You shut up you skinny ninny, I'm solid, not fat." He whined to Drew, "Tom-tom's pickwickian too but you got him up."

"Hey," Tom-tom squawked from above. "I am not fat my ma says I'm just large boned."

"I'm ready. C'mere," Drew said, taking a long deep breath.

Pil wriggled between Drew's hands. Drew maneuvered his palms under Pil's ample butt, scissoring his legs like mad, and using the wall to push off, with a couple of grunts he pushed him up to where Juan and Santiago caught him and huffing and puffing hauled him over the ledge.

Drew climbed up behind him and threw himself on the ground rolling onto his back. He laid there for a second, panting. Then he rolled over and kissed the ground like Juan had.

"I'm so water-logged, look at my wrinkled fingers!" Rocky said, holding up his digits in amazement. "I'm a raisin!"

"I always said you were a prune-face!" Pil teased him.

Matty sat back on her heels grinning hugely. "Hey, look at us, we're clean! At least the sopping we took made one good thing happen. It feels so great to get all that dirt and gunk off. I'll never complain about Gram making me take a warm bath ever again."

The cheerful mouth straightened when she thought of her grandmother.

"I'm taking showers from now on, no baths for me after spending hours in that stinkin' lake," Pil claimed.

"And caves, when I get outta here I'm never going in a cave again," Santiago swore.

"Yeah," Jamie agreed, "and we didn't even get to see a bat."

"Or Batman," Rocky said.

Simone pulled up the hem of her pink shirt to view it. Her pearly whites glowed. "I'm me again! Pink!" She pulled the pink bow from her hair surprised that it was still there and finger combed her blonde ringlets then clipped the bow back in.

Teddy sat cross-legged squeezing water from her coffee colored braids. Her shirt was powder blue again but her jeans had holes in them. "I swear on Christine, my favorite doll's life that I will never, *ever* go swimming again!"

Lips pressed tight, Tom-tom shook his head deliberately side to side. "Me neither. Never."

"I was so scared…" Jamie whispered, his chin trembling.

The realization of the treacherous situation they had been in, the hours they had spent in the water, swimming under a solid wall not knowing if there would be an end to it hit them. They all grew quiet reliving their harrowing experience. Tears flowed, relieved happy ones this time.

Jessy stood up. "Hey guys, we keep crying buckets like this and in a second we're gonna be back in a river, except it'll be a salty one." Smiling, he pushed his drying black curls behind his ears.

"Listen, we survived a really, uh, tra- traumatic experience. But like my minister says, what doesn't kill us makes us stronger." Matty stood up next to the angelic child brushing off the back of her jeans.

Juan got to his feet too. "Well, we've had our rest. Now, let's blow this popsicle stand." He pulled his wet cap out of his back pocket, twisted the water out of it then shook it. Frowning ruefully at it he tried to smooth it back out then plunked it on his head with the bill backwards.

Matty pulled out Drew's pack of cigarettes and lighter and handed them to him.

Drew gave her a smile of thanks. It had been an unspoken moment they'd shared when he had handed them to her for safe keeping. At the time, Juan and Drew really thought they wouldn't make it back to the others when they had set off to explore the lake.

He regarded his soaked, crumpled pack of cigarettes as he took them from her. They were destroyed, he was about to toss the pack on the ground when he saw Matty watching him. Her arms crossed, one foot sticking out a bit and tapping.

"Really Matt, like who's gonna be here to find litter?" Sighing, he rolled the pack up since it was already ruined, and stuffed it in his pocket.

Grinning at her, he removed his jacket and the black and white striped shirt wringing them like Juan had twisted his cap. He pulled the soggy shirt back on then tied the jacket around his waist. He said to Juan, "Yeah, let's get the heck out of here."

The children gathered in a loose bunch preparing to leave but chatting about their experience in the water and what they were going to do the minute they were home safe; eat a burger, sleep in their own beds, hug their dog.

Teddy wandered in small circles kicking at loose stones. She made bigger circles, tired of waiting for the others then stopped and looked up at the arched stone tunnel in front of her.

It was the largest tunnel and opening they'd seen since being dumped in the miserable mountain. Standing dead center under the arch, suddenly her head tilted forward, her arms fell from her hips to stick out rigidly at her side with the palms flared and fingers spread, her mouth dropped open.

"Oh my goodness….hey guys…" Wonderment filled Teddy's voice. The children didn't heed her call, they chatted and wrung out wet clothes to get ready for what they could only imagine would be another precarious journey to who knows where-

"Guys!" Teddy squealed and twirled around so hard her braids swatted her in the face. "Come look!"

Juan and Drew stopped talking when they heard her shout. They looked over. The tiny cinnamon girl stood under the stone arch, her arms and legs out like a spinning wheel. An aura of light shone around her.

Juan called out, "Teddy are you all right, you-" he broke off when he saw the halo of light behind her. A bright natural light. Astounded, he moved towards her slowly, afraid that he was only seeing an illusion, a mirage.

The other kids finally turned their attention to the young girl. Amazement struck each child's face as they saw her standing aglow. But they too were scared to move, to be disappointed once again.

Juan approached Teddy, she turned slightly aside so he could stand with her under the arch. His mouth wide open, he expelled a hushed, "It's out, Teddy. It's out, I can see the sky." He turned back to the other kids and exclaimed, "I can see the sky!"

Simone covered her mouth with her hand, the kids stood stock still afraid to believe what he said.

Juan turned back. He and Teddy stood side by side. Now the glow surrounded the two of them. Teddy jumped in the air squealing and skipped back to the other kids.

She threw her arms around Simone, they jumped up and down in glee. Matty and Jessy held hands, grinning ear to ear. They walked tentatively closer to the arch stopping a few feet in front of it.

Juan strode back to the group. "Yeah, it really, truly looks like the way out. We need to make sure we're not on a cliff or something, but I'm sure we can get out!"

Rocky happily clapped his hands. "We're free! We're free! What are we waiting for- let's go!"

Quickly the kids gathered their shoes and drying clothes off the ground. Rocky and Drew hugged, Santiago and Juan hugged. The two little girls were still skipping and leaping in joy. Pil and Tom-

tom linked elbows and jigged around the group. Barty and Jamie jumped up and down grinning.

"Okay everybody," Juan said. "Let's check it out! Wait 'til you see how blue the sky is, and the sun is shining bright as I've ever seen it!" The kids maneuvered into a wrinkled two by two and started walking towards the arch. Matty and Jessy stood a few feet in front of the arch waiting for them.

Too excited to wait, Teddy skipped over to stand underneath the arch. She impatiently peeled at the group and shouted, "Come on, let's go!

Simone screamed- an ear splitting piercing, blood-letting scream. Shock struck the kids' faces like a vicious slap.

Standing just on the other side of the arch was Dusty Troicasi, or according to his own personal testimony, Judas Iscariot.

His clothing in shreds, strips of tattered fabric hung and swung from his angular arms and legs, bruises and gashes like spattered paint only added to his murderous appearance.

Covered in dirt, bits showered from his scraggly hair. A bedlamite monster with the pitchfork in one hand and an axe clutched like a battle sword in the other. He could have been a mutinous pirate from a scourged ship. Pure malevolence blazed from his furiously insane eyes.

"Where do you kids think you're going?" His voice hoarse and grainy slavered through sharp teeth. Sweat dangled in a drop from the tip of his long sneering nose. The words slithered over his putrefied tongue as if they could reach out and strangle them.

Chapter Fifty-Seven

Like a flower blossoming, golden petals unfurling after a long deep sleep, the sun's rays threaded through the last of the morning haze. Fingers and toes of brilliant light stretched, pushing their way through lingering cloud puffs.

Crystal blue sky shimmered; tree tops and blades of grass blinked awake in the warm welcoming solar rays.

A stellar day burgeoned, spires of minty pine drifted, flavoring the air with its fresh clean scent. Birds soared like mini airplanes surfing on currents from fringed tree top to tree top chirping greetings. Such a beautiful gleaming morning, it was hard to comprehend the dark jeopardous reason for the mission the men were on.

At the foot of the mountain, Michael, Lucas and Hollis spread twenty feet apart to cover part of the side but stay in shouting distance.

They decided to zigzag up then down the mountain then move over a hundred yards or so and start over until they had combed the monolith thoroughly. If they didn't find an opening, they'd keep fanning around and up and down until they did.

Michael was positive the children were being held inside the rocky conical cage. And hell or high water, devil or be-damned anti-disciple, nothing was going to keep them from finding the kids. The only scary question was, were they already too late? Were the children still alive?

Scrambling over rocks and boulders they hastily climbed, scanning the area around them looking for any opening or change, or disruption like an indentation left from a moved boulder or disturbed dirt that may indicate a concealed passage into the mountain. Although it was moderately steep, the men picked their way steadily up the incline.

"Here!" Michael yelled. The others got over to him as fast as they could scramble over the rocks. "Look, it's an opening," he indicated a slit between two big boulders.

Hollis chewed the inside of his mouth, shook his head. "No way, Mike, it's way too narrow, Troicasi never could have gotten the children through it."

Already sidling his body through the crack Michael said, "I know it's not the way he got in, but it's a way. I'm going. You guys keep looking."

"Michael wait-"

Michael disappeared.

Hollis and Lucas stared blankly at the crack. Lucas said, "You heard him, let's go." He turned and picked his way around the mountain. One last look at the crack and Hollis followed him.

Separating, they hadn't gotten twenty feet past the crack climbing over boulders and then a grassy slope heavily sprinkled with cheery wildflowers when Lucas heard a commotion in the distance. "Wait-" Lucas called out. He could see Hollis' tanned pate catch a ray of sunlight reflecting like a brown mirror flash way over to the left of Lucas.

Lucas wiped his forehead with his sleeve, cheeks shining with perspiration. Unshaven for two days, the blond bristles made his face appear more chiseled and less boyish. He pushed back a thick blob of blond hair that was irritating a maple syrup colored eye. Not so waffle looking now, more like a burnt pancake.

Hollis pulled his handkerchief out of his back pocket and wiped the sweat and dirt off his bald head and patted his face and neck before stuffing it back in his pocket.

Smoothing his handlebar moustache, the half smoked cigar clamped in a corner of his mouth, Hollis squinted across the waving green grass to where Lucas signaled with his hand to get his attention.

Lucas motioned down the mountain. Behind a boulder Hollis stepped carefully horizontally so he could get a better vantage point. Digging his western boots into the hard pan, he grasped a protruding stone to hold onto.

Shading his eyes with a hand over his brow, he strained to see what had gotten Lucas' interest.

The duo looked down the mountain, surprise struck the men. "Well, would you take a gander at that…" Hollis drawled marveling at the spectacle below.

A parade of people trooped along a trail and wound around the very bottom rim of the mountain. Citizens of both Halo Valley and Cleasaí, including volunteers from Strowell and Glenfall were sweeping across receding flooded marshland and highly hazardous terrain.

Mothers and fathers, sisters and brothers, grandmas and grandpas, friends and neighbors and total strangers, even the worst of the criminals, Boris O'Neil, Greg Van Ostrand, Antonio Arcangelo, on and on the people marched. Word had gotten to them; they came to find the children.

The roads had significantly cleared for the people to wend their way through the dangerous peats and bogs, over holes hidden by standing water, rocky terrain, wild dogs and waning severe weather, bottomless gorges and sudden rockfalls to come for the children. The word Michael had left with the station had gotten through.

Lucas and Hollis grinned from ear to ear. The villagers had come together. They'd put aside their petty issues and infighting and criminal acts to search for and hopefully save the children. It didn't matter if someone didn't have a child missing, they were all united in the mass effort.

Through determined expressions, they chatted amicably, smiling and offering encouragement to the families that had children taken.

Cat led the parade with Justin beside her. A white cloth bandage wrapped around the red-headed officer's injured head, the wiry officer leaned on a walking stick, but his step was strong and steady.

Spotting the men climbing up the side of the mountain, Cat waved fervently at them. Justin raised his stick in a jaunty hello.

Lucas and Hollis waved back, the parade of people hooted and whooped up at them.

The crowd surged and swelled around the mountain, a compassionate pool of humanity. As if their hope and faith, and strength of presence and solidarity could literally pull the children out of the walls of the mountain.

They gathered, milling at the foot of the mountain. They looked to Cat to tell them what to do next.

Smiling brilliantly, Cat nodded towards the mountain. "Let's go up."

Chapter Fifty-Eight

Troicasi stood, blocking the children's way to freedom, to home and family. He raised the pitchfork and axe above his head and screamed as if about to charge into battle.

"You will not leave this mountain cave alive!" he thundered. "*I* am in control, this is *my* story, *my* mountain, *my* legend- *my* destiny- *I* will say who goes- and how- Me! Everything is wholly and infinitely *my* choice!"

Stepping forward, still on the other side of the stone arch with bow-frog legs akimbo, Troicasi brandished the pitchfork, raving maniacally. His repulsive demon face bloated purple with rage, insane ghoul eyes, he screamed, strident ear shredding inhuman sounds.

"You will not leave me! I am the king, I am your lord!" Putrid saliva slobbered down his dagger chin, shaking off with every word.

He took another step forward, almost into the arch. Sunlight streamed in behind him, lighting the stirred dust, sparkling particles and flying bugs. "You *will* bow to me, pray to me, sacrifice *to me-*" he jabbed the pitchfork at Teddy who stood frozen in front of the arch.

The triton stabbed across her arm digging a jagged gash, slicing the skin open like a ripe peach, a frenzy of blood gushed. Too shocked to move or scream, the petrified little girl stared at her brown arm, blood poured out of the gash like red water from a hose.

"You will die-" the demented Troicasi screamed, raising the axe in one hand over the tiny cinnamon girl preparing to strike her again.

Louise Furley

She stood ice still, eyes bulging like popcorn, brown pigtails down her chest like suspenders, blood spurting and streaming down her arm. Tossing the pitchfork behind him Troicasi grasped the ax with both hands and raised it to cleave Teddy in half. Screaming in a rabid furor the axe arced, he swung it down like he was splitting a log-

"Arrggggggggggggggghhhhhhhhhhhh!" Jessy pulled his hand from Matty's, beside him Jamie screamed, and the two boys raced across the ground then leaped in the air-

Launching themselves as hard as they could at Troicasi- the boys roared a tribal scream and struck Troicasi square in the chest knocking him off his feet and hurtling the trio backwards out of the arch. More screams, then silence.

"Oh my gosh!" Juan and Drew ran through the arch. Santiago shook himself out of a shocked stupor and followed them.

Matty sped to Teddy who had crumpled to the ground. Pil, Rocky and Tom-tom gathered in a circle, kneeling beside Matty who had dropped next to Teddy.

"Give me something, something to stop the bleeding!" Matty hollered, pressing her hands against Teddy's wound. Running over, Tom-tom tore off the bottom of his shirt and frantically handed it to Matty. Together Matty and Barty wrapped it around Teddy's arm, tying it tight to suppress the blood.

Simone scurried over and dropped to her knees. She held Teddy's other hand. Her voice shook as she tried to reassure her friend that she was going to be all right.

Pil and Rocky helped Teddy sit up then climb up on wobbly legs. The kids waited, watching the arch. But no one came through it.

Holding Teddy between them all, tentatively the kids squeezed into a huddle and cautiously inched to the arch. When they passed through, they could see a few feet on the other side.

Juan, Drew and Santiago were kneeling at the edge of the opening of the mountain. Sunlight radiated into the entrance lighting the children into precious jewels. They were looking down. Juan dropped to his stomach, Drew and Santiago joined him, their arms hanging over the rim, reaching down. "Here- here- grab ahold-" Juan yelled.

"What's happening? Where's Jessy and Jamie?" Matty cried.

Teddy clung to the red-pigtailed girl. She swept terrified big brown eyes around the enclosed area frigid with fear looking desperately for Troicasi to come pounding out swinging the axe and bellowing- but the demon was nowhere in sight.

"Okay, we got ya, hold on guys, hold on to our hands, that's it," Juan was talking over the edge of the opening. The three boys squirmed on their stomachs, stretching and pulling until what seemed an eternity passed, then the boys pulled frightened and banged up Jessy and Jamie up and over the edge. The five boys collapsed on the ground, chests heaving.

Jessy sat up, dark eyes beaming, a giant grin split his cherubic face. He raised his arms straight up in the air crowed in triumph, "We did it! We made it! He's gone! He's gone!" he cried gleefully.

The boys got to their feet and hugged each other then they ran to the other kids and all the children hugged and wept.

"Is- is- is the monster gone?" Teddy asked timidly peeping from Matty's nurturing arms.

Drew grinned broadly and went to the girls. He wrapped his arms around the two. He said, "Yeah," nodding, "yeah, he's gone. Jessy and Jamie knocked the son of a bitch right over the edge, right into a huge gorge.

He totally disappeared into the abyss. He's a goner. Jessy said he heard his screams go on for a long time until they disappeared entirely. Thank God our guys managed to catch a hold of jutting stones and saved themselves from following the freak down the hole."

He threw his hands up in the air and yelled, "The monster is dead! The monster is dead! We're free! We're free!"

"We're free!" Santiago yelled. All of the kids cheered, jumping up and down, hugging and dancing.

"Enough frivolity, guys. It's time for us to get the hell out of this cavern," Juan proposed, laughing with joy.

"Frivolity?" Rocky mocked.

"Yeah kid, frivolity." Juan grinned at the boy, ruffling his hair. "Let's go".

Jubilantly the kids stood in front of the fissure that Troicasi had fallen into. Pil spat into the hole. "Good riddance you ugly freak." Tom-tom patted Pil on the shoulder. He parroted solemnly, "Yeah, good riddance freak."

"Look!" Barty squealed, flapping his skinny arms excitedly. "The ravine isn't really wide, just deep. We can easily walk around it." He looked to Juan as their appointed leader for confirmation.

As an answer, Juan strode directly to the side of the crevasse, and right around it to the other side. He turned triumphantly to the other kids. "Come on! It truly is the way out! I can see down the mountain a few hundred feet I think. It slopes easy. We can get down."

He hesitated at his own words then lit up.

"We can get down!" He shouted, "Let's go!"

Chapter Fifty-Nine

Stumbling through the tunnel with his hands pressed against both sides of the wall for balance and direction, Michael tramped in total darkness with one focus, find the children. A ways in he halted. "What the hell?" he muttered, cocking his ear.

The hair stood up on his neck, he could hear rushing water. "Shit. That crazy bastard did it, he opened the dam. The town-" galvanized into frantic action he raced through the tunnel dragging his palm against a rocky wall to guide him in the pitch black. He prayed he wouldn't run head on into a rock wall.

He could only follow the sound of the water, it sounded closer and closer the roar was so loud now he couldn't hear himself think. He had to slow down to make sure he wasn't going to fall into the flooding water himself.

Then he discerned a faint light. Gingerly moving closer, he reached a rocky ledge and peered over. He could see out through a hole.

"Oh my God," he cursed a few filthy words. He could see all of the people, with Cat and Justin at the lead, marching up the mountain.

A drop of water plunked on his head. He looked up and winced. No wonder the sound was deafening, the water hurtled over his head down a wide tunnel, a huge rushing river heading straight to an opening just above where the villagers were.

If it spewed out of the mountain it would hit the people like a tidal wave, knocking them as if they were matchsticks into the ravine below where the weight and strength of the water would crush them and drown them in seconds.

In the light, he could see he was standing over the dam. The miners must have been plagued by the lakes and reservoirs that developed inside the mountain and built the dam to control them.

Frantically rooting around to find the mechanism that might control the dam, he muttered, "The lousy freak must have gotten the dam partially open and the weight of the water pushed it further until it broke free gushing out. Where the hell is it? Where is the lever?" The water thundered over him like a runaway train.

He was running out of time.

Chapter Sixty

Surging as one, the children burst out of the opening in the mountain like a slammed piñata, a handful of colorful confetti kids tossed into the air, set free, a fiesta of cheers and thrills and the wondrous feeling of being alive!

The radiant sun illuminating their faces, the children streamed down the mountain. Under a dome of piercing blue sky they ran through the wavy green grass, pretty wildflowers glistening around their battered knees.

They giggled and screeched and danced and skipped, breathing in crisp clean fresh air, an electric charge of happiness blazed around them.

A great roar blew up from the bottom of the mountain as the townsfolk saw the children coming down the mountain.

The people were scattered from the foot of the mountain to where some had already reached Lucas and Hollis. Parents frantically searched each child for their own beloved son or daughter.

Holding her breath, Cat counted the youngsters. Her hand covering her mouth, she released a heavy sigh of relief when she got to twelve. *They were all there, all alive, all safe.*

She searched the mountain- *Where was Michael?*

Chapter Sixty-One

Through the cleft in the rocks, Michael could hear the roar of cheers from the villagers and the children, he uttered a silent prayer of gratefulness, *Thank God they're alive*!

But the water was jetting like a rocket through the pass, in seconds it would explode out right between the children and the town anxiously running up to meet them, and it would massacre them all in moments-

Jerking his head around, up and down and around looking, searching, his hands bleeding and raw from the rocks, he chanted, "Where, where, where-"

Water dripped on his head, in his eyes on his shoulders, he only had seconds, seconds and it would all be in vain, the searching and panicking, and profilers, and Lucas, Hollis, Justin and, he couldn't think about it, couldn't think about Cat, or Matty, Gram, Korey.

"Where, where," then- he hit his elbow hard, hard enough he heard it crack but he didn't feel the pain because he saw what he hit, the lever,

"There you are," he muttered, jumped up and grabbed the lever that was straight up against the wall. Falling to his feet, his palms torn, the lever hadn't budged.

He pushed a loose rock out and could see the side of the mountain at least two hundred yards around the curve of the mountain. Something moving, a flash of red, he leaned closer to the hole and squinted.

Dee Troicasi or Herodias or whoever she was, was running down the other side of the mountain away from the villagers. She must have still been in the mountain, hadn't left like Troicasi had said.

He looked up at the lever and realized he wasn't where he could close the dam and stop the flood of water, he was at a diverting area. One last look out at the fleeing Dee, he brushed his hands on his pants to dry them.

If he pulled the lever the water would divert from the villagers but it would gush like Niagara and kill Dee Troicasi.

The water yowled over him, some of it leaked through the tunnel on his head and shoulders and in his eyes, he could no longer hear the people outside.

One last fleeting glance at the fleeing Dee, he jumped up, grabbing the lever and fell, and jumped again and again, until he caught the handle and held on, he dug his boots into the wall and using his weight he pulled with all his might, all his strength, straining.

The lever moved slightly, a wall, a portion of the dam squealed like a rusty hinge then stopped.

He dangled holding onto the lever jerking his body to use his own weight to pull it down, kicking his legs back and forth, his shoulders screamed in agony but he kept pulling and kicking-

Chapter Sixty-Two

Spotting the bright blond hair of his daughter Simone, Justin, bandaged head and all, bolted up the mountain hobbling crookedly on his stick like a wounded soldier. Her battered arms raised high, Simone screamed, "*Daddy*!"

Reaching her, tears blinding him, Justin didn't stop to take in her grubby appearance or tired purple shadows under her blue eyes, he threw his stick to the ground and gathered her up in his arms sobbing into her soft dusty hair.

A grown up twinge to her voice, Simone said calmly, "I am fine, Da. You didn't need to worry about me, I can take care of myself." Justin gazed into her serious eyes. There was a new selfless maturity there. "Mama!" Simone squealed with delight, as her mother Emma hurried to them, the three hugged and praised God for Simone's safe return.

The rest of the families, John Artzi left his wife Francine in his wake as he ran and threw an arm around each of his boys, Rocky and Drew. Francine and daughter Salome and third son Alexander, scurried to catch up, the family melded into a huge hug.

"We were so frightened for you boys. We never thought we'd ever see you a-" John's voice broke, tears gushed, he crushed his sons to him.

Wringing her hands, Francine looked puzzled. "You boys look different somehow, changed. Rocky looks taller, and- and like a young man, and you, Drew," she exclaimed, "you seem at peace, as if you've grown a lifetime, matured. We were so scared you were never coming home again. "

Rocky and Drew exchanged smiles, their arms around each other's shoulders. A twinkle in his eye, Drew said to Rocky, "There was never any doubt that we'd make it, was there?" Rocky shook his head, smiling so hard his ears curled up.

Jim Two-Feathers and his wife Adoette buried their son Tom-tom in their arms, plastering his pudgy face with kisses. Through a sheet of tears, Adoette said to her son, "Baby, you look so different, so much leaner, and stronger. You look like your great-great grandfather, the brave warrior leader, Running Wolf. What happened to change you so?"

Tom-tom pulled his shoulders back proudly, a new confidence deepening his voice he said, "Let's go home, Mom."

Paul Philo and wife Darby with brother Cody surrounded Pil taking turns hugging and kissing him. "We missed you so much boy," Paul admired his son, tears streaming down his face. Surprised, he said, "You look so- so strong son, slimmer, confident what on Earth happened up there?"

Pang, Mai, and sister, Lin-Lin Ming cried over the safe return of their little boy Jamie while hugging the stuffing out of him. Mai clasped her hands together marveling at her once fragile son who now stood tall before her with a new aura of strength and self-assuredness. "My baby has grown up..." she sighed in wonderment.

Juan and Santiago were crushed in the relieved arms of their parents Zebedee and Sophia Trueno. Zebedee examined his sons. "Why," he said dumbfounded, "you boys look somehow different. Like..." he held them each out at arm's length.

"Like you're bigger, straighter, there's a- a sense of pride and courage about you boys. Juan has a wise glint in his eye, and Santy, I swear your shoulders are broader, more muscular, more sure. What the hell happened in there?"

Juan and Santiago glanced at each other and grinned. "It's a long story, Dad," Juan said. "Yeah," Santy agreed, "we'll tell you all about it."

Lucas picked up Jessy in his brawny arms and carried him down to his mother. Black ringlets bounced against globby blond curls as they strode down the mountain.

Petite Mary Montebello and her brood of Jessy's stepbrothers and sisters joyfully drew Lucas and Jessy into their throng. Mary knelt on the hard ground in front of Jessy, her fingers laced, long dark hair draped in a veil over her face, she thanked God for her son's safe return. Jessy's siblings danced around him thrilled to find him safe and sound.

Happily, Jessy stood grinning, black eyes radiant, basking in their love.

All the rustling about stirred up the butterflies; they fluttered around beautiful sashaying bright kites. A balmy breeze wafted bringing an invigorating smell of spring, tousling hair and dresses and lime green leaves sprouting on trees.

Skinny Barty stood shyly, unsure, but his father, Joseph Solomon and mother Becky shrieked at the sight of their son. Joseph hugged him so tightly Barty could hardly breathe. "Son," Joseph's voice broke with emotion, "we were so afraid we'd lost you!"

Becky's tears washed over his face. She held his arms out. "Let me look at you." Her eyes widened in wonderment at her son. "You're standing so tall, strong, different. You've grown into a robust young man."

Barty was relieved to see his older sister Rachel with tears streaming down her face holding his baby sister Persia. Persy waved chubby hands at her brother. Barty had been so worried about her. When Troicasi had approached him on the street near the woods, Barty had felt safe enough to talk with him.

But when Barty declined to leave his sister in her carriage to go into the woods, as Troicasi had said he had something fabulous to show him, Troicasi had hit the boy on the side of the head, stunning him, then carried him off into the woods leaving baby Persia sleeping in her buggy.

Barty hadn't known if she was okay or not until now, the fear of the infant left alone on the wintry street had gnawed at him the entire time of his imprisonment. While his parents hugged him, he took his sister, cradling her in his arms. He kissed her tiny nose, beaming head to toe from the love his family soaked him in.

D'Wayne Keegan howled when he saw his baby girl Teddy with her arm wrapped up and her pretty face all scratched and bruised. Her mother Quineisha and sister Lacole wept as they hugged and kissed her like mad. "My baby, my poor baby," D'Wayne cried, cupping her tiny face and inspecting her arm, he sorrowfully studied her injuries.

Teddy puffed up her little chest proudly and said, "I'm fine, Daddy. You don't need to worry about me!"

D'Wayne leaned back in wonderment at this child who only weeks ago was selfish and lazy and timid. It was amazing how even scratched and bruised, her arm slashed open, she stood brave and strong like a priestess. Self-reliance, her new coat enveloped her. Strength radiated from her brown eyes.

D'Wayne picked her up holding her to his burly chest, hugging her like he'd never let her go again. All that was visible were two cinnamon braids looping over his beefy arms.

Michael sprinted up the rest of the mountain, Matty flew into his arms, he wrapped his hands around her waist lifting her high in his arms, pigtails flying like red robins, a great giddy grin split her face, chicklet teeth dazzling. He cradled her tightly to his chest, tears streaming down his unshaven face. "Matty, you're safe, you're safe, thank God, thank God."

Matty grinned up at Michael, she fluffed the back of his hair that grew well past his collar. "Uncle Mike, you sure need a haircut, you look like Tarzan." He laughed out loud and hugged her tighter. "Let's go find your grandma, she's been beside herself with worry."

Matty gazed seriously at her uncle. "We were just fine, Uncle Mike. We took care of each other. Jessy and Jamie killed that creepy monster that took us. He's gone for good. We'll all be happy and safe again now. Hey, you're all wet!" She giggled.

Michael patted her head. "I always had faith in you, Mat. I knew you'd take good care of the other kids. I'm so proud of you." Matty laid her head against Michael's neck as he carried her down the mountain.

Michael didn't trust himself to speak any more, hearing Matty's courageous words and clear confident seriousness in such a young child twisted his heart.

He hadn't let himself dwell or even think about what could be happening to his niece while she was gone. He tried to let the relief flood his limbs, but it was painful, the fear still scraped and gouged as it coursed through his veins.

A beige blur streaked up the mountain barking for all his worth. Banny caught up to Michael and Matty, jumping and barking he hopped up and down trying to jump up Michael's leg to reach Matty. Giggling, Matty called down to the little dog, "Hi Banny! I sure missed you!"

Michael smiled at the happy dog. "You can lick her all you want once we're down this damned monolith!" The dog leaped and bounded, tail wagging, tongue flapping next to Michael all the way down.

Michael carried Matty down to where Korey was waiting with Grandma Zinny. Korey gripped Zinny's arm tightly to hold her back from running up the mountain to embrace Matty. He didn't want to have to have the EMT carrying the elderly back down on a gurney.

Zinny was so fraught with anxiety and excitement and relief at seeing Matty held in Michael's arms as he victoriously carried her pixie, pig-tailed great-granddaughter down the mountain, her entire body trembled. Her hands steepled in prayer, she opened them wide as Michael set the girl down in front of her.

Great sobs wracked Zinny's body as she bent and hugged the dear child to her bosom. Korey grinned at Michael, they clasped hands, patted each other's shoulder. Korey laid a hand on the top of Matty's head. "I knew you'd do it," he whispered to Michael.

Cat and Hollis joined the joyous foursome. Michael caught Cat's shoulder and drew her into the fold. Hollis muscled his way in between Korey and Matty so he could pinch the pixie's cheek and tease her like the way he used to, he quickly dashed away an errant tear before the child could see it.

Cat whispered in Michael's ear, "Yellow flower." He shot her a lop-sided grin and squeezed her close to him. "Yeah," he said, "yellow flower." Then he said, "What's that supposed to mean again?" Her laughter ringing in his ears he led the ecstatic crowd down the mountain.

"What a glorious day!" Mallory O'Leary exclaimed. Flaming hair swinging in the soft wind, a head taller than most of the people around her, the pretty reporter gave the thumbs up to her news crew. She had quietly kept her crew waiting patiently at the bottom of the mountain. She let the town welcome back and revel in finding their lost children in private.

When everyone had calmed, she would strike up the cameras and microphones and get to work. Until then, she was content to listen to the mayor.

Rotund, Mayor Ashton Whitworth attired in a three-piece gabardine suit, babbled gleefully at her side. Plump, cherry red cheeks, reading glasses peeping out of his breast pocket, thumbs tucked into his waistband, sweat beads of relief dotted the Mayor's balding forehead.

"Everything is good again in the valley," Whitworth boasted, strutting, his big belly straining against the starched white shirt. "Halo Valley is at peace and safe again. Our own precious utopia is back to normal, all is right with the world!"

"They're coming down!" Holding a microphone in one hand, Mallory fluffed her hair with the other and broadly smiled, every tooth flaunted like a rising starlet at her main cameraman.

"Let's go!" Hips undulating underneath a skintight pantsuit Mallory raised her hand like a sword, motioning for her crew to follow her. With the rest of the village residents closing in behind them, they pooled around the exuberant families victoriously marching down the mountain linked together like a human chain, hand in hand in hand.

Epilogue

A few weeks later the park resonated with boisterous laughter. Two young boys, half eaten burgers in hand chased each other through the lush park.

They raced between Michael and Lucas, the men juggled their beers to keep them from spilling, and stepped back laughing as the kids ran off to join a pack of children flying kites up on a hill.

The officers finally enjoying a day off stood side-by-side, drinking their beer and contentedly watching the park come alive with people and food and amusements. Grilling hot dogs, sausage and peppers, and hot soft pretzel aromas cruised the currents, Lucas was practically drooling.

Trying to flatten his unruly lump of hair, he smiled when Michael snickered next to him. "Yeah," Lucas said ruefully, "I know, give it up, my glob will never cooperate and lay neatly. But, my new motto is 'never give up!'" He laughed and swigged.

Nodding, Michael said, "I think that's everyone's new motto. Hey," he nudged Lucas gesturing with his head.

Lucas grinned watching his girlfriend, Kenzi, hurrying over the thick grass towards the two men with a tray in her hand. The pretty young woman with shoulder length lemony yellow hair leaned in for a kiss when she reached Lucas. "Hi hon," she greeted him.

"Hey babe, it's great to see you but even greater to see what you have there." Lucas spied the food steaming on the tray. "Whatcha got?"

Kenzi held the tray out so the men could see. "Here, help yourselves, boys, I brought it for you. I know you get so involved helping other people you often don't get the chance to eat."

Lucas kissed her cheek again. "Your heart is as beautiful as your face, Kenzi. I love how you take care of me."

He eagerly unwrapped a burger and took two huge bites, ketchup dripped down the side of his mouth which he quickly lapped up with his tongue. Kenzi broke out laughing, Michael shook his head at his friend's antics and took a burger himself.

"Here," Kenzi said, she picked a cup of beer up off the tray and handed it to Lucas. "I figured you'd need a refill by now."

"You can so read my mind, Kenz." Lucas accepted the cup slipping it in the empty one he was holding.

"So," Kenzi started, smiling slyly at Michael offering him a beer off her tray. When he took the beer she dropped her arm to her side holding the tray against her thigh. "What's up with the coordinator, Miss Sylvester? I heard you two were like Tarzan and Jane while trying to find the children?"

Lucas sputtered, choking on his beer. "Kenzi!" Coughing, he frowned at his girlfriend.

The sassy blonde ignored him. She was a tall, athletically slender girl that could almost see eyeball to eyeball with the former football player. But right now her full attention was on the handsome sergeant. "Come on Luke, everyone's talking about it. I heard Gramma Zinny just loves her."

Michael calmly finished his burger and sipped his beer.

"Well?" she asked. "Is she staying here, going back to upper Ireland, are you going with her, give me the goods man!"

At that moment, Lucas shifted his eyes crazily at Kenzi trying to signal her, until she swung around to see Cat striding across the park directly towards them.

Long hair tossing in thick waves behind her, golden highlights glinting in the sun, she looked purely happy. In jeans and a blouse, she carried a hot dog in one hand and a soda in the other, a small purse dangled from one shoulder.

"Hi!" she greeted, cheerfully joining the group. "I've heard a lot about you, Kenzi. You're as pretty as Lucas has described." The girls faced each other with warm smiles.

Kenzi's Irish blue eyes appraised Cat. "Oh, and I've heard tons about you, Miss Sylvester," Kenzi burred through a thick local accent. "And I must say, you are even more beautiful than you have been described."

"Oh, uh, thank you, please call me Cat."

"Okay, Cat." Kenzi sidled up next to her. She leaned in conspiratorially and said, "So, now that the children are safe and the storm is over and Cleasaí is almost habitable again, people are already preparing for the cleanup and move back, what are your plans? Hey!" She squealed as Lucas grabbed her arm and pulled her away, off across the park.

Michael and Cat could hear her berating Lucas all the way across the verdant lawn. "But why shouldn't I ask? What's the big deal? Why shouldn't-" their voices dwindled.

Lucas turned and saluted them with a cheeky grin then they disappeared into the crowd.

Silently watching the people dancing and eating and playing games, Michael drank his beer and Cat consumed her hot dog then licked her fingers.

Finishing his beer, he crushed the cup and took his empty wrappings and Cat's and tossed them in a nearby trash can. He walked back to Cat and stood in front of her, his thumbs tucked over his belt.

Children ran back and forth screaming and pulling brightly colored kites, the kites soared and sailed, ribbons of tails flowing in the sky.

He cleared his throat then said, "So, ah, have you made any plans yet to leave?"

Cat stared at his knees, he stared at the top of her head, the warm breeze stirred the gold-striped wisps. Michael moved closer to her, he smoothed back the wisps then slipped his hand under her chin and raised her head so they could look directly into each other's eyes. They'd had a few dinners together, but both were quite busy getting the villages back in order.

She shrugged one shoulder. "I guess I need to start making some plans. I mean, everyone is perfect, the village is perfect, the weather is perfect..."

Michael tipped her chin up and kissed her so softly his lips barely brushed hers. "You're perfect. And we have unfinished business," he whispered against her mouth then let her go.

Sighing, he stuffed his hands in his pockets, hunched his broad shoulders, but didn't take his eyes of hers. "Maybe you can stay awhile. I think some folks could still use some guidance, and Cleasaí won't be fully livable for a few months or so, you know..." He trailed off.

Cat shrugged one shoulder again, clasped her hands together. She stared down at them. "They don't really need me anymore. My job is done. I won't ever forget this fantastic unbelievable experience I had here. Finding the children was so- so amazing, incredible, I can't describe how I felt when I saw the first child cresting the mountainside. I-" she sighed heavily.

"I'll never forget it. Nothing will ever be as precious as seeing those kids all safe and sound and drawn into the bosom of their loving families, and the entire community. The way the residents came together, was just extraordinary, I mean, I heard that even a bunch of hardcore felons learned of the children's plight and joined up in the search."

Cat paused, her smile tender. "And, I'm glad I found a new friend through all this." She gazed up at him, a tear slipped out and rolled over her cheek.

Michael touched the tear with a fingertip scraped and calloused still healing, then held her hand. "I think you are also amazing, incredible, precious, mind bogglingly beautiful." He took her other hand urging her to look back up at him.

His voice husky, he confessed, "You've boggled my mind since the first second I saw you. Sassy, smart as a whip, hot as hell and with a huge heart of gold, I could hardly work for thinking of you.

That's why I was so furious when you went out in the storm that day.

"My heart caught in my throat when I saw you slumped in front of the car with the snow piling so fast over you that if I'd looked out the window one minute later you wouldn't have even been visible. I can't bear to think what would have happened if…"

Cat tugged from his hand and smoothed a lock of black hair off his forehead then drew the back of her hand tenderly down the side of his face. He'd shaven but hadn't yet gotten his hair cut. He still looked like the wild warrior.

"I know, Michael, I was foolish to have tempted the storm. All I could think of was that the computer held the key to the kids. I was wrong for taking that chance but, I- well I can't go back and un-ring that bell. I will always be grateful to you for risking your own life to come and rescue me. Thank you-"

Michael caught her arms and roughly pulled her to him, holding her so hard against his chest she could feel his buttons pressing into her breasts. He cradled her face with his steely fingers and mercilessly crushed her mouth with his.

The victorious warrior taking his prize. In seconds, dangerously out of control, hungry and achingly inflamed, he wrapped his arms around her so tightly she was in excruciating pain, exquisite agony, and she wanted more.

"I don't want your thanks, Cataleigh," he growled in her ear. "I don't want to be just your friend." Cupping her face in both hands he told her, "I want more, I want you, freely given," he captured her lips again.

Fiercely he caressed her back with his strong hands, their heat pressing through the fabric of her blouse, his fingers moved down cinching her waist.

She lifted her head, her breathless, "*Michael,*" inflamed him more. His hand stroked back up to grip the back of her neck, groaning against her mouth, his voice low and gruff, a raw slur he rasped, "I could take you now."

Cat could feel his heart pounding against hers, she threaded her fingers in his tangled mane pulling him harder against her. Their bodies melded tightly together, the heat seethed between them-

Again she was the one to pull back, remembering they were in a public place. Gazing into those ebony eyes burning with arousal, she drew a long, shaky breath to calm herself.

His pupils so huge his eyes looked like dark mesmeric moons, round black magnets pulling her into their depths, she had to stop herself from falling in.

"Michael," she said softly. She could feel his grip lighten. For moments they held one another, the intense emotion pouring off them.

Stepping back, he blinked, smiled crookedly. "Don't worry, I'm not a barbaric caveman. Not totally anyway. Actually, that's not a bad idea, throw you over my shoulder and-" he reached for her.

"Michael! Don't you dare!" She wriggled in his grasp, but he didn't let go. "Where's all that rigid control?" she asked him.

He held her in a rock hard but loose embrace, smiling, he leaned over and kissed the top of her head. "You're like a drug to me, Cataleigh, the more I have the more I want. It was all I could do to keep my hands off of you through this whole ordeal. Knowing you were just down the hall those days at my house, all those cold showers…but," he leaned back to look at her.

"I can wait. As long as it takes. If you give us a chance."

She smiled up at him. "I think the two towns can carry on without me. Although there's probably already a new mission on my desk right now. I-"

"Tell them you need a long, long vacation. I can come out to you if you can't, but," he took her hands again and pulled her back to him, chest to chest. His hands around her neck, his thumbs stroking her jaw, he coaxed, "Stay with me, Cataleigh, stay for a while. Make that forever."

He kissed her again then pulled apart. "I need you, want you, Cataleigh. Stay with me forever, my yellow flower. I mean it, marry me, I want my forevers to be with you." He took a breath then said, "If that's what you want. Do you?"

Tears slipped out and down her cheeks. He frowned, "Don't cry, why-"

On tiptoe she drew his head down and kissed him hard, until both were breathless. Smiling, she whispered, "They're happy tears. They're yes tears."

He grinned, kissed her again not wanting to say anything to cause her to change her mind. Sliding his arm around her shoulders, he pulled her next to him.

Cat's head drifted to Michael's shoulder.

They watched the park fill to overflowing with the lively animated throng laughing and eating and playing.

The laughter and camaraderie were beautiful melodious chords energizing the land.

In the background, the Maru Mountains like a dark majestic halo, cradled the town.

The End